THE
NOTORIOUS
SCARLETT AND
BROWNE

ALSO BY JONATHAN STROUD

The Outlaws Scarlett and Browne

The Bartimaeus Sequence
The Amulet of Samarkand
The Golem's Eye
Ptolemy's Gate
The Ring of Solomon

Lockwood & Co.
The Screaming Staircase
The Whispering Skull
The Hollow Boy
The Creeping Shadow
The Empty Grave

Buried Fire
The Leap
The Last Siege
Heroes of the Valley

THE
NOTORIOUS
SCARLETT AND
BROWNE

JONATHAN STROUD

Alfred A. Knopf
New York

THIS IS A BORZOI BOOK PUBLISHED BY ALFRED A. KNOPF

This is a work of fiction. Names, characters, places, and incidents either are the product of the author's imagination or are used fictitiously. Any resemblance to actual persons, living or dead, events, or locales is entirely coincidental.

Text copyright © 2023 by Jonathan Stroud
Jacket art copyright © 2023 by Stephanie Hans
Map art copyright © 2023 by Tomislav Tomić

All rights reserved. Published in the United States by Alfred A. Knopf, an imprint of Random House Children's Books, a division of Penguin Random House LLC, New York. Originally published in paperback by Walker Books Ltd., London, in 2022.

Knopf, Borzoi Books, and the colophon are registered trademarks of Penguin Random House LLC.

Visit us on the Web! rhcbooks.com

Educators and librarians, for a variety of teaching tools, visit us at RHTeachersLibrarians.com

Library of Congress Cataloging-in-Publication Data is available upon request.
ISBN 978-0-593-43040-8 (trade) — ISBN 978-0-593-43041-5 (lib. bdg.) — ISBN 978-0-593-43042-2 (ebook)

The text of this book is set in 10.65-point Berling LT Std.
Interior design by Megan Shortt

Printed in the United States of America
10 9 8 7 6 5 4 3 2 1
First American Edition

For Sam, Roy, and Robin

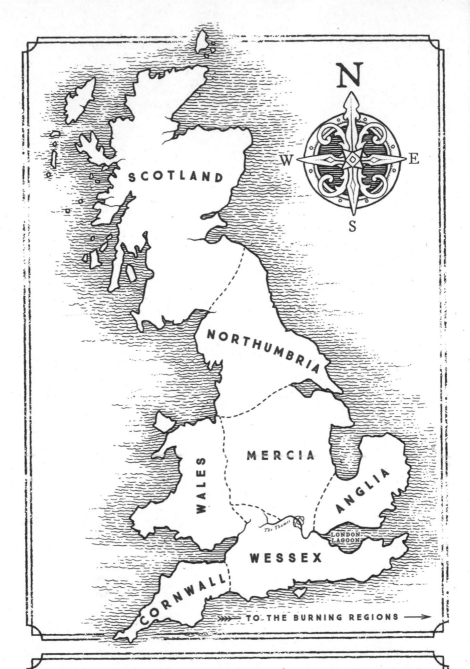

N

W   E

S

SCOTLAND

NORTHUMBRIA

WALES

MERCIA

ANGLIA

The Thames

LONDON
LAGOON

WESSEX

CORNWALL

TO THE BURNING REGIONS →

THE SEVEN KINGDOMS

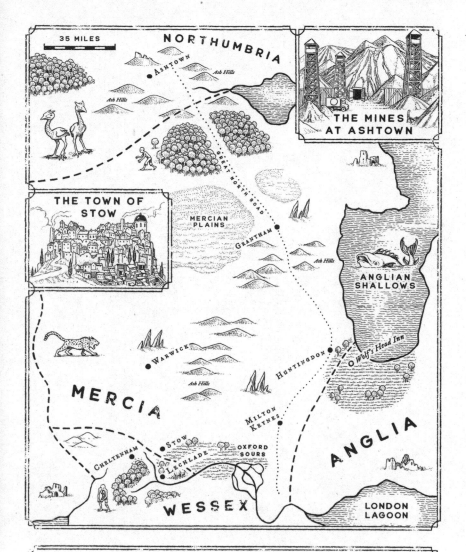

THE GREAT NORTH ROAD

I

THE WARWICK
JOB

1

That evening, with the sun setting over the ash fields and the curfew bells ringing out above the cities of the plains, three murderers gathered at a crossroads. They wasted no words in greeting. The youngest climbed the broken tower to survey the land; the oldest took up a position of concealment in the ruins beyond the ditch. The third, the bandit captain, strolled to a concrete slab that lay amid the sagebrush and black foxgloves beside the road. He lit his pipe and sat at ease, waiting for travelers to come to them.

The crossroads was a good place for an ambush, which was why the bandits had selected it. The tumbled walls of the old watchhouse provided cover, while the surviving tower gave a clear view in all directions. They were close enough to the towns to guarantee foot traffic, and far enough away for the militia not to bother them while they chatted with their prisoners. Also, there was a ravine nearby where the bodies could be tipped.

The bandit captain enjoyed his work, and waiting was part of the pleasure. He felt like a fisherman on a riverbank, scanning the surface of the water, knowing that sleek fat trout were close at hand. He sat with his leather coat open, one booted leg extended, sucking on his pipe. Through half-closed eyes he watched the fragrant smoke twirl skyward. Yes, patience was the key. . . . Presently the fish would come.

Sure enough, soon a low whistle sounded from Lucas on the tower. The captain glanced up toward the parapet and noted the direction of the boy's outstretched arm. From the east, then: the Corby road. Traders, probably, hurrying to reach Warwick before nightfall. The captain rubbed his bearded chin and glanced at the pistol in his belt. From Corby might come spices, furs, black tektite jewels . . . A Corby haul was rarely disappointing.

How would they be traveling? On foot? In a motor vehicle? He could not hear an engine.

He got to his feet unhurriedly, took his pipe from his mouth, and set it on the slab to await his return. Stepping through the sagebrush, he stood ready at the side of the road.

The ash fields were soft and sugary in the evening light. Long shadows, sharp as coffin nails, stretched from the pines behind the ruins. To the east, the shadow of the tower was a slash across the red-brown earth.

And now two bicycles came into sight, making for the crossroads.

The bandit captain frowned in mild surprise. Bicycles were not unusual in the safe-lands, but the Corby road was long and arduous and had deteriorated in the period of the Rains. As he watched, the lead bike weaved smoothly to avoid a pothole. The one behind swerved at the last minute, teetering on the brink of disaster, righted itself, and rushed on.

Both riders were heavily laden with rucksacks and packages. Despite this, and even at a distance, he could see how slight they were. If they were young, this suggested further possibilities. There was a slave market in Warwick, and the bandit captain was on passable terms with its overseer.

He waited until he could hear the rattle of the wheels. Then he walked out into the dying sunlight and took up a heroic posture, legs straddling the center of the road. He flicked his coat aside and tucked his thumb into his belt, so that his palm cupped the gun hilt loosely.

Smoothing back his glistening mane of hair, he held up his hand.

The leading bicycle came to an abrupt halt, wheel twisting, raising a cloud of thin red ash. The other nearly collided with it. With a squawk of woe, its rider veered away and skewed to a standstill too, his rucksack pitching drunkenly to the side.

They *were* young. A blinking, bewildered, dark-haired boy. The other was a girl in a broad-brimmed hat.

The red dust settled slowly around them.

This was always the best bit for the bandit captain. He liked the theatricality of the moment. Him blocking the road. Seeing the shock on their faces, the slowly awakening fear.

"One moment, travelers!" he called. "A word with you."

"Bandit," the boy said.

"Yeah?" The girl's head tilted slightly. "I'd never have guessed."

Her face was in shadow, but the bandit captain could see twirls of red hair spilling down below the angled hat. She wore a battered brown jacket and dark jeans stained with ash. She had a rifle on her back; also a rucksack with packs and tubes strapped to it. There was a pistol tucked into a slouched gun belt just inside her coat.

"A friendly conversation," the bandit captain said. "That's all I require of you. I should mention that I have armed men watching us. I must politely request that you remove your weapons and dismount from your bicycles."

He waited. The riders didn't move.

"Hat," the boy said.

The girl lifted a hand slowly, lazily—but not to remove her pistol, as the bandit expected. Instead, she took her hat off, propped it on the handlebars. She sat back on the saddle, one boot resting on a pedal, the other on the ground. Long red hair, dark with sweat, fell in a mess of ringlets either side of a pale and sullen face. No more than nineteen, the bandit guessed. Nineteen and healthy. Certainly worth keeping alive.

But she had still not dismounted from the bicycle. Or taken off her gun. And nor had the boy moved. He wore an old gray militia jacket, which hung long and shapeless on his feeble form. He was slender-faced, dark-eyed, almost girlish in his features, and was gazing at the bandit captain with an expression of vacant intensity. A simpleton, perhaps. The main point was, he carried no weapon, and the bandit instantly disregarded him.

He returned his attention to the girl. "Did you hear what I said?"

"Yeah." Her voice was surprisingly calm. "You want my guns."

"So then."

"We'd prefer to negotiate."

"I'm sure you would." The bandit captain smiled suavely; he made an expansive gesture in the direction of the ruins. "Sadly, that's not an option, my dear. You'd do well to obey me. I have five men concealed here, each a crack shot, each with a rifle trained on your heart."

The girl wrinkled her nose in mild distaste. She looked at her companion. "Albert?"

"Two men," the boy said. "One on the tower, one at the window of the ruins."

"Rifles?"

"Pistols."

The bandit scowled. "Enough of this jabbering. Five men, I say, who—"

But the girl was glancing up toward the ruins.

"Left and up a bit," the boy said. "Yep. You've got him. The other's at the top." The curious thing was, he wasn't looking at her *or* at the ruins but was still watching the captain with his big, dark eyes.

"Okay, that's fine," the girl said. "Which would I take first?"

"The one on the tower is the best shot. He's the fastest. The one at the window sucks."

A muffled voice came from the ruins. "Hey!"

"This guy?"

"Was good, but his nerves are shot. He drinks too much."

The bandit captain had run a pub before his rages got the better of him and he killed a man in a brawl. He had a thirst on him now, and he could feel his anger swelling in his belly as the conversation ran away from him. Just looking at the boy's bland, blank face made him oddly furious. That and his disconcertingly accurate chatter. He had the sense that he was missing something, and that infuriated him too. If it hadn't been for the girl, for the price she'd fetch at auction, he would have taken out his pistol and shot them both where they stood.

"Excuse me," he said. "*If* I could get a word in for a moment, we're agreed that several guns are trained on you, correct? The point is—if you go for your weapon, we will kill you. If you try to run, the same."

"Cycle," the boy said.

"What?"

"We'd cycle. Not run. Look, we're sitting on bikes."

"Talk some sense," the girl said.

"Gods above us! It makes no difference!" The bandit stamped his boot upon the road. "Cycle, run, or flap your arms and fly like two toothed birds, the outcome will not change."

A breeze blew a curled strand of hair across the girl's forehead. She brushed her face clear. She had green eyes, as bright and cold as glass. The bandit found it hard to look at them. "All right," she said slowly, "keep your pants on, mister. No need to get upset. So what happens if we do as you ask?"

The bandit captain flicked irritably at a dusting of ash on the side of his tight black jeans. He had lost his calm, and that made him feel put out. Lucas would have seen that, and Ronan, too; they would needle him about it later. "Well," he growled, "suffice it to say we are gentlemen of the road, and we have our own code of honor. We will look through your bags, perhaps take a few trifles, things that appeal to us. . . ." He shrugged. "That is all."

"And after that?"

"We let you go."

"Albert?"

"They'll kill us," the boy said.

The bandit started. "I assure you—"

"At least they'll kill *me*. Shoot me or cut my throat, dump me in a ravine for the wolves to find. You they'll keep alive, Scarlett. Maybe sell you to the slavers. If you're lucky."

"Oh, dear," the girl said. She stared at the bandit captain with her bright green eyes.

The captain found his own gaze flickering uneasily to and fro. He adjusted his position slightly in the road. "Whatever your fate," he said thickly, "it is ours to decide. Throw away your gun and dismount. I will not ask again."

"Good," the girl said. "I'm glad about that. Here's my

counterproposal. It's late. The sky is growing red. We've ridden all day across difficult country. There was a collapsed bridge in the hills and we had to ford the torrent. We came through ash squalls and sand slips and had a pack of spotted fell-cats following us for miles across the scarp. Plus, Albert got a puncture and fell into a bog. We're tired, our backsides are saddlesore, and we want to get to town before they close the gates. We have work to do in Warwick tomorrow. We don't need trouble with you gentlemen of the road, and I don't want to waste my bullets. So stand down and let us go by."

Again the bandit captain experienced a vague sense of unreality, that things were not going quite as they should. He could imagine Lucas crouching on the parapet, pistol ready, watching everything with his cold gray eyes. Looking at the girl and the loaded rucksacks, waiting for the talking to be done. He would be impatient now. These days he was kicking too often against orders and was happy when his captain faltered. The little swine thought he was the better shot, too, and quicker, when all he really had was the arrogance of youth—

"He's not listening, Scarlett," the boy on the bicycle said.

The girl nodded. "Okay. Tell me when."

The captain drew himself up. His fingers tightened on the pistol.

"Last chance," he said.

"Yeah," the girl said. "It is."

There was a pause.

The way it always worked was: The captain drew his gun, then Lucas and Ronan fired too. He moved first, then came the barrage. The travelers never had a chance; Lucas, in particular, was too fast. But the captain didn't quite feel his usual confidence. Nothing was right here. Somehow, he didn't want to start things. All at once he thought of his pipe waiting on the concrete slab.

"You can always go back to it, Will," the dark-haired boy said. "You'll find the tobacco's still alight."

The captain's eyes widened. He felt the world pressing in on him, the natural order of things turning upside down. A stab of shock went through him, curdling into fear and hatred.

The boy's smile faded. His gaze was sad.

The captain looked at him, looked at the girl.

The girl said nothing.

They stood in silence, the three of them, in the dust of the empty road.

"Now," the boy said.

Three shots.

Silence again.

What was really galling to the bandit captain in his last moments, what *really* offended his dignity, was the way the boy knew he was going to shoot before he did himself. Throughout his life, in moments of panic or rage, the captain had been like a machine driven by levers. When enough of them were pulled, he acted, and the conscious thought came after. So, now, in his terror and confusion, he had drawn his pistol before his mind framed the intention—yet the boy had already predicted it. Not only that, but two shots had already been fired while his gun was still in the process of rising. And neither bullet was his own. The third shot followed, but *that* wasn't his doing either. He could not quite understand it, nor why his finger refused to tighten on the trigger. . . . He felt, rather than saw, the pistol fall from his nerveless hand. There was a sudden impact to his knees. He realized he was kneeling on the ground.

For some reason, he could not move his eyes. At the edge of his vision, he caught sight of a swift black shape flashing downward—something heavy dropping from the tower. He heard the crunch on the stones beneath, then a brief cry from a window in the ruins.

His eyes were locked. He saw the bicycles, the boy and girl still standing there, the ash on the wheel rims, the dust on their boots. The girl was tucking her gun back into her belt. He could no longer focus on them. Then he realized he was lying on his face in the road. It was curious how he hadn't noticed the transition. There'd been no sensation of falling.

He smelled the cordite from the pistol. It made him think of his pipe again.

Now there were no sensations at all.

2

I t was midnight in the town of Warwick. Even at such an hour, the day's heat radiated ghostlike from the cobblestones. Across the plaza, the cafés were closing. The last customers idled at their tables, watching the slave girls sweeping up beside the empty market stalls. Soft fragrances hung in the air. At the militia station fiery braziers illuminated the posters on the Wanted Wall, making the faces of its outlaws shift as if alive.

From beyond the boundary wall of the Faith House gardens, bells and incantations sounded. Evening worshippers began to exit the gates and disperse across the square. At a discreet table, Scarlett McCain took a sip of coffee, adjusted her tinted glasses, and watched them leave. Ten minutes remaining. Everything was going like clockwork. In ten minutes the compound would be locked, and the great heist could begin.

For four days she and Albert had covertly surveyed the Faith House, the oldest such establishment in Mercia and famous for the wealth locked in its vaults. No one had detected them. Thanks to their disguises, no one had noticed that two of the most notorious outlaws in the Seven Kingdoms had infiltrated the crowds. Right now, Scarlett wore a knee-length green cotton dress, white pumps in the local Mercian style, and a neatly bobbed blond wig. She had her legs crossed, a bowl of coffee at her hand, and a cloth bag of weapons at her feet. In her neatness and sophistication, she looked a typical rich young Warwick woman and nothing like a certain disheveled red-haired robber whose face was pasted a few feet away on the militia wall. Scarlett disliked the dress, and the wig itched like a bastard, but they had kept her incognito for four days.

Snatches of conversation drifted to Scarlett as the townsfolk passed her. There had been a delay with the supply trains. . . . A convoy on the Great North Road had been set upon by the Tainted, several lorries overturned, the guards eaten, the products lost. . . . In better news, two slaves and a religious dissenter would be whipped for deviancy at the House tomorrow. . . . The chief Mentor would give an accompanying speech, with tea and cakes available. . . .

Scarlett's eyes narrowed behind her glasses at the mention of the whipping, but she kept her face impassive. She waited. Now the gates to the Faith House compound clanged shut, and bolts were drawn to seal it for the night. As the worshippers moved off, a slight, slim figure broke away from the back of the crowd. He wandered over as if to inspect the shop fronts, looped past where Scarlett sat, and disappeared up a narrow lane beside the compound wall.

Scarlett finished her coffee. She placed a pound note under the bowl, picked up her cloth bag, and left the square. She too entered the quiet lane. The bag was heavy in her hand. As she went, she mentally itemized its contents: her gun belt, a rucksack containing ropes and twine, a crowbar, cotton dampers, lockpicks, torches . . . Yeah, she had it all. The rest of their kit was with the getaway bikes, stowed in the wadi outside town. Nothing had been forgotten. All that was needed now was to carry out the job with professionalism and cool efficiency.

"Yo, Scarlett!"

A scrawny shape lurched from the shadows. Scarlett jumped aside. Like her, Albert Browne was in disguise. He wore the local Warwick fashion—a crumpled linen suit, a white shirt, blue deck shoes. He lacked a wig, but his hair had recently been combed. He carried a wodge of glossy documents and a sticky paper bag.

Scarlett glowered at him. "Don't leap out at me like that! And don't shout my name!" She glanced back up the lane, but all was still. "Are you okay? You survived the evening, I take it?"

"More than that." His smile was as guileless as ever. "I found it very interesting."

"I bet you did. I see they gave you some religious brochures. What's in the bag?"

"Two massive buns. They were handing them out after the services. Nice Mentor lady practically thrust them into my hands as I was leaving. Fancy a nibble? They're good."

"No, thanks. Did you get the last piece of information we needed?"

"I got it. I had to do a lot of sieving before I found some-one who knew the secret."

"Excellent. So where's—"

"Turns out," Albert said, "that half the Mentors aren't al-lowed into the inner sanctum. Only the senior ones know the hidden door. The one I found was a little pimply guy, but by the point I'd got to him, I'd chatted to everyone else during the breaks between the rituals. Goodness, I read a *lot* of minds, and it was teas all round each time, which I don't mind admitting is putting a bit of a strain on the old blad-der right now. *And* my head's spinning from all the incense in the rituals. I had to sit through a Muslim salah, a Chris-tian Mass, a Hindu puja, *and* a reading of the Sikh Gurbani, which is fairly heavy going for one evening. . . ." He hesitated. "You seem impatient."

Scarlett spoke softly. "I'm just wondering if you'll ever finish."

"I've finished now. No, wait—there was a super Animist dance too. Lots of high kicking from the ladies of the town."

In six months, Scarlett had learned the arts of patience and perseverance. She took off her sunglasses, rubbed her eyes, and suppressed the urge to clout him. "*Albert*. Where is the secret entrance to the vaults?"

"Main public chamber. Behind some drapes."

"Booby-trapped?"

"Yes."

"Any other dangers?"

"Just what we already know. Poison gas, pitfalls . . ." He shrugged. "I got the visuals. We shouldn't have any problems. Oh, and I saw glimpses of the vaults themselves. Gold, jewels, piles of banknotes . . . You know, all that stuff you like." He opened the paper bag, took a bite of bun. "Are we still going ahead with it?"

The old thrill was running through Scarlett, dark joy at the imminence of action. "Of course we're going ahead. Did you learn anything else?"

"Yes. There are two watchmen in the foyer tonight. Plus, a Mentor sentry walking in the gardens. I spoke to him in person, and he had lots to say about building up my religious portfolio. He said I should pick two starter faiths—Judaism and Shintoism, say—and see how they worked for me over a twelve-month period. After that, I could diversify into—"

Scarlett held up a hand. "Yes, fascinating. Right now it's the guard himself I'm interested in. What can you tell me about him?"

Albert chewed, considering. "He's big and hairy, and his name is Bert."

"Any *relevant* information?"

"He carries a gun under his robes. Also a ritual sword. He's been trained, knows how to handle himself. Violence in his past. Judging from the few minutes I was reading his mind, these days he's mainly interested in rice wine, poker, and girls from the Kenilworth district." Albert spoke thoughtfully. "You know, for a Mentor, I don't think he's particularly spiritual."

Scarlett snorted. "Of *course* he's not. None of them are. All right, you've done brilliantly, Albert. We don't need to wait any longer. Let's go."

They continued down the lane, Scarlett leading, Albert eating his bun. Moonlight cut diagonally across them, silvering the far verge, but the side by the wall was black. Scarlett's senses crackled with anticipation. This was it: this was what she lived for. Now she was alive. Now the drab world leaped into exquisite focus—the shadows pooling darker, the moonlight gleaming brighter, her clothes tingling against her skin. Each sound, each smell, the very taste of the air was invested with rich significance. Danger or opportunity might be hidden in each detail.

Scarlett had already surveyed the wall, found a spot where the flaking mortar between the bricks gave good purchase. She had left a stone in the gutter to mark the place. When they reached it, she waited again, watching, listening. The sounds of the town were faint, or at least fainter than Albert's chewing. Moonlight and shadows. She opened the cloth bag, drew out her gun belt, and strapped it on. For the first time in four days, she felt properly dressed.

She set her fingers to the wall—and hesitated.

"Albert," she said, "will you *stop* eating so loudly? You're like a marsh-ox from the steppe. All that slurping and chomping will bring the militia down on us."

"Sorry. It's my nerves, I think."

"No, it isn't. We've done six bank robberies. This is no different. Put the bun down."

"It is a *bit* different, Scarlett. You know the stories about this place."

"Yeah. And I don't believe a word of any of them. Apart from the details about the gold."

"If you say so." A final frenzy of chewing and swallowing followed. The pamphlets were cast aside; Albert wiped his fingers on his jacket. "There. I'm ready."

"Right. The rucksack's in the bag. Put it on. Wait till you hear my whistle, then join me."

The wall was maybe twelve feet high; it took Scarlett eleven seconds to scale it. At the top, she straddled the stones, keeping low, looking out over the compound. The treelined gardens of the Faith House formed a great black rectangle, surrounded by the huddled lights of modern Warwick. To the north, immeasurably greater, the vast ruined arches and girders of the Old Town gleamed like bones against the stars.

There were one or two lights burning in the separate dormitory building beyond the trees, where most of the Mentors would now be retiring to rest; but the Faith House itself was a gray moonlit mass, a blocky, sprawling shadow sleeping beneath its minarets and spires. Robbers had never penetrated it. Even the formidable criminal fraternity known as the Brothers of the Hand, Scarlett's old employers, was said to have tried and failed. Its reputation—for both its gold and the intricacy of its dark defenses—extended across the kingdoms. It was supposed to be invulnerable.

Scarlett grinned. But *that* wasn't reckoning on the unusual abilities of Albert Browne.

She whistled quietly. Presently she heard a tremendous puffing and groaning coming from below. Albert appeared, very out of breath, and hauled himself atop the wall. A drowning one-armed man clambering into a lifeboat would have made less fuss about it.

Scarlett glared down at him. "What's the matter?"

"It's all that tea I had. I can hear myself sloshing."

"Always do a heist on an empty stomach. Rule Number One."

He perched awkwardly beside her. "Have we got to drop down? I think I might burst."

"Really? *That* would be worth seeing. . . ." Scarlett swiveled on the wall and lowered herself swiftly, frowning at the feel of her bare legs against the cold stone. Good disguise or not, a cotton dress wasn't cut out for this kind of work. She missed her trusty old coat and jeans, stowed with the bikes outside town.

Hanging for an instant, she dropped lightly into darkness. The fall was not far; she landed on soft, dry earth, with the smell of aromatic flowers all around. She stood, alert and silent, listening to the eager beating of her heart. She exulted in the moment, as she always did when she entered the territory of her enemies. Now there was no going back.

Noises overhead. She stepped away from the wall. There was a squeak, the briefest rushing sound, a muffled impact where she'd just been standing. Scarlett sighed and turned her attention to her gun belt. Yes, all the clips and pouches were in the right position: ammunition, lockpicks, knives . . .

Behind her, she heard Albert get totteringly to his feet, brushing soil from his clothes and rucksack.

He drew alongside. "This poor suit is never going to be the same again."

"Who cares? We're never going to be in Warwick again, either."

"True. It would be unwise. I'm sad about that, in a way."

Scarlett was moving softly off between the trees. The moon was bright and had lent the earth its silver sheen. "Sad? Why?"

"Well, it's like every place we rob. There's so much history here. The eerie ruins, the curious local customs . . . Some of the people are quite nice, too."

Scarlett snorted. This was the amazing thing about Albert. Six months of an outlaw's life, and he still managed to retain his incorrigible positivity. "Albert. You've seen the posters. We're Public Enemies Number One. If they catch us, if they find out who we are, they'll string us up in the central square. They'll torture us, then kill us horribly. Everyone wants us dead."

"I know. . . . But aside from that."

"There *is* no 'aside.' These are people of the Towns. They're cruel, vindictive, and hateful, as I keep saying. And the Mentors are worst of all. Look at the post there. It's all the evidence you need." She slowed; they had come to the edge of the trees. A gravel path and a broad strip of silvered grass ran up toward the Faith House. Not far away, the path bifurcated around a circular pool, dark as ink, its rim of white tiles symbolizing the all-encompassing circle of the Faith Houses, the way it embraced every permitted religion. But here too was a dais, on which stood a slim and upright pole—the whipping post. Scarlett's eyes glinted. Tomorrow the Mentors would use it again on three more victims.

They did not move for a while, but stood still and watched the gardens. It was always as well not to be hasty at such times. Nothing stirred at the House itself. The great façade was blank white plaster, pitted and stained with age. You could see the curved brick steps that led up to the entrance foyer. Light showed from a single small window above the door.

Presently they moved toward the building, keeping to the trees.

"You mentioned our Wanted posters just now," Albert said. "Did you take a look at them while you were passing? A proper look? Seems the reward's gone up to twenty-five thousand pounds."

"Yeah. I saw that."

"You realize it used to be twenty thousand just for me. That means you're worth five thousand pounds now, Scarlett. Well done."

He was smiling at her, and she grinned back. "Get lost. We'll be worth a whole lot more after tonight, if all goes well. . . . Okay, we need to cross the lawns. We go straight to the door, burst in, deal with the watchmen inside. Are you ready?"

"Yes." There was a pause. "Well, actually not quite." Albert cleared his throat. "You know, it's all that tea. . . ."

Scarlett rolled her eyes. If he didn't, he'd never be able to concentrate. "Shiva! All right, but be quick about it. The nearest tree."

He departed with stiff-legged strides, and Scarlett stood looking out across the gardens. The whipping post was lit by moonlight; almost against her will, her gaze kept returning to it. A cloud passed across the moon, and the post vanished. For a moment Scarlett's focus changed; she saw three different posts, standing in the sunshine of a golden dawn. . . .

She blinked fiercely, wiped the image away. Footsteps on the grass: Albert returning from the bushes. Only it wasn't Albert. It was a man in the long black robes of a Faith House Mentor, appearing from round the corner of the building. The sentry had a squat, broad torso, a ruddled face, black hair slicked back long over his high white collar. He and Scarlett noticed one another at the exact same time. Scarlett was the first to react. She started forward, reaching for her belt. The sentry moved swiftly too. His right hand pulled clear of his robes, holding a pistol. In the same instant, a knife left Scarlett's hand; it struck the man's wrist, handle first, knocking the gun from his grip.

They were both still moving forward. Now the Mentor's left hand appeared; it held a long knife curved like a bird's beak. He lunged close, swiped viciously at Scarlett's arm. She swiveled aside; the blade tip cracked against the ground. The guard lashed sideways at waist height. Scarlett dropped forward onto her hands—the knife swept over her head, passing through her upflung hair like a fish through waterweeds. She swung a leg in a horizontal circle, connecting with the man's shins and making him stumble away. A moment more and she was on her feet again. He swung the knife desperately. Curling round it, she kicked out again, so that her heel made contact with the softest, most central portion of his trousers. There was a noise like a deflating balloon. The sentry folded inward. As his chin came down, Scarlett met it with an emphatic uppercut. Another noise: this one like an egg cracking. The man seemed newly boneless. He went flying back, landed heavily, relaxed into a spread-eagled star shape on the ground.

Scarlett blew her blond fringe out of her eyes and straightened. She rubbed briefly at her knuckles. They ached.

Albert came out from behind the trees, fiddling with his buttons. "Phew, *that's* better. . . . I feel much lighter now." He pulled up short. "Oh, who's this?"

Scarlett glared at him. "*I* don't know, do I? Was it Bert or Bill? You're the one who met him. Now hurry up and take hold of his legs. We need to tie him somewhere out of sight."

She was pleased to see that Albert didn't hesitate, didn't ask questions, but just did what he was asked. The heist had properly started. The body on the ground had snapped him into line. Six months it had taken to iron out his quirkiest, most life-threatening idiosyncrasies, but she'd just about managed it. In an emergency situation, he was almost as well drilled as she.

They removed the unconscious sentry, gagged and bound him, left him trussed against a tree. Then they returned to the Faith House. Brightness still shone from the foyer window.

The night was silent. The House and its contents waited.

Albert went to the door, looked toward the wood a moment. He glanced back at Scarlett and in silence held up two fingers. Then he raised his thumb.

Two men, as predicted. They were expecting nothing.

Scarlett nodded, took out her pistol. She moved toward the door.

3

All things considered, Albert Browne felt that his life of crime was going rather well. Yes, there *were* drawbacks, but this was to be expected with any career, and the benefits more than outweighed them. He was confident of this because, in quieter moments—whenever he wasn't being chased, hunted, or shot at—he'd gone so far as to compare pros and cons.

The top four drawbacks were:

1. The constant prospect of violent death.

2. The abusive language that frequently came his way.

3. The endless nights camped out in the wilderness, with thorns poking into intimate areas of his anatomy and wolves and dire-bears prowling avidly beyond the sulfur sticks.

4. The twinges of guilt that afflicted him from time to time.

Number four was bothering him a bit that evening. Take Bert the Mentor. One moment he'd been chatting agreeably with the fellow; an hour later he'd been tying his lolling body to a stump and gagging him with one of his own socks. No doubt the fellow deserved it; nevertheless, the disconnect was real. And now he had the sensation again as he looked at the two black-suited watchmen lying trussed and gagged on the floor of the Faith House foyer. Scarlett was just dragging them over behind their Welcome Desk, out of view of the door. Albert couldn't help feeling sorry for them, despite their furiously bulging eyes, their muffled curses, and the naked hostility of their thoughts. He flashed them an apologetic smile as he tidied the brochures that had been scattered in the fight. It would be so much nicer to live in a society where he and Scarlett could share pleasant conversation with such men, instead of bursting in, knocking them smartly on the heads, and tying them up with fifteen yards of prime knicker elastic, purchased at a Warwick fabric store the previous morning. Perhaps one day the world would change for the better. Albert certainly hoped so.

Meanwhile, the four top benefits of the roving outlaw life were:

1. Being with Scarlett.

2. Being free.

3. Being fit (this due, in no small part, to the endless getaway rides).

4. Traveling the length and breadth of the land, seeing its wonders, meeting its people, uncovering its beauties and its mysteries, and so satisfying the craving for knowledge that hunkered at the depths of his being.

On this current expedition, point four had been particularly satisfactory. They had left the fens and open skies of Anglia, crossed the ruined Tarmac stripway of the Great North Road, and cycled through the hills and gorges of the ash belt, sampling some delightful karst scenery, before passing several days in the fascinating town of Warwick.

Now they were about to explore its celebrated Faith House too.

Scarlett was on the move again. She crossed the room, her blond wig shining, her gun and burgling tools swinging incongruously against her dress. Albert pattered over to meet her, past the plastic charity box with its collection of pennies, the rack of brochures, the tea urns, the rows of simple wooden chairs. . . . He smiled ruefully: a short while ago, he'd been standing here, disguised as a prospective worshipper—now he was robbing the place! Yes, it was the sheer variety of experience he appreciated. No two jobs were ever the same.

They reached the door at the end of the foyer, where Scarlett paused to listen. Albert adjusted his rucksack and looked back at the huddled men. "Are they okay?"

"Well, I haven't given them each a pillow, but I think they can just about breathe. . . ." She pushed at the door with a cautious boot. "Don't look at me like that. I've got this far without shooting anyone, Albert. You should be pleased."

"It certainly makes a change." He scanned the room beyond: everything was still.

"I think I'm very restrained these days. Apart from those

bandits the other night, I haven't shot anyone for . . ." Scarlett frowned slightly, trying to recall.

"For almost a week. The sentry at the Mercian border, remember?"

"Oh, he doesn't count—I just winged him. He shouldn't have tried to stop us riding past." She slipped through the door. "Which way is it now?"

"Hall Two. Far side of this atrium. All the same, that Mercian sentry . . . a simple 'sod off' would have sufficed, surely."

"Oh, don't worry. I think I said that too."

The central atrium was a cool, dim space of smooth tiles and pitted brick, lit with soft electric lights and hung with drapes of gray and gold. It smelled strongly of incense. Neutrally colored doors opened to halls of worship on either side, and there was a curtained arch at the end. They strode straight toward this without delay.

Scarlett's efficiency of purpose was one thing she'd taught Albert during his six months at her side. There were countless others, too—some of them even legal. He knew how to choose a safe spot for a camp; how to make a cooking fire; how to set snares for mud-rats and weasels; and how to keep blood-moles from surfacing under your sleeping bag during the night. He knew the six top uses for a V-shaped stick; the best way to skin and debone a rabbit; how to find his way across a tektite field, where compasses were useless and the buzzing in your head could not be stilled; how to draw water from a gourd-tree; how to walk safely through black marshland; even how to cross a burning zone without a pair of fireproof boots. He had bartered with vagabonds, broken bread with thieves and lepers, joined zealots in their odd devotions. He had traveled on the motorized convoys that braved the Great North Road and the barques that hugged the Anglian coasts. He'd seen the Iron Mounds from afar and felt their magnetic pulses jolt his bones. In short, he'd *lived* a little, and the shuttered privations of his childhood in the prison of Stonemoor seemed an age ago.

It went without saying that Scarlett had taught him certain *other* abilities too, techniques of stealth and silence that came in handy during their expeditions. Skills at lock picking, window easing, and door jesting; little flourishes of knife and jimmy that helped gain access to safes and filing cabinets and desk drawers . . . This is not to say that Albert was particularly good at any of them, but these days he rarely put their lives in danger through sheer natural incompetence, which was itself a result.

They arrived at the archway at the end of the atrium. Hall Two, beyond it, was a place of shade and silence, lined with purple drapes. Scarlett paused now, listening. "So," she murmured, "the entrance to the secret rooms is here, behind the curtains?"

"If the pimply guy had it right."

"I suppose he'd know, pimples notwithstanding. Other Mentors inside?"

"Possibly."

"Traps?"

"Definitely. The real defenses start here."

The smell of incense was stronger in the inner room. Ranks of low stools curved around a blank, semicircular space where ceremonies of worship could be held. A neat display stand still held the list of the rituals that Albert had attended earlier that evening. It was not the first Faith House they had broken into, and he had come to understand the way the Houses worked—their mix of the theatrical and the mundane. They were places of order, first and foremost, no matter which god you worshipped, which rites you chose for your portfolio. Orderliness was all. Here you could see it in each room, in the carefully arranged drapes and candles, the gold and glimmer, the coziness, the comfy chairs, and the tea urns in the vestibules. It was a place of public chatter, of warmth and well-made things. Everything was kept on a human scale, and the world beyond was barred to it. Nowhere were there windows facing out to stark reality—to the fractured ruins of old Warwick or (worse) the beast-haunted hills beyond. But there *were* artful glimpses of the numinous: portals into blackness, high windows looking onto painted stars, thin alcoves with statues of gods and saints standing in husky dimness. It was deliberately created to be a house of mystery and shadow, and—

"Albert."

"Yes, Scarlett?"

"I just asked you a question."

"Did you? What was it?"

"Stay focused! We're on a job, remember! I said: 'Where's the hidden door?'"

"Left-hand curtain. Be careful with the levers." Albert hefted the rucksack more comfortably onto his shoulders. It was his job to carry that. Scarlett had the tools and gun.

She pulled aside the drapes, revealing the flat outline of a doorway and three short, plastic-handled levers protruding from the wall. She looked at him questioningly.

"The one on the right," Albert said. "The other two will kill us horribly."

"Uh-huh . . . okay. Do I pull it up or down?"

"Up. The door swings inward, I believe."

"Anyone behind it?"

Albert concentrated, opened his mind to the dark and the silence. "No."

"Fine." She pulled the lever without hesitation, and the door indeed swung inward, much more swiftly than Albert had expected. The entrance corridor of the inner sanctum of the Warwick Faith House stretched away in darkness. Far off was a lantern, burning.

They stood and looked at it. Somewhere beyond, if the stories whispered across the Seven Kingdoms were true, if the startling images Albert had sensed when sieving the Mentors were not deceptive, untold wealth was waiting.

It was a very inviting corridor.

Neither of them moved.

"Well, it *seems* all right," Albert said.

Scarlett scowled at the glimmering lantern in the distance, at its little halo of molten gold. "Doesn't it? That's what I don't like. Anything in anyone's thoughts about this corridor?"

Albert considered. The images he had stolen from the Mentors' minds shimmered dimly in front of him, like fragments of a dream. "Not specifically. There are definitely flipstones somewhere, but I couldn't get the exact locations. I asked lots of leading questions about the defenses of the House, but most of the people were too busy trying to give me brochures. I *do* know the way to the vault. It's down the end there, make a right, and then straight on."

"All in good time. . . ." Scarlett took her torch from her belt and slanted its light ahead of them. The floor tiles were large and gray and rectangular, each extending the width of the corridor. Every fifth one was slightly discolored—paler, somehow, than the rest. She wrinkled her nose. "They don't look *quite* so trodden on, do they?" she said.

Albert nodded. "Dusty with disuse, in fact."

"Yeah. . . . Let's keep them that way."

They moved slowly down the corridor, adjusting their strides to step over every fifth tile. As ever, Scarlett was calm, deliberate, unruffled. She kept the torch circling systematically, looking for oddities in the walls or ceiling, but the plaster was blank and bare. Whenever she paused, Albert looked back over his shoulder at the open door behind them, where a tiny strip of Hall Two could still be seen beyond the drapes. It was a deep gray space, empty and still. Albert realized he rather disliked it.

"We should have shut that door," he said.

"No. We may need a rapid exit. . . ." She snatched at his arm. "Careful! Watch your step!"

Albert gave a shimmy of fright, staring at the innocuous pale tile he had nearly trodden on. Certain unpleasant rumors about the Warwick Faith House returned unbidden to his mind.

"Scarlett, what do you think's down there?"

"Under the flip-stones?" She grinned back at him. She was already moving on. "Well, I don't reckon it's giant man-eating frogs, if that's what you're worrying about."

"You don't believe those stories? Good. Why?"

"Because of the logistics. How d'you keep a bunch of whopping frogs healthy, trapped down there? What do you feed them on? How d'you stop them eating each other?" She gave a shrug of her thin shoulders. "Nope, it's nonsense, take it from me. But hey, we'll never know, will we? Because we're not treading on the tiles. And now, what do you make of this?"

They were almost at the end of the corridor, with closed arched doors to the left and right. Ahead of them, the lantern glimmered enticingly on a high shelf, below which was a wooden lectern with a book resting on it. Albert stopped short: the image was identical to one he'd seen in a Mentor's mind when he had asked about their defenses.

"It's one of their holy books," he said. "It's bound in Tainted skin, and it's got gems pasted on the spine. Looks tempting, but it's a trap." His gaze flitted to the ceiling. "Yes, there! Above the door. See the tiny pipe? It's where the gas comes out if we take the book."

Scarlett grinned at him. "Well spotted. I'd have missed

that one. Give me a bunk up, will you? Then look away. It's awkward clambering about in this stupid dress."

She opened a wallet on her belt and took out the cotton wool padding they had brought for such a purpose. Then she stepped onto Albert's hands and so jumped to the lectern and then the shelf. From here she leaned out, plugged the pipe, and jumped lightly down again.

While waiting for her, Albert had been obediently glancing back up the long, blank corridor. It was still empty. "What about this holy book?" he asked.

"We nick it. Joe can get a good price for the jewels." Scarlett plucked the book off the lectern. There was a slight click, but nothing else happened; she handed it to Albert, who put it in his rucksack. "And now we go right," she said. "Anyone behind this door?"

He concentrated, searched for nearby thoughts. "No."

"Fine."

She opened the door; beyond it was a large, square room, lit by flickering electric light. There were several doors out, tables and comfy chairs, and ranks of display cabinets lining the walls. These contained the usual Faith House mementos—artifacts dating back to the days of the Frontier Wars. There were guns with which the pioneers had shot the Tainted; papers showing grants to the people of Warwick to reclaim the ruins and plow new fields. There were photos too: of the big-mustached first Mentors; of executions of deviants in the central square; even of the first traveling Faith Houses from which the Mentors spread the doctrine of hope and spiritual connection to the scattered Surviving Towns. The Houses in those days were little more than curtained booths, each set atop a wooden wagon and reached by scaling a simple ladder. Albert tried to imagine the wagons trundling through the wilderness, avoiding the dangers along the way. How had the Mentors kept safe? Perhaps there were fewer Tainted in those days.

As ever, he found himself lingering at the cabinets; as ever, he would have liked to stay and study the old pictures properly. But it was impossible. Scarlett was waiting in the center of the room.

"Will you hurry it up?" she hissed. "You're like an old duffer admiring a view. I want to get to the vault."

"But don't you think it's fascinating?" Albert bustled over, his shoes falling softly on the rugs that lined the floor. "So much history! This House is stuffed with it."

"It's the fact it's stuffed with *gold* that interests me," Scarlett said. And sure enough, her thoughts bore this out. Albert was doing his best to ignore them, out of courtesy, but he could see the images swirling around her head—the vats of coins, the gold and silver bars. Now that she was close to success, her avarice was swelling, pressing in on her cool practicality.

"I don't think it's piled up *quite* as high as that," Albert said.

She glared at him. "Not reading my mind, are you?"

He spread his hands. "If I am, it's not *my* fault. We're on a job, so you're not wearing the hat, plus you're practically throwing your thoughts at me. It's like you're hanging colored flashing lights on them, they're that brash and gaudy. Anyway, it's not how the Mentors saw the vault, that's all I'm saying."

"All right. Stop grumbling. Where *is* the vault?"

"Door straight ahead."

"Okay. Watch out for that big pale tile here. Don't tread on it."

They circled carefully round, approached the door. Scarlett grasped the handle, pushed her blond hair out of her face. "Not locked. Anyone behind this door?"

Albert concentrated. "No."

"Fine."

She opened the door. Behind it stood a tall bald man in a black suit, holding a long, thin-bladed knife. Without a sound he lunged forward, stabbing at Scarlett's heart.

4

lbert opened his mouth to give a cry of shock but found he didn't have that luxury. Instead, he was knocked smartly backward by Scarlett, who had dodged desperately aside as the knife sliced down. He lost his balance, stumbled back another step—and trod heavily on the large pale floor tile behind him. It subsided with a click, seesawed around a pivot in its center, and pitched him down into a yawning void.

Scarlett was ducking under a second wild blow from the Mentor. Even as she did, her hand shot out behind, grasping Albert by his upflung wrist. She braced her legs and took his weight. Instead of plummeting straight into the pit, Albert fell against the side of the hole. His midriff struck the lip of the flagstones; his fingers scratched for a handhold as his feet kicked frantically in nothingness.

From somewhere below came a draft of cold air and a hollow sucking and splashing of things moving urgently in dark water.

The Mentor slashed outward with the knife. Scarlett jerked back. In doing so, her hand dropped down, and Albert found himself plunging farther over the edge. He clutched at the lip of tile. Close below him there was a wet impact against stone—then a splash, as a large object dropped back into the depths. Something bunted the tip of his shoe. He heard a soft scrabbling sound, then another splash.

Scarlett hauled furiously on his hand, dragging his arms back up and over into the light. She let go of him, flowing onward and away to engage with the shape of the Mentor. Albert thrust hard with his elbows, flopping his torso forward onto the tiled floor. He clawed himself up and out of the pit. As he shuffled onto his knees, he looked down and glimpsed several pairs of pale and bulbous eyes perched in the darkness below. They were peering up at him from distant depths. The flip-stone closed abruptly on them.

Somewhat unsteadily, he got to his feet. As he did so, there was a gasp, a cry, a thud, a crack of metal on tile. When he looked, the thin-bladed knife lay spinning on the floor. The Mentor was a crumpled mound close by. Scarlett was standing in the doorway to the Faith House vault, clutching at her head.

Albert's stomach lurched. "*Scarlett!* Are you all right?"

"Sure." She wasn't out of breath; perhaps only a little irritated. Her wig was askew, a great chunk sliced from the top of it. "Look at this," she growled. "Ruined. What's Joe going to say? It took him ages to get this for me. He's going to be livid if we have to find another one." She pulled the blond mess away and cast it aside. Her long red hair fell untrammeled about her face.

Albert took a deep breath. "But *you're* not hurt?"

"Of course not. What's up? You're shaking."

"Nothing. Nothing at all. I'm fine."

"What was in the pit?"

He looked at her. "Water. Jumping things with bulgy eyes."

"Oh." She paused, then rubbed her hands together briskly. "Well . . . *that's* why we don't tread on the pale tiles, see? Got to watch where we're going. And speaking of which—what's with this guy?" She nudged the body beside her. "How come you didn't sense him?"

"I'm so sorry, Scarlett. But there's iron bands on the inside of the door—look. Iron blocks my talent, as you know." He saw the inquisitorial light in her eyes click off. It was one of Scarlett's many virtues: she didn't dwell on things unnecessarily. With his explanation given, the matter was closed. She was instantly satisfied, ready to move on.

He stepped over the Mentor's outstretched leg. It had long been a source of fascination to him that Scarlett had acquired so many illicit skills at such a young age. Someone, he knew, must have taught her, but she never spoke of it. Like most things in her past, it was hidden just below the surface, out of view. He didn't care to sieve for it: she was his friend.

"He isn't dead, is he?" he asked.

"Nope." She bent to the man's side, plucked a set of keys from a pouch at his belt. "But he'll have a mare of a headache when he wakes up. Which serves him right—he tried to stop us getting into *there*."

Albert looked past her. He could see the spyhole in the

open door through which the Mentor had been watching them and, beyond, a room of metal shelves and tables stretching away beneath soft electric lights. And *on* the tables: boxes, boxes, neatly stacked—with here and there a glint of gold. There was a familiarity about the room—he had caught echoes of it when sieving the Mentors earlier. Like all borrowed memories that were suddenly made real, they gave him the sensation of being an interloper, of fleetingly wearing someone else's life rather than his own. In some ways, it was not an unpleasant feeling.

But he was getting left behind again. Scarlett was striding into the vault, moving at that pace she always maintained during a heist. Brisk, balanced, supremely controlled—ready to react to whatever sprang at her, seldom glancing back. Albert had long ago realized that back was her least favorite direction. It was like there was something awful following behind her. Scarlett knew it was there; she could not escape it. But she would never let it catch her up.

She was flourishing the keys now, unlocking cashboxes, flinging open lids, springing between the shelves. "There are clearly Mentors in the building we didn't know about," she said. "We should spend ten minutes here, no more. Let's have the bags."

Albert took the burlap bags from the rucksack and threw one to Scarlett. Holding his own bag open, he approached the nearest aisle. Yes, here were the things that always got his partner so excited: the piles of banknotes, the coins, the jewels, the gold and silver bars, the rows of statuary and other luxuries that had been traded from specialist towns across the kingdoms. The Faith Houses hoarded wealth in a manner unimaginable to the average citizen. Since they were barbaric in their treatment of anyone who disagreed with them or failed to meet their genetic requirements, Albert had no compunction about taking what he could.

He was about to start with a stack of notes when he noticed something more interesting. On an otherwise empty shelf was a small see-through plastic box, perhaps as long as his forearm. Inside it, resting on plumped pink satin, was an irregular metal object, very black and corroded. Albert could see brittle plastic-coated wires sticking out of it, a long thin tube, and something resembling a curved hook. He knew that artifacts of ancient days were sometimes retrieved from drowned or Buried Cities in the wastes, and he had long wanted to see one. A strange tang reached his nose. It was sharp and sour and musty—the smell of things lost and rediscovered. The smell of the past . . . He bent close to the box, frowning.

"Albert, will you *stop* your daydreaming?" His head jerked up. Scarlett was glaring at him from across the aisle. Her bag was almost half full.

"Sorry."

"Your mouth's hanging open as wide as this sack. What have you got so far?"

"Um . . . nothing."

"*Nothing*? Shiva! How many times have we discussed this?

You can stare gormlessly into space as long as you like *after* we've completed the job. This isn't 'after,' is it?"

"No."

"So concentrate. You know the priority: banknotes first, then coins, then gold that can be melted down. Then jewels. If there's space left, we take ornaments that Joe can sell. Okay?"

"Yes, Scarlett."

She was moving away. "Good. You're doing fine. But we need to finish here and get out. And don't forget to keep listening—or whatever it is you do."

"I won't." He looked back at the open door. The anteroom was still quiet, the display cases and sofas gleaming darkly beneath the electric lights. The Mentor lay as before. Albert looked and listened, but the iron on the door impeded his efforts. The only thoughts he could discern were Scarlett's, and they were fierce and full of gold.

He passed among the boxes, obediently shoveling coins and notes into the sack. Scarlett was right. He *did* feel as if he was doing fine. Aside from the skills she was teaching him, his control over his own powers was improving all the time. Take mind reading, for instance. It was much more precise than it had been when he left Stonemoor—he could delve with impunity into individual minds. And he could do it in crowds, too. The hubbub in his head was still there, of course—he'd still see the swirling thoughts of those around him. But he had learned to damp it down, to dull its sharpness, so the old panic didn't well up inside him. Crucially, that meant he was no longer prey to the Fear, to the eruption of psychic violence that wrought such havoc on his surroundings. It meant he could sieve people with greater confidence, even in stressful moments, even in banks and Faith Houses. . . . And what was his secret? Focus! Focus and concentration!

"Shiva's ghost, Albert, you've drifted off again."

"Sorry, Scarlett, sorry."

"Will you bloody well fill that bag?"

"Of course, of course. . . ." He hurriedly collected a few more trinkets. As an afterthought, he picked up the plastic box containing the strange metal relic too. Then he rejoined Scarlett, who was strapping her bag to her back with an air of satisfaction.

"We should always hit Faith Houses from now on," she said. "Nothing else. Forget the banks. I'm carrying three times as much gold now as we got from that two-bit High Plains Bank in Bedford, and—" She broke off, frowning. "What have you got there?"

He held the box up reverently. "I don't actually know."

Scarlett blinked at it. "I do. Looks like a relic from before the Cataclysm. Bin it."

"Why? Don't you think it's special?"

"No, I think it's a lump of old crap. Empty out this crate instead—look, it's crammed with money."

"I thought it might be valuable. . . . It's on a pretty cushion. We could see what Joe says."

"I *know* what Joe will say. That piece of tat isn't going to help him build his boat, is it? Gods above us! We've got half the wealth in Mercia at our fingertips. Our main problem is choosing what to carry. And *you're* interested in the one thing with no commercial value. Throw it away."

"Oh, all right." He knew better than to argue. All the same, when she wasn't looking, he put it in the bag.

The sacks were full; Scarlett and Albert met beside the door. Scarlett's eyes shone with a green flame; she was still deep in the exultation of the heist. Albert, by contrast, was conscious of a sudden melancholy. It often happened this way. He gazed back at the vault, at the boxes left unopened, the secrets unrevealed. . . .

He realized she was watching him. "We've got all that we can carry," she said.

"I know. But it doesn't seem right to leave *any* of it." Albert gave a heartfelt sigh. "Think of all the poverty out there . . . the outcasts, the slaves. . . . Did you see those kids sweeping the main street this evening? They were practically dressed in rags."

"I know." Scarlett glanced ostentatiously at her watch. "And your point is?"

"I'm not sure. We should help them somehow."

"We *do* help them."

"Scarlett, we should do more."

"Yeah, well, this philosophizing will have to wait till we're safe beside the campfire tomorrow." Scarlett turned back to face the antechamber. "Just think, you can alternate it with all your gormless staring. It'll be a blast for you. But now we need to choose the best way out before—" Her voice broke off. "Albert, where's the Mentor?"

Albert looked around the room. In many ways it seemed much the same. There were the cabinets and comfy chairs, the quiet closed doors, the rugs, the big pale flip-stone. . . . There too was Scarlett's discarded wig, wedged like a giant caterpillar against the base of the wall.

But no Mentor.

He bit his lip. "That poor man! He must have rolled over and fallen down the hole."

Scarlett scowled. "Yes. Or, in another distinct possibility, the bugger's got up and run away." As she spoke, there came the clanging of a bell. She cursed softly. "Yeah, right on cue, that's the alarm. . . . This is *your* fault, Albert. I blame you."

"*My* fault? You're the one who hit him! You obviously didn't do it hard enough."

"Exactly! It's all this stupid stuff about not killing! I should have just chucked him to the frogs—then we wouldn't *have* this problem. All right, all right—forget it. Listen, you need to concentrate now. You sieved the Mentors; you know the layout of this inner sanctum. What can you sense, and where?"

Albert was ahead of her. He had already closed his eyes, trying to ignore the thrumming of his heart. "Okay . . . I hear thoughts. Men coming."

"Good. From which direction?"

"Er . . . from all of them."

Sure enough, thoughts were stirring all around. They were

still a way off, maybe, but getting closer on every side. As Albert opened his mind to them, their strength redoubled; they spilled over and through each other. He could discern pictures, too—unpleasantly coherent ones, laced with violence and retribution.

He shook the images away. "The best bet is this door on the right," he said. "It leads to higher floors. There'll be windows overlooking the gardens. But there are Mentors there—"

"Not for long, there won't be." Scarlett took her pistol from her belt. She checked the bullets, glanced coolly up at him. "This could be tight. Just saying, and don't take this the wrong way, it might be a good moment for you to . . ."

"*I can't.*" The words tumbled from his lips; he felt a cold clamp of panic in his belly. "You know I can't," he said. "I mustn't. It's too dangerous. It's not possible."

She snapped the gun shut. "In that case," Scarlett said, "you're going to need to lock onto my mind. Do what I do, soon as I think it. There won't be time to talk."

It was true. From somewhere near at hand came the grinding of cogs, the sound of hidden mechanisms. Bolts shutting across the Faith House, escape routes being closed down. From neighboring rooms came the thump of boots and terse commands. . . . Scarlett and Albert didn't wait to hear more. They were already gone.

They met six Mentors in their progress upward through the inner sanctum of the Faith House. Six Mentors, with more behind. At least Albert *thought* that was the number. The specifics were hard to recall. In part this was because of the kaleidoscopic madness unfolding all around—the swift changes of direction, the figures hurtling toward them, the bullets cracking against stone, the flashes of knives and swords, the screams and squeals, the buffets, blows, and curses, the sequence of livid faces and clutching hands. Yes, partly it was all of that. In his experience, such close-quarter stuff always served to scramble one's memory, and when (as today) the chase took place in a series of half-lit corridors and stairwells, some thick with chalky incense, it only added to the confusion.

But it was Scarlett who *really* shielded him from the details of what was going on. Throughout their flight, he remained close behind her, focused on *her* mind and what *she* saw. And—as ever in such circumstances—her thoughts were sharp and measured, ringing with clarity and light. *Up the stairs . . . stop . . . duck now . . . step back . . . wait . . . leap over the body . . .* Each intention was signaled a split second before she carried it out; each action merged smoothly into the next. By latching onto thoughts and actions, by repeating them, by echoing them as best he could, Albert was able to remain close beside her and alive. *Through the arch . . . behind the chairs . . . dodge left . . . spring right . . . now crouch and run . . .* Somehow, in this manner, the chaos was filtered out; events flowed past him like water, and he retained his calm.

They barreled into a chamber on an upper floor. Bullets flew between their heads and struck the bags tied to their backs. Scarlett spun round and slammed the door. She drew a bolt into the latch. It was a small stone room; moonlight from a single window spilled against the walls.

Impacts sounded on the door. Albert and Scarlett crossed to the window, looked out of it and down. It was not the smallest drop. The gardens of the House stretched black below.

"Well," Scarlett said, "I've seen worse exits. So we jump to the parapet on the left and swing down to the one below. From there we can throw ourselves to that narrow tree branch—see it?—and after that it's a scramble down the trunk and away."

Albert had seen worse exits too, but not often. "Looks a bit tricky," he said.

"Only if you don't trust me." She gave him a flash of the old grin. "*Do* you trust me?"

He looked at her, standing there beside him. Scarlett's hair was a cascade of defiance. Her pale face shone. There was a cut on the side of her forehead and another on her hand. The dress had seen better days now; the sword slashes didn't help. But she stood poised, lightly balanced in her neat white pumps, ready for another explosion of decisive movement.

Did he trust her? Albert hitched his trousers a little higher.

"Always," he said.

"Then let's go."

5

They had not escaped. Their pursuers were in sight again. From her position on the hilltop Scarlett could see a faint cloud moving along the white thread of the Warwick road. The cloud was sharp and tilted at the front, diffuse and ragged to the rear. Its dust rose silently between the hills. She adjusted her elbows and took up the binoculars. Yes, there was the convoy: the truck with the militiamen, the black-sided van that held the tracker dogs, lastly the three motorcycles coming along behind. It was too far away to hear the screaming of the engines, the howling of the dogs, the bloodthirsty cursing of the men as they followed the outlaws' trail. But Scarlett could imagine it all vividly enough—and what would happen if they caught them.

The binoculars felt loose and sweaty in her hand. She put them down; the hunting party was once more just a faint cloud on the horizon.

"Well, this *is* exciting," Albert said. "Think they'll fall for it?"

He lay beside her on the dry earth of the slope. Like Scarlett, he was flat on his belly, arms bent, legs outstretched, his clothes so covered in ash, dirt, blood, and gunpowder that he merged with the rocks around him. They were like two spindly outcrops of the hill.

"They're townsfolk," Scarlett said. "They're stupid. Of course they'll fall for it."

"I hope so. I can't cycle any longer. My legs will drop off. I don't think my bum has ever been so sore."

"What joy. Another detail I could do without. But don't fret. They won't come this way."

"Are you one hundred percent sure?"

Scarlett hesitated. She wasn't one percent sure, but she wasn't going to let Albert see it. "Definitely, yeah."

"Oh, good." Albert reared upward like a sand-whale breaching; in a trice, he was sitting cross-legged on the hilltop and cheerfully reaching for the bags. "So—I fancy an apple while we wait," he said. "You? Or I've got some cracking Uppingham plums."

"For Shiva's sake!" Scarlett grappled his arm, pulled him furiously down beside her. "Don't get up yet, you fool! They'll have binoculars too."

Albert subsided obediently and they lay in silence, side by side. Scarlett remained propped on her elbows, chewing a strand of hair. Her wide-brimmed hat was safely on again, but she still wore the green dress, stained by the dust of the getaway ride. She could feel sunlight on the backs of her legs, the hem fluttering in the warm breeze coming up from the gully. It would have seemed quite pleasant if it hadn't been for the exhaustion and pounding fear.

Well, there wasn't any use complaining. Everything now

depended on the trick. It was the last roll of the dice of what had been a taxing day.

Leaving Warwick had been a difficult experience. Simply getting out of the Faith House gardens had been strenuous enough, and the chase through the streets was worse. The militia had been out in force, and it had taken Scarlett and Albert almost till dawn to reach their bicycles. Departing at speed, they had blown the bridge over the ravine at the edge of the safe-lands to delay pursuit. To leave nothing to chance, they had also set off in the wrong direction, only doubling back to the south when they reached the hill country. It hadn't been enough. Trackers had spotted them from afar across the ash fields, and they'd been hounded ever since. At last Scarlett had been forced into a desperate tactic to buy them time.

They had ignored the turnoff to the tiny hill path, cycling a further mile along the main road before strapping their bikes to their backs and climbing a scree slope to get onto the ridge. To make the ploy effective against the dogs, they'd scrambled up a hill stream for the first two hundred yards. Then a zigzag route through sagebrush to meet the path. . . . With luck, it would be enough. Scarlett's neck ached with tension. Her stomach was a knotted fist. If it wasn't enough, she and Albert would be dead within the hour.

Even with the binoculars, you couldn't quite see the place where the turnoff was, where the path diverged from the road. Still, you'd be able to tell from the dust cloud what the militia was doing, whether the ruse had worked.

"They've chased us a long way," Albert said. "It feels much longer than usual."

"It is." Scarlett's lips were parched from the chase; there was water in their bags beside them, but now was not the time to move. "We did desecrate their holy Faith House," she said. "We also smashed up half the market during our escape *and* destroyed their bridge."

Albert nodded. "*And* you knocked over two of the town elders when we cycled off."

"Three. There was a small one you didn't notice."

"It's no wonder that they're mad. Shh! This is it!"

Scarlett stiffened; she caught her breath. The dust cloud had neared the turnoff. Looking through the binoculars, she saw the trucks stop first, the motorcycles skid to a halt alongside. Figures got out, started moving by the road. Yeah, they were thinking about it, inspecting the ground.

"Our cycles went straight on," she muttered. "So you'll go straight on, too."

The men seemed unsure. They were locked in conversation. Scarlett felt a ribbon of sweat trickling down from under her hat. At last the militia returned to their vehicles. The convoy set off. They went straight on. The dust cloud vanished beyond the slope of the hill.

Scarlett expelled air in a rush. She put the binoculars down. "We did it," she said.

"So *that's* all right." Albert was already at his ease and opening the lunch bag. "I don't know why we were worrying."

* * *

They sat where they were on the brow of the hill. It was wild territory. Below the high escarpment, the dirt slope steepened and fractured into a wide declivity, choked with a river of tumbled stones. At its base opened a broad, sunlit canyon, peppered with saw-brush. There was a stream down there; it glittered in the afternoon sunlight, winding between great tilted slabs of black rock. Beyond was another slope, rising again to the salmon-colored hills.

Albert took an apple from their supplies. They had not had time to eat all day. Scarlett's first move was to finish her bottle of water. Then she pulled her bags close—the loot, her rifle, her prayer mat in its plastic roll, everything she owned. She took her cuss-box out and hung it round her neck. It had not been advisable to wear it while in disguise. She felt the familiar bite of the grubby cords; its weight, as ever, was both painful and reassuring. From a pannier she took a few coins and slotted them into the box to make it heavier still.

"You might want to put a few more in," Albert observed. "After four days' swearing, you've got a bit of a backlog."

"Yeah."

"Golly, I've never heard you cuss so much. My eyes are still watering. You should swap that box for a barrel."

"Of course I swore. Do you blame me? We nearly died a dozen times. Give me an apple."

"I think there's cheese left too. I sat on it just now when you pulled me down, so it's a bit squashed and dribbly, but—"

"The apple will be fine."

A warm wind was coming up the gully. Scarlett tilted her hat back and let the breeze break gently against her forehead. It was good to sit there, with the warmth and the light and the wind on your legs and arms. And with sacks of stolen plunder at your side. It was the feeling of righteous freedom. Once again, Scarlett and Browne had successfully thumbed their noses at the Faith Houses and the wicked Surviving Towns.

But it hadn't exactly been easy. . . . A thought occurred to her.

"So," she said. "Albert. How did you reckon it went today? The heist. All that."

He looked at her with his big dark eyes. His hair and face were red with dust, his suit ripped and ruined from the exigencies of the chase. "The heist? Good, I think."

"Yes?"

"I sieved the Mentors well. You kicked them in the groin with your traditional finesse."

"And what about our escape? Cast your mind back. Is there anything we could have done better, perhaps?"

Albert's brow furrowed. "Well, now . . . perfection is so hard to come by. I'm sure there's always some little detail we could improve. But, you know, all in all I think it's gone jolly smoothly."

"So nothing to mention, then?"

"No."

"Not even that bit at the start of our desperate ride, when

you stopped your bike beside the Warwick slave pens, saun-
tered over to the cage, and freed the captives there?"

Albert nodded smilingly. "Ah, yes. I felt sorry for them.
There were no slavers around. I just broke the lock and let
them out."

"I know you did. With sharpshooters firing from the walls
and half the town howling at our backs. Why?"

"Simple. They were friendless, poor, and desperate. I think
some of them were Welsh. They needed a bit of help, Scarlett. It gave them a chance in life."

"No, it didn't. They'll have been rounded up in ten minutes after we left. . . ." Scarlett scratched irritably at the side
of her scalp. The hat was uncomfortable on her head. But she
didn't want to take it off. She was weary, and when she was
weary her thoughts had a tendency to become uncontrolled.
Things bubbled up that Albert, sitting nonchalantly beside
her, might easily observe. The hat was her safeguard. It protected her against this. She shook her empty bottle, looked
down the steep slope at the stream far below.

"Are you hot?" Albert asked. "There's a lovely breeze."

"I'm not removing the hat right now."

"I won't sieve you."

"Not purposefully, maybe. You probably do it without
thinking. You probably do it in your sleep." She finished the
apple and tossed the core carelessly toward the gully. "The
point I'm making is: you risked our lives on impulse. It was a
generous impulse, sure, but we lost valuable time with those
slaves. All that was important was to get away."

"Was it? Truly? I don't know. . . ." He frowned at her; she could see his frustration, see him summoning the words. She waited. "Why are we doing this, Scarlett?" he said.

"Robbing the Towns? To irritate them, to undermine them. To steal back some of the wealth the Faith Houses have spirited away. To enable us to redistribute some of that money to those who actually deserve it. Especially us. That's our life, Albert. We're outlaws—it's a noble calling. Would you rather be back in Stonemoor, kowtowing to the High Council all your days?"

That discomfited him, as she knew it would. He shuddered. "I never want to think about Stonemoor again," he said. "But we mustn't ignore the other victims, all the same."

"We *don't* ignore them. Thanks to you, we give half our cash away these days. To Joe, to the folk at the Wolf, to other outcasts that we meet. . . ." She shrugged. "I'm not complaining. I'm glad we're doing it. In fact, I'll be stopping off at Huntingdon tomorrow to distribute a little more."

There was a silence. "Without me?" Albert asked.

"I'll catch up with you at the Wolf's Head. Huntingdon's not a big diversion. I can give some of the money to the freed slaves there."

"Sure that's all you'll be doing?"

"All that concerns you," Scarlett said.

Neither spoke for a time. Scarlett was aware that a slight peevishness had entered her voice. She regretted it—fatigue aside, it *had* been a wildly successful day. The Warwick Faith House had been on the agenda for a long time. And they'd done the job beautifully, confidently, working as a team. Yeah, those posters in the square had it right. SCARLETT AND BROWNE: PUBLIC ENEMIES NO. 1. Each heist they tried, they got better and better, and there was nothing the Towns could do about it. It was a good feeling. Well, good up to a point. . . . Strange how, even with the glow of satisfaction that came from a successful heist, her emptiness and agitation remained. . . .

Which was exactly what Albert was getting at, of course. She glanced at him. He was staring out across the valley, his hands on his ragged knees. His face displayed no emotion. "Sorry," she said.

"That's all right."

"You did really well at Warwick, Albert. We both did. Where do you fancy going next? Northumbria, maybe? Anglia again?"

He shrugged. "Yes. Or Wessex."

"Not Wessex." She gave a brief, dry chuckle. "The Brothers of the Hand are still looking for me. They want my head."

"Still? You don't think they've got over it yet?"

Scarlett had a mental glimpse of Soames and Teach, the dreadful leaders of the Brotherhood, sitting brooding about her in their grim fastness at Stow. It wasn't a wholly comforting picture. "They *never* get over losing money," she said. "Well, we'll discuss plans with Joe at the Wolf. Right now, we need more water. I'll go down and get it, if you like."

"I'll go," Albert said. "I could do with stretching my legs. And those black rocks in the valley are quite interesting." He stood abruptly, a thin, ragged figure framed against the light.

Without looking at Scarlett, he gathered up the bottles and was slithering down the scree.

When she was alone, when she could see him at the bottom of the slope, picking his way between the saw-brush and the black splinters of rock toward the river, Scarlett took off her broad-brimmed hat and dropped it on the ground beside her. Her hair beneath was dark with sweat, frozen in low, disordered waves. The thin iron band that circled the top of her head felt sticky to the touch. The wretched thing had come free from the hat again. She'd have to fix it back to the fabric somehow.

Twisting her lips in discomfort, she reached behind her and unclipped the band, letting it come loose from her head like the opening of a flower. She laid it in her lap and rubbed furiously with both hands at the itchy weal it had left behind. Ordinarily it didn't bother her too much, but in conditions of heat like this it was more annoying than the cuss-box. She scowled. How had Albert's old jailer, Dr. Calloway, worn something like this all the time?

Her companion's slim shape was still visible below, moving hesitantly near the riverbank, looking for a place to fill the bottles. His shadow trailed behind him like a stain, like something dark had melted out of his body. Seen from here, he was nothing, just a fragment moving in the wilderness. Close to, he didn't seem much to write home about either.

But he was something. Every day he surprised her.

She stretched out like a hill-cat, lying back on her elbows and letting the hot wind come up from the gully to dry the knotted fronds of hair. A toothed bird was riding the thermals above the valley, and Scarlett watched it as it went about its hunting. The hills seemed quiet, but there was evidently life out here, stirring under the stones. . . .

It was growing late. They needed to get on.

She'd been unfair to him—she knew she had. Not about the slaves, but about him sieving her. About the hat.

It wasn't that he *meant* any harm. It wasn't that he'd ever *intend* to spy on the deep things, the secrets that were fused to the heart of her being. But he *could do it*. He could do it and she'd never know. Sometimes Scarlett could live with that knowledge, and other times not. Sometimes she just needed to wear the hat.

Albert was away from the gully now and out on the valley floor, moving with caution, the water bottles slung over his shoulder on their tie cords. It was difficult ground, dotted with boulders and the tilted black pillars of stone. A portion of the rocks not far behind him was rippling in a heat haze. It would be hot down there in the canyon, out of the breeze.

She followed his progress idly, letting her mind drift. Six months. As many heists. And in each one he was more controlled, his skills more accomplished and impressive. He was better in emergency situations, better in crowds; he could sieve almost anyone he—

Her head jerked up.

Wait. Something about the heat haze—

Scarlett's gaze snapped back to the rippling ground behind Albert.

Not a haze. Too long, too thin, too sinuous. Like a twist of ground had melted and was running slowly, lavalike and purposeful, in his direction.

In an eyeblink, the pistol was in her hand.

The body of the giant rock snake was three times Albert's length and probably two feet wide. It was perfectly camouflaged, its scales a mosaic of browns and grays and salmon pink. Only when it broke out from between the shadows of the rocks did she see the sharp pale zigzag pattern on its back.

The pistol was no good—she couldn't shoot that far. But she *could* alert him.

She raised the gun, fired the shot into the air. The noise rebounded down the gully, plunging back and forth between the rocks—a booming avalanche of sound.

Albert looked up. His small, thin figure turned. At the same moment, the snake increased its pace. It shivered, looping forward, building rapidly into its kill strike. The body flexed up in a mighty undulation; the great chisel head lifted, reared twice as high as Albert. The death-white zigzag on its back caught the sun, shone briefly like a lightning bolt.

Gods above! The rifle!

Scarlett threw herself over to the rucksack, ripped the weapon clear.

As she did so, she felt a pulsing in her temples. There was a crack like distant thunder.

She swung the gun round and up, scrabbled to a kneeling position, sighted between the rocky bluffs—

And stopped.

And lowered it again.

The giant snake was no longer there. The ground beside the river was veined with red splashes, splotches of flesh, twisted flecks of sun-brown skin. A great wedge of the valley floor stretching out in front of Albert was different too. There was debris everywhere. Several rock pillars had vanished; others were broken. Nearby boulders had split and shattered. Above the river a cloud of red rock dust was drifting silently away.

Scarlett's eyes were fixed on Albert. He raised one thin arm to her in casual acknowledgment, gave what was almost certainly a rubbish thumbs-up. Then he strolled off to crouch on the shingle by the stream. He filled the bottles one after another, standing them on a rock beside him. He did it carefully, almost competently; only once did he lose his balance and nearly fall in.

Scarlett sat back on the hill. She let her pulse slow, let the breeze dry the new sweat on her brow. Her knee was bleeding where she'd rested it on the stones. She sat cross-legged in her dirty green dress, with the rifle cold against her thigh. Her hair blew hard across her face.

"Bloody hell, Albert," Scarlett said. "Why won't you do *that* on a job?"

She put another coin in the cuss-box. There were two birds out riding the thermals now. Scarlett watched them soaring above the crags. They flew effortlessly, banking and dropping with little adjustments of their wings, and presently vanished toward the sun.

It was peaceful on the slope. The wind blew; the sky deepened. It took Albert a long time to toil upward among the rocks and stones of the gully. All the while he was doing so, Scarlett McCain remained sitting there, alone and quiet, gazing out beyond the hills.

II

THE WOLF'S HEAD INN

From the top of the rise you could see the green folds of the hills stretching back as far as Cornwall, and there was a rock by the path where the child could sit and catch his breath. The girl sat with him, her thin legs drawn up, her plimsolls flat upon the stone. She had her chin resting on her arms and her arms resting on her knees. She was watching the toothed birds down in the sunlight of the valley, circling the soft green domes and minarets of the highest trees. The valleys were filled with forest. On the tops were thickets of gorse and bilberry.

The child had adopted the same pose as his sister. Every now and then a knee escaped his circling arms and fell to the side; he would draw it carefully back into position.

"Can I have another berry?"

"No way. You've had millions."

"I'm still hungry."

The girl was hungry too, but she had put their pots of bilberries into her satchel and wrapped them in her jersey to keep them from knocking together. She wasn't going to undo all that now. "When we get home."

"But Mummy's going to make them into jam."

"So she'll give you something else."

They went along the brow of the hill, following the faint

chalk path, the little boy in front, the girl behind. Some days they would meet other homesteaders on the top, but today it was just them, the landscape, and the wind. The brow was curved like the back of a sleeping dog; they followed the gentle knobbles of the spine, down and up again, the gorse bristling against their legs.

The girl went with a steady rhythm, red pigtails bouncing against the back of her neck. She was thinking about the jobs that needed to be done when she got down. The goats, the chickens, helping her mother with the tea, going with Florence to the Masons' to ask about the ram, restocking the firewood from the shed, putting Thomas to bed, working in the garden if she had any time at dusk. . . . In her serious, practical way, she itemized everything, put it all in order, checked and rechecked to make sure nothing was forgotten. It was good to make a list; it satisfied her. She felt as if the jobs were already half done.

They dropped down into the hollow, where, as usual, the little boy stopped to have a pee, then angled steeply upward again to the hill above the house. The girl supported her brother's bottom on the most difficult bits, encouraging him upward, but he was getting bigger now and didn't slip or fall.

It was when they reached the top of the final ridge that the girl saw the ribbon of black smoke rising from the pleat of the valley. She stood with her hand on her satchel strap, staring at it, thin-faced, her mouth a tight, wide line.

The little boy was looking back at her. "What is it, Carly?"

"I don't know. They've set fire to the haystack or something. Shiva, I can't turn my back on them for a bleeding minute. . . ."

"Don't cuss, Carly. Mummy doesn't like it."

"Yeah. Well, Mummy's not here, is she? And if Mummy's set fire to the haystack, she's going to be hearing a whole heap more cusswords very shortly. . . ." The anger in her voice was forced; she could not sustain it. It was a black smoke, thick and greasy, holding its form even when the wind caught it, angled it toward her over the side of the hill.

She took the little boy's hand and pulled him with her along the path. He was tired and didn't want to run, but his sister was determined. After a while she grew exasperated at his protests and slapped him. Then he cried and came after, trotting and stumbling. The girl went erratically. She moved fast but kept stopping to look at the smoke, trying to gauge its exact position.

Not the Masons', or the Fowlers'. Too near. Not the bonfire either. Too big, too thick. She looked at the black fragments dancing against the sky.

"Why did Mummy set fire to the haystack?"

"What?" She was biting a twist of her hair.

"The haystack."

"I don't know if it's the haystack. Shiva, I don't know what it is. Hurry up, will you, Thomas? Come on."

They came down off the brow, over the broken stile, and into the trees. Green shades enveloped them. The bright chalk of the path ran white as a bone below the summer's bracken, going steeply down.

The girl marched ahead; the child came behind, snapping stalks, ferreting in the dry, secret, vaulted spaces below the ferns.

The wind shifted, coming up from the valley through the wood. It brought with it hints of smoke and something else: a sour taint. The girl stopped in the ferns, wrinkling her nose. She stood quiet and still and watchful, looking down the hillside between the trees.

The little boy crashed behind her through the bracken, alternately jumping, sliding, and skidding on his bottom. He tumbled to a halt beside her.

"Carly, look, I found a yellow stone."

"Yes. . . ."

"Look how round it is."

"Uh-huh. . . . Yeah, it's nice."

"Carly, you're not *looking*."

She was. The girl was looking as she had been taught to do. Looking and listening. The path dropped away over the hill's curve into the green shade. The fern heads were bent like a cowled congregation, silent, infinitely grieving.

Silent.

No birds. No animals. Nothing.

She sensed the silence sweeping toward her up the hill.

The girl swiveled at the waist, hoicked the child up, and carried him off the path, plunging away to where the bracken was deepest. The stalks slapped and broke against her chest like seawater. She ducked them both down into the depths. It was dark and green and dry.

"Thomas," she said softly, "we're going to play a game. You're good at games, aren't you?"

The child was crouched beside her, pudgy knees under his chin, almost as he had been up on the ridge. He was frowning. "My stone."

"What?"

"When you picked me up, I lost my yellow stone."

"We'll find it in a minute. Thomas, we're going to play dead lions. Both of us. But we have to stay as still as still. Can you do that?"

"Yes. But—"

"Let's do it now."

"But—"

"I'll give you a treat if you win. A good one. But I *bet* you'll move before I do. Yeah? Ready? Okay. Three, two, one. Go."

The idea of a treat had a concentrating effect. The little boy toppled forward. With a flurry of exaggerated kicks and wriggles, he pressed himself against the earth. He grew quiet. The girl hunched herself over him, arched like a tent, ready to press down and cover him brutally, to smother any noise.

They lay there. Soon the taint that was stealing upward through the wood found its way to them, curling invisibly between the fern stalks, brushing against their skin, rendering it unclean. It was more invasive than the smoke, more insidious. The boy was quiet. The girl's eyes were wide open in the half-light. She did not blink or move.

Presently she heard soft rustlings, the movements of a company climbing swiftly up the path. As it swept closer, she heard the swish and creak of the ferns flexing and the drum of feet on the hard chalk earth. Bare feet. Clawed nails in the earth. There were no words, no conversation; only, once, a shrill whistle, right on the edge of hearing. A great fear came over the girl; she lay like one already dead, her teeth and gums bared.

The taint grew thick; it ran in the sweat down the back of her neck and fell to the earth in drops beside the little boy. They were on the path but also coming through the bracken on either side. How close they would come she didn't know.

The noises became loud and local; shadows moved, the ferns above them quivered. A stench broke over them and was rapidly pulled away as the company continued on. The girl didn't move. The little boy was motionless. They lay together in secret in the wood.

After a long while the girl relaxed, but she still didn't change position. She stayed where she was. She began crying and cursing under her breath.

The child had grown drowsy in the warmth, but now he was bored. "Don't cuss so, Carly. That means I win."

"Yeah. You win. You win for sure."

"What is my treat? Why are we not getting up?"

"Oh, Thomas. I don't want to get up."

"We've got to."

"No."

"We've got to go home."

She struggled to her feet at last, breaking above the fern crests, staring all about her in the silent wood. Her eyes were large and pale, like those of a rabbit inching out of a hollow. She was holding one of the pigtails that her mother had tied for her, that morning at breakfast, after she'd come in from the goats. She was holding it like it was her mother's hand.

Traces of the taint still hung about the wood; she imagined it tangled invisibly about them, exposed and taut and white, like tendons running between the trees, but there were birds calling with tentative voices, and the feel of the place was clear.

They returned to the path, where the ferns were ripped and ragged and where, after some searching, the child found his yellow stone among the grasses of the verge. He was very pleased with it.

She took his hand, and together they went down through the wood.

At the edge of the first pasture they found the haystack intact, with the black pitchfork leaning against it, as the girl had left it earlier that day. She took the pitchfork, held it in front of her as they went on toward the column of black smoke behind the trees that fringed the homestead.

In the second pasture they found the goats. The girl picked up the boy and hid his eyes.

"Don't look," she said.

He had gone very still. "What's happened? Where's Mummy? Where's Florence? What's happened to the house?"

"You mustn't look." She hugged him to her fiercely, furiously, pressed his head against her shoulder.

"Ow! Why won't you let me look, Carly? Let me go."

"I'll never let you go, Thomas. You understand me? Never. I'll be with you always. But you mustn't look, sweetheart. You've got to close your eyes. Close your eyes now."

She started forward toward the burning house, a thin girl with a satchel of bilberries over one shoulder and a child on the other. The wind had switched, and there was turbulence in the air. The column of smoke was breaking overhead. Gray and black particles were falling on the grass about them, pattering slow and heavy, like rain.

6

It was one of those storms come over from the Burning Regions. Even inland it was raining ash. At the so-called motor-town of Huntingdon—two strips of bars and doss houses clamped either side of the Great North Road—the night was thick with it. Brown-black slurry was collecting on the Tarmac and along the raised wooden sidewalks. From the window of the Sunrise Inn saloon, you could see a few figures scuttering along the sidewalk, springing in and out of focus as they passed the bars and diners. They seemed to hang on the edge of existence, at the frontier between solid and liquid things.

Scarlett let the net curtains fall and swiveled back unsteadily to survey the saloon. The entertainments were in full swing. Beneath the dangling rows of lanterns, travelers stood at the bar or sat around tables in the company of the women of the inn. Everyone was drinking; some played cards, some shot darts; a group flipped coins into a hollow Tainted's skull. In one corner an upright piano of surpassing age was being played by an elderly lady in a flowery cotton dress. The atmosphere was thick with alcohol, with grimly determined levity.

A curved wooden staircase led to a balcony level, heavy with drapes and further gaming tables. It was there that Scarlett had lost all her money at skull toss a few moments before.

Well, not *all* her money—just the money in her pocket. Albert, now presumably over the Anglian border and half-way to the Wolf's Head, still had much of the plunder from the Warwick job. As for *her* portion, she had given away some of it in her first hours in Huntingdon—to the group of freed slaves in the favelas on the edge of town, and also to the women of the Red Rose Café. In the past six months, at her partner's prompting, Scarlett had grown used to making such random donations; she took pleasure in passing Faith House gold to people on the margins of society. But there were other impulses to be obeyed too, and so she'd let her hair down with the rest of the loot, as Albert had known she would.

Sometimes she won big at such games, sometimes she didn't. Scarlett didn't much care either way, and she felt no guilt about it, despite Albert's disapproval. It was all about losing herself, about offsetting that particular hollowness that she always felt after a job. The problem this time was that she'd gone too far and borrowed cash from some of the watching haulers in a last-ditch attempt to change her run of luck. And now she'd lost *their* money too.

Scarlett sat back with her head against the wall, eyes half closed. She'd sworn blind to the men that she had the cash upstairs and would fetch it after finishing another drink. They were waiting for her to go and get it. She could see them watching her from the bar—suspicious, but not yet suspicious enough to do anything. They all had guns, though. They were tough long-distance drivers, used to getting their convoys through the Tainted-haunted Wilds. It would get messy if she tried to sneak off to the door.

Well, the night was young. She'd think of something.

She rubbed her eyes and turned back to the window. Her head hurt. She thought of Albert wobbling off on his bike under all his packages. How she'd kept reassuring him she wouldn't lose it all. . . . Promises, promises. . . . Who was more stupid: the one who made a promise or the idiot who believed it? She moved the net curtains aside and leaned her brow against the raindrop-studded window, letting the cold seep into her through the glass.

Outside, the storm had intensified. The neon light of the steak bar opposite looked like it was melting in the rain. The road was a black strip, the sidewalks abandoned. . . . Or almost so. Scarlett squinted past the raindrops. Where the long-distance bus stop was, beneath the plastic awning where the ash rain bounced and spun, a man was standing.

The traveler wore a brown wool greatcoat with silver buttons, the collar drawn up against the weather. The coat was patinated with rain and the encrusted dirt of a long journey. His hands were in the coat pockets, his shoulders slightly hunched; his head was bent as if in meditation, with his eyes cast down at the water running between his shoes. Despite the wind and the water, he wore no hat; his hair, cropped short at the back and sides, lay plastered in black ribbons on his scalp. His face was straight-nosed, hollow-cheeked. The eyes could not be seen. There was a stillness about him that was remarkable amid the tumbling squall.

The cold glass throbbed against Scarlett's forehead. She pushed herself back from the window, got to her feet, took her hat from where it hung on her chair. She felt a sudden impulse to leave the inn, leave Huntingdon, get on the road despite the storm. In the course of her life she had learned to obey such intuitions. She had no more desire for the half-drunk beer on the table beside her, but she picked up the bottle and started out across the saloon.

"Heading up to your room?" They had been waiting for her move. A barrel-chested hauler, all jeans, tattoos, and red-checked shirt, whose black beard began where his chest hair stopped, swayed out of the crowd into Scarlett's path. "We're looking to get our money."

Scarlett grinned easily, raised the bottle in greeting. "Just moseying up now." She had borrowed quite a lot from him.

"You're not thinking of cutting out on us, I hope?"

Scarlett was at that very moment thinking of sliding down a drainpipe from an upstairs window. "Not at all. Want to hold my beer? I'll be back in three minutes, maybe two."

"The boys and I reckon you need an escort. Just so's you don't get lost coming back."

"Nope. I make a point of never taking a man to my room. But I *will* offer you, personally, a game of blackjack when I come down. I've got a feeling my luck's about to change."

She smiled up at him, held his gaze coolly in a way

that might mean anything or nothing. The hauler shifted, scratched at his beard. "It might at that. Two minutes, then."

"Sure." Scarlett turned away, pretended to take a casual sip of beer.

There was a gust of fresh air. Across the room, the door to the street clinked shut. Scarlett, with the bottle at her lips, paused minutely.

A man had come into the saloon.

She knew instantly he was the traveler from the bus stop. He was younger than she'd thought—a youth, even, with a clear, clean-shaven face. Ash and rain studded his shoulders and the lines of his slicked-back hair. Standing on the stone step, with the beer light glinting on the folds of his greatcoat, he surveyed the saloon, head turning side to side. He did not walk into the room but just stood there, eyes ranging blandly across the company.

Scarlett set the beer bottle on a nearby table. She pulled her hat down low. Her hand moved to her gun belt.

The youth stepped forward, began drifting through the crowd. He did not look at her; still, Scarlett could see he was making in her direction. Any lingering doubt that he had come for her was gone. On closer inspection, the greatcoat was slightly too big for him. You saw it mostly in the steep caldera of his collar, at the center of which his slim neck protruded incongruously; also at the cuffs, which threatened to engulf his hands. He was slight of frame, girlish and unmuscular. He looked as if a breath of wind might blow him down.

Scarlett realized she was very frightened of him.

Her hand closed on her gun hilt. She began to move too, seeking a way out. Her first plan was to reach the stairs, but the route the young man was taking looked as if it would cut her off. She altered course. Aside from the saloon door itself, there was a door behind the bar. Other exits were possible, too, but there were people and tables in the way. She wasn't close to any of them. She cursed herself for being sloppy.

It was too crowded to use her pistol, too crowded to cut and run. Scarlett inched through the throng, moving circuitously, chopping and changing direction. Across the room the youth did likewise, responding to her movements, trying to predict them. His progress was not entirely smooth; once or twice he was elbowed aside by laughing women and red-faced men. Nevertheless, each time, he frowned, stopped, took a different path that somehow brought him ever closer to Scarlett, who discovered her options were being systematically shut down.

She found herself beside the bar. A couple took their drinks and moved. The youth was there.

He smiled at her; his eyes were a deep blue.

"Scarlett McCain?"

The rest of the people in the saloon: they were still present but suddenly shaken clean away from her, separate and discarded, like so much snakeskin.

She kept her face blank. "No."

"That's a shame. Well, let me buy you a drink anyway."

His voice was soft, the quality of his gaze piercing. There

was the suggestion of his entire concentration being focused upon her, a disconcerting intensity of interest.

Scarlett felt a cold prickle at the back of her neck. She had seen that look before.

She shook her head. "Sorry, pal. I'm leaving."

"Oh, let's have a talk first." The youth raised an arm. "Barman! Two Alnwick Lights."

The barman of the Sunrise Inn—an enormous figure, menacingly bald, muscles spooned with difficulty into his black shirt and jeans—plucked two bottles from the icebox, knocked their tops off with the back of a knife, and set them spinning down the counter to come to rest at Scarlett's elbow.

"Thanks." The young man was leaning carelessly on the counter. He pushed some neatly folded notes toward the barman and smiled at Scarlett. "Got to keep it civilized," he said. "What do you say, Miss McCain? Crowded spot. Innocent bystanders . . ." He broke off to eye the wheezing haulers and brightly painted women and boys thronging close by. "Course, when I say 'innocent,' I'm probably stretching the term." His eyes dropped to her hand resting on her gun. "Anyway, it's not really the place for an altercation, is it?"

They regarded each other for a moment. The youth seemed to be unarmed. Scarlett considered whipping out the pistol and shooting him at point-blank range. Something dissuaded her. She took her hand away from her gun, leaned against the bar too, put one boot on the footrest. She eyed the door behind the bar—it might lead to a side exit or simply fade out in a cellar or a storeroom. Gods alive, she was getting careless. She should have done a proper reconnaissance. She should have left earlier. She shouldn't have come here at all.

"Well, this is very pleasant," the youth said.

"Yeah."

"Do you want some peanuts with that?"

"No, thanks." He was no older than her, taller maybe by an inch or two. His voice, his manner, even his smallest movements were modestly underplayed and utterly self-assured. The two aspects coexisted in everything he did. His quietness contained both.

"Do you know who I am?" the young man said.

Scarlett turned the bottle on the table. "You're one of two things," she said. "From the fact that you've got all your fingers, I assume you're not a member of the Brothers of the Hand. That makes you a Faith House operative. I must say, I thought the High Council might have sent someone a little . . ."

"Older?"

"I was going to say 'more impressive,' but 'older' will do."

The operative grinned. His teeth were very white. His eyes sparkled. He said nothing.

"How did you know where to find me?" Scarlett said.

"Word travels fast on the Great North Road. We're not that far from Milton Keynes, where the Council is. There are Wanted posters up, even in Huntingdon. Pamphlets, too."

"Pamphlets?"

"Detailing your stirring exploits." The smile broadened. "Your fame is spreading. In short, you were observed this morning by someone who thought you stood out a little. I came up to check it out."

"And do I?" Scarlett asked. "Stand out?"

"Oh yes. I could see it, soon as I came into the room. If I may say so, you're better-looking than on the posters. I was hunting for a hideous redheaded crone."

Scarlett curled her lip. "That meant to charm me?"

"Not at all. Obviously the hard living doesn't help, and nor does making faces like that. But you move differently from the others. Faster, more intentionally. Like you've got purpose. Like the thread of your life is hung taut and true, not frayed and sagging like most everyone else's here. I knew it was you," the young man said. He winked at her. "Also, you're the only person in this room who's shielding her mind with an iron band."

Scarlett froze. She pressed her teeth together tightly. Her heart, already beating fast, jolted like it had left its mooring, then redoubled its pace.

"Where's Albert Browne, Scarlett?" the operative asked.

She had to clear her throat to get the words out. She took a sip of beer. Her mouth was dry. "Somewhere around."

"I don't know. . . . Is he? I'd have thought I'd sense him. . . . Well, we can go somewhere quiet," the youth said easily. "You'll soon tell me."

In the glass curve of the bottle, Scarlett could see other drinkers pressing close on every side, including several of the haulers with whom she'd been playing skull toss an hour before. All at once, the saloon was a place of refuge. "That's not going to happen," she said. "You said it yourself, it's not a good place for an altercation. And I'm staying right here."

The quality of the youth's smile did not alter. He gave a discreet shrug; the shoulders of the greatcoat rose and fell. "You don't think I truly give a tinker's damn about any of these losers in here? We can involve them if you want. The High Council of the Faith Houses is very keen to make your acquaintance, Miss McCain. And Albert Browne's, naturally. I'd like you both on a bus by morning. Finish your drink, and we'll go outside."

Scarlett hesitated. Then she smiled. "All right," she said loudly. "You win. We'll leave this joint. Let's go."

Movement in the crowd. The black-bearded hauler materialized at Scarlett's side; behind him, her other creditors stood glowering, each one bigger than the last.

The hauler's beard was bristling with indignation. "What's this? What's going on?"

"Sorry, boys," Scarlett said. She touched her hat. "There's a change of plan. I'm out of here. My friend's taking me away."

Several sets of eyes swiveled in the youth's direction. He was cast into shadow by the looming men. He blinked up at them, adjusting his coat slightly. "Evening, gents."

"Evening," the hauler said. "Sorry to stick a pole in your spokes, sonny, but we've business with this girl. We can't allow her to leave."

"Business?"

"She owes us money."

"Ah, yes. Gambling." The young man nodded. "I can only imagine your pain. Well, I'm sorry too, my bushy-faced friend. It doesn't have to be a problem, but she's coming with me."

The attention of all the men was on him. Scarlett took a slow step backward.

"What did you just call me?" the hauler asked.

"You heard." The youth's smile vanished. "Oh, and I wouldn't try it if I were you."

"Try what?"

At that moment, the young man noticed Scarlett's subtle movements. He frowned. Before he could speak, the black-bearded hauler had reached out and grappled his collar, tugging him away from the bar. The boy almost disappeared inside his coat. He lifted a pale hand. Something happened. The hauler was jerked upward off his feet. He let go of the boy's coat. He spun on his heels, whipping like a top, making his companions fall back around him. Faster, faster—his outstretched beard formed a blurred ring about his head. The motion halted; before his beard could finish moving, the man flew up and backward over the crowd and out through the nearest window in a storm of splintering wood and glass. The night swallowed him. There was a distant impact as he hit the road.

Silence.

"That," the boy said.

It had happened so suddenly, so shockingly, that Scarlett had forgotten to move. She and everyone else in the room were frozen, staring.

The youth brushed at his coat. "Honestly, what a godless place this is. Everybody back off—including you, barman." The man behind the counter had risen into view with a baseball bat in his hand. "Miss McCain—you stay where you are."

Several of the women and boys in the saloon gave shrill moans of distress. One of the haulers, hair as bright as summer corn, hurried to the door and out into the street. Over in the corner, the lady at the piano put down the lid, took up her sheet music, and tiptoed away.

"Piano player's gone," Scarlett said. "That's always a bad sign."

"Is it?" The youth nodded. "Interesting. Now, Scarlett, if you'd like to come with me . . ."

Scarlett didn't stir. "Never start fights in a saloon," she said. "That's the first thing they teach you. Only brings trouble."

The boy rolled his eyes. "Heavens above us, *I* didn't start it. He did. Well, I expect he'll think twice about doing it again."

The door to the saloon swung open, bringing with it a squall of rain. The hauler with the yellow hair burst back inside. "Honest Bart's dead! He's broken his neck!"

There was a collective gasp. The company was silent, stricken, gauging the dreadful news. Heads turned to look at Scarlett and the young man in the coat. All across the room, hands moved toward gun belts. Beards bristled. Eyes widened. Brows corrugated like Venetian blinds. Women headed for the stairs. There was a fusillade of guns being cocked.

"Looks like you killed the most popular guy in town," Scarlett said. She moved very slightly back from the bar.

The youth frowned. "Oh, this is ridiculous." His voice rose; he glared around the saloon. "Do you hicks know who I am? I am a representative of the High Council of the Faith Houses! I have jurisdiction here, and if—"

Scarlett launched herself forward and shoved him violently in the ribs. The young man stopped talking. He fell to the floor. Scarlett threw herself to her left, vaulted onto the countertop, rolled across it, and disappeared over the other side. As she landed heavily among the empty bottles and beer crates, the shooting started. Bullets shattered the mirror above her and thudded into the front of the bar. She pushed herself into a sitting position, hearing round after round being emptied.

She imagined the youth lying there.

Well, no one could say he hadn't asked for it. She adjusted her hat, then scuttled on hands and knees behind the counter. Glassy fragments from the mirror bathed her in a silvered shower. Still the firing continued. She passed the curled body of the bald barman, who had dropped down and was cowering on the floor. She met his eye, crawled past him, reached the little door, and so slipped out into a back room.

Cold air, white tiles. A smell of beer and cleaning fluid.

Scarlett saw steps to a basement—but also a small hinged window. She didn't hesitate but leaped up onto a dirty sink, drove herself headfirst through the window, wriggled once, twice, and fell out into the night.

She landed on a pile of sodden cardboard boxes, rolled head over heels, and was up again. Along an alley and out onto the Great North Road. She could see gun flashes still going on behind the glass of the saloon door. Scarlett sprinted across the road and down another alley on the opposite side, where her bicycle was waiting behind a heap of bin bags.

As she reached it, there was a deep, soft thump behind her.

The gunfire stopped quite suddenly.

The rain had dropped. The town was silent. There was no noise from the saloon. Scarlett crouched where she was beside her bicycle, in the alley's protective shadow. She was breathing hard. She had her pistol in her hand.

She waited, looking across at the saloon door. She could see the lanterns shining through its window. She could see the broken glass, the body of the bearded man lying in the road. She heard drops of water falling onto the bags of refuse, the sound of its trickling in the mud around her boots.

She watched the door. Surely they would start coming out now, one or another of the haulers, sickened by the shooting, wanting air, or hoping to get out before the militia arrived. If not, surely she would hear them. Hear something, at any rate: the boasting, the laughter, the forced high spirits that always came after a drunken killing. That old girl would be wheeled out with her sheet music, they'd start the piano up again . . .

Not nothing.

A shape swelled behind the pane of the door, a fluid thing distorting against the lantern light. It drew together, became a slender silhouette. The saloon door opened, letting a lozenge of light spill out over the wooden porch. The thin young man stepped out. His long coat swung slightly as he halted, perhaps to let his eyes adjust to the darkness. He looked up and down the street with a questing air. He held his head cocked to one side as if listening.

Scarlett pushed her hat down harder on her head. She gripped her gun more tightly. She pressed close to the alley wall. The bricks were hard and wet against her neck.

Whatever the young man was hunting for, he didn't find it. With his left hand he brushed something off the lapel of his coat—perhaps a trace of plaster, fallen from the ceiling. It was the same gesture he'd made earlier, when he'd thrown the hauler out of the window. He stepped down off the porch, pattered away from her along the line of bars, in and out of pools of light.

Silence. Just the water dripping.

After a few moments Scarlett realized she was still crouched there, rigid, watching the operative fade away into darkness. It was as if he had trawled her willpower with a line and was pulling it away with him down the road.

With a soft curse, she snapped her gaze free. She stood. Quietly, she eased the bicycle away from the wall.

On the other side of the Great North Road, the light burned from the open door of the saloon. It was still quiet. There was no movement from inside.

7

The Anglian weather had performed one of its about-faces. After several days' rainfall, the sky had become a platinum-blue shield. The sun blazed; the cornflowers opened in the reedbeds; the mud on the levees crusted over, growing a pale gray skin that in places was strong enough to withstand the weight of a bicycle and in places not, so that the wheels cracked through to the purplish ooze beneath. Albert had camped along the edge of the marshes. Now he took unobtrusive paths through the fenlands and in due course arrived at his destination, a refuge and rendezvous point for wanderers between the kingdoms: the celebrated Wolf's Head Inn.

As a toothed bird flew, the Wolf's Head was scarcely five miles from the nearest trading post on the Great North Road. Nevertheless, it was surrounded on all sides by broad expanses of reeds and still black water and was not an easy place to find. Casual travelers were dissuaded from the attempt by reports of blood-otters, leeches, and bog-worms in all seasons, and of mosquito swarms in summer. One benefit of these dangers was that the Tainted, the worst peril of all, were rare visitors to the fens. Even so, the inn had two antique machine guns set in embrasures above its iron door and a rumored system of concealed pitfalls in the long green grass below the walls. Mags Belcher—Old Mags, the proprietor—was said to possess a mummified Tainted in the cellar, the relic of an attempted raid in her grandmother's time. No one doubted her ability to repeat the trick with future assailants—or indeed anyone who failed to pay their bar bill, a fact that helped maintain good order in the taproom.

The inn stood in the center of a broad field—sunken below the level of the fens, but protected from them by a raised circle of earthen levees. The lower two floors of the building were made of neatly fashioned stone blocks, angled outward at the base and carving like a snowplow into the muddy pasture. On one side was a little courtyard, from which a single flight of winding stairs climbed steeply to the entrance at first-floor level. Above the door were the machine-gun slits, and beyond that the stone was replaced, for two more stories, by walls of brick and timber, from which protruded the mullioned windows of the guest rooms. Everything was topped with a steep, red-tiled roof. Fixed to the chimneys were three lightning catchers shaped like leaping wolves. When storms swept in, the wolves sparked and crackled, channeling lightning strikes down copper wires to discharge in the field below.

Albert had loved the Wolf's Head ever since his first visit with Scarlett, and he could feel his anxieties fall from him as he parked his bike in the rack, crossed the cobbled courtyard, and climbed the steps to the iron door. In the little paneled hallway beyond, a small and smiling dark-skinned man with a withered arm waited to collect his weapons. When Scarlett was there, this operation always took some time: she would unload her pistol, two throwing daggers, a flick-knife, a knuckle-duster, and a length of cord that she claimed was a spare bootlace but that Albert suspected had a more sinister purpose. All of this was secured in a great black chest in a corner of the hall. Today the procedure went rather more quickly, Albert's only contribution being some toenail clippers with a slightly pointy end.

The air smelled pleasingly of tobacco smoke and leather. The ceiling was low, straddled by blackened beams. From its hook beside the door hung the old wooden sign, daubed with faded letters. It read:

THE COVENANT OF THE WOLF'S HEAD

No KILLING
No VIOLENCE
No SLANDER OR ABUSE
Here, outcasts all,
WE WEAR THE MASKS OF FRIENDS.

Anyone breaking these RULES
will be taken to the cellar.

Albert had always been struck by the awful simplicity of this last injunction. He had asked Scarlett what awaited wrongdoers in the cellar, but she had been unable to help him. "No one knows. That's what's so terrifying. One thing's for sure: they never come out."

On this visit Scarlett was elsewhere and he was alone. He passed between a pair of heavy curtains into the apricot half-light of the taproom, populated today by groups of traders, white-robed cultists, furriers, fugitives, and ne'er-do-wells—and also Gail Belcher, Mags's daughter, a robust and pink-skinned woman who presided over everyone from a swivel chair behind the bar. However, Albert wasn't looking for any of them. He stood and surveyed the company. It took a moment for his eyes to adjust to the smoky dimness, but already he detected laughing thoughts close by. His heart swelled. He followed the sensation. . . .

And there were Joe and Ettie, waiting at benches by the window.

Six months had passed since Albert had taken a voyage on Joe's raft, *Clara*—six months since he had destroyed *Clara* in a single violent outpouring of the Fear. That had been a pivotal moment, and the intervening period had seen changes in both their lives.

Albert had begun his career with Scarlett, during which he had worked hard to suppress the Fear. Her reassuringly effective presence helped with this: snakes aside, these days he rarely felt the surges of terror or fury that might unleash the uncontrollable forces inside him.

Meanwhile, Joe had arranged the creation of a new raft, using the money he had earned from the original trip. Built in a fishing village in the Thames estuary, *Chloe* was bigger and broader than *Clara*, with a more powerful engine and with extra hidden compartments for contraband. Joe and his granddaughter, Ettie, had since resumed sailing in it, up and down the river, and he had plans to build a seaworthy boat as well. Officially, Joe was a kipper trader; unofficially, he fenced gold and other treasures that Albert and Scarlett acquired during their heists. Such things were hard to dispose of, but Joe had the contacts to make it feasible. His profits were passed to the poor and sick along the Thames. It was to facilitate such business that Scarlett, Albert, and Joe regularly met at the Wolf's Head, where news could be shared, arrangements drawn up, and pleasure be had at seeing each other again.

Little Ettie gave a squeal of delight as Albert crossed to the benches. Joe nodded at him soberly. "So, you're back again, dirtier and more squalid than ever. But in one piece?"

"More or less."

"Scarlett?"

"Will be here in a couple of days."

The old man grunted. "Minus her share of the money, no doubt. I know what she's up to. Well, if neither of you's been hanged, drawn, and quartered, and had your bits stuck on poles for the ravens to peck at, I'd say you've done quite well." Joe flourished a bony arm. "We've got plenty of beer here. Sit down."

Albert shuffled up alongside them. Sitting at the window, silhouetted against the green-black fen, old Joe was gaunt and darkly weather-beaten, his hair a puffed gray sphere. His joints were knobbly; his bones jutted like scythes and plowshares beneath the skin. But Albert was pleased to see that his gaze remained quizzically acute and that the thoughts flickering above his head were vigorous. Albert, who did not generally sieve the minds of his friends, whatever Scarlett might allege, kept his own gaze politely averted. It was easy enough to do on this occasion: he was too busy smiling at Ettie.

In the month since he had seen her, the child had grown perhaps a little taller, but she was still essentially the same: small and blond, red of cheek and sparkling of eye. She was a whirligig of affectionate energy, rarely inactive, coursing with life. She was also entirely mute and, after her initial squeak of excitement, made no further sound. She hugged Albert as he sat down, then pressed close against him, resting her head companionably against his arm, as she had once done on the raft.

Albert had found a bright green feather from a lyrebird while crossing the fens. He presented it to Ettie. The girl's mouth formed a silent O of wonder. She held it up against the window, twirling it between her fingers, watching its iridescence play against the light.

"Where's *my* feather?" Joe took up a stone pitcher and poured Albert a cupful of beer.

"Sorry, I've only got a great big pile of loot to share with you."

"I suppose it'll have to do." The old man raised his cup; they drank each other's health. "So, Warwick, was it?" Joe said. "How did it go?"

"Very well, all things considered. We robbed the Faith House and survived." Albert sat forward in his seat. "I tell you, Joe, Warwick is an extraordinary place! The town is built within a forest of giant ruins—great black arches, thin as spiders' legs, that tower above the modern walls! And a strange thing about the lands around: In the hills, there are black rocks that protrude from the ground at savage angles. Some are big as houses, and their surface is like glass. Now, these rocks all tilt toward the *same* geographical point. Near Warwick, they face southeast. Up near Grantham, which is farther north and east, they all face south!"

He paused to catch his breath. Joe raised his bushy eyebrows politely. "A remarkable fact."

"*Isn't* it? How were those rocks created? How were they put there?"

Joe shrugged. "How indeed? Perhaps they are a product of the Cataclysm."

"Perhaps! It's almost like they were blown here by some single tremendous force. What *was* the Cataclysm, I wonder?"

"Who knows—or indeed cares? Now, returning to the substance of your expedition," Joe said. "I take it the Faith

House didn't disappoint? Were the tales of its wealth exaggerated?"

"Not at all!" Albert smiled. "I have a sackful of gold, jewelry, and ornaments for you to trade, and money that can help you with your sea boat. And that's not all—" He opened the bag beside him, took out the plastic box with its blackened relic, and set it on the table with a flourish. "Behold and marvel! An eerie survivor of ancient days!"

The old man stared at it. "It looks like fossilized poo."

"Really?" Albert was a little hurt. "I thought you would appreciate its mystery."

"The only mystery is why you lugged it on your back across the kingdoms. Why would anyone want a moldy piece of rusted gun? Use it as a doorstop, or better still, sling it in the fen." Joe gave a chuckle. "No, I'm more interested in the gold. It's a relief to know your partner didn't have *all* of it when she slunk off to the gaming tables."

"Yes. . . ." For a moment, Albert's enthusiasm waned, to be replaced by the slight sadness that had ridden with him since his parting with Scarlett. "I wish she did not feel the need to act this way," he said. "There is something in her past that pains her deeply, but she never confides in us. Why? We are compassionate. We are gentle. We are her friends."

The old man snorted. "Are you mad? The last thing she wants is compassion! Gentleness? It would only arouse the anger that burns inside her. She would hate us for it. No, she must carry her pain alone."

There was a brief silence. "Those are wise words, Joe,"

Albert said. "Scarlett would be surprised at your understanding. She says the nearest you've ever got to knowing a woman is selling kippers to them at a market stall."

"Is that so? How does she think I've ended up with my granddaughter Ettie here?"

"She thinks you found her under a bush. Or stole her or something. But come, let's talk of something more cheerful. Lighten the mood. Tell me of your carefree life on the Thames."

Joe took a sip of beer. "It's about as carefree as kissing a blood-otter. On our last journey, we called at the river town of Henley. People at the wharf noticed that Ettie is mute. We were accosted; stones were thrown. The authorities let us leave, but we were fortunate to escape the cages." He gazed off across the parlor of the Wolf's Head, at its milling crowd of outcasts. "See the company we keep today?" he said. "Persons of every shape and size, with missing limbs, with birthmarks, with strange beliefs that the Mentors insist are wicked or forbidden . . . This is where Ettie and I belong now too. . . ."

For a moment Albert could not speak. He ruffled Ettie's tousled head and hugged her to him. The little girl had put down the feather. She now had a fistful of colored pencils and was drawing something on a piece of scrap paper—an impossibly complex mess of colored lines. Albert could make nothing of them. "I am so sorry to hear your story, Joe," he said at last. "It is an unjust world. But you told me once you might travel away in search of a better life. Is this still your dream?"

"That's why I'm building a sea boat," the old man said.

"One day I shall set sail around the coasts to Wales or Cornwall and leave the cruelties of Wessex and Mercia behind. . . ." He rolled his bony shoulders and stared out at the fens. "You ask about the Thames. The river is awash with rumor. The Tainted are spreading. They are no longer confined to the wilderness but threaten the safe-lands of many towns. In some areas, the crops have failed and there is talk of famine. I have heard of riots taking place, which the Faith Houses and the ruling families are struggling to suppress. Meanwhile, the High Council is seeking to crack down on nonconformity of every kind. . . ." Joe straightened abruptly; he chuckled to himself. "But what am I thinking? That reminds me! I *can* lighten the mood. Let me show you something."

From a bag beside him he brought out a small, folded pamphlet and held it up for Albert's inspection. It was printed, rather inkily, on cheap yellow paper. A woodcut illustration on the cover showed a pair of crudely drawn stick figures, each firing a brace of pistols as they bounded across a rooftop. There was a gibbous moon in the sky and a small but unmistakable gallows in the background.

Albert regarded it with interest. "That's a pretty design." He looked again. "Hold on, isn't that—?"

"Yep," Joe said. "Presenting 'The Ballad of Scarlett and Browne,' the latest quality chapbook from the Wessex Press. I picked this up in Marlow the other week. They were selling them behind the hot-dog stall for two pence."

"'Being an account of their daring crimes and unnatural

vices,'" Albert read. "Golly. Some big words in that subtitle. What's 'unnatural vices' mean?"

Joe grinned. "That becomes clear when you dip in."

Albert was still staring at the picture. "I'm not sure I have quite such a mess of hair as that. And does Scarlett really look that old?"

"Well, they got her scowl right," Joe said. "True, if they had you tripping over your own feet and falling down a chimney, it would be more lifelike, but how can anyone draw you accurately? You're too busy running away the whole time. Still, I'm sure they'll capture a cracking likeness of you both for a future edition when you're dangling peacefully from the gallows."

Albert took the pamphlet; after some hesitation, he turned to the first page and read out the opening verse.

"In Lechlade town, where old Thames runs
And morals are quite forgotten,
There was a thief with bright red hair
And a simply enormous—"

"You'd better stop right there!" Joe ordered. "It's not appropriate for Ettie. I'll let you read more once she's gone to bed."

"I can't wait." Albert set the chapbook reverently on the table. "Shame Scarlett's not here to enjoy this. Our very own pamphlet! Fancy!"

Joe nodded. "It's a sign you're on the way up. All the most famous outlaws have been celebrated this way. Sprightly Mick, the 'Wessex Rover,' had several ballads detailing his merry exploits, and Sam Goodfellow, known as the 'Ladies' Highwayman,' featured in a whole Northumbrian song cycle, in which his many conquests were recounted in forensic detail. I used to have a stack of those pamphlets under my bunk when I was a lad."

"Sam Goodfellow . . ." Albert's mind was full of swashbuckling heroes, tight jerkins, outrageous deeds. "He sounds a colorful rogue. What happened to him?"

"Oh, he was recognized from a pamphlet, captured, and shot from a cannon at Bamburgh docks."

"And Sprightly Mick?"

"Boiled in oil in the square at Newton Abbot."

"Right. . . . So getting a ballad written about you isn't necessarily that lucky?" Albert asked after a thoughtful pause.

"Not always," Joe conceded.

"Not *ever*," someone said. "It's not lucky at all. You can bloody well take that from me."

The voice came from above them. Albert and Joe looked up. Ettie gave a squeak of pleasure. Albert flinched back in surprise and alarm. Scarlett McCain stood there. She was covered in lashings of dried mud, her coat was torn, her hat was askew. One side of her hair had been tied up in a rudimentary pigtail; the other side hung like a mosquito net across her face. Her rucksack and prayer-mat roll were slung at a crazy angle, half off her back. She was gray-faced, hollow-eyed; her body had a brittle quality, as if it would shatter to the touch.

Albert started to his feet. "Scarlett—"

"I'm okay. Been up all night. Hiding in the wastes, then riding three hours straight. Hey, Ettie. Joe."

"You look like something spat out by wolves," Joe said. He moved across the bench to let Scarlett sit down. "Beer?"

"Beer, sausages, bath. In whatever order." Scarlett took her hat off and tossed it on the table. She ran her hands wearily across her scalp. "Had a spot of trouble in Huntingdon," she said. "News has been spreading about us. Pamphlets and such." She reached out for the jug.

Albert was watching her. No sooner was the hat off her head than her thoughts came swimming up. Almost without trying, he saw the embedded image of handlebars, the endless whir of the moving road. And there was something else, too. A handsome, smiling youth.

She looked up at him. "Don't."

"Sorry. Who was he?"

"A Faith House operative. He was after you, after both of us. He almost got me in the bar in Huntingdon. I had a nice little chat with him before getting away."

Albert assimilated this. "What was he like?"

"I suppose you've just seen his face. Physically? Thin and weedy. Coat slightly too big for him."

Albert frowned. "Doesn't sound like much."

"Oh, and he was shot repeatedly at point-blank range by a saloonful of angry men and strolled out of there alive."

"Ah."

"Yeah."

"So you didn't kill him, then?" Joe said. "That's not like you."

"Nope," Scarlett said. "I didn't." She rested her head back against the bench; a little curl of dried mud fell from one cheekbone. "I don't think that would be very easy to do. He's got powers, Albert. Powers like yours. . . ." She blew out her cheeks. "Might even be a product of Stonemoor—I don't know."

Stonemoor. Until that moment, until that word, the warmth and murmur of the little parlor at the Wolf's Head Inn had enfolded Albert quite securely, kept the world beyond at bay. Now it was as if the walls had cracked like eggshells and fallen open, and a bright and bitter light had been let in. He looked beyond Scarlett, saw far away a wet plain studded with great stones, drab forests on either side. The sky was gray and black, heavy with rain, but here and there the sun broke through and washed the landscape. The patches of light rolled slowly over the moorland, exposing the contours, picking out the stones. One patch moved on the horizon, shone on a great gray building set between the hillsides. White walls sprang into view, a long and undulating band like a piece of exposed chain. It seemed to Albert suddenly that the chain was not broken but ran invisibly across countless miles, to reach him in this parlor where he sat among his friends and twine tightly round him.

He sank back in his seat. Ettie was still drawing. She had taken another pencil and was swirling it on the paper, covering the pretty colors with a spiral of jet-black lines.

8

As it turned out, Scarlett got her bath first, and the sausages had to wait. She was in no fit state to enjoy a meal. Even some of the least savory customers of the Wolf's Head were eyeing her askance from neighboring tables, and Gail Belcher was grimly sweeping up the trail of dried mud she'd left strewn across the floor. Fortunately, the inn had a chamber free, and the bellows were working in the steam room. Scarlett gave a serving girl her clothes for cleaning and retired to the baths, where she soaked and dozed in a tin tub for an hour. Without being quite invited, Ettie accompanied her; the little girl sat on the towel basket, beside Scarlett's discarded gun belt, making faces at her through the steam.

Pink and tender, her muscles loosened, her crust of mud quite gone, Scarlett went to her room to await the return of her clothes. Again, Ettie came too. She sat on the bed, jittering about on the straw mattress, while Scarlett lit candles, opened the plastic tube, and laid her prayer mat on the floor.

"You know the rules," she said severely as she settled

herself upon it in her T-shirt and shorts. "Don't disturb me while I'm meditating. If you do, if you so much as brush this mat with your smallest, plumpest toe, I'll put you over my knee and smack your bottom. Don't think I won't! I've done it to Albert. I'll do the same to you."

The little girl smiled at her. She picked up the empty tube and peered inside.

Scarlett closed her eyes, let the gently moving candle-light play softly against the darkness of her lids. As she had been taught long before, she took deep breaths and rose swiftly through her body's heaviness, past the warm weari-ness of her muscles, past the smell of lilac soap and the damp tumble of her hair, up and out of the room, out of the Wolf's Head Inn altogether, and so to a distant place with the fens spread out beneath her and the glow of a few scattered settlements shimmering in the immensity of the dark. With detachment thus attained, she next pursued clarity of thought. She imagined the weave of the prayer mat far below, how all its ragged complexity was actually formed of single threads, woven together in an orderly way. Holding that concept in mind, she began to smooth out and separate the threads of her own life, which (as they so often did) seemed tangled and obscure.

It had been three days since she'd last meditated—in the blue dawn at Warwick, on the morning of their heist. So much had happened since: the Faith House raid, the chase, the snake, the disastrous night in Huntingdon, her cycle ride across the fens . . . So much noise, exertion, danger, violence. And yet, considering it now, it mostly seemed of little consequence. Already the details were blurring in her mind.

Except for one thing. The operative, of course. The fact that he had traced her so quickly—that he had relied on word from local spies and arrived in Huntingdon almost at once—was disconcerting. Such purpose and efficiency wasn't usual in the fragmented kingdoms. It suggested the Council was focusing its efforts in ways Scarlett hadn't seen before. As for the young man himself . . . if he truly had Albert's abilities, but without Albert's silly scruples and self-doubt, he would be formidable indeed. He, the operative, was someone who was not afraid of himself, someone who took the trouble to master his powers rather than agonize about them. There was a coldly impressive quality about that. Sitting in the warmth of the little bedroom, Scarlett saw the youth's face again. She remembered his casual smile, his decisiveness, his speed. . . . She realized she had not asked his name.

In any event, his appearance had serious implications and threatened to overshadow the success of the Warwick heist. And it *had* been successful. A job of infinite difficulty had been carried out with panache, enterprise, and minimum destruction. So, all right, there was a saloonful of dead men in Huntingdon, but *that* wasn't Scarlett's fault. It was yet another crime to set at the Faith Houses' door! The main point was that she and Albert had once again outwitted the cruel rulers of the Towns.

Strange how the thought did not have quite its usual potency. She kept seeing the open door of the saloon and the soft dead light within.

Well, what matter? There was injustice everywhere. If you were weak, you suffered. If you were strong, you made damn sure nothing happened to you.

No. . . .

That wasn't right.

If you were *truly* strong, you made sure nothing happened to those you loved.

Scarlett could not sustain her detachment. She dropped like a stone; dropped back into herself, into her body. There was an ache in her stomach. She sighed, bent her head so that her wet hair fell round her like a curtain. She let her inner weariness capture her at last.

A soft touch at her side: Scarlett started, sat upright. She opened her eyes to find that an unknown time had passed, and that Ettie was sitting beside her on the mat. The child had her head bowed, her legs crossed in a fair approximation of Scarlett's posture. Her hands were plumply folded in her lap. She was breathing deeply, giving little snores.

Scarlett opened her mouth in automatic disapproval, then closed it again. Whether or not it was the effects of the mat, she could not summon the necessary indignation. She sat for a moment beside the sleeping girl, then got up and nudged her with a foot. Ettie yawned and stretched.

"I'll smack your bottom *next* time," Scarlett said. "Right now I need some food."

* * *

Evening was seeping up like mist from the fens. The last light in the sky was reflected in the watercourses, in the deep blue strips between the blackness of the levees. Curlews called: a hollow, haunting sound. In the west, a bank of clouds hung like a slowly purpling bruise.

Scarlett's clothes—cleaned, dried, and roughly folded—had been left outside her door. She and Ettie returned to the bar, where they discovered Albert in the process of buying their meal. He had ordered beef sausages, turnip mash, and purple kale, and another round of beer. Gail Belcher prepared the order. She was a handsome woman, large-boned, straw-haired, possessed of a somewhat brusque and brutal femininity that Scarlett knew made Albert nervous. In a backroom beyond, Old Mags, the wizened matriarch of the inn, sat knitting in her rocking chair. Her fingers were a blur; they moved the needles with amazing speed.

"There's someone asking after you," Gail Belcher said, piling heaped plates on a tray. "You and Albert both. Been waiting a day or two, hoping you'd drop by. Says there's a job on offer, might be up your alley. An illegal one. You know the kind of thing."

In previous months, several proposals had come their way in the convivial atmosphere of the Wolf's Head. So far, Scarlett had rejected them all. She glanced across the taproom. "Who's asking? Those merchants? Those cultists? Those burly ore smugglers?"

"Nope." Gail gestured with a great pink arm. "There by the fire."

To Scarlett, the little gray-haired woman sitting in a corner booth was so unobtrusive as to almost merge with the substance of the inn itself. She blended with the shadows, a diminutive birdlike person perched among cushions. Scarlett could imagine sitting on her by mistake. She had an untouched beer and a bowl of pickles at her elbow and was engrossed in a solitary game of cards.

"That old girl?" she said. "Who is she?"

"Sal Qin. A merchant-trader from up north. Stops here from time to time."

"Trustworthy?"

"As much as any of us."

Scarlett pushed her hat brim up and grinned. "That's not exactly a ringing endorsement."

"Sal's honest in her way, but otherwise a shrewd business-woman with no more scruples than a stoat. Your sort of girl, Scarlett," Gail Belcher said. "Enjoy your food."

The sausages and mash *were* good, which was lucky, as it was all the Wolf's Head served. After the meal, they sat with Joe. Ettie dozed in the corner of the booth, her small fair head resting on a pile of cushions. Scarlett told her story of the operative again. Joe listened with many tuts and exclamations. Albert was silent. He seemed unusually subdued.

"This youth," Joe said at last. "What was his name?"

"Not a clue."

"Did he sieve you? Did he read your mind?"

"No. . . . He *tried to*, though. He knew I wore an iron band. I never took my hat off, never showed it, but he knew."

Albert made a sound between his teeth. He was staring out through the dark windows. "Ah, yes," he said. "Your precious iron band. You've got it on now, I see."

Scarlett nodded. "Yeah, and it's a good thing I had it in Huntingdon, too; otherwise he'd have sieved me, found out about the Wolf's Head. He'd have known we were here."

"If you hadn't *gone* to Huntingdon in the first place," Albert pointed out, "he wouldn't have had the opportunity at all."

Scarlett set her hands flat on the table, arranging her fingers with studious care. "As you know, I went to distribute some of our takings. There are many needy people there—ex-slaves, orphans, refugees from the plague lands . . ."

"Not to mention many barmen, croupiers, sots, and fellow gamblers who *also* benefited from your visit," Joe said. "Where's the rest of the cash? You blew it, didn't you?"

"So what if I did?" Scarlett drew herself up. "That's my business. The important thing in the circumstances—as I'm sure we all agree—is I managed to save my life."

The old man snorted. "Yes, what joy that gives us. I can scarcely stop myself from dancing. Well, you'll be pleased to know that while you were wallowing in the bath upstairs, Albert and I put the rest of the money into one of Gail's strongboxes for safekeeping. Just in case you fancy losing it at poker tonight. Now we need to discuss your next move. I don't think you can stay here long in case that operative

111

shows up. This inn's not far from Huntingdon—it's an obvious refuge. If the High Council doesn't know about it, that devilish boy can easily sieve someone who does. He may have done so already and be on his way."

There was a silence. Darkness glittered at the windows. Scarlett remembered the dull, unnatural thud she'd heard in the saloon, the sudden silencing of the guns. Another memory surfaced, as if from deep water: a conversation six months before, high on a concrete platform at the edge of the sea.

"Do you think he's from Stonemoor, then, Albert?" she said suddenly. "The operative? It would make sense if he's got the same powers as you."

He looked at her, his face blank. "I don't know. Maybe."

"Dr. Calloway told me you were *almost* unique—those were her words. What do you think? Maybe this is another of her protégés. One who *didn't* try to rebel."

"I was kept apart from the other inmates most of the time," Albert said. "I rarely saw what they could do. They had powers, though. That was why they were there. . . ." He made a swift, impatient gesture, casting the issue aside. "But a much more important question is about tomorrow. What are we going to do? Where shall we go?"

"You could come south with us," Joe said. "There's always room on *Chloe*, provided you don't blow us to smithereens again. Travel the Thames once more for old times' sake. Or are you still running scared of the Brothers of the Hand and their lust for bloody vengeance?"

"I'm not running scared at all," Scarlett said. "It's called being sensibly cautious. But all the same I should avoid Wessex and southern Mercia right now."

"Where else, then? East into Anglia? North?"

They sat in silence for a moment. "If it's a question of *north*," Scarlett said, "there may be something we can do to make it worth our while." She swiveled in her seat and looked at the booth in the corner of the room.

Close to, the merchant-trader Sal Qin seemed even smaller than when seen from a distance. She was dwarfed by the dark wooden back of the booth and almost smothered by a heap of stained cushions that provided comfort for customers of the inn. She was as slim-boned as a child, as unobtrusive as a sigh. Her legs did not reach the floor. Her gray hair was cropped very short; the skin of her face was covered with tiny wrinkles, as if it had been scrumpled up like a ball of wastepaper and hurriedly smoothed out again. She wore a leather coat with a high collar and epaulets, a black shirt, black jeans, and black boots with silver filigree. As Scarlett and Albert approached, she was still playing patience. Her swift hands moved across the table, shifting cards between stacks. She was building up runs of the court cards—Mentors, Mayors, and Sheriffs—trying to complete the seven suits before drawing an Outlaw card. Scarlett watched the colors of the kingdoms dancing between her fingers—red for Mercia, green for Wessex, blue for Anglia. They merged and melted, blending and separating again.

"Ms. McCain, Mr. Browne." Sal Qin did not look up. "Join me. Take a pickled radish from the bowl. I'm just finishing my game."

They sat. The woman played on; all at once she drew a card with a scowling ruffian on it and tossed it into the center of the table.

"Bloody Outlaws," she said. "Always pop up when you least expect it." She grinned at them.

Scarlett grinned back. Albert's smile was functional, his gaze slightly unfocused. Scarlett could see he was concentrating on the woman. While she was assessing the proposal, it was his job to assess the proposer. "I hear you may have a suggestion to make, Ms. Qin," she said.

The face crinkled. The eyes were black and bright and full of humor. "I do, I do. There's a job needs doing. I am looking for a team with rare skills that might carry it out."

"You'd find we're efficient and professional."

"You're *lots* of things, if a certain ballad is to be believed. Some of your vices sound positively eye-popping." The diminutive lady sat back among the cushions. "Anyway, let's not waste time. Have you heard of the Buried Cities? How a fiery storm swept over during the Cataclysm? How it covered the cities and their people, entombing their secrets forever?"

Scarlett frowned. "We know about the Buried Cities. In fact, I've *been* to one. It was just a few ruins sticking out of the ground. Half-buried towers, walls, endless holes and pits filled with big hunting spiders that'll eat anyone dumb enough to go poking about in them. Everything valuable was rifled long ago."

"You're talking of the Wessex one, perhaps?" Sal Qin said. "Yes, in the south the ashfall was relatively light. The city *I'm* talking about is different. Up in Northumbria, where I come from, the falls were deep and hot, and the settlements they covered have remained far below the surface. Except at one place only: Ashtown."

Scarlett could feel the intensity of Albert's interest. She remained impassive. "Go on."

"It is in a remote region where savage horn-beaks roam. Here a river has cut through a band of hills and revealed a hidden city of incalculable extent. Since it was discovered many years ago, miners have been exploring it. Even now, with a honeycomb of tunnels stretching below the grasslands, the outer limits of the ruins have not been discovered. Still the excavation work goes on."

"Why?" The excitement in Albert's voice was clear. "What do they find there?"

Sal Qin's voice dropped low; she scanned the taproom, but no one was near. "The Buried City is a vast necropolis," she said. "They say there are whole streets down there, perfect and entire, nestling within the excavated tunnels— with buildings, streetlights, roads, and squares, all of a scale and sophistication to stretch the eyes. They *also* say that the houses are still inhabited by the dead—by twisted, shrunken corpses, clustered in the deepest places, still seeking refuge from the terror that engulfed them centuries ago. . . ." She took a pickled radish. "But that's by the by. What interests *me* is what they dig up. The mining company requires its employees to sign contracts of secrecy, so the precise nature of the most precious artifacts is mostly barroom rumor. Certainly they are objects from the ancient world: curios, pieces of art, books . . . Who can tell? Only one thing's for sure—all these prizes make their way to the vaults of the single organization with enough money to pay for them."

"The Faith Houses," Scarlett said.

"Correct. The gods alone know what the High Council does with them," Sal Qin said. "But honest merchants, such as me, are frozen out of the process *and* the profit. Ashtown is the small, modern settlement that's grown up on the surface to serve the needs of the miners. I've been there. I've tried to negotiate access to the trade—without success." The woman shrugged; her epaulets shifted. "I have customers who have expressed interest in acquiring these treasures. They are impatient. They have suggested I try . . . alternative options."

She was smiling at Scarlett again. Scarlett glanced aside at Albert. As she had silently predicted, his mouth was slightly open, his eyes elsewhere. She knew his mind was lingering in imagined catacombs, in sunless streets below the arid hills. . . . She kicked him subtly in the shin. "These 'alternative options,'" she said slowly, "sound as if they might be risky."

"Risky," Sal Qin said, "and extremely profitable. That's why I've approached you."

Scarlett considered a moment. "When the artifacts are brought up from the mines," she asked, "where are they processed?"

"In a depot built into the side of the hill. They are shipped out once or twice a week in armored trucks, which cross the wilderness by way of the Great North Road at top speed. Most are bound for the headquarters of the High Council in Milton Keynes. A long and lonely journey, Ms. McCain. I was thinking such a transport might easily fall prey to ambush."

Scarlett frowned. "There are guards on the lorries?"

"Yes, and they are heavily armed. To ward off bandits and the Tainted."

"It sounds impossible to me. Why not rob the depot above the mines?"

"Too well protected."

"The Buried City itself?"

"Is accessible only by iron gates set into the hill. The gates are staffed by teams of guards and engineers who control the mechanisms. Everyone going in or out is frisked for items they might have stolen. Then there are the giant carnivorous grubs you might meet, the white blood-moles, the pockets of poison air . . . No, the robbery would have to be done aboveground. I'm sure an ambush could be arranged," Sal Qin said, smiling. "Why not? Inventive highwaymen have done such things before. Think of the legendary Sam Goodfellow!"

"Yeah. And he ended up being fired from a cannon into

the sea," Scarlett said. She rose. "All right, Ms. Qin. Thank you for the offer. We'll sleep on it, then talk again."

"Of course." The little woman picked up her pack of cards. "I've nowhere else to go."

"What did you think?" Scarlett asked. They were walking back across the bar. It was late now, and the crowd was thinning out. Joe and Ettie were no longer at their table.

"Of Sal Qin or her proposal?"

"Qin. It goes without saying that the *proposal* is crazy and suicidal."

"If *you* think that, it must be bad," Albert said. "So we're not doing it?"

"Not a chance. But I quite liked her."

"Me too. She's honest, I think. What she said about the mining place was certainly true. I saw images of hills, big motor trucks, a fenced compound silhouetted against a blood-red sky . . . Basically, her thoughts matched what she was saying, which is a sign she was telling the truth. Where do you suppose Joe's gone?"

"He'll be putting Ettie to bed. So Qin's not connected to the Faith Houses, then?"

"No. She's a black marketeer of some kind. As she said, she's got a customer who wants the artifacts. I saw an image of them, too: a thin, bald man or woman—it was hard to tell." They had reached the table, still covered with a mess of plates and Ettie's discarded papers. "You know, I think retiring early might be the best option for us, too," Albert said. "I'm bushed, and we can decide where to go in the morning. Or do you want to wait for Joe?"

"He'll be in bed as well." Something was tugging at the back of Scarlett's mind, a dark thought, dressed in rags. It kept flitting out of view; she could not quite focus on it. She stood beside the table, with the fens black outside the window. "What did you say just then?" she asked. "About the customer? Sal Qin's contact?"

"You know, I'd have thought Ettie'd want to take these drawings with her," Albert said. "She loved doing them. . . ." He picked up one of the scattered pencils. "Qin's customer? I said it was a thin, bald person. I got a visual of them, but I couldn't quite make out if—" His voice broke off abruptly. He was looking at something on the tabletop.

Scarlett had likewise gone quiet and still. "Albert," she said softly. "This person: Were they wearing a sort of creepy patchwork coat? All black, but made of patches sewn together, rather like lizard scales?" She waited. *Albert.*

"Sorry. Yes. Yes, they were. . . ."

But even then he wasn't concentrating on her. Instead he reached out to the ketchup bottle in the middle of the table and picked up something small and squared that was propped against it. He set it flat where she could see it, turned it slowly round.

It was a slim metal token, stamped with the image of a four-fingered hand. The little finger was bitten off at the base.

9

Just for a moment Albert thought the shock would master her. Scarlett wobbled, leaned against the wall to steady herself. Her face was a ghost's at a window. Her mouth was white like an old scar.

He saw her take a deep breath, summoning her inner strength. Color re-erupted in her cheeks; life returned to her eyes. She put her hand to her belt, only to realize that her gun was locked in the hall chest with her other weapons. She swore softly and turned to face the room.

Albert's own realization had been just as rapid. He knew the symbol of the criminal organization known as the Brothers of the Hand. He knew their reputation as thieves, extortioners, and black marketeers. He knew that, by Scarlett's account, they had betrayed her and tried to kill her, which was why she had run off with their money. Of course, there were two sides to every story. Since, in the case of the Brothers of the Hand, *their* side included stern penalties for anyone who crossed them, including dismemberment, premature burial, and being fed alive to giant owls, Albert had long been happy to have nothing to do with them.

And now the Brothers were here.

The implications gathered thickly, blackly, like a flock of crows roosting in his mind. With Scarlett, he scanned the taproom of the Wolf's Head Inn. A few late-night drinkers sat in booths; Gail Belcher dried glasses behind the bar. The lanterns hung soft beneath the roof beams; there were clinks, gentle noises, the murmur of tired conversation. No one paid any attention to Scarlett or Albert. How strange that they couldn't sense his terror; how strange they weren't startled by the hammering of his heart.

There were no hostile thoughts that he could see, and no sign of anyone who was obviously a Brother. But nor was there any sign of Joe or Ettie.

"Perhaps they haven't got them," Albert said.

"Oh, they've got them."

"We should tell Gail. Get our weapons."

"She won't give them to us. We need to go carefully, so keep your voice down. The Belchers don't react kindly to any disturbance, no matter what the provocation. There's absolute neutrality in this house. Remember the cellar."

"But if Joe and Ettie have been abducted—"

"We can't prove they have." She was looking at the table, at their discarded plates; as Albert watched, she took three knives, wiped them on a napkin, pushed them one by one up her coat sleeve. "If somebody lured them away on some pretext," she murmured, "lured away Ettie so that Joe had to follow, that's all perfectly aboveboard as far as Gail's concerned. And once they set foot outside the inn . . ."

Albert didn't hear her finish. A flare of rage and terror erupted in his skull. He had a hard, metallic taste in his mouth. A buzzing filled his ears. He shook his head, trying to fling the agitation off him. *No.* When it had burst out with the rock snake, it had torn up half the valley. It *mustn't* happen here. He thought of the devastation it would cause.

He thought of Ettie being lured away.

"We need to hurry," he said. He saw that Scarlett was picking up more utensils, stowing them in places about her person. "What are you taking *those* for?"

She looked at him. "Don't ask. There's things you can do with spoons."

They walked swiftly across the room. In the corner booth, Sal Qin was busy with her cards. Scarlett nudged Albert as they passed. "She's the one who brought them here."

"So should we—"

"I *think* it was unintentional. You sieved her, didn't you? You said she was honest. She wasn't wise to this. They must have set her up and followed her when she came to find us."

"You mean her bald customer in a patched black coat? Is he or she a Brother?"

"It's a he. His name is Teach. And yes: very much so." Scarlett shook her head. "If he's here, we've got our work cut out for us. Sal Qin can wait. We'll deal with her later."

At the bar, Gail Belcher nodded to them from behind a bank of shimmering beer glasses. Scarlett gave her a wave. "Hey, Gail. Did you see our friends leave? Were they alone?"

The landlady rested one large pink hand on the bar top.

"I'm not sure. It was crowded. The kid went off with some-one, I assume the grandfather. . . ." Her eyes narrowed. "No, wait . . . that can't be true. I saw the old man hurry out on his own, not long after. Trouble?"

"Not at all. Just wondering. Good night, then, Gail."

Out in the hall, the attendant had left his post. The lights were dim. The great weapons box was padlocked. Albert rattled it briefly.

"We could try upstairs," he said. "Check their rooms."

"They won't be upstairs, will they? The Brothers want us outside."

The door to the Wolf's Head was never locked before midnight. Scarlett raised the latch, and they stepped out onto the top of the steps. It was very cold. Below them, the courtyard was a dappled well of silver. No one was in sight. The Milky Way was a bright sash strung across the chest of the heavens.

In two quicksilver leaps, Scarlett was down the entrance steps. Albert came stumbling after her. He felt a tightness under his ribs; his legs were leaden, his mind fogged. The Fear was building. It was like with the bad old times when he lost control. He knew this was a time for calm, for con-fidence in Scarlett's abilities and in his own. He needed to stabilize his emotions. But he couldn't do it. He kept think-ing of Ettie.

Lamplight gleamed in the bicycle sheds. It threw a hard stripe across the center of the cobbled yard. The sheds were empty. He could see customers' bicycles in their racks, the tools hanging there, the hoses and pumps for cleaning. Scarlett's mud-caked racer leaned against a wall.

She was waiting in the middle of the yard, very poised and still. "What do you see?"

Albert closed his eyes. At once he picked up thoughts nearby: dark thoughts, coiled and watchful, pregnant with ill intent. And somewhere beyond, traces of a mind he recognized: a small one, vulnerable and scared. The pulsing in his head redoubled.

"They're waiting behind the outbuildings, near the gate," he whispered. "I don't hear Joe. I can hear Ettie—very faintly. She's farther off, maybe on the track."

"Is she all right?"

"She's alive."

"But you don't sense Joe?"

"No." There was a pause. "But that doesn't mean—"

"Sure."

He waited for her to move. The noise in his head was growing louder. Pressure pulsed in his temples. "They're taking Ettie," he said. "We've got to go after them."

Scarlett nodded. "They're aiming to draw us out onto the fens. Get us away from the inn. Then the men hidden here will come up behind us." She looked at him. "Are you okay? Is it the Fear? If so, you could—"

"No. I can't. Don't ask me. It might hurt you—or Joe and Ettie."

She wrinkled her nose; the subject was shelved. "All right.

Then you can be bait. Start walking along the track. I'll fol-low. Go quickly, go quietly, and *don't look behind you."*

He swallowed. "Think they'll come after me?"

"Yeah." She patted him cheerfully on the shoulder. "Or maybe shoot you stone-cold dead." With that she flitted away.

Albert didn't try to second-guess Scarlett's plan. He squared his narrow shoulders and shuffled off across the cob-bles. As he neared the outbuildings, he sensed the thoughts of the hidden men ruffling suddenly, like trees in a summer breeze, and knew they'd seen him.

Ahead were the posts that marked the limits of the Belchers' lands, where their edicts of neutrality would no longer hold sway. He passed between them and up the fen-land track onto the levees. Behind him the thoughts moved too. The men were following him. Whoever they were, they knew their job: when he listened by conventional means, he couldn't hear a thing.

The top of the earth bank was silvery with starlight, with rushes steepling downward on either side. Below him the fens stretched glittering to the horizon's curve, an immense silver dish supporting the sky.

A hundred feet or so ahead, the levee turned beneath a single willow tree, contorted by wind and storm. Albert walked slowly toward its bent, black shadow. The thoughts kept pace behind. They were drawing nearer, gauging their moment. Somewhere, faintly, he heard the noise of a furtive boot on stone. The hairs rose on the back of his neck. He felt an overwhelming urge to look behind him. With a savage effort of will he kept his eyes fixed on the tree.

Closer, closer . . . He could feel their eagerness now.

He knew they were about to strike—

A thud.

A scuffle.

A complex sequence of other sounds—gurgles, gasps of surprise and pain.

After that, succinct and muffled, a single solitary swearword. Then nothing.

Albert walked on toward the tree. Three steps later, Scarlett was at his side. She was breathing slightly hard and carried a pistol, a cartridge belt, and what looked like a silver cane. She fixed the belt in place and tucked the cane and gun into it.

"All right?" he asked.

"Yeah."

"Was that you swearing?"

"Yep. Stubbed my toe on some rocks."

"I'm sorry to hear it. How many were there?"

"Brothers or rocks?"

"Brothers."

"Four. The last one was very well equipped. Look at all the stuff I got from him. Even a sword stick! Just in time, too— I'm all out of spoons."

They turned the corner at the willow tree and followed the line of the next levee between the silver reeds. Straight ahead was a ragged cluster of windblown trees and bushes that formed a short avenue around the path. Albert could see starlight at the far end, but the center, under the branches, was a tunnel of black.

"Good place for an ambush," Scarlett said.

That was Albert's thinking too. He could detect new thoughts from several sources, but their locations were not clear. Worryingly, he could not sense Ettie. The buzzing noise in his head was a constant burr, interfering with his talent. He tried to shut it down.

"Hat," he said.

Scarlett took her hat off, squashed it down, tucked it in the back of her belt. With the iron band removed, her mind was opened to him. He could feel her cool intention and her anger, but also an anxiety she did not normally exhibit. She was thinking about the thin, bald man.

Their pace slowed; the undergrowth rose high on either side. Slowly, Albert's eyes grew accustomed to the shadow, and he saw an object on the track in front of them.

It was a narrow metal cart with an open back and shafts at the front end. The shafts fed into a kind of double bicycle, with two seats, two pairs of handlebars set on parallel frames. The cart was at rest, skewed across to block the path. The bicycle seats were abandoned, but in the back of the cart were two limp forms. One was long, the other short.

They lay side by side. They didn't move.

Albert felt a sudden wash of terror. A crack opened in his head; energy pulsed through it, making the branches of the nearest trees shiver. With an almighty effort, he forced the crack closed again. He concentrated. What he *wanted* to do was to run forward, to tend to his friends. What he *did* was sift the thoughts that hung half hidden among the trees.

"Four men," he said softly. "One at two o'clock, lying under the tallest tree. One at three o'clock, crouched in the grasses. One at ten o'clock, behind the trunk. And the fourth—"

Someone stepped out from behind the cart and began to walk toward them.

Even in the half-dark, Albert recognized the man. He had seen him in both Sal Qin's and Scarlett's memories. A small-boned person, no taller than he was, elegantly proportioned, in jeans and a white shirt, and with a black coat of sewn patches, shimmering like scales. He was entirely bald, with a delicately constructed face, neat of chin and curved of cheekbone. He had big, bright, long-lashed eyes. There was a sword or sword stick at his belt. Perhaps a gun too—Albert couldn't see. He strolled with fluid, ostentatious ease around the cart, trailing the fingers of one hand along its side, and stopped, facing them.

"Hallo, Scarlett," the man said.

"Hello, Mr. Teach."

"Been a while, girl."

"Yeah. Not long enough."

A chuckle like dry leaves shifting. "Still our fierce little pigeon," the man said. "Flying solo, dangling her broken chain . . ." The smooth face was expressionless, and the voice was papery and dead. It put Albert in mind of airless rooms, of things lying at the bottoms of old wells. It was soft, but without softness. Like a bed of nettles, it offered no comfort or respite.

"Not solo anymore, actually," Scarlett said.

"More fool you," the bald man said. "It makes you weak." He glanced toward the cart and the bodies lying there. "Makes it easy to catch hold of the chain and pull you in."

"You'd know better than to hurt them, of course," Scarlett said.

Teach did not respond. The words were of no consequence to him; Albert, scanning the man's thoughts, saw that Joe and Ettie literally weren't on his mind. Mr. Teach was instead imagining his men opening fire on Scarlett and Albert, catching them from every side. Albert saw his own body crumple, his death imagined as a simple and negligible thing. . . .

Anger pushed against the crack in his head; leaves and twigs on the path around him began drifting outward in a slowly expanding circle. Scarlett's hair fluttered against the side of her face.

Her eyes flicked briefly to him.

"We been keeping tabs on you since you betrayed us, girl," the man said in his flat, dead voice. "Newssheets, pamphlets, all manner of wild publicity. You been busy."

"You oughtn't to believe everything you read, Teach," Scarlett said. She moved her hip subtly, letting the side of her coat fall away, giving access to her gun. "Well, so you've pulled me in. What do you want? The cash? Thing is, I'm more or less skint right now. I had some bad luck in Huntingdon recently."

The chuckle came again. "Bad luck, you say? *That* don't surprise me," the bald man said. "You never could stay solvent. How'd you lose it *this* time? Skull toss? Cards? Or d'you just pee it up the wall in a stupor of self-pity? That always was your story since the beginning."

Scarlett was silent. For a moment Albert felt a trapdoor open in her mind. But even now she had control of herself. The door swung shut, and her voice was calm.

"Albert?" she said.

"Teach will give the order. He's fastest and he'll fire with the others."

"Anything else?"

"No."

"Okay," she said softly. "Tell me when."

Mr. Teach made a slight movement, similar to Scarlett's, exposing the butt of his gun. "So this is the boy?" he said. "We've been wondering about him." He stepped a little closer. "I suppose you've killed the others? Nice to see you ain't forgotten everything I learned you."

"I can get you the cash," Scarlett said. "But first I want the old man and the girl."

"It's not the money we've come to take," the man said.

"What, then?"

Teach did not answer.

Scarlett shrugged. Albert could feel her mind narrow to a point. She was thinking only of her fingers, of the pistol at her side. "That truly the way it is?" she said. "I'd have thought my little life clock would still be ticking nicely back in Stow."

"Scarlett McCain," Teach said, "that clock of yours has just about run out. Throw the gun away, put your hands on your head, and kneel d—"

"Now," Albert said.

The thing about sieving, the thing you always had to do, particularly when your life hung by a thread, was strain out the distractions. Albert had long since learned this art. So right then he ignored the evidence of humanity from the three men in the bushes, the humble thoughts of home and hearth, beer and fellowship, that flitted like pale butterflies in the dark. He ignored the sight of Joe and Ettie lying in the cart; he ignored the fury it awoke in him. Instead, he watched the hidden cords of Mr. Teach's mind, watched them grow taut with purpose, and knew he would give the order to shoot in the next few seconds.

So he spoke first. And before he had closed his mouth, Scarlett fired her gun four times.

The reports were instantaneous; the swing of her arm was just a blur. Four shots, four bullets. Three hit their mark. Two of the flitting butterflies winked out. The third grew tremulous with pain.

Only the fourth shot missed. Fast as she was, Teach had danced aside. A spark at his hip; his gun spat once. Scarlett's pistol flew from her hand.

She jumped back, cursing. In a single, seamless movement she tore the sword stick from her belt and threw herself at the slim, bald man.

Teach's lips parted; the man was smiling. Now *his* sword

was in his hand. He swayed toward Scarlett, met her frenzied blade strikes casually—once, twice, and then again. Their weapons were twirling shards of starlight. Each clash they made rang like a bell. Albert looked about for Scarlett's gun. He couldn't see it. The pulsing in his head was growing stronger. Dimly he heard noises in the bushes from the wounded man. The other two were silent, dead and gone.

He wanted to get to Joe and Ettie in the cart, but Scarlett was in the way. And Teach was too good. He was a twist of smoke blurring in the wind, no longer defending, but dancing in from every angle. No matter how she spun and ducked, no matter how she cut her desperate patterns in the air, the man was more than matching her. He anticipated every move. Albert could feel Scarlett's helplessness. The end was near. She fell back, weakening. Teach feinted, swiveled, feinted once again—

And struck.

As the blade pierced her side, Albert shared the explosion of Scarlett's pain. He cried out with her—and in that moment of rage and terror, the Fear exploded too.

The energy that burst from him hit everything indiscriminately. Teach was knocked flying, out and over the edge of the levee. Scarlett toppled to the ground and skidded away along the path. The cart moved, swinging sharply sideways toward the bank, with Joe's and Ettie's bodies rolling violently against the sides. Branches in the trees were bent and snapped, went tumbling off across the fens. Cold starlight shone suddenly on Albert's face, on the torn, uprooted bushes, on the cart wheels tilting toward the sky. . . .

And Albert knew this was only the start. He would rip the cart and trees to matchwood. He would rend the living and the dead, his enemies *and* his friends. The Fear would scour them, break them, destroy them all! And he was helpless to stop it. Helpless! There was nothing he could do—

He scarcely noticed the heavy footsteps stumbling behind him. An instant later something connected brutally with the side of his head.

10

The first thing he heard was the ticking of the clocks.

"Albert," Scarlett's voice said.

"Yes?"

"You're awake. I know you are. Stop trying to doze off again and open your eyes."

"Do I have to? I'm dreaming I'm in a goose-feather bed in the Wolf's Head Inn, and somebody smelling of lilac soap has just brought me my breakfast. Porridge and honey, Scarlett, and lashings of buttered toast and coffee."

"Hey, the reality's almost as good, Albert."

"Is it?"

"Yeah. Come on. Take a peep. You won't regret it."

"Oh, all right." Albert opened a tentative eye—a difficult operation, as it was welded shut with something sticky. The first thing he saw was Scarlett sitting a few feet away. She was tied to a chair, her ankles and wrists bound with loops of yellow wire. Her weapons were gone, her coat had been removed, and the side of her jersey was stained with a flowering of dried blood. Her hair was in wild disorder; matted clumps of it hung over her bruised face. Short of being dug up from a cemetery, it was hard to think how she could have looked worse.

Albert didn't feel that he was doing much better. His hands and feet were immobile too, and he had a pulsing pain in his head that was only partly due to the recent eruption of the Fear. One of his eyes barely opened at all, and the same was true of his jaw, which felt as if it had been disassembled and reattached by an enthusiastic amateur surgeon, possibly underage.

He frowned, but only briefly. It hurt. "What kind of reality do you call this?" he croaked. "Where's the buttered toast?"

Scarlett gave him a wonky grin. "I'm sure someone smelling of lilac soap will bring it in very shortly. Stop complaining and look around. The good news is we're *here*."

Refocusing on his surroundings took Albert another painful effort. After much blinking, the blood caked round his eye fell away and he was able to take in the scene.

He was in a great circular domed hall, cavernous and dim. Its stone walls were black with age, the windows shuttered; far above Albert, scarcely perceptible galleries hung in concentric tiers. The general darkness was intensified by one brightly lit portion of the hall, where four electric arc lights had been erected on stands. They illuminated this area like a stage. Here sat an enormous desk without a chair and, on the wall behind it—Albert had to squint to be quite sure of what he saw—shelf after shelf of clocks, rising high into the haze. *Clocks:* any number of them. They were all different—some familiar wind-up ones made by the horologists of central Mercia; others weird antiques with meaningless glyphs and symbols, perhaps dating from the days before the Cataclysm. There were clocks with wooden cases, clocks of metal, clocks with garish plastic housing. Clocks as wide as rib cages, clocks as small as a clenched fist. They were all ticking, and the ticking was out of step. The sounds tripped over each other, like the beating of a faltering heart, and blended with the humming of the arc lights to create an undercurrent of unease that extended through the empty space, fizzing and vibrating through the dust and cobwebs.

Behind the desk was a broad oak door, smartly polished and utterly out of keeping with the decrepitude of the hall. This door was closed, but a light was trained upon it so that its surface shone. It too was part of the theater of the room.

The chairs where Scarlett and Albert sat were positioned between the desk and the center of the hall, where several immense ropes and chains dangled, some fixed to concrete weights, others wound around pulley wheels in the floor. The ropes rose up and up, to be lost amid the dimness of the galleries. At the trailing ends of two of them were complex harnesses that seemed to consist mainly of barbed hooks, buckles, and leather straps.

Albert took his time absorbing everything.

"Yes," he said. "Tell me—in what precise way is any of this actually 'good'?"

For someone with a sword wound in her side, who'd been roughly tied to an iron chair, Scarlett seemed in fair spirits. "It's good, you idiot, because they *didn't kill us*, which is what I thought they were going to do. If Teach wanted us dead, he'd have cut our throats last night and rolled us into the fens. Instead of which he's exerted considerable effort bringing us sixty miles by bicycle cart and motor van to Stow. He's even got someone to patch up my wound."

"This is Stow?"

"Yup. We're in the headquarters of the Brothers of the Hand."

Albert felt an inner dislocation that was almost as acute as the pain in the side of his head. "But, wait . . . the last thing I remember—"

"Don't worry. It's all a bit foggy to me, too. Enough of the Brothers survived our fight to cycle us across the border into Mercia. They got us to a road, where a van was waiting."

Sudden memory coursed through Albert. He jolted in his chair. "Ettie! Joe and Ettie—"

"Are alive too. They were with us in the back of the van. Joe had been coshed, but he was waking up when we were dumped beside them in the cart. Ettie just seems to have gone to sleep. Nothing bothers her at all. I was mostly worried about *you*. The guy hit you hard. You were out cold for ages. At last you started drooling, and I was able to relax."

Albert stared at her miserably. He could feel the self-confidence that he had gained over the past six months seeping out onto the dusty floor. "I'm sorry, Scarlett," he said. "I wanted to help, but . . . the Fear came. It's what I always dreaded. In a real crisis, I lost control."

Her groan resounded around the hall. "For Shiva's sake, don't apologize! I'm *glad* you used your power! It's about time! The only problem was, you didn't lose control *enough*."

Albert thought of the Fear coursing through him, its hunger, its glee at being liberated. He could still feel it tingling in his fingers, feel the echo of it running up and down his skin. It was separate from him, untamable. It would never have stopped. It didn't want to.

"No," he said softly. "I'm glad they hit me. I'd have killed you all."

"You think? All you did was prune a few trees and knock Teach into the fen."

"Did I? Was he hurt?"

"Afraid not. You just made him very wet. And angry."

"Oh."

From somewhere far off came an enormous clanging sound; the reverberations boomed away across the hall. Albert and Scarlett sat waiting, but no one came.

"All part of the buildup," Scarlett said. "They'll be along."

Albert pulled at his wrists. "I want to see Joe and Ettie. I'm worried about them."

"I expect we'll see them shortly. Soames will make his grand entrance, tell us what he wants, we'll do a bit of bartering. We'll negotiate Joe and Ettie's freedom, he'll make me rob a bank or something in return, and all will be sweetness and light." She grinned again. "Main problem right now is I want to scratch my nose. Got an itch."

"You weren't so relaxed when we met Teach yesterday," Albert said.

"Oh, Teach is an old stick. Soames is chatty. I get on with him."

It didn't seem *very* likely to Albert. He looked around the terrible, gloomy hall.

"Grim, isn't it?" Scarlett said. "It used to scare me, too. But it suits their purpose. Everything's carefully designed to instill maximum terror in those who are brought here."

"It's doing a decent job of that right now."

"And you haven't even noticed the bell tower. For the owls."

Albert stared at her. He followed her gaze to the dangling mess of pulleys, ropes, and chains in the center of the hall. He raised his head with difficulty, peered toward the ceiling.

Silence. Shadows . . .

"Yep," Scarlett said. "Up there."

Somewhere directly behind them a door opened. Footsteps came toward them across the hall. They could not turn round, could not see who it was. Albert shifted in his chair.

"More theater." Scarlett gave an ostentatious yawn. "Just stay relaxed. They're like wolves—they get savage if they sniff any sign of fear. Hey, Teach!" she called. "Albert was wondering if you'd dried off yet! Hope you didn't get a cold!"

Mr. Teach's neat, small-boned figure came into view

around the chair. He moved like a dancer in black shoes, his hand on the hilt of his sword. If his black coat *had* been covered in mud, it was now in sparkling fettle. Its patchwork surface shimmered glossily under the arc lights like animal pelt. His skin clung tight and pale upon his skull. When he was smiling, as now, jagged ripples like quotation marks hovered about his mouth.

"Chipper, are you, girl?" he said. "That's good."

Behind him came two larger persons, men in dark suits with flat caps on their heads. One carried a lidded plastic bucket, the other a long knife. They came to a halt beside him.

Scarlett blinked at Teach lazily. "Waiting for the boss?" she asked.

Teach's smile did not alter. "My partner's on his way," he said. "But there's things to do in the meantime." He motioned to the man with the bucket, who lifted its lid.

From on high came a faint and feathery rustling, a soft and plaintive hooting.

"The owls smell the blood," Teach said.

Taking a pair of tongs from the bucket, he brought out a piece of meat, very red and flapping, which he hurled straight up into the dimness of the tower. There was a tremendous fluttering and snapping, a jingling of chains. The piece of meat did not come down.

Teach put the tongs back into the bucket, wiped his hands on his jeans. "They're restless this morning," he said. "Want something bigger. They haven't been fed for days."

Albert was trying to think of something to say to this

when he heard a clang beyond the arc lights. The spotlit door swung open. Beyond was darkness. There was a pause.

A rumbling and squeaking. Through the doorway came a wheeled contraption. It was formed of a great wood-and-leather chair—the leather green, the wood black—fixed to a metal armature and raised high on four enormous cart wheels. An immense man sat upon the chair. He filled its volume; he extended over it in folds. He wore a gray suit with pink pinstripes, a white shirt, and a pink tie, with a pink handkerchief blooming from his breast pocket. The stripes of the suit followed the shelves and slopes of the man's broad chest and spreading belly. Albert had never seen someone quite so large. Two short, conical arms hung uncomfortably on either side, as if welded there on a whim.

With one hand, he held a steering bar fixed to the front wheels of his chair. Behind came two more Brothers with black suits and flat caps. They pushed; the immense man steered. His short, conical legs dangled from the front of the chair. One of the man's shoes was swaying jauntily, as if obeying some internal rhythm. Squealing, complaining, the chair maneuvered between the lights, between the wires that coiled across the floor like a nest of snakes, and so to its position behind the desk. The Brothers retreated; with a delicate gesture, the immense man took a pair of gold-rimmed spectacles from his jacket and perched them on his nose.

His head was pink and round and gleaming, all dripping jowls and wattles, like an ice cream left too long in the sun. He had a thick mat of golden curls, graying at the temples, and a bright and beaming face of surpassing ugliness. The mouth was very broad, the nose small, the eyes almost lost in the enfolding flesh. But it was a face that smiled. Where Teach was stiff and tight and dour, all skin and skull, the newcomer radiated expansive bonhomie: he beamed and twinkled as he peered through his glasses at his captives in their chairs.

"Scarlett McCain!" he cried. "It *is* you! I thought Teach might've been making it up! Splendid! Delightful! It's been too long!"

"Wotcher, Mr. Soames," Scarlett said.

"It's good to see you again, dear girl!" The man's voice was rich, deep, pleasantly modulated, full of sprightliness and vigor. "But—what is this?" He adjusted the spectacles in consternation. "Bound and trussed like hoodlums? Gracious me, untie them, Teach! Untie them! Are we savages? Are we Cornish? Are we Welsh? Let them get up from their chairs!"

Teach rolled his eyes but made no protest; evidently he had expected this. He nodded at the man with the knife, who bent to Scarlett first and then to Albert. The wires that bound him to the seat were cut. The man lacked a finger on his left hand.

Scarlett was pacing stiffly, letting the blood return to her limbs. When Albert tried to do the same, his legs almost gave way. He wobbled; his head felt light and woozy. Scarlett stepped close and raised a supportive elbow, letting him lean against her.

"Why, the poor things are *famished*," the immense man cried. "Have they not breakfasted this morning?"

"I was hoping to give the owls the breakfast," Teach said.

"Now, *is* that hospitable?" Mr. Soames snapped his fingers at the man with the bucket of meat. "Emerick—be so good as to fetch coffee for our guests. In the meantime—Scarlett, Mr. Browne, step closer! Come, let's look at you! Don't be shy."

In his prison at Stonemoor, Albert had often stood before Dr. Calloway's desk, awaiting painful reprimand. The unpleasantness had been heightened by uncertainty: he never knew what punishment would be meted out to him. He had a similar sensation as he and Scarlett shuffled toward the desk, with the enormous pink-faced man smiling down at them. He felt small and helpless. He felt about six years old again. No doubt that was the intention.

Close inspection of the desk didn't improve matters. There was a pile of newssheets arrayed before Soames, but also a rack on which was a range of metal devices, hinged, bladed, pronged. Implements for piercing, stabbing, slicing. The handles were black and scuffed with use; the cutting edges shone evilly under the arc lights. Albert's soul shrank at the sight of them.

Beside him, Scarlett was the model of relaxation. "You look well, Mr. Soames," she said. "Your setup's improved. Got more clocks and better lighting. The owl ropes are the same."

"If something works, why change it?" Soames's neck folds

quivered; his black eyes sparkled with merriment. "Ah, still the same Scarlett. Proud, defiant, and in sore need of a hairdresser. There's Mabel Snips in Bottle Street, remember—here in Stow."

"I'll bear it in mind."

"And your career is going from strength to strength, I see." Soames rested a heavy hand upon the newssheets. "Wessex, Mercia, Anglia . . . My, you *have* been far afield. Doing all sorts of naughty things. You're not always named in the accounts, of course. But *I* knew."

"Got a ballad now and all," Scarlett said.

"I know. Appalling doggerel. But it shows what we in the Brotherhood have always known. You have a whiff of stardust about you. You—and your formidable companion. . . ."

The folds of skin shifted; Soames turned his head, and he, Teach, and Scarlett regarded Albert, who was still looking at the horrid devices in the tray.

"Hello," Albert said.

"He's not to be underestimated," Teach said.

"I think he's charming," Soames said. "He looks like a melancholy goblin. Talents?"

"Yep," Teach said. "But he don't know how to use them. In a scrap, I could close my eyes, spin round twice, put a knife through his eye at fifty paces. My aunt could do it. My aunt's dog would give it a good go. His fighting skills aren't why the girl sticks with him."

The deep burr of Soames's chuckle sounded again. "Oh,

I think we all know why she keeps his company. I'm glad you've found someone, dear Scarlett. A replacement of a kind."

Albert glanced at Scarlett. He could see the flush spreading across her cheeks.

The man was returning across the hall; instead of the bucket, he bore a tray on which were cups of coffee, piles of scones, and clotted cream and jam. His passage precipitated a great agitation in the bell tower. The hooting and rattling noises were louder; one or two white feathers drifted down through the grainy light of the hall.

"There," Soames said. "Take some coffee, Mr. Browne. Take a scone. Personally, I favor spreading the jam on it first, and then the cream. Teach does the reverse: a barbaric act."

Albert accepted some coffee. The man with the tray passed him the cup. He too lacked a finger on one hand.

Scarlett had taken a scone and had wolfed it down in two big bites. She radiated insouciant unconcern. Albert suspected this was a front, but the Fear had left him too weary to sieve her or anyone else around him. "Nice," she said. "Right—we should talk business. We should talk about certain misunderstandings. We should talk about my friends."

For the first time, Soames's expression darkened. His eyes became slits behind the golden spectacles. His soft body stirred within his suit like a pupa inside its cocoon. "Hasty, hasty," he said. "We are just getting reacquainted, and in the case of this boy with the saggy jumper, getting to know each other. I saw you eyeing my tools here, Mr. Browne." The tips of the great fingers brushed lovingly against the rack on his desk. "Tell me, what do you think of them?"

Albert swallowed. "They're a bit sharp."

"Sharp and subtle. Yes, indeed. And what do you think they're for?"

"Torturing your helpless victims, I suppose."

A smile blossomed. "Great Siddhartha, no! They're for my clocks. Observe."

As he spoke, Soames reached beneath his desk and unclipped a long hooked pole. With unexpected deftness, he spun one wheel of his chair, turning to the shelves behind. Flicking the hooked pole higher in his hand, he plucked a small clock down from its shelf and drew it to his lap. A spin of the wheels; he was back at his desk with the device before him.

"I have made adjustments to all these timepieces," Soames said. "You'll note the hands run backward, and see how the numbers represent not hours but other units of time. Each marks out the destiny of someone in my power. It counts their remaining weeks and days. . . . Take this one, now." The clock was plain and made of brass; it gave a tremulous ticking sound. Soames turned it over. He reached to his rack and selected a thin-bladed knife, with which he prized open a hatch at the back. "This clock," he said, "is bound to a Mr. Abbott—a prominent grocer of Lechlade. I believe you have been to that town? Well, thanks to my support, he is a prosperous man. He pays me regular small fees to remain so."

The soft lips pursed. "But will you believe it, Mr. Browne, in recent months these fees have not been forthcoming!"

"Perhaps he is in some difficulties," Albert said. "Have you asked him?"

"Naturally. He blames a local famine and the depredations of the Tainted, but that is not my concern. Troubles come to us all—do they not, Mr. Browne?" Soames prodded with the knife at the flicking innards of the clock. "See Mr. Abbott's fluttering heartbeat here? How fragile a thing it is! And when the hands wind down and the frail bell rings—in, let me see, two days—*if* he has not paid his debt, all will be over for him." He clipped the casing shut.

"All will be over?" Albert repeated. "You mean—"

Soames's eyes snapped wide, and he formed his mouth into a small circular rictus of exaggerated shock. The flesh on his face rippled outward from the three round holes thus formed. "I mean the owls, dear boy," he said in a deep and plangent voice. "The owls."

Albert stepped back from the desk. "That seems a little harsh."

"Chain them up and hoist them high," Mr. Teach said. "Nothing ever comes down."

"Well, only a few pellets," Soames said. "Ah, don't look so queasy, Mr. Browne. You've done worse, by all accounts. Which brings us to the subject of *your* blood debt to us—you and Scarlett here."

Scarlett made an impatient gesture. "Shall we speed it up?" she said. "Let's take the conversation as read. *You* say I owe you money. *I* say I got that money for you in Lechlade, only for your man there to try to kill me anyway. *You* say I took the lives of some of your Brothers last night. *I* say I was only acting to save my own. We can agree to disagree on all of this. So: we cut to the chase. You have our friends. What do you want for them?"

Albert had been watching Soames as she was speaking; the great body had slowly shrunk backward in its seat, hands together, fingers steepled, eyes disappearing behind the surface shimmer of the little glasses. The bonhomie was suddenly absent, as if wiped clean. The face had no expression.

"Yes," he said softly. "Your friends. The child is a charming little snip of a thing. She and her markedly less charming grandfather are our guests now, as you know. Let us return to you and Albert Browne for a moment. Teach loathes you for your betrayals. He wants to feed you to the owls. Me, I've read the newssheets, and I know the pair of you to be a formidable proposition, too good to waste. Prove me right and your friends live. Fail and they die. Is that cutting to the chase enough for you, my dear?"

Albert looked between them. There was silence in the hall.

Scarlett shrugged. "Just tell us the name of the bank."

"The *bank*?" A reverberation passed across Soames's body; the little legs shivered with exquisite pleasure. "My dear, we're not interested in *banks*. We know you can rob banks with your eyes closed. As can we. Surely your sweet little girl is worth far more than that."

"What, then?" Scarlett asked. She scowled. "What do you want? Spit it out."

"You already know the proposal."

"I don't understand."

Realization struck Albert. It wasn't often that he was quicker on the uptake than Scarlett, at least when it came to practical matters like bank jobs, safecracking, and other such activities. But he had made the connection now. "The mines!" he said. "Ashtown! The Buried City! You want us to steal the artifacts from there!"

"Sal Qin's job?" Scarlett said.

"*Our* job, really," Soames said. "Teach is the client who spoke to her about it. Teach and I are the clients who want it done. We have often had business with Ms. Sal Qin. She is an excellent source of black-market goods from across the kingdoms." He smiled. "However, I confess that our primary purpose in employing her in this case was actually to hunt you down. We gave her your names and suggested she use you for the tricky Ashtown job. Most helpfully, with her Anglian contacts, she traced you to that horrid inn, and so—as you see—we were swiftly able to get you back into our power. But there is such a thing as killing two birds with one stone, and our desire for the mysteries of the past still holds. We *are* interested in Ashtown's secrets. The Faith Houses should not have a monopoly on them. So yes—I want a cargo lorry full of the Buried City's treasures. I want it driven here to Stow."

Neither Scarlett nor Albert spoke. Albert was thinking

of Sal Qin's description of the mine and its horrors, of the heavily armored high-speed lorries that burst out of the gates and thundered down the roads. . . .

"That's foxed them," Mr. Teach said.

Scarlett shrugged. Albert could see she was working hard to maintain her composure. "It's difficult, sure. Some would say impossible. . . ."

"Ah," Soames said, "but when you think of that dear child being drawn up slowly into the darkness of the loft . . . The owls are each as tall as a man, Mr. Browne. I'm told their feathers are quite translucent, their eyes blood-red. Perhaps it's a pigment thing, like creatures of a cave. They have been up there for years."

"A difficult job, but not impossible to *us*," Scarlett clarified. "How long do we have?"

"I am not an unreasonable man." Soames opened a drawer in his desk. "Let's see . . . yes, perhaps this one . . ." He brought out a small metal alarm clock, decorated with rusted white and yellow flowers. "A pretty little timer for a pretty little girl." He set the clock on the table and spun some dials, pressed a button. The clock shivered and began to tick. "There . . . ," he said. "The time is almost noon. You have precisely one week. One week from noon, the treasures must be in our possession. If not, we hoist her up."

"One week?" Scarlett said. "Ashtown is in Northumbria! We'll have to get there. . . ."

Soames made a dismissive gesture. "There are buses. Consult your *Tompkins's* timetable."

"We'll have to figure out a plan."

"Not beyond someone with your quick wits, I'm sure."

"We'll need weapons . . ."

"Pinch them."

"Money . . ."

"Steal it."

"First you've got to show us Joe and Ettie are alive."

Soames gazed at her. All at once he gave a roar of fury. He exploded forward in his seat, slammed a fist upon the desk so that the clock tools leaped and clattered. Scarlett and Albert jumped backward in fright. His lips frothed. His face was incarnadine, red to the roots of his hair. "Do my shell-like ears deceive me?" he cried. "Do you dare make demands of me? After what you've done? You are in no position to give orders to anyone, Scarlett McCain! You are lucky not to be dangling in the bell tower at this instant! You will return here within a week, with the cargo we request, or I swear to every conceivable deity that that pudgy brat and her arse-faced grandfather will be fed to the sodding owls!" Mr. Soames sat back in his chair, seemingly exhausted by the emotional exertion. From his breast pocket he took out the pink handkerchief and dabbed his mouth and forehead. "You may take my word that the two of them are currently alive and well," he said. "That will remain the case for seven days. And now this interview is over, unless there are further questions."

"I have one." Albert had been listening pretty hard, and most things were clear enough. But one thing puzzled him.

"These artifacts from the Buried City," he said. "What exactly *are* they, Mr. Soames? What do you want them for?"

"An intelligent question, which I will not answer." Soames signaled to his men, who hurried forward. "All I will say is that if the Faith House Council is interested in something, my organization is interested in it too. And we are very good at seeing potential, even in ruined, worthless things. . . . After all, we took Scarlett in—didn't we, my dear?" He smiled at them benignly. "I'll see you in a week. Show them out, Mr. Teach!" The men pulled on the chair, turned it; on squeaking wheels Soames was ferried to the door.

Teach was already heading for the exit on the other side of the hall. He paused for a moment by the ropes and chains. "Very clever system," he said. "See the counterweights? They make it easy to lift something high into the tower." He twanged a rope. Reverberations reached the bell tower, arousing a distant fluttering. "That girl, we'd rattle her up in seconds." He winked at them. "Wait here. I'll get your things. You've a long journey ahead of you."

He departed the hall. Albert and Scarlett stood alone amid the gloom and shadow and the rustling of the owls.

"You *worked* for these people?" Albert said.

"Yeah." Scarlett's face was a mask. "It seemed like a good idea at the time."

III

THE BURIED CITY

Precisely what the men had said, and in what order, the girl couldn't remember. Nor who had started it, them or her. She was pretty sure the one she'd upended in the water trough had been a bystander; *he'd* just looked at her funny. But the other three—the guy she'd pitched through the plate-glass window, the man draped over the postbox, the one crumpled moaning at her feet—hell, they sort of blurred in the mind.

Still, they were all as bad as each other, no doubt about that. And the onlookers were the same. The surrounding ring of townsfolk undulated in and out like a jellyfish as she turned on her heels to spit and snarl at them. Men with poles swiping and prodding at her; boys throwing stones; the rest just laughing and cheering as she snatched at them with clawing hands. . . . *Townsfolk!* If they had but a single chin for her to punch! She'd do it now, punch all of them . . . but they kept on moving away.

It didn't help that the ground was tilting, that her head kept hurting so; it didn't help that the bottle in her pocket was empty, too. But that was the way the world was. Bad things just kept on happening. Trouble kept toppling in on her, out of the bluest sky.

Like now. A sharp, shrill double whistle sounding. A militia-man in his green bowler hastening through the crowd.

Shiva, if there was one thing the girl didn't like, it was the militia. Well, she didn't like the Mentors, either. Or *anyone* in the Towns. . . . Gods, could anyone tell her why, each time she moved, it hurt her eyes so? All she'd wanted was to buy some bread.

She turned slowly, trying to blink the present into focus. The militiaman was a big one, bullnecked, shirt tight on his belly. Baton. Handcuffs. No pistol, though. Making the mistake they all did. Looking at her, seeing just the tattered clothes, the dirt, the hair like knotted string . . . Seeing just a small female. Funny how *that* registered with him more than the unconscious men strewn all around.

Well, it was a rookie error. She danced aside of his grip, let the baton crack through the air behind her. A shimmy, a swivel. A boot in the backside to send him floundering. She shook her head to disperse the pain and decided to disperse the crowd, too. Spreading her arms wide, she charged—howling like a wolf, screaming out her despair and rage. That scattered them fast enough, but they didn't go far. It was like they were at-tached to her with elastic—soon they were pressing in behind, reaching again with their hooks and sticks.

She weaved among the striped market stalls, hunting a way out. Here, there: this way, that . . . Looking at the in-teresting merchandise as she went—the woolen goods, the ceramics, the metal tools, the bicycles. Imports from Wessex, at a guess. She hadn't seen a proper factory here in . . . in this two-bit Mercian border town, whatever its bloody name was. . . . Ooh, here was a nice array of hats, all greens and blues and crimsons. She reached out for one—and saw the crowd re-forming up ahead. Men blocked the way. A pole slashed down at her. They weren't laughing so much now. She swore at them and leaped up among the hats, crushing the straw boaters and ladies' Sunday specials beneath her muddied boots.

There was a wall beyond, and no way onward other than a drainpipe. Without thought, the girl jumped halfway up, braced her arms and legs, skittered up the rest. Something struck her side, making the bones rattle in her hip. Stones bounced against the brickwork by her head. She hoisted herself up onto the roof, teetered for a minute on the gutter, turned to shout abuse at the pursuers below. Scrabbling at the tiles, she clambered up the steep rise to the roof crest, hopped over, and skidded down the other side. A momentary pause, a sharp drop onto a porch roof, then to a rain barrel, and so to the street beyond.

She set off, limping only slightly from the fall.

A voice, calling her: "Hey!"

She slowed, gazing dully all around, saw steps cut into the sidewalk by the side of a house. A cellar. A splash of candlelight. A door opening below.

Someone looking up at her and beckoning.

"In here!" he whispered. "Come on. . . ."

The girl halted, looked at him. Her head hurt. She couldn't focus. But she sure as hell didn't know him. He was a townsman who wouldn't do her any good.

She made to continue on her way.

"Exactly how stupid *are* you?" the voice called. "The crowd is coming round by Glass Street and Execution Row. They'll head you off at the junction. Their blood's up. You just trampled across a stall of Faith Day hats. You broke the nose of one of the sons of the ruling family. Can you hear them? It won't be the felon box for you now. I think they'll tear you limb from limb." A flash of teeth, a grin in the shadows. "Or you can haul your butt in here."

She stood, staring down the street, letting the words filter through her brain; and sure enough, she *could* hear the buzz and rumble of encircling pursuit, the whoops and gabble of the swarm. It almost attracted her—the idea of swift death in this way. *Almost*, but she didn't want to give them any further satisfaction. They'd think they'd won. They'd think they'd beaten her. When it happened, it would be on her own terms.

"Clock's ticking," the voice said.

With sudden speed, she was down the steps, past the small man standing there, and inside.

She realized at once that she might have made a mistake. The room was a low, dark space. It was lit only by semicircular barred windows wedged below the ceiling, looking out to the street at boot level, either side of the house. There were empty crates and barrels, a flagged floor, tamped dirt, and mold; in one corner a rusty pile of chains.

The girl turned and regarded the man narrowly.

He made a placatory gesture. "The door's unlocked," he said. "See—I'm moving away from it. I am unarmed. I have no doubt you could kill me. I just wish to talk to you."

He was a little one, sure enough, not quite her height, and with a tight-fitting plaid jacket and olive-green corduroy trousers that emphasized his narrow shoulders and mouse-like frame. But they were good clothes, and he knew it. He was pleased with them and himself. His patent leather shoes glimmered as he stepped beneath a window. His small-boned face was almost overpowered by an extravagant flick of light brown hair, like a giant curl of icing crowning an uninspiring cupcake. His movements were brief, nervy, those of an animal scenting danger; they came and went in double-quick time.

"Keep your distance," the girl said.

She wiped blood from her nose with her sleeve. One of the men must have struck her; it was only now she was noticing the pain.

"I will, with pleasure." A smile flickered in and out, neat teeth displayed and sheathed again. "Distance is imperative—I can smell your breath from here. So now: sit down if you wish. There's a barrel over there."

But the girl had remembered the flood tide of profanities that had escaped her lips during the fight. She was fiddling with bloodied fingers at a purse at her belt, pulling coins out of it, and transferring them to a dirty string bag tied around her neck. She performed the ritual with grim intensity; only when several coins were transferred, and the weight around her neck was appreciably greater, did she look up again.

"Did you say something?" she asked.

The little man's mouth flexed. He put his hands into the pockets of his jacket. "Gods above us," he said. "You're a mess."

The girl was squinting through the gloom. Her hip hurt. Her legs were weak. All she'd wanted was to buy some bread. She slid down the wall to crouch on the tiles.

"Got anything to eat?" she said. "Or drink?"

"No." The man glanced toward the window behind him. He was listening, but the crowd was some way off and its baying could not be heard. "So what was all *that* about?" he asked. He waited. "Your little contretemps. Your scuffle. Your disturbance of the peace. Can you remember? It's all of five minutes ago."

For the girl, the circumstances were already hazy. She rubbed one eye with the base of her hand. "I don't know. They insulted me."

"And so you beat up several grown men and flattened half the town." His nostrils twitched. "It seems excessive. And impressive, also, in a way. Do you have a name?"

"Scarlett McCain."

"Where do you come from, Scarlett?"

"Nowhere near here."

"Do you have a family?"

"No." She looked at him red-eyed. "Is there a point to this?"

The shiny shoes rocked back and forth in the dirt. "Let me turn that around a moment. Is there a point to what *you're* doing, Scarlett? Picking fights with fools in marketplaces? Shouting and swearing and breaking arms and windows. How's that working out for you?"

"I don't care. Have you got anything to eat? Or drink? A drink would be fine."

"You already asked me that. Not yet. Maybe presently, depending how you answer my question."

"And which question," the girl asked, "might that be? Because I've got to go."

"And do what? Go sleep in a bin someplace?" The man shook his head. "Shut up a minute and focus on what I say. I was watching you in the market. You have clear talent, of a kind. Plenty of anger in you, too."

"Oh, you think?" The girl gave a derisive snort. She made to get up, but her boot slipped in the muck of the floor. Her balance was off, or something.

"Both those things are useful, or could be made to be so. At least, that's the view of Soames and Teach, who are the heads of my organization."

The girl could hear noises swelling in the road outside. She experienced a spasm of queasiness in her belly that made it hard to concentrate. "Your organization?"

"The Brothers of the Hand."

"I don't know what that is. I don't know what you're talking about."

"Does this mean anything to you?" The man took his hands from his pockets. He held up his left hand so that it was silhouetted against the window. Even in the grime and gloom of the cellar light, the girl could see that the little finger had been cut neatly away at the base.

She winced, pushed herself up to sit straighter against the wall. "What the hell happened there? Who did that?"

"It's a sign of my devotion to the organization. I took it off myself."

"You must be crazy."

"Says the starving, ragged girl lying in filth in a cellar while a raging mob hunts for her outside." The little man folded his hands in front of him and smiled at her. "Look at me—do I seem in a bad way, generally? Do I seem hungry and humiliated? Do I seem poor? Quite the reverse. The Brothers look after their own."

The girl spat into the dirt. "Oh, sure. You're wealthy. Of course you are—you're of the Towns. I want nothing from you. Let me out of here." She struggled to rise.

"Your hatred," the man said, "shines out of you like a black gemstone lying in mud. I don't see much evidence of intelligence, though. The Brothers are no more 'of the Towns' than you. We are not like the Mentors, the bank managers, the militia. We hate them, just as you do. Only we use them, we feed off them—and we do it carefully and cleverly, choosing the time and place and method. We do it from places of security and comfort, not skulking in the bushes like two-bit vagabonds such as you. And now I think we will, just for a moment, lock the door. . . ." He stopped talking, flicked two bolts into place. Through the bars behind him the girl saw the street become alive with running boots and shoes, bouncing like raindrops in a thunderstorm, like sparks struck between a flint and steel. The ground shook with it.

The girl got to her feet, supporting herself against the wall. She stared out at the rushing, faceless malice of the crowd. Opposite her, the man raised one of his intact fingers to his lips.

The mob reached the end of the road with no sign of the girl. The boots milled about in a chaos of frustration.

Something rattled at the door; it shook briefly, became still.

A new energy coursed through the boots and shoes. A different street had been suggested, another possible refuge for the fugitive. Away, away! The hue and cry swept back along the road, fading but never quite snuffing out. It hung like a smell in the margins of the room.

The man's smile flicked on and off. "They do want you quite badly," he said.

Whatever energy the girl possessed seemed to have departed with the crowd. She said listlessly: "You talk a lot without saying anything. This outfit of yours, the Brothers of the Hand, these activities you mention. I take it you're a criminal organization?"

The little man stood in shadow at the edge of the window, smiling at her, a dusky corona around him. "And so the intelligence returns," he said. "No, we're a business, that's all, and Soames and Teach are businessmen who seek opportunities outside Faith House control. They've asked me to be creative in finding new blood, and I believe that's what I'm doing. The way you climbed the roof . . ." He let the words hang, let her reach for them.

"It's nothing. I've always climbed." For the first time in a long while, she let her eyes refocus. There in the musty cellar she had a glimpse of hills and trees.

He waited for the moment to play out, for her to resurface in the room. "If you think about it sensibly," he said, "you'll know it's unlikely you'll leave the town of Stow alive. There's only so many roofs to climb. But it doesn't *have* to be that way. I could take you to meet some people while things die down. Get you food, too. Somewhere to sleep."

She was staring at the window and its bars, imagining climbing the steps, slipping out into the street. . . . A wave of exhaustion washed the thought backward, pressed it, wriggling feebly, against the wall. The noise of the crowd was still audible, not too far away.

"Sounds good, doesn't it?" the man said.

"Your finger," she said. "Would I be required to do that? Because if so . . ."

"That would be up to Mr. Teach and Mr. Soames. I don't know. But you won't be meeting them yet, not till you've got yourself cleaned up. Small steps and all that." He waited. "Well?" he said.

A shrug. He was offering her sleep and food and safety. "Sure," she said. "Okay."

"Excellent. In that case—" He took a penlight from his pocket, shone it on the darkest side wall of the cellar. Behind the mess of barrels, wood, and jumbled debris was a waist-high door. The girl had not noticed it, though she'd been standing just six feet away.

She stared at it. "What's through there?"

"Your new life. My name is Carswell. All you have to do is follow me."

11

When the door of the Trans-Kingdom Country-man bus opened and Scarlett stepped out onto the concrete platform at Ashtown, the first thing she noticed was the color of the earth. It was a deep, rich black, tinged with red. You could see it showing through the thin covering of grass beside the highway. You could see it smeared at the base of the stockade wall. You could see it on the boardwalks on the main street, on the splash-boards of the white clapboard houses, on the wheels of the ale vans, on the men's boots, on the women's skirts as they hurried along. It was everywhere, and it was tolerated. Just as it had destroyed the ancient city far beneath them, so had it assured the wealth of the modern community that owed its existence to the mines. Ash was the source of all prosperity. It had made the town.

There was no sentry waiting to see their papers. Scarlett stood on the platform, blinking in the day's freshness, while Albert clambered stiffly down. They were the only persons alighting in Ashtown. She pulled her coat close around her. It was cold. All morning, they had been steadily pulling upward out of the Mercian plains into Northumbria. The hills above were a shimmering pastel green, fringed with wet cloud.

The bus thrummed, revved its engine, and drew away toward the stockade gate in a burst of diesel fumes.

"Ah, Scarlett, have you ever tasted air like this?" Albert took an expansive breath and exhaled with lip-smacking gusto. "It's so lovely and fresh! So clear! I wonder why that is."

"We're farther from the Burning Regions, maybe? I don't know. Well, I'm glad you're happy. You've been snoring in my ear the past three hours. You *ought* to be feeling good."

Albert's hair was skewed sideways; he had a rumpled look. "I am indeed. True, six buses in twenty-four hours has left me somewhat sore, and I may have constipation from sitting down too long. Other than that, I'm in excellent fettle to carry out a daring crime!"

Scarlett glanced along the main street, but no one was near. "Our brief stay here should be a lot more comfortable than the buses," she said, "so happily your bowels will soon recover—*provided* we are cautious and keep on the right side of the locals. One tip, incidentally, is not to talk so brazenly about how you're going to rob them."

Albert's face fell. "I know," he said. "I just feel jittery, Scarlett. We have six days left to return to Stow, and we haven't even begun our work. I need to *do* something."

"Me too." Scarlett adjusted her hat. "But we can get started now. We're here."

The bus stop was almost at the end of town. From where they stood, Scarlett had a good view back up the main street. Yeah, two curving rows of bars and doss houses, hotels, a food market, a casino, some shabby tobacco stores: it reminded her of Huntingdon, of Stow, of many frontier towns. A few young women stood in pockets of sunlight, twirling parasols, taking turns to laugh and talk. Limping, misshapen men—perhaps unlucky victims of the mine— loitered on the porches, blowing cigarette smoke, waiting for something to happen. Nothing did. The shop windows were dark and unreflective. In late afternoon, Ashtown had a shuttered, mothballed air.

Scarlett knew what kind of place it was. When evening came, and the miners returned from the Buried City, the street would blossom violently like a garish nighttime flower.

The long journey north had left her feeling irritable and cooped up. She had an urge to be alone. "Albert," she said, "can you find us a hotel? A quiet one, not expensive. I'm going to take a walk out of town, get a sense of the geography, maybe take a gander at the mines. I'll meet you back here in an hour. And *be careful*. This is *not* a normal Surviving Town. It's a tough burg, where even the sweetest-looking waif will cut your throat for the pennies in your pocket, then blow them at the gaming booth next door. Keep a low profile and try to fit in."

She looked at him. Albert was listening gravely, giving an impersonation of sober competence that might have fooled a passing stranger. "Scarlett, you can rely on me!"

She walked out through the open gates in the stockade,

where the sidewalks ended and the rich black soil began. There was a low hill behind the town. The grass was thick and flourishing. Wet seed heads brushed her jeans as she began to climb.

From halfway up, she could already see where the mine road left the highway, see where it looped toward the ridge, a mile distant on the other side of the valley. Directly below her, Ashtown itself was exposed. As she'd surmised, it was essentially no more than a single street, backed by unkempt yards and surrounded by a stockade to keep out the Tainted and the beasts. Away from the main drag, the buildings quickly deteriorated into shacks and storehouses. Everything was workaday and unexceptional. The special stuff was hidden underground.

It did Scarlett good to have the cold air on her face, to breathe deeply and stretch her legs. She went on climbing. At the top of the rise, out of sight of the buildings, she unclipped her binoculars. The clouds were low, sagging with rain; on the ridge across the valley, mist drifted along the tops of giant spoil heaps excavated from the mines. In places, where the ash layer was thinner or had been bitten into by rushing streams, the ancient ruins were near the surface, their spars protruding like gray teeth in black gums.

She moved the binoculars slowly, following the zigzag slashes of the mine road. Two-thirds of the way up the ridge, a narrow plateau had been cut into the slope, with a cliff rising behind it. Here a wet spattering of lights hung bright beneath the cloud. Strong lights. Watch lights. A high fence ran around the edges of the plateau, with sentry posts every hundred yards and a gate onto the road. Inside the compound were a few low gray buildings. Scarlett could see figures moving about. Men with dogs. Men with guns. Behind it all, a great door was set into the cliff face. The entrance to the mines.

"Yep," she breathed, "that's where the action is. So how the hell do we get in there?"

It was a question that, in one form or another, she had been asking all the journey up from Stow. Not consciously at first, not at the forefront of her mind. There had been too much to organize, too much to figure out, simply in getting across the kingdoms. At the outset, Teach had returned her hat and coat and given them a battered copy of *Tompkins's Complete Bus Timetable*; fortunately, Albert still carried a wodge of Faith House money in his trouser pockets. Other than that, they'd had nothing. A good deal of ingenuity had been used up buying or stealing the bare equipment they required—the binoculars, a revolver for Scarlett, sufficient ammo, rucksacks and ropes, knives and provisions—all while taking a succession of rackety buses across the wastes of Mercia. There'd been no chance of traveling back to the Wolf's Head for their proper belongings. They'd had to hit the Great North Road.

Six buses, little sleep. There was no use in complaining about it, or in wasting her energies in fury at the Brothers;

still less in getting anxious about Joe and Ettie. She had to be practical now—and fast. Time was their main problem.

Far away on Soames's desk, Ettie's clock was ticking. One day had been used up already. It would take the same to get back to Stow. That left five days, max, to carry out some kind of raid. For something this difficult, that wasn't long.

Well, they'd do it. She just didn't have a clue how.

She stowed her binoculars and with long, brisk strides headed back to town.

Albert was waiting for her near the bus stop at the end of the main street. He was leaning against a lamppost. Not just leaning. He had his collar up, his hat down low, his hands deep in his pockets. He was slouched at an implausible angle, shoulders back, crotch jutting forward alarmingly. He seemed to be wearing his own portable shadow, from which his eyes glinted with incoherent menace. A chewed matchstick hung twirling from his lips. The effect was disconcerting. Rugged northerners looked at him askance. Mothers escorted their children in wide circuits across the road to avoid him. Even Scarlett flinched.

"Hey there, Scarlett."

"Why is your voice so low? Why are you standing in that weird way?"

"You told me to fit in."

"Bloody hell. I'm surprised no one's shot you. Stop loafing and come on. Did you get us a hotel?"

"I chose the Spade and Compass. I've booked us in already.

It's over here." He led the way along the raised sidewalk. "It's quiet, as you wanted. There were just a few ladies sitting about in the saloon. Seemed friendly. Two of them blew me kisses as I looked in."

"Uh-huh. Did they. I imagine it'll get a whole lot busier when the mine shift ends."

"It will be nice if it gets lively," Albert said. "Also, it's got a mummified arm in a case above the reception desk. It was brought up from the Buried City, the guy said, and is very rare."

"That's meant to recommend it to me?" Scarlett shook her head. "All right, if you're sure."

Grudgingly, Scarlett had to admit the Spade and Compass was suitable for their purpose. It was shabby, gaudy, and broad-fronted, as were many of the women sitting in the saloon. Still, it was by no means the most down-market hotel on the strip, in that you could check in without being immediately mugged by the staff. The receptionist was dour and uninterested; the mummified arm was appropriately shriveled; their room was spacious and moderately watertight and clean, with its own privy and a window overlooking the street. The only problem, in fact, was that it was *their* room. To Scarlett's irritation, Albert had booked them in as a married couple, a Mr. and Mrs. Johnson.

"Look at this!" she growled. "A double bed. Why didn't you say anything?"

Albert's expression was vague. "The man sort of assumed, I guess. I went along with it. Also, one room's cheaper than two."

This was a valid point, which Scarlett ignored. "Well, why 'Johnson,' for Shiva's sake?"

"I don't know. I always use that pseudonym whenever I have to stay in a Town." He smiled genially. "You could say it's my trademark."

"Don't use it too often. Someone might spot a pattern. There's that operative out there hunting for us, don't forget. All right, I'm having the bed; you can sleep on the floor between the sink and the bin. Now we should get to work, gathering information."

They went down to the street, bought noodles at a kiosk, and settled themselves on a stoop to observe the evening activities of Ashtown. These weren't long in starting. Shortly after six o'clock, a dirty white bus brought the miners down from the hill. They wore blue overalls and heavy boots. Their faces were black with dust, their eyes red-rimmed and weary. Almost at once, the main street came to life. Lights flickered on, music started in the saloons; there were raised voices, laughter, rapid movements everywhere.

Scarlett and Albert watched the people as they headed to the bars or queued for noodles and fried chicken. Albert sat with his eyes half closed. Scarlett knew what he was doing.

"Anything?" she said after twenty minutes had passed.

Albert nodded distractedly. "I've got any amount of fragments. It'll take a while to build up the full picture, but the mine compound is heavily guarded, like Sal Qin said. Not only that, but they fill up the trucks *inside* the hill behind some iron doors. I don't see how we can get in there."

"Yeah, it looked impregnable from across the valley," Scarlett said. She rubbed her chin. "So . . . maybe we'll have to hijack the trucks on the road. That's *got* to be easier, surely."

At that moment, the boardwalks began to rattle. Lanterns swung in the shop overhangs. Babies cried, people hurried off the street. Scarlett and Albert turned.

With a roaring of gears, a vehicle came rumbling through Ashtown. It was an enormous green-gray truck, speeding along on six pairs of colossal wheels, each almost as tall as Scarlett herself. The body of the lorry was iron, marked with the white circle symbol of the Faith Houses. Gun muzzles protruded from hatches in the sides. The cab had reinforced iron doors, and a narrow windshield, through which a driver and a guard peered grimly. Atop the body of the truck was a rotating plastic turret, with another guard sitting at his ease, a machine gun held ready. The cargo truck roared past, making the ground shake. It splashed through a puddle below the stoop, spraying water over Scarlett's coat and jeans.

Albert was untouched. He watched the juggernaut as it dwindled into the distance. "*Or,*" he said, "maybe we need to keep thinking."

For the rest of that evening, and through the following day, Scarlett and Albert continued their reconnaissance. Albert wandered between the saloons, engaging people in conversation and sieving them to discover what he could about the security of the mines and the movement of the trucks. He sat outside the hotels and at the window tables of the coffee houses. He spoke to miners, barkeeps, and the ladies with their parasols. His aim was to build up a picture of the Buried City—and what it contained.

Scarlett adopted a different course. Shortly after dawn, she climbed on foot to the hill above the town. Drawing close to the mines, she wormed through the gorse under the shadows of the watchtowers and lay in secret, watching activity in the compound. From time to time the iron doors opened in the cliff and rattle cars of compacted ash were brought out from below. Otherwise, the doors were shut. Guards were a constant presence; she recorded the duration of their patrols along the inside of the perimeter fence, and the times when sentries changed. At length, withdrawing with care, she left the plateau and climbed to the ridge above the compound, where thirty spoil heaps from past excavations rose like gray milk puddings against the clouds and sky. She walked among the heaps and peered down into the brick-lined shafts that carried air deep into the mines.

Toward the end of the afternoon, she sat on a promontory as the great iron doors below her opened a final time. Two white buses emerged. Scarlett watched as they descended the zigzag road to Ashtown. One—carrying the miners—went as far as the main street. The other did not go so far but parked at a small building just inside the town stockade; even through her binoculars she could not see who got out of it. Other than these buses, the only visible activities all day were the sentries wandering about and the rattle cars bringing up debris. Everything significant happened inside the hill.

Scarlett returned thoughtfully to town. Break into the fortified mines or hijack a heavily armed lorry on the road? Neither option was too thrilling. Either way, she needed inside information. Perhaps Albert would provide that now.

As she approached the hotel, she became aware of a man in faded blue dungarees sitting on its stoop. His hair was white, his beard bushy, his face etched deep with age. He lacked the lower portion of his left leg; his trouser was neatly folded just above the knee. The man's stick leaned against the step beside him. An empty metal bowl sat by his boot. A small white dog lay at his elbow, resting its head mournfully on its forepaws.

Scarlett hesitated, then came to a decision. She went to the kiosk opposite. She crossed the road holding a paper carton, sat beside the man. "Noodles?"

Bright blue eyes blinked at her from above the beard. "I'd prefer money, but I'll accept noodles in place of anything better. Your charity is appreciated, albeit with the caveat that I expect you want something in return. Acts of random kindness are seldom what they seem in Ashtown. Here, everything is a transaction. What are you after? My clothes? They will not fit you. My wealth? I have none. My begging bowl is rusted, my walking stick brittle. If you want my dog, he has mange and a terrible stomach complaint. If you want my body—"

"Are you going to have the bloody noodles or not?"

"I will. Thank you." The beggar took the carton. "They seem a trifle cool."

"That's not *my* fault, is it? You've been waffling on so long." Scarlett sat glaring while the beggar ate the noodles, spooning out portions with his fingers to give his little dog. At last he tossed the carton aside and sat back with a sigh. "I take it you worked in the mines," she said.

"Long ago." The man brushed fragments from his beard. "Till a blood-mole took my leg."

"I am sorry for it."

"Worse things happen in the Buried City. Life on the street is dull and hard, especially when the black storms sweep in from the east, but I am not sad to be out of the mines. It is an evil place, particularly in the abandoned zones."

"Evil? Why?"

"Well, the blood-moles don't help, nor any of the other beasts that infest the tunnels. There are problems with the Tainted, too, from time to time. But in a deeper sense, it's wrong to meddle with the past. The city is a tomb and the resting place of the wicked dead. It should be left untouched, yet we defile it for our profit. . . ." He scratched fondly under his dog's ear. "Alfie here wouldn't do anything so stupid, you may be sure. But that is the whim of our blessed Faith Houses, and who are we to contradict them?"

"Who indeed? Why do you say the dead were 'wicked'?"

The blue eyes glinted. "If you saw their faces, you'd know."

Scarlett regarded him a moment. "I am a tourist with interest in the mines. I would like to hear your thoughts about it. I can always bring more noodles, if you're willing."

The beggar nodded. "Feel free. I'm not going anywhere. Not very fast, anyhow."

Late that evening, at the Spade and Compass, a council was held in Scarlett and Albert's room. Scarlett drew the curtains over the windows, set the lantern glowing. They sat on the bed together. Music sounded dimly from the saloon below.

"So," Scarlett said, "what have we found out?"

"Enough." Albert's face was weary; it carried the shadows of the people he'd been sieving, their disappointments and sullied dreams. "Essentially Sal Qin was right: the Buried City is vast, and they've been digging there for years. Areas 1 to 3 are flooded; Areas 4 to 6 are unsafe for a variety of horrid reasons. Only Area 7 is currently being worked. This bit has got lighting and equipment and is relatively safe—and it connects to the underground loading bay inside the iron doors. The artifacts are boxed in special rooms near the bay and loaded into the trucks. At night the miners leave. Only a few guards remain. But the doors are locked from the inside. No one gets in. In the morning, it all starts up again." He rubbed his tired eyes. "One other thing, Scarlett. Children work there too."

"What do you mean, children?"

"Just that. They're miners, I suppose. Or slaves."

"We didn't see them on the bus. . . . No, wait"—she snapped her fingers—"the second one! I saw it from the top. Goes to a place on the edge of town. What do they use kids for?"

"I don't know, but I'm not sure they're treated kindly. I don't like little children being locked up, Scarlett. I saw too much of that in Stonemoor. And some of the things I sieved about the mines—"

Scarlett knew the way the conversation was going, and she wanted to forestall it. Albert had a tendency to drift off into inessentials. She held up a hand. "Okay, you may be right, but it's not our concern. We're trying to help Joe and Ettie here. *They* won't be treated very kindly if we're not back in a few days. So let's consider the options. The first is to tackle the cargo trucks on the open road. Correct?"

Albert nodded reluctantly. "Yes. The cargo lorries leave the underground depot when they're full, which is every few days. One went yesterday, so there's probably one being readied now. But we've already established that they're much too fast and too heavily armored for us to ambush." He looked at her. "*Aren't* they?"

For a moment Scarlett thought of mentioning that even a well-armed speeding truck might struggle to cope if Albert could be persuaded to unleash the Fear. But she knew it was no use. For six months he had worked to close off that talent; he would not be persuaded otherwise. "Yep," she said easily, "and that means we have to fall back on the alternative."

She could hear doubt in his voice. "We enter the mines?"

"Sure. We do it at night, when everything's quiet. Just us and a sentry or two. We get in, steal a truck from the loading bay, open the cliff doors, and drive it out and away." She stretched luxuriously, tipped her hat lower over her face. "Simple."

"Your definition of 'simple' is interesting," Albert said. "Let me count out the problems for you on my fingers. You may have to lend me yours. There's the fence, the guards, the dogs—" He broke off abruptly. "Uh-oh."

"What? I'm only smiling."

"You're not—you're grinning. It's that horrid grin I never like. It's the grin that never ends well, particularly for me."

"It's the grin that tells you I've got the solution." Scarlett put her arms behind her head and settled deeper into her pillow with a sigh of satisfaction. "You're not going to like it, but there *is* a way."

12

If it hadn't been for the knowledge that he was about to drop down a hole into the land of the dead, Albert would have enjoyed his walk into the hills. It was a pleasant-enough stroll in the late-afternoon sun; there had been no rain, and the heather on the slopes was dry and fragrant. Far below them, the two silvered rows of Ashtown's buildings lay like an open zipper, their deep blue shadows stretching to the east. He was not sorry to have left the place. A sense of oppression had been growing in him during his two days sieving the inhabitants—a kind of moral claustrophobia that came from living their lives by proxy. His head was awhirl with their hopes and hates and appetites; he felt tied to their saloons and gaming houses, to their chophouse brawls and silent tenement rooms. It was the kind of thing that got to a fellow after a while. Albert was happy to breathe fresh air again.

The way to the ridge was long. They went slowly, for their packs were cumbrous and weighty: they had spent the morning in Ashtown's hardware stores and were carrying torches, sulfur sticks, and several coils of rope. Six months ago Albert would have struggled to make the climb *without* such a burden: in fact, he would have collapsed into the first bush he found and lain there with his trainers wiggling feebly at the sky. But he was hardened now, and sinewy; and Ettie's face was there before him whenever he closed his eyes.

"I can't stop thinking about her," he said. "I hope she's okay."

"She's fine." They had stopped for a breather halfway up the slope. The floodlights of the mine compound were visible above them, around the curve of the hill.

"But if your friends mistreat her . . ."

"They're not my friends! And they won't: if anything, it'll be the reverse. You can guarantee Joe will be making the Brothers' lives a misery in one way or another." Scarlett took a drink from her water bottle. "Soames knows I won't bring him anything without proof they're well. They'll do nothing to them until we get back with the cargo."

"And after that?"

"We'll think of something." She clipped the bottle to her pack. "Won't we?"

Albert nodded briefly. He walked on; presently Scarlett fell in beside him.

"They were *never* my friends," she said. "But they *did* save my life, a long time ago."

"I can only go on what you tell me." Albert looked up suddenly; faint on the wind, the six-o'clock bell was sounding in Ashtown. An answering ring came from the mine compound.

The gate in the boundary fence swung open. Albert and Scarlett crouched low in the heather, watching the two battered buses start off down the mountain road. Albert looked especially at the second bus: he thought he saw a row of small heads behind the dirty glass, but it was too far away to be sure.

The gates swung closed. Albert knew that a host of defenses were now being deployed in the compound. Keys would be turned, bolts slammed, guard dogs let loose. Sentries would take up position in the watchtowers. And the great iron doors in the cliff behind would stand silent and impassable through the night hours. They'd not be opened until dawn.

None of which mattered a squashed fig, because that wasn't how he and Scarlett were getting in. They continued climbing.

On the ridge above the mines, the spoil heaps sprouted like newborn hillocks clinging to their mother. Grass grew on areas of the bumpy clag; other heaps were bare, despite the passing years. It was cold in the shadows between them; the ground was uneven and studded with thistles. Albert, imagining the city beneath them, was beset by an inexpressible sense of loneliness, seeping up through the roots of the grasses and the soles of his shoes.

They came to the place at last. Scarlett halted suddenly beside a thicket of thorns and brush. Peering uneasily through the brambles, Albert glimpsed a low brick wall, curving round to make a circle perhaps ten feet in diameter. A metal screen was fixed across it, two bricks down, to prevent leaves and other debris falling in. Below that was a gray void.

"The air shaft," Scarlett said. "There are others, but this is the best. See how rusted the screen is? We can cut through that. According to the old beggar with one leg, the shafts lead right to the center of the mines, to bring clean air to the miners. They drop vertically to start with, then curl gently down to reach the levels. Once we get to the bottom, it'll be a cinch to stroll through the tunnels and reach the loading bay with the lorries. This is our back door in."

Albert craned his head out over the lip of stone. Cool air rose from the deeps, making his skin thrill and tingle with the touch. He felt sweat break out on his palms.

"Scarlett," he said, "I have a question that I wish I had thought of earlier. How can we be sure that our combined ropes are long enough for the shaft?"

"We can't." Scarlett had taken some bolt cutters from her rucksack; bending out over the abyss, she was busy snipping through the rusted grille. "Next question."

"But what happens if we reach the end of the rope and we are still not at the bottom?"

"We let go and fall the remaining distance. Even you can manage that."

"Yes. And I can manage the bone-breaking, teeth-scattering landing as well."

"You forget that the shaft becomes a chute. According to the old beggar, anyway. Have I calmed your nerves?"

"Not entirely."

"Well, quit worrying. It's not as if it's the first time we've climbed down a rope together. There was that fortified bank in Sedgefield, remember?"

"Yes. But that was a twenty-foot drop, not two million or whatever this is. Also, at Sedgefield I lost my grip and landed on your head."

Scarlett pushed at the grille; a circular section dropped silently away into the shaft. "True. If the same thing happens now, do me a favor and scream so I have time to move."

With what seemed indecent speed, she took a coil of thin blue rope from each of their bags and tied them together to form one long length. She fixed one end of the rope around the root of an ancient hawthorn tree. The rest she played out over the edge. Then she performed numerous tests on rope and root, checking they would bear their weight. Albert watched in silence. Scarlett tolerated a certain amount of panicked gabbling in such moments, but there was always a cutoff point, beyond which he tended to get a thick ear.

At last she was satisfied. She shouldered her pack, put on some gloves, held the rope loosely in one hand. She hopped up onto the lip of stone and looked at him.

"All right?" she asked.

"All right" was possibly stretching it. Albert only nodded.

"Give me ten minutes," she said. "I'll see you at the bottom."

She turned her back to the void, jumped out, and began to rappel down. The last Albert saw of her was her grin, her hair flaring in the sunlight. . . . Then it was just silence and the calling of the birds. Also, the usual questions. Where had she learned to *enjoy* such danger? Where had she learned not to care?

For a while the rope head jerked and trembled on the lip of the stone. The movements lessened as Scarlett dropped away. Albert sat on the edge, putting on his climbing gloves, trying to distract himself from thoughts of imminent death. As so often with a job, he already had snapshots in his head—images of the Buried City, taken from the miners of the town. Strange doors, walls, and passages hung in darkness, oddly lit and floating—he could make little sense of them. But there *was* a pervading sense of horror in the memories. . . .

He sat silently. Light was fleeing to the west. The sky was ragged with black cloud.

Despite Scarlett's bravado, Albert was under no illusions about the difficulties ahead, and he knew he was relying on his partner to survive. He knew *she* knew it too. She seldom mentioned it, but what she wanted was for him to use his other power in tricky situations. She thought he should use the Fear. But *that* was easier said than done.

There was a stone on the ground beside his shoe. Not a very big stone. Round, yellowish, ordinary . . . Albert looked at it. He concentrated. After a moment the stone wobbled, then grew still. He took a slow breath and tried again. This time the stone moved smoothly upward off the soil. It rose as high as his head, hung steady. Albert looked to the left; the stone shifted in that direction. He looked to the right; the stone moved likewise. Albert sat on the lip of the shaft, hands clasped in his lap, the stone following the movements of his eyes. Presently he looked down and fitted it back into its original indentation in the mud.

He got up with a grimace. All very well. In quiet times, when he was alone, such skills were easy enough. But it was a different matter trying anything when he was angry or upset. Then, as with the rock snake, there was no hope of precision or control!

Ten minutes had passed. Back in his early days with Scarlett, Albert would have spent considerable time and energy loitering up top, tightening his rucksack, doing his shoelaces, finding interesting insects on nearby bushes, and generally putting off the inevitable. Now he simply sighed. He caught hold of the rope, turned for a last look at the sun, leaned back and outward. Then, dropping through the hole in the metal screen, he started climbing down.

To begin with, he had the circle of sky above, the curve of the bricks around him, the silent, cold immensity of the hole below. Gradually the sky receded; little by little the darkness swallowed him. All he had now was the sure sensation of his shoes moving down the wall, his hands scuffling along the roughness of the rope. . . . A sense of futility rose in him. Try as he might, he felt he was simply hanging, like his tentative movements were getting him nowhere.

He lost track of time, focused entirely on the mechanical repetition of the task, trying to ignore the aches in his back and shoulders. His existence was reduced to air and silence, to the faint white glow of his trainers scuffling on the brick.

And still the shaft went down.

Albert let himself drift into a protective reverie. How lucky he was! How fortunate to be dangling on this rope! Through all his years in the prison at Stonemoor, he had desired to explore the secrets of the kingdoms. And the secrets of the past were surely the most evocative ones of all. Now, with every trembling handhold, he was inching back across the epochs—to a city that had existed before the Cataclysm. What marvels might he find?

At last he realized that his feet, far from being level with his waist, had swung beneath him, and he knew that Scarlett's assertion about the shaft becoming a chute was correct. He went on with growing confidence, and by the time he reached the end of the rope, he was able to stand on the brickwork. With only the barest hesitation, he let go and skidded down the final stretch. There was a suggestion of light and space. The chute bent decisively, became fully horizontal, opened into a corridor. Albert plopped out of an opening and landed on his bottom. Scarlett was leaning against the wall opposite, looking bored.

"*There* you are," she said. "Have fun?"

"If not dying horribly counts as fun, then yes, I had a super time." Albert got up, rubbing at his aching arms. "Ooh, wait— what are these things?"

"Your biceps: I'm glad you're finally acquainted." Scarlett shone her torch along the tunnel. "Well, we're in. Now all we need is to find the cargo trucks. Come on."

The corridor was squared, roughly hewn, and unlit, but there was a soft light glowing up ahead. Albert followed Scarlett toward it. The air was cold and dry and dead. It smelled of stone and dust. Apart from their footfalls, he could hear no sound.

Almost at once, they entered a chamber with electric lights bolted to the walls. The lights were off, but the room was lit by a phosphorescent mold that hung about the ceiling. A mechanism of cogs and wheels was visible within a heap of rubble. There was a big white sign beside it. Beyond this, a broad tunnel floored with plastic matting led away into the dark.

Albert and Scarlett approached the sign. It was dirty, coated with the dust of years. Brushing it clear, Albert discovered a set of rules and warnings for employees of the mines. "Look," he said. "You're supposed to wear a helmet, boots . . . and breathing apparatus in case of gas. We haven't got *any* of that. I'm only in trainers."

Scarlett grunted. "Yeah. It's the bit below that bothers me."

The bottom half of the sign was a checklist, with chalk stubs hanging at its side. The table showed silhouetted images of a range of unpleasant creatures, presumably potential visitors to the mines. Albert didn't recognize all the shapes, though some had a worrying number of legs. Next to each, a series of numbers had been scribbled.

"See that?" Scarlett said. "Shows what areas they've been found in. Ack, we've got blood-moles, giant lizards, bore-worms . . . and I don't know *what* that horrible, segmented thing with wings is. Gods, look at them all! They infest the place!"

"Especially Areas 5 and 6," Albert said. "Don't go anywhere near *those* bits, or you might meet something nasty." He scratched his nose. "What area *are* we in, I wonder?"

Scarlett tapped him on the shoulder. Turning, Albert saw an enormous number 6, practically man-sized, painted blood-red, daubed across the opposite wall.

There was a longish pause. "Well," Scarlett said, "not to worry. We won't be here long. We're just going to nip over to Area 7, find some boxed-up artifacts, nick a truck, and drive away. We probably won't see much of the Buried City, and we *certainly* won't see any of these critters."

"Even that horrid segmented one?"

"Especially not him. It's almost a shame it's going to be so boring." She flashed Albert the old half smile. "Right, this wide tunnel is a good bet. If we follow a main route like this, we'll soon find stairs to a working region. Then it's onward to the artifact packing rooms and the loading bay! Come on."

They pattered down the tunnel, a wide highway scuffed red with the footprints of many boots. In the pale light, Albert could see the marks of miners' tools on floor and ceiling. A few rusted oil cans lay in a corner, old axe-heads, other undefinable debris. There was a feeling of disuse, as if no one had come that way for a while. It was very quiet.

After rather longer than they'd expected, they reached a junction where the tunnel split into three. Here Scarlett's confidence about the clarity of the route wasn't quite borne out. Each branch was lit by the same eerie phosphorescence. Each had plastic matting. There was no means to tell which of them, if any, was the correct way.

Scarlett adjusted her hat, frowning. "What good is a crossroads with no directions? Where's the signage in this place?"

"Maybe it's been eaten."

"Well, we've got to make a choice. What do you think? Is the middle way a trifle wider?"

"I was going to suggest right."

"Let's go left, then. We've got a terrible record at this sort of thing. We're almost certainly both wrong."

Whether or not the left-hand route was correct Albert never knew. Soon all thoughts of the loading bay and the trucks were driven from his mind. The tunnel ran on for a stretch, then turned a corner and opened out into a high, wide space. There was a gulf above them. Strings of electric lights glimmered along the distant roof, casting a soft white illumination over the cavern and what it contained.

There were houses in it.

Albert and Scarlett stopped dead.

The floor of the cave was ancient, blackened concrete, smooth in parts, cracked in others. On either side, housefronts blossomed from the gray-red stone, growing from it organically, as if the crystals in the rock had mutated into doors and archways, pillars and gable ends. They were ghost houses.

The buildings were half formed, fragmentary and dreamlike, their outlines hazy beneath the remaining coating of rock. In some places the excavators had seemingly been at pains to reveal the intricacies of the ancient constructions; in others they had hardly bothered to reach the brickwork, contenting themselves with cutting through to the doors and windows and so gaining access to inside. Sometimes, narrow holes had been burrowed into the interiors—presumably the work of human agency, though it made Albert recall the giant bore-worms. Balconies of uncut stone had been left high up to form walkways to the highest apertures. These were reached by ladders of appalling slimness, which Albert could scarcely imagine a grown person having to scale. He thought of the child slaves again.

He realized he had forgotten to breathe. Even Scarlett was momentarily subdued.

"So much work," he said. "Think of the effort needed to create this place."

She nodded. "They must *really* want whatever's down here."

They walked on, torches swirling, following the line of matting across the cave. They went silently, for it was a place of echoes; the softest footstep created murmurous reverberations that rushed through the hollow spaces, gathering strength, bounding and rebounding, and calling back at them from far away, so that it seemed an army of the dead was converging on them from every side. . . .

But there was no one there.

"This bit must've been excavated years ago," Scarlett whispered. "There's no tools, no carts, no heaps of stone. Keep your eye on those holes, though. I don't like them."

They came to what had perhaps once been an intersection of the ancient streets. Here the corner of a building had been entirely uncovered, and another hollowed-out cavern extended away under striplights. The walls were striated with black lines, implying they had been torched by tongues of fire. . . . Albert tried to visualize the living city. It was hard, but not impossible. The architecture was similar in style to some of the Surviving Towns he had visited, only muffled and distorted, as if seen through a broken lens. It was a place of visual echoes too.

A set of orange cones had been placed across the side cavern. Scarlett and Albert regarded them.

"What do you think these mean?" Albert asked.

"'Keep out.' 'Danger of death.' 'Giant insects up ahead.' It'll be something like that."

"It will, won't it? Shall we go the other way?"

"Let's."

They moved off. Almost at once, Albert held up a hand. "Hear that?"

Scarlett did. Her face was taut with tension.

It was a soft but definite *clicking.* Random clicks, at an unknown distance, and from an unknown direction. Unhelpful images came into Albert's mind. He thought of claws tapping on stone, of giant jagged mandibles slicing together . . .

"Probably a generator," he said. "Some harmless machine."

She met his gaze. "Exactly. That's what I think too."

They kept on, following the line of the ancient street, and moved through an ash-stone arch into a smaller cave. Here the houses had hardly been exposed at all. Holes had been drilled in search of the hollow cavities locked inside the buildings. They were not very large holes. Albert found it difficult to envisage one of the big miners from the saloon squeezing his way inside. The roof had collapsed in places. He picked up speed: the prospect of entombment didn't appeal to him.

The passage split again. Rough miners' stairs hewn in the stone led upward, but straight ahead an arch showed in an ancient concrete wall. They paused again in doubt.

"Up, you think?" Albert asked. "Might get us to another area."

"Yeah. But would it be Area 7? We don't actually know."

"At least the clicking noise has g— *Scarlett!* There's someone watching us!"

A gray shape crouched beyond the arch. Albert jumped back, blood crashing in his ears. Scarlett's revolver was already in her hand. He heard her swift, tight breathing.

They waited. The shape did not move. With fumbling fingers, Albert aimed his torch toward it. His beam inched shakily nearer, transfixed the figure with a spear of light.

The crouching person was very thin and motionless, its bony arms crossed protectively above its head. There was a softness about it that puzzled Albert. Even in the torchlight, the outline was fuzzed, not sharp. The limbs were soft and granular, merging with the body.

Scarlett lowered her gun. "Relax . . . it's one of the inhabitants from ancient times."

They stepped cautiously into the hollowed chamber. The walls were seared with marks like giant fingers, radiating inward from the doorway. The hunched, dry form was twisted awkwardly, as if still trying to avoid whatever had entered the room.

"It's so thin," Scarlett said. "Like it's made of burned paper. Like it would disintegrate to the touch. . . ." She crouched close, peered under the brittle, shielding arms. After a pause, she stood again.

Albert had been watching her. "Scarlett, what were you doing?"

"Looking at its face."

"Why? What did you see?"

"Nothing. Nothing. . . . Don't look at it."

They stood there.

"What do you think *happened* in the Cataclysm?" Albert asked.

"Gods know. Something very bad."

They retreated to the steps, climbed to a new level, and went onward through the mines. It was not Area 7. The tunnels wound in and out of entombed houses in a confusing manner. The sense of abandonment deepened. The air was musty. After an unknown time, Scarlett suggested they return to the stairs and try another way. But they could not find the stairs.

Since the discovery of the mummified body, their mood had changed. Albert noticed Scarlett's responses were more abrupt, her decisions less considered. She was moving faster, treating each junction with impatience, eager only to get on. He too was conscious of a growing disquiet, a pressure stemming from the ceaseless silence. They were both thirsty. Scarlett had drained one water bottle and started on her second. Albert's torch battery had run out.

They went through caverns filled with shards of concrete debris, once passing an enormous brick wall that stretched up into unknown space. They went through areas where the phosphorescent mold covered the floors and was tacky beneath their boots. They saw other bodies, too, always in the far corners of empty rooms. Some were still bonded to the rock, as if seeking to prize themselves free; others had been brought from other locations by the miners and dumped there, lying in interlocking mounds. There was evidence that sometimes they'd been used for fuel. Albert disliked the corpses, but this treatment upset him, he didn't know quite why.

They came out at last on a broad tunnel undulating away to left and right through the hill. It was lit by strings of light bulbs bolted to the wall. There was a narrow-gauge track beside the rubber walkway, and a smell of diesel oil hanging in the air.

Scarlett pushed her hat back and scratched at her

scalp. She was perspiring; her cheeks were flushed. "Smell that? It's been used recently. We just have to figure out which way."

Albert nodded. "Perhaps that clicking will help us decide. I can hear it again."

"Shiva! Where?"

"It's coming from behind us. I can't imagine what it is."

"Well, it's not going to be *good*, is it? Think back to that sign and take your bloody pick. I reckon it's following our scent. See anything?"

Albert looked back along the curve of the tunnel they had just come down. "No."

"Good. So: left or right? One of these *must* lead to the loading bay. . . ." She squinted at her watch and cursed. "*Two o'clock!* How did *that* happen? The night's half over!"

Albert stared at her in shock; he, too, had a sense of wild dislocation. He'd thought they had been walking for perhaps an hour.

They chose the left-hand way, going in silence now. The track wound back and forth and presently entered a long, high chamber. One length of the cave was of rough, protruding stone; along the other ran the smooth face of an enormous concrete building, exposed to a height of three stories, studded with ranks of squared, gaping windows. There were bodies in this cave too, a great number of them, stick thin, heads bowed, tucked in sitting positions in half-excavated recesses along the base of the wall.

A string of pale lights hung in loops halfway up the

blank side wall, painting patches of ground with a tremulous sour-milk glow. Other areas remained deep black. Halfway along the cavern, a ladder stretched to one of the higher apertures. Two small mine carts sat on the track nearby, one filled with rubble, the second with an array of digging tools.

Scarlett grinned in satisfaction. "There's our proof. This *has* been recently worked. We're getting warm. If we keep following the track, we'll reach the head of the mine."

Albert hung back, wrinkling his nose. "Smells bad in here," he said.

"Gas pocket, maybe. We can hurry through." She picked up the pace. "Come on."

They moved swiftly along below the empty windows, past the row of blackly crouching bodies. Albert tried not to think of their shriveled limbs, their yellowed, grinning teeth. He felt a quickening of purpose, a burning desire to feel the open air again. He hoped Scarlett was right, that they would soon be at the loading bay.

A thought occurred to him. "The guards," he said. "If there are guards at the trucks, we should avoid bloodshed if we can."

Scarlett made a noncommittal noise. "Depends if they play ball."

"We don't *have* to shoot them, do we? We could just bop them on the head. Rough them up a bit. It's no different from the banks, is it?"

"I don't know. They could be pretty tough customers. We'll see."

They walked on, following the string of lights. After a bit, Albert looked back down the hall. The clicking sound had faded. There was no sign of anything with lots of legs following them in the tunnel.

"Still clear behind," he said.

"Good."

"Maybe our luck's changed at last."

"I think so, Albert. I definitely think so."

He took a few more steps. Really, it was unnecessary to check again so soon, and he could not have explained why he did. There had certainly not been any sound. Maybe it was intuition, maybe there had been something else: some subtle anomaly his conscious mind had missed. Either way, he looked over his shoulder once again—and was just in time to see one of the crouching bodies swing round, stretch its bony legs out of its recess, and step down onto the floor.

13

The thing moved in utter silence. For Albert, its smooth fluidity, its quietness, its stealth—above all, the sheer impossibility and horror of what he saw—all of it was simply an intensification of the dreamlike quality of the Buried City. A sense of unreality had hung about him since he'd entered the tunnels—a place where time had no meaning, where there were streets of houses drowned in solid rock. . . . If the dead returned to life too, there was at least an evil logic to it. Terror snaked around him, constricting his limbs. His jaws were clamped tight shut. He watched the figure step clear of the wall. It went jerkily, stiff-legged. It was at the margin of a pool of lamplight, swathed in shadow. How pale it was! How thin! The head swung loose on the bone-thin neck. Black eyes glimmered, white lips grinned. A white-skinned, bony leg hinged out into the light. Sharp teeth snipped together—and with that scissors click of sound, the endless moment finished and the spell upon Albert was broken.

He gave a strangled yelp.

Scarlett spun around. The single word she said was decidedly undreamlike.

Her revolver appeared in her hand; she fired it three times close to Albert's ear. Sound exploded round him. Bullets struck flesh. The creature fell backward, landed, rolled head over heels across the track, got to its feet again. Teeth shone in the darkness.

The cavern rang with ricocheting noise. Along the row of recessed ledges, other forms began to stir. Bent backs uncurled. Limbs extended like spider legs, languorous and slender.

Blood-dark thoughts winked into life along the hall.

It was only then that Albert's conscious mind caught up with what his instincts had known all along. In this particular chamber of the Buried City, he was *not* in the presence of the dead. But nor precisely of the *living* either—or, at least, not living *humans*.

It was a horror of a different sort.

"Tainted . . . ," he whispered.

"Albert—" Scarlett's voice beside him. "Get to the ladder and climb."

Her calmness cut through everything. Turning, he saw the ladder angled against the wall beyond the rail carts. It stretched to the haze of the third story. There were figures emerging from ledges behind it, but he ignored them, ignored the blaze of Scarlett's gun as she fired twice more at shoulder height, sending pale shapes spinning. He ran; she backed away alongside him, in and out of lamplight. Gun smoke hung about them. It was hard to see.

The ladder was a child's one—light and thin, impossibly tall. Albert did not think he could reach it. He had not yet even reached the rail carts. He was about to put on a desperate spurt when a pale hand grasped his shoulder from behind. He glimpsed a wrist like veined marble, a bracelet of bone and iron. Black nails ripped his flesh, pulled him backward with hideous strength. Pain flared. Albert screamed. There was a stench, a howling. The thing lunged close, all mouth and teeth. Scarlett was there. She stuck her revolver in its face and fired. The howl cut off. The hand fell back. Albert stumbled on.

They reached the rail carts. Scarlett's gun was empty. She snapped it open, tipped the spent cartridges away. No time to reload . . . Forms converged through swirling smoke; there were hoots, whistles, a scraping of taloned toenails on the ground. Scarlett jammed the gun back into her belt, grabbed herself a pickaxe, tossed it to her other hand.

The hoots became screeches: the Tainted were all around them. Scarlett's pick swung left and right. Albert jumped for the ladder, went up it three rungs at a time, propelled by the screaming from below. Up, up . . . He felt the wood sag beneath his weight. Glancing down, he saw white shapes congregating, some beginning to climb, others grappling with the ladder as if to tear it down. Scarlett was just above their outstretched arms, standing straight and perfectly balanced, climbing slowly backward. She wasn't holding on. The bloodied pick was in her belt. She was reloading her revolver. The ladder swayed. Albert clung on. Scarlett flicked the gun closed, fired six shots between her boots. The ladder stopped its shaking.

Albert reached the top, almost at the ceiling of the cave. There was a great squared window, an excavated room beyond. It was a black space. Anything might be inside: a blood-mole, a snake, a bore-worm . . . Albert didn't care. He threw himself off the ladder and into the ancient room. Almost at once, Scarlett was with him. She shoved him aside, kicked the ladder away. Albert watched it fall back, out and sideways across the cavern. It cut through the wires supporting the dangling electrical lights, carrying them with it in a shower of fizzing sparks. Half the lights went out. The ladder clattered down across the rail tracks. The Tainted cooed and chittered in dismay.

Albert and Scarlett looked at each other.

"You all right?" she asked.

"Yes." He ignored the throbbing in his shoulder. "You?"

"Just livid." She dragged her fingers across her forehead. "What was I *thinking*? I should have recognized their smell! This place messes with your mind. . . . Are they giving up?"

Albert was watching the frenzy far below: a lapping sea of white heads, fringed with wisps of hair. Bony arms reached for the ladder; they picked it up, began to return it to the wall. "Not exactly. . . . I'd say we've a minute, not much more."

Scarlett swore under her breath. She flicked her torch on, swung it round the room. It was a chamber of fractured concrete, empty apart from a pile of rubble and the suggestion of an aperture beyond. "There may be a way out," she said, "but we've got to buy ourselves time. Help me roll that stone across."

She sprang to one of the rocks that formed the stack of rubble. It was a great thing, big as Albert's chest. He crouched beside her, wrestled at the stone to free it from the pile. It wasn't easy work. His right arm was hurting; his shoulder felt numb. As they struggled, the top of the ladder reappeared at the window. It shook rhythmically as something began to climb.

Scarlett's hat was askew, sweat running down the side of her face. "Albert."

"Yes."

"Can I make an observation?"

"Of course."

"You do know this would be a decent time for your talent to break out, don't you? It would be *so* much simpler if you could just blow the bastards to pieces down there."

He looked at her. Did he feel the Fear? He certainly had the pounding in the head, the racing heart, the tingling in his wrists. . . . Yet he was reacting to it as *Scarlett* did—by running, jumping, fighting, rolling stones . . . letting out the pressure in a practical way, just as she'd taught him by example. The old Albert couldn't have done that—he'd have been helpless. The Fear would have exploded. He'd probably have brought the whole cave tumbling down.

They had the rock halfway across the room.

"I'm sorry," he said. "I can't. It's there—but it's like I've suppressed it too well."

"But the other night, with Joe and Ettie—"

"I *can't* just switch it on and off, Scarlett. The Fear doesn't work like that!"

"No? That Faith House operative seemed to manage it okay."

The ladder top was shaking. He heard a growling and a slavering from just below.

A final frenzied effort. They rolled the stone the last few yards. The rock went out through the window. There was an awful crunch, then a splintering and crashing as the ladder disintegrated and fell away. Out in the cavern, the whoops and whistles stopped abruptly—then started up again.

Scarlett and Albert flopped back on the floor, chests heaving, groaning.

Albert stared at the ceiling. "You just compared me to the Faith House operative," he said.

"Oh, forget it." Scarlett struggled to a kneeling position, peered out over the ledge. "They're going," she said. "They're swarming away up the cave."

The howling faded. Albert was newly conscious of the pain in his shoulder. He could see blood running there. He gripped his arm, watching Scarlett leaning out of the window.

"Think they'll try to follow us?" he said.

"Yeah. They'll try to cut us off. We can't hang around." She shone the torch toward the hole at the back of the room. "Our only choice is this tunnel."

"Did you see them all curled up back there? What were they *doing*?"

"Sleeping? Hibernating? Who can tell with them? Maybe they just like being underground. The old beggar said the miners had trouble with them from time to time."

Albert had been slowly getting up. He froze. "The one-legged beggar said what?"

"That they had occasional trouble with the Tainted." She brushed a fleck of dust from the tip of the torch. "Didn't I mention it?"

"No. You didn't. You never thought to tell me that little detail."

"Okay, so I forgot. It's no big deal."

"No big deal to you!" He glared at her. "I almost had my arm sliced off just now!"

"But you didn't. Look, it's still hanging on as feebly as ever. I really don't know why you're making so much—" She trained the light on him. "Albert, your shoulder!"

He turned away. "Don't bother yourself."

"Shut up. That cut . . . Did it bite you?"

"No."

"Certain?"

"Yes. Its teeth were snapping, but you shot it before it could bite. This was where it got me with its nails." He saw Scarlett was still staring at him hard. "With its *nails*," he repeated. "Why?"

"No reason. Hold this torch for me." Wrestling her backpack off her shoulder, she flung it open and pulled out the waterproof medicine pouch. She took out a small plastic vial, bit the top off with her teeth, and spat the end away. "Only it's good that it's the nails. You get *bitten* by the Tainted, it's a different story." She poured a colored liquid onto a piece of gauze and jammed it on his shoulder. The sting made Albert flinch. "Hold that there. Keep it on. . . . Yeah, they've got bacteria in their mouths or such. It infects you when they bite. If that happens, you get sick fast, lose fluids. . . . After an hour you swell up black and die. They just follow casual like, wait until you're dead before starting on their feast. But hey, it was the nails, so it's okay." She glanced at him. "If you're one hundred percent sure?"

"I *was* sure before you started talking. I'm not one hundred percent clear on my own *name* now."

By the light of Scarlett's torch they wormed their way through the narrow tunnel at the back of the room. At points it was so low they had to take their rucksacks off and push them first. It was a child's route, Albert knew, and again he wondered at the inhumanity of the miners, to send children into such places. Everything was quiet, but Albert could easily imagine bare, clawed feet speeding down dark paths, and the silence did not reassure him.

Presently the tunnel opened into a second room, similar to the first. A window led onto a solid spur of stone, with open fissures either side, and glimpses of an excavated street below. They passed into another house, through gaping arches, along corridors of blackened brick, then back into miners' tunnels again. At every junction they listened but heard nothing.

They reached a staircase of fractured concrete, going up

and down into the earth. Rocky outcrops protruded through the walls. It was difficult to guess which way to go.

Just as Albert was about to speak, a long, low whistle drifted up from round the stairs. Scarlett scrabbled at her torch and switched it off. They stood there frozen. . . . Now, from just around the corner, came sniffling, snuffling sounds of noses questing for their scent. . . . With infinite care they stole up the curve of the staircase, fearing at every moment to hear the hateful hoots and screams breaking out behind them. But pursuit did not yet come.

They fled onward through the maze of tunnels, in and out of bones of buildings, with silence and terror at their back. Albert had no eyes now for the wonders of the past. It seemed as if he had been running forever, down endless loops of stone. At last, with almost shocking abruptness, they broke out upon a miners' highway. It was a broad tunnel, with matting underfoot and a narrow rail track running purposefully toward a dim light in the distance.

A rectangular wooden box lay on a pallet beside the track. Scarlett levered up its lid, to discover a stack of gelignite sticks, furry with dust. White fuse wires extended from the ends. Without words, they took as many as they could. They kept their torchlight locked close to them, the darkness curving all around.

Albert closed his bag. "Should even things up a little," he whispered.

Scarlett nodded. "And I've got six bullets in my gun. That's all *I* need. Here, you take this bloodied pickaxe."

"Really? For me? Thanks."

She straightened. "It's a race to the finish now. They can't be far behind."

They advanced along the track. Slowly, insensibly, the grainy haze ahead of them became a glow and the glow became a stronger light. It swelled around them. The walls of the tunnel fell away, and they stood at the upper edge of an enormous rough-hewn cave.

There were two wooden rail carts standing beside them on the track. Beyond this, the floor of the cave sloped away steeply, as if the whole vast slab had been upended in a great convulsion. Perhaps this *was* the case: at the far end, the floor finished abruptly in a clifflike step with a drop beyond. Scaffolding protruded from the depths. There were other diggings far below, the suggestion of dim tunnels, piles of debris. The rail track ran straight down the center of the sloping cave to the brink of the hole, where it ended in a broken ramp of shattered wood. There had once been a bridge across the gap. The bridge had crossed to a brightly lit opening in the cliff face opposite.

Albert stared at the opening on the other side. It shone like a promised land. But the bridge had been blown and a metal mesh placed across the space, severing the connection.

He saw from Scarlett's face that she understood what they were seeing, too.

"Yep, that's Area 7 over there," she said. "They've got a full-powered generator working those lights—look. But they've closed it off. They know all about the bad stuff on this side."

"They must've been talking to that one-legged beggar," Albert said.

"Was that an attempt at sarcasm?"

"Possibly."

She shifted her pack. "The question is: How do we get across before our friends arrive?"

Albert glanced back along the empty tunnel behind them. There were other openings into the cave too. Several tracks emerged from side tunnels and connected to the central one. He could see platforms with great squared wooden hoppers, mostly filled with rubble. There were broken carts, some lying on their sides; coils of rope; and splintered tool racks. It felt as if the chamber had been abandoned in great haste not long ago. It was all a bit forlorn.

"We could blow that mesh fence with gelignite," Scarlett said. "That's easy enough."

Albert nodded. "But first we've got to get across the gap."

"Yeah."

"Which is impossible. Unless we climb down the hole and up again somehow. And we'd never do that before they came."

"You're right, Albert. There's no point trying that. But there *might* be another way. . . ."

Albert had experienced six months of Scarlett's company, with all the joys and surprises it brought him. He didn't need her to take off her hat to know she was studying the rail carts. "I hope you're not thinking what I *think* you're thinking," he said.

"Maybe I am."

"We'd fall into the ravine!"

"Would we? Look how steep the slope is! We'd fly across."

"Yes—and hit the fence and bounce like berks back into the ravine."

She grinned. "I'd lob the gelignite across first, of course. Blow the mesh."

"No! No way! It would never work. It's a stupid idea. I'd go further. I'd say it's the stupidest, most misguided, most pants-wettingly awful plan you've ever had."

"It's also *quick*," Scarlett said. "And if you've got a better suggestion, spit it out, because I can hear sounds behind us."

They turned to face the tunnel at their backs. They looked. They listened. They didn't do it long.

"It's a cracking plan," Albert said. "One of your all-time greats. Got the matches?"

"Yep. Get pushing. I'm going to break the barrier." She was already away from him, wrestling with her pack.

Tucking the pickaxe into his belt, Albert hurried to the rail cart nearest the top of the slope. He set his weight against it, the wound in his shoulder protesting at the effort. Upper-body strength wasn't really Albert's thing, but the wheels were oiled, and he felt the cart begin to move along the track. His satisfaction was mostly canceled by the oncoming sounds behind, which were now resolving into howls and whistles and slaps of rushing feet.

He pushed still harder. All at once the ground steepened beneath him, and the rail cart picked up speed. To start with he embraced the change; then he realized the cart was moving away from him. One trip, one stumble, and it would be gone. Albert grappled at the wooden rim and pulled himself up just as the momentum changed decisively. He was clinging to the rail cart as it rolled down the track. Cool air hit him; ash dust blew upward from the cart bin, making him blink. He could see Scarlett silhouetted far ahead, against the light of the barrier fence. She was on the broken bridge, in the act of throwing the stick of gelignite across the gap. He saw her face flash palely as she looked back at him.

Down went the cart, picking up speed, rattling and jumping as it struck small pebbles on the track. Risking a look over his shoulder, Albert saw thin white forms emerging from the tunnel. They spilled past the other cart and over the wooden platforms, haring after him.

Albert hung on. He was watching the fence on the other side of the gap. The gelignite had landed successfully; it rolled against the barrier, fizzing. He waited for the explosion, but nothing happened.

From tunnels on either side, more Tainted came running.

He looked at Scarlett. What was she *doing*? She was running *away* from the track. . . .

The Tainted surged forward. Some ran upright, others bounded on their hands and feet. The cavern filled with their howls and screams. Scarlett stopped and turned. She started sprinting back at an angled route that would intersect her with the rushing cart. . . .

The slope steepened; the cart went faster. Straight ahead

was the shattered bridge, the broken rails projecting into nothingness.

Albert's hair streamed back. Clinging with one hand, he eased the pickaxe from his belt.

Scarlett ran, her red hair flowing. Her hat came loose. She snatched at it and stumbled. The Tainted were right behind. They reached for her with long white fingers.

Down came the cart.

Scarlett jumped, a Tainted at her back. She hit the side of the cart, fell over it and in.

The Tainted leaped too. Albert swung the pick to meet it.

Both shape and pick were torn away, lost in the onrushing air. The cart hit the bottom of the slope, shot up the broken ramp and out over the ends of the track.

The gelignite exploded.

A pulse of light erupted against the base of the barrier, swelling outward, swallowing the mesh in a circle of white flame. All sounds cut out.

The rail cart hung in space a moment.

Then it plunged straight into the light—and searing heat and brightness reached out for Albert like cupping hands.

14

It occurred to Scarlett afterward that it had all worked out for the best. If there was one good thing to say about hurtling in a cart over a gorge into the mouth of an explosion with a horde of cannibals champing at your heels, it was that you didn't have time to fret. What if the mesh barrier had only partly torn? They might have been kebabbed on a forest of red-hot spikes. What if the gelignite had exploded a couple of seconds later? Their smoldering pieces would have been scattered far and wide. There were a dozen other horrible fates on offer, but none of them bothered her at the time, mainly because she was upside down in the rearing cart, legs scissor kicking in midair.

What happened next didn't leave much room for contemplation either.

The gelignite *had* blown a ragged hole in the center of the barrier, and the cart *almost* passed neatly through it. Only the back wheels caught against the spines of twisted metal—caught and held, so that the cart flipped suddenly forward, pitching Scarlett out.

She flew through air still rippling from the blast, through

a rain of metal fragments, through smoke and flecks of fire. Her boots touched ground; her onward movement became an instinctive somersault, then (more controlled now) a body roll. She landed on her feet, went stumbling on for a few more flailing strides. From behind she heard the crunch and crash of the cart spinning over, splintering, disintegrating. . . . She skidded to a stop, crouched low into a ball. Pieces of wood sheared past at an angle out of the smoke, but nothing struck her. Close by, a set of wheels trundled gradually to a standstill.

Smoke dispersed around her. Scarlett got up somewhat dazedly. She was in a bright hall under strings of ceiling lights. Her pack was still on her back; her hat was gone, and her hair hung tumbled around her face. She looked down at herself. Miraculously, she seemed all there.

Turning, she was confronted by a mess of smoking wood and metal, the torn bloom of the exploded fence, and a black void beyond, from which the howls of the Tainted echoed.

"Albert?" she said.

No answer came. Scarlett approached the shattered rail cart, slowly at first, then at a limping run. She began pulling the debris aside. He had been clinging to the back of the cart. The cart was reduced to splinters, the chassis contorted and hot to the touch. It was a scene of devastation. Nothing solid had survived.

"*Albert . . . ?*"

"Over here."

Scarlett stopped her increasingly frantic searching, stood abruptly.

Albert was sitting neatly on the floor, far off across the hall. He had his legs splayed, his trainers akimbo, and was blinking at her sleepily as if he'd just woken in a comfy bed. His face was a little sooty; his hair pointed to all hours of the clockface. Apart from that, and a few pieces of shattered wood, there was nothing to show he'd been in a high-speed collision.

Relief flared in her. "What are you doing over there? Why didn't you say anything?"

"Had the wind knocked out of me. Are you okay? Looked like you were panicking."

"I wasn't panicking." She scowled, patted her head. "Where's my bloody hat?"

"Over there. It fell off while you were doing all your trademark flips and twiddles." He got up stiffly. "And, by the way, you *were*."

"I so wasn't."

"You were all fluttery and anxious."

"I was *cross*. I just thought you'd done something stupid and got yourself killed."

Scarlett located her hat in a pile of pieces of rail cart and jammed it on with what dignity she could muster. The metal band seemed a bit bent, but it would function.

"It's not a crime to worry about me," Albert said. He had moved to the broken fencing and was looking out over the gap. "Particularly when we've carried out the escape of the century. Look what we got away from."

Scarlett drew near the ruined barrier with caution and squinted back into the deeper mines. The creatures had stopped their screeching. But they were still there. They were standing quite motionless, clustered at the edge of the pit, staring across at them.

At this distance, the eyes and mouths were black smudges on the bone-white faces. Stick arms hung at their sides. They were like pale stalagmites fixed to the cavern floor. One of them clicked its jaws together, teeth closing like a bear trap. Otherwise they made no sound.

Their taint drifted across the gap. Scarlett closed her eyes. For a moment she was on a forest slope, crouched among ferns, holding a child's hand . . .

"How long do you think we've got?" Albert said.

She blinked her eyes clear, adjusted her hat on her head. "We're safe for now. They *might* try to climb down into the pit and back up here, but by that time we'll be in a loaded truck and gone." She turned away and walked briskly off under the bright lights of the hall, leaving only silence behind.

Unlike the disused levels, the working area of the mines was sufficiently signposted and easy underfoot, so it did not take them long to find the loading bays. This was just as well, for by Scarlett's watch it was almost morning. Not long after dawn, the buses would return up the hill, and Area 7 would come to life again.

The chambers that they walked through now were different from the older tunnels they had explored. The ceilings were studded with proper lighting, the floors swept, the rubble bunkers and rail carts free of rust. Broad tunnels led off to new tracts of the Buried City, but here were equipment lockers and sorting rooms, walls hung with tools, racks of coats and helmets, rows of scuffed boots, dining halls that smelled of cleaning fluid, boards with work rotas, tables scattered with discarded mugs and plates—and stacks of pamphlets, too.

Albert gave a delighted cry. "Hey—it's 'The Ballad of Scarlett and Browne'! They've got one of ours!"

"Just when I thought this place couldn't get any better," Scarlett said. "Well, don't *take* the stupid thing."

"Why not? It's a lovely souvenir. Besides, I want to read about our unnatural vices on the way home."

Tucking the pamphlet into his bag, he strolled happily on, with Scarlett trailing somewhat blankly after. It never failed to amaze her how fast Albert could shake off a trauma. He was like a butterfly flitting to the next flower: a butterfly that remained miraculously unharmed. Looking at him now, minutes after crashing through the barrier, she saw he hadn't a scratch on him, while she could scarcely move for bruises. There were moments—this was one—when her companion seemed almost as alien to her as the Tainted, albeit a lot more harmless.

Though of course he *wasn't* harmless. Or wouldn't be, if he chose.

They came to a broad white room with a ceiling of metal strips and walls of wooden beams. There were many tables in it, and crates piled on the floor. The crates were stamped with the white circle logo of the Faith Houses. Some were closed, some open and empty except for linings of straw. Others, to Albert's great excitement, had objects in them. He bounded to their side.

"It's a packing room," he breathed. "This is where they select the best things from the mines. Let's see what we've got. . . . There's gold and silver items, predictably . . . lots of metal scraps that might be melted down and reused . . . several burned fragments of old books—because they're after knowledge too—and, wait, what are these devices? This long tube might be a sighting barrel, Scarlett, and there's a kind of trigger on this one. . . ." He frowned up at her. "It's just like the thing I found in Warwick. Joe said that was some kind of gun."

To Scarlett's mind the blackened, corroded objects were markedly less interesting than the pale light she could see coming through a wide doorway at the end of the room. "Okay, so they're old weapons," she said. "No doubt the Ancients tried to kill each other just like we do. Who cares? The important thing for us is, these boxes aren't properly packed up yet. There may be finished ones in the loading bay. Let's go."

"Yes, but why do the Faith Houses want such relics? Why does Soames want them too?"

"It doesn't matter *why* Soames wants them! We just have to make sure they reach his sweaty little hands as soon as possible. Stop wasting time. I can see *daylight* there!"

She could hear the excitement in her own voice. After the hours spent under the earth, the glimpse of fresh, frail light was like a balm to her spirits. Albert felt it too. He hastened; they stole to the door, peered round—and got their first sight of the loading bay.

It was a great concrete-lined hall. High on the walls at the far side was a row of wide, rectangular windows, dirty and flecked with rain. Through these the drab dawn light was radiating. Below the windows stood the metal doors that led out to the compound on the side of the hill. There was a lever beside them, a motor, cogs, a hinged mechanism.

This was not the best of it. In the center of the loading bay sat an armored truck, enormous and silent, like a great beast drowsing on the steppe. Hazy light spilled slowly over it, grainy with ash dust from the tunnels. The outer shell was scratched and pitted; the treads of the immense rubber tires were cut and torn. Its gun turret was a gray hump on its back. Its rear doors hung open, revealing an interior piled with wooden crates. Further crates, yet to be loaded on, were scattered close at hand. A cargo lorry, bound for the distant south! *Exactly* what they had come here for. Scarlett grinned in satisfaction.

She scanned the rest of the hall. Everything was still. Other arches led into dimness. Along the near side was an enclosure of high wire fences, surmounted with barbed wire, and with a couple of corrugated metal huts inside. She saw a stack of petrol barrels, a mechanics' area with tools and tires . . . There was a smell of petrol. The important thing was that no guards were visible. Nobody was around. It was almost too good to be true.

Scarlett chewed a strand of hair, considering.

Would they have heard the explosion in the mine? Might they be lying in wait?

Albert touched her arm, startling her. "Scarlett . . ."

"Yes? You see something?"

"I do. That pen just there."

"Yes?"

"It's where they keep the children."

"What?" Her brain, heavy with fatigue, mired in thoughts of guards and snipers, had trouble shifting gears. "What children?"

"The slaves who work in the mines."

And when she looked again at the enclosure, she saw details she had missed before. On the dusty area of ground beside the huts were tables in bright colors, a row of tiny chairs . . . Yes, and toys, too: a faded wooden rocking horse, a mess of toppled blocks, a single, sorry colored ball. Scarlett glared at the pathetic details. She imagined the noise when they came back on the bus, the pattering of shoes, the thin, high voices, the little coughs and sighs . . .

Scarlett felt a tightness forming in her middle. She pulled her arm away from Albert's hand. "Why are you talking about this now?" she said. "It's not important."

"Don't get angry, Scarlett. Think about it. They come here at dawn, go home at nightfall. That means they *never see the sun*. It's worse than in Stonemoor. At least there we had the grounds to walk in."

"That's not our problem! We're here to save Joe and Ettie. So shut up and do something useful. The truck's there—and so is our way out. You sense anyone?"

He glared at her, concentrated briefly. "No. But I'm not likely to—there's so much iron around."

"Okay. . . . I'm going to run for the truck. If all's well, I want you to nip to the lever and open the doors. I'll start the engine and we're away."

He was still staring at the little enclosure. "And the gates to the outer compound?"

"We smash straight through. Albert . . . are you listening? We've *got* to focus now."

"Of course." The lingering frown had gone; his face was blank and calm.

There wasn't any more to be said. Scarlett took the gun from her belt, held it at her side. She slipped out into the vastness of the room.

Her boots made no noise as she crossed through shafts of soft dawn light. It made her skin tingle to think of the ease with which someone concealed behind the crates or oil drums might pick her off. But no one shot at her. The loading bays were still.

Negotiating the crates scattered on the floor, she drew close to the open truck. Looking in, she saw that stacks of crates sat neatly in mesh storage cages, together with a pile of empty boxes, as yet unfilled. Beyond the cages was a living area with two seats for its guards, a weapons rack, a ladder reaching to the gun turret above. . . . Also, an internal hatch connecting with the driver's cab.

Scarlett glanced back at Albert, hovering like a fretful ghost across the hall. She motioned toward the door mechanism. Without waiting, she hopped into the truck and slipped to the forward hatch. Scarlett had done some driving during her time with the Brothers, helping ferry black-market goods across the Wessex-Mercian borders. Nothing fancy, nothing as big as this, but the workings would be the same. All she required was a key, and that was probably in the ignition. She pulled open the hatch and ducked inside.

There was a man in the driver's seat.

He was slumped low, as if he had steadily been melting through the long solitariness of the night—a swarthy, unshaven man in a gray-green uniform and a dark green bowler, with a white circle badge of the Faith Houses fixed to the side of the crown. He had his hands resting on his stomach, a coffee cup wedged between them. Technically, he was presumably a sentry. In reality, he was sleeping heavily. Scarlett frowned at the rank unprofessionalism, even as she prepared to take full advantage of it. He wasn't *quite* wearing a woolly nightcap on his head, but it was close.

The man's eyes opened as she crouched beside him; he was just in time to see her tap him on the shoulder with her gun. With her other hand she plucked his pistol from his belt.

"Wake up!" she hissed. "And do your panicking quietly."

The man gave a yelp; the coffee cup went spinning. "Murderers! Killers! Deviants!"

"None of those, provided you calm down."

"Robbers? Brigands?"

"Close enough. Now give me the keys to this truck."

The man's eyes flicked left and right. "It would be a dereliction of my duty."

"And sleeping isn't? There's dribble on your shirt. Cough up the key and be quick about it."

"But I am under oath to the High Council! I must defend these treasures with my life!"

Scarlett flourished the pistol grimly. "That can easily be arranged."

The guard hesitated; he began rummaging in his trouser pocket. "Perhaps we can come to an agreement. I think I have the key . . . but why take it? You can never leave the compound alive. The sentries will gun you down as you drive away."

"We'll take that chance," Scarlett said. "In fact, if that's the way of it, maybe we'll make *you* drive."

"You could not be so cruel!" The man gave a whinny of distress. "Where is your better nature, my dear? You're just a girl!"

"A girl whose better nature shriveled long ago," Scarlett growled. "A girl who has just spent twelve difficult hours crossing the mines in order to steal this wretched truck. And not just me. . . ." She pointed out of the window, where Albert was flitting toward the door control: an enormous chest-high lever sticking from the floor. "That is my associate, a boy of appalling viciousness. Beside his ruthless depravity I am practically a saint. Would you prefer his attention directed upon you?"

The man stared at Albert, who was now wrestling with the lever, straining with the utmost effort, and failing to make it budge an inch. "I don't honestly know. It's hard to say."

Scarlett cocked the pistol. "I'm losing patience. Where's that key?"

"It's kind of wedged down by my thigh."

"*Un*wedge it, then. I'll count to three."

The guard reared; there was a flurry of desperate movements in his trousers. "Here!"

"Ack, why is it so sticky? All right, sit quiet. Now we wait for the doors to open."

They waited. At the lever, Albert's exertions continued, accompanied by a remarkable array of bug-eyed grimaces. Scarlett could feel her jaws tightening in frustration.

"You say you came from the deeper mines?" the guard said. "But there are barriers . . ."

"Broke them. Gods, don't you ever oil that bloody thing? Just how stiff can a lever be?"

"It's not stiff at all. It would help if he pulled it the right way."

Scarlett groaned, rapped on the window with the gun, and made appropriate gestures. After a few moments' bafflement, Albert understood. He gave a hearty thumbs-up and pushed instead of pulled. At once the lever shifted. Even from inside the truck, she could feel the floor shudder, hear a hum of moving cogs. The great doors squealed, began to open. There was a broadening column of pale blue light and drizzle.

Scarlett signaled again. Albert had seen the guard in the driver's seat; he came round the back of the truck and scrambled in through the rear doors. "Who's this fellow?"

"Don't bother to get acquainted," Scarlett said. "He'll be leaving us as soon as he's driven us out of the compound. Shut the doors and come up here."

Albert swiveled and pulled the rear doors to; he drew a bolt across. Scarlett checked ahead of her. The mine gates were almost open, and rain was coming through. The sour but hopeful light of dawn shone onto the cab. She could see the watchtowers of the compound. At the edge of the plateau, the boundary fence was framed against a blue-red sky.

The guard was becoming restless. "Don't make me drive! They'll shoot me!"

"Quit moaning. We'll hide out of sight. They'll recognize your ugly face and let you through."

"They won't! The truck never leaves this early! And I'm not authorized to drive!"

"You are today, my friend. Take the key. Albert, crouch down here."

Albert crouched; Scarlett reached out with the key. At that moment, something collided with the back of the truck.

Everyone jolted into each other: Albert into Scarlett,

Scarlett into the guard. There was a thump against the driver's door beside them. A face pressed at the window, all black pupilless eyes and fish-white skin. Shark teeth bared.

The guard's scream drowned out any noises Scarlett and Albert might also possibly have made. Thuds sounded on the sides of the truck; the back doors rattled. For a single second, Scarlett was motionless with shock. Then she grappled the guard by the collar. His face was boneless, bubbling with fright. She shoved the key into his hand.

"Drive."

He stared at her. The white form was scrabbling at the driver's door. Claws scratched lines into the glass.

"You want to live, don't you? *Drive!* Drive for the boundary gates! Albert, take the gun! Shoot him if he disobeys."

Writhing forms leaped at the windshield, things of bone and claw and skin, blackening out the light. Scarlett pushed past Albert—who was slowly gathering his wits—out through the hatch into the body of the truck. Past the crates and boxes in their cages, straight to the gun-turret ladder. She began to climb. As she did so, she felt the engine start. The truck was shaking with the assault from outside.

At the ceiling hatch, she flipped the locks and crawled out into the gun turret. The machine gun was there, fixed to its swivel chair, nose protruding through the clear plastic dome. The lights of the compound swam in the blue dark beyond. Rain from beyond the mine doors beat on the plastic. There were things crawling on the truck roof. Scarlett pulled herself into the chair, flicked the safety catches, kicked with a boot to make the chair and gun spin. She squinted along the sights, emptied a round of shots into the white things crowding close, blowing them off the roof and away. Her head rang with the sound of the firing. Too late she saw the ear guards hanging over the muzzle of the gun.

The truck was inching forward, gears roaring. Scarlett swore roundly. "Albert! What's the delay? Get us out of here!"

Albert called something; she could not hear what. She spun the chair; the Tainted were pouring from the arch at the back of the hall. She opened fire, raking them with methodical sweeps; some fell, others flowed around the truck, began clambering up toward her. Scarlett veered side to side, shooting. Bodies rolled and tumbled away in a flurry of flailing limbs.

The truck jerked, gained speed with great rapidity. It narrowly missed the mine doors, passing so close that the Tainted hanging off that side were scraped away. It rumbled out into the open air. Visibility was poor. The truck turned this way and that, with white things clinging to it or falling in its wake like foam churned by a speeding boat. Its movements were increasingly frantic; Scarlett could sense the desperation of the guard as he wrenched at the steering wheel, trying to fling the creatures off. Some lost their grip, fell, and were crushed beneath the truck. Others clung on. Lights came on in the watchtowers at the fence; sentries began firing. Bullets bounced and rang off the metal surface of the roof, sending sparks dancing; a nearby fence collapsed in a shower of splinters. The truck rushed on.

There were no Tainted remaining on the roof. Scarlett stopped shooting. Through the rain-blown plastic she had a glimpse of the folds of the hills, the lights of Ashtown below them in the valley. The truck made directly for the gates of the perimeter fence through a hail of bullets and rain.

She reset the safety catches on the machine gun, slid down the ladder, returned to the cab. The guard and Albert were grim forms hunched in their seats. The windshield was cracked and smeared in red. There was still one Tainted pressed against it. She could see the blue tattoos winding across its belly and chest. A sentry's bullet struck it. It met her eye and flexed its jaws at her in a long and soundless howl.

The gates loomed close. Scarlett braced herself.

They struck with a force sufficient to lift the front wheels off the Tarmac. Scarlett was jerked forward to bang against Albert's seat, then thrown back through the hatch behind. When she opened her eyes, the thing clinging to the wind-shield was gone. The truck was moving along the curve of the mine road. They tilted over the head of the plateau and ran down between slopes of black soil and windblown grass into the teeth of the coming day.

15

There was a red light in the sky that morning. A bank of cumulus clouds hung high over the kingdoms, and the glow of the Burning Regions was reflected in it. If you looked up through the cracked, stained windshield of the truck, you could actually see the movement of the flames. Red striations, impossibly vast and distant, flickering and pulsing on the undersides of the clouds. To Albert they seemed the only things alive. The earth was dark and flat beneath their shadow.

The truck rumbled on. In the cab, the great wheels made no more noise than the purring of a cat. The Great North Road ran steadily southward, a gray strip in gray country, through arid scrub and encroaching forest. From time to time Albert saw fortress villages on nearby hills, but never anything nearer to the road.

They had rattled through Ashtown in a blur, stopping shortly afterward to eject the trembling guard and let Scarlett take the wheel. Albert had felt rather sorry for the man, who had endured a difficult half hour. Still, looking at it another way, they had probably saved him from the Tainted, and he could ever afterward boast of meeting the notorious Scarlett and Browne of widespread pamphlet fame. He pointed this out to the guard to cheer him up, but there was no audible response. They left him trudging off toward the town stockade.

Scarlett drove, Albert sat. They were too exhausted to talk, and the first leg of the journey was brief. After an hour the road began descending toward the Mercian plains between thickly wooded foothills. Scarlett found a place where loggers' tracks diverted from the highway; she negotiated a trail until they were out of sight of the road. Here she switched off the ignition. Her hand dropped to her lap. The truck was quiet. Albert and Scarlett slept where they were, upright in their seats in the darkness of the cabin, while traces of reflected fire played silently across the sky.

When they awoke after perhaps three hours, they were surrounded by dancing green shade. The sun had broken through the cloud bank and it was hot in the cab. Neither felt much better for their rest. Their adrenaline had evaporated in the silence, leaving only crystallized fatigue. Scarlett's hat had fallen off as she slept, and her hair hung like tangled webs across her face. Albert's body felt achy and lopsided, the wrong size for his skin. He told himself that they had succeeded against enormous odds, with three days yet before their deadline. But it was hard to feel elation. The road ahead was long, and Soames and Teach waited at its end.

Scarlett wanted to be off. While she started the engine, Albert investigated the interior of the truck. It was a surprisingly well-equipped space, with its chairs, a foldout table, and even a foldout bed. A corner cupboard was stocked with bottles of water, a paraffin stove, and tins of meat, biscuits, bread, and coffee. In short order Albert assembled a hearty breakfast, which he brought to Scarlett at the wheel. She balanced it on her lap with a grunt of appreciation, keeping one eye on the road.

"Is there anything else I can get you?"

"Some better wipers would be nice." She gestured at the bloodied windshield, then took an enormous spoonful of tinned meat. "No," she said, chewing, "this is fine, and we're in good shape. But we need to keep on. The mining company will be sending messenger pigeons south—we've got to go faster than the birds."

"Think they'll try to follow us?" Albert asked.

"The company? Don't see how they can. They've the Tainted to deal with now."

Albert thought of the swirling white horde bursting from the gates, the sentries firing from the watchtowers . . . The horror of the night hung over him; he didn't have much to say.

The road came down into Mercia through a region of open grasslands. It was sparsely populated. Once they saw a herd of horn-beaks far off, grazing in the ruins of a town. They met few other travelers: just one convoy of ten armored vehicles and a single long-distance bus. Gradually evidence of occupation increased; they rolled through straggling villages, past horse-drawn carts and steam-powered wagons.

Toward noon the road split into two equal forks, each meandering into the blue distance. There was a dilapidated road station at the junction, defended by walls of tumbled stone. A man in grubby overalls sat outside a hut beneath a broad straw parasol, offering for sale petrol, water, and good fresh orchard fruit. Ancient apple trees grew in the grass of his sunny compound, and armored messenger pigeons fluttered in cages atop the walls. Albert bought a bag of apples while Scarlett asked questions about the route. The right-hand fork was suggested and taken. Albert noticed the man watching them from the shadow of his parasol as they revved away.

The afternoon wore on. Heat haze hung over the yellow scrubland. The slopes were sandy and dotted with clumps of firewort, saw-brush, and ilex. It was a desolate region. A low line of rocky hills rose against the sky, drew close, and clustered on either side of the road.

"We should stop soon," Scarlett said. "If all goes well, we could be in Stow this time tomorrow. But first I need to rest again."

Albert grunted. *He'd* been wanting rest for hours. The wound in his shoulder was stinging, and he was growing oppressed by the monotony of the ash lands. Not only that, but Scarlett's spiky, sleep-deprived thoughts were clustering about him in the confinement of the cab. Without the hat to hinder them, he couldn't stop them drifting close, radiating a brittle self-satisfaction at their triumph in the mine. Albert had done his best to ignore them, but he felt weary, irritable, and out of countenance. He was worrying about what would happen with the Brothers. He wished Scarlett would focus on this too.

"A rest would be good," he said. "But before we get to Stow, we need to figure out our plan. How do we get Joe and Ettie safely away? It's no use us just showing up with the stuff. Soames will obviously betray us."

"I know he will. He and Teach are keen to feed us to their owls." Scarlett made an airy movement of her hand. "But it's no big deal. I'll come up with a scheme to fool them tomorrow. I can't think straight just now."

Albert shrugged. "As long as you share it with me in advance," he said.

"What's that mean?"

"It means don't keep it to yourself. Like you did yesterday about the Tainted being in the mines."

"Oh, you're not going on about *that* again? Come *on*, Albert. I didn't know they were in the mines at all. It was just a possibility."

He could hear the impatience in her voice, and it annoyed him. "A possibility I'd quite like to have been party to," he said.

"For Shiva's sake! We got through it okay, didn't we? And

it wasn't all bad. Sure, we met the Tainted—but that horrid clicky thing that followed us never showed up, did it? *And* we never met any of those giant blood-moles or bore-worms. I call that a fair result."

Albert didn't answer. He folded his arms and gazed out at the cracked Tarmac, the flashing blur of sand and stones beside the rushing wheels. It was the usual story. You'd never get an apology from Scarlett. Not about the small stuff, and not about the big things, either. It was because of *her* that Joe and Ettie had been kidnapped, for example. It was *her* past that had got them in this mess. But would she ever properly admit it? Would she express regret? No. She *cared*, of course—she'd move heavens and Earth to help them—but she'd never let that compassion show. It was the same when he'd mentioned the children in the mine. . . .

His eyes widened. He jerked upright in his seat. "The children!"

"What?"

"What about the children? The Tainted are loose in the compound, and when they go up there in the bus—"

Scarlett made a dismissive noise. "Pipe down. The kids won't go anywhere in the bus today. That guard we saved will have sounded the alarm in Ashtown."

"But if they do . . ."

"I repeat: the kids won't be taken to the mines. We've actually done them a favor—they'll enjoy a nice day off. Now shut up, will you, and help me find a place to stop."

"*A nice day off?*" He knew they were both tired, he knew he should probably stay silent, but her glibness overrode his caution. "Don't be so horrible! Those kids are slaves!"

"I know." Scarlett stared out at the road. "It's bad. But it could be worse for them."

Albert looked at her. "How?"

"They have company, don't they? They have each other. . . ." Out of nowhere, he felt Scarlett's anger push back against his own. Its intensity startled him. He saw her fingers gripping white on the steering wheel. "And what exactly do you propose we could have *done* about it, anyway?" she added. "Hang around to set them free?"

"I don't know," he said.

"No. Exactly. You *don't* know, Albert. Now be quiet."

He sat there silent, his fury pacing like a tiger. He stared out at the dull gray strip of road.

"I'd have thought those kids would mean something to you, that's all," he said.

There was a silence. "And what does *that* mean?"

"Nothing."

"It does. You know it does."

"It doesn't mean anything." He spoke wearily. He'd regretted it as soon as he said it, but it was too late now.

"I've told you never to read my mind. I've told you countless times."

"I've *not* been reading your mind. I've been doing my level best *not* to, all journey."

Scarlett stiffened suddenly, looked round her in the seat.

She uttered a soft curse. "My hat! Where's my hat? It's fallen off. Put it on me."

"Forget the stupid hat," Albert said.

"I can't reach it. Put it on my head."

"No."

"Albert—"

"Do it yourself!" Even in the moment he knew how watery and false his surge of anger was, how driven by exhaustion, but he couldn't stop. It was like it was happening to someone else. "I'm not helping you put that iron band on your head!" he cried. "Why are you so obsessed with me reading your mind? It's the last thing I'd want to do!"

She snorted. "Yeah? I think you love it. Mind reading's easy. It's safe. It carries no risk whatsoever—"

"—and is usually completely tedious," Albert interrupted. "Particularly in *your* case. There's stuff deep down you *should* be telling me, but I leave that well alone. On the surface, your mind's nothing but bad temper and bodily functions. In fact, if I read you now—"

"Albert, don't you dare!"

"Too late, I'm afraid. Yes . . . you're tired, you're hungry, and you're worried sick about how we're going to stop the Brothers killing Joe and Ettie. But you don't want to admit it, that makes you angry, and you want to take that anger out on me."

Scarlett glared back at him. "Is that it?"

"That's it."

"It had better be."

"Oh, and if you want the loo, we can stop the truck and you can go behind one of those big dunes."

Scarlett's hand jerked slightly; the truck swerved in the road. "I don't need the— Well, I'm certainly not going to go *now*."

"I know."

"No, Albert, you *don't* know. You know *nothing* about me or who I am." She gave a hiss of rage. "Will you get away from me?"

"Pleasure. That's all I want to do. Pull this thing over."

Scarlett wrenched on the wheel. The truck turned hard across the road with a squeal of tires, left the Tarmac, crashed through a clump of brush, down a bank of stones, and along a dried-up riverbed between low hills. The engine roared, the suspension squealed; Scarlett's arms were locked, her jaw set, her hair a furious tangle. She jammed the accelerator down. They followed the riverbed until there were steep slopes all around; then she braked so sharply, Albert almost banged his nose on the dashboard. She turned off the ignition.

Dust settled around the cabin, blocking out the sun. They sat gazing straight ahead.

"I'll say one thing," Scarlett said. "I could do with less of your mind-reading tricks and a lot more of your *other* power. It's no good telling me you've suppressed it. I saw what happened to that rock snake. I saw what happened when Teach took Joe and Ettie. It's still in you, right enough.

Trouble is, you're too scared to use it when it counts." She didn't look at him. "Also, you're much too happy to rely on *me*."

"I thought we relied on *each other*," Albert said. He could scarcely speak, he felt so angry. He shook his head. "And of *course* I'm scared of it. I'd be crazy not to be. You haven't the first idea what the Fear is like. It's cruel, it's unstoppable. It can't be controlled."

"Rubbish. That operative controlled it, back in Huntingdon. He seemed to master it fine."

"And *that* led to a saloonful of dead people. Which bothers *me*, even if it doesn't you." Albert rattled the door handle beside him. "I've had enough of this! I'm getting out."

"Be my guest."

"I'm out of here."

"That's fine." She waited. "Well, get on with it, then."

"I'm trying."

"It might work better if you *pull* the handle."

Albert gave a curse. He pulled. The door flew open. Without another word, without a backward glance, he jumped down and strode off across the sand.

Despite his fury, he could see Scarlett had chosen a good place for a stop. The upper regions of the riverbed were surrounded by high mounds—it was a stretch to call them hills—of sand and grit and tektite stone. The Great North Road could not be seen. Albert clambered up and over the crest of the nearest slope, until the truck fell away behind him and he was firmly out of sight of Scarlett too.

He scuffed onward purposelessly for a few minutes, his energy swiftly ebbing. At last, with a sigh, he threw himself down.

Evening was approaching. The day's heat was leaving the wasteland, and the hollow black stones strewn about were emitting little pops and whistles as they contracted and the air was driven from them. The blue of the sky had been bleached almost to whiteness, and the soil was white also. There were no clouds. It was a vision of the world scoured clean.

Albert sat and let it scour him too.

Really, it was a pity Scarlett had stayed cooped up in the truck. She would have liked the peace and emptiness. . . . Not that he *wanted* her with him. No! He was far too cross for that.

Why had he got so cross? Partly her pretense of callousness. Of course, she was right in one way: they *couldn't* do anything about the slaves in the mines. But he'd been needling her for a reason. It irked him that she tried to ignore the injustices of the world.

In part, also, it was her connection to the Brothers. A little more humility from Scarlett about the matter wouldn't have gone amiss. Still, her criminal past wasn't new to him, and Albert knew he couldn't *really* object—not after *his* enemy, Dr. Calloway, had pursued them both for so long, not with this unknown operative hunting them too.

No, it was something deeper than that, and it underlay everything else. Why had she joined up with the Brothers in the first place? Why did she keep that affected indifference curled round her like a cloak? Both questions had the same answer. And Scarlett refused to give the answer to him. She dodged and ducked, and wore the stupid hat, and kept that piece of herself imperfectly hidden. She was deliberately shutting him out—and on a day of little sleep, a day when he'd been clinging to a rail cart as it flew across an abyss with the Tainted at his heels, that fact irritated Albert immensely.

The *other* thing that irritated him was she'd been right about the Fear.

The colorless sky was darkening, and the stars were coming out. He could feel his annoyance cooling, his anger contracting like the whistling stones of the Mercian wilderness. He knew he needed to go back and apologize. . . . Though apologizing to Scarlett was a dicey business. You risked snorts, sarcasm, frenzied eye-rolling, and occasional knives flicked close to your ear. And that was if she'd already forgiven you.

Still, maybe she'd have taken the chance to meditate. Maybe she'd be in a better mood.

Better get on with it. Albert got up, smiling slightly, shaking his head at his foolishness. He clambered back to the top of the rise, pattered down the slope with brisk, quick steps—

And halted.

There was a young man sitting on a rock beside the way.

Albert resumed his descent. He went slowly, but he did not change his course or run. He kept on walking. There was nowhere else to go.

He looked at the truck. It was very quiet; one rear door hung open. Albert had not opened that door. The cab door, which he *had* left open, was closed. There was no sign of Scarlett. There were crickets chirruping, the sun blazing up at him off the rocks. With every step he felt the powdery sand crunching beneath his shoes.

He could not see Scarlett anywhere.

He could not sense her thoughts.

The young man sat with one foot resting on the rock, his leg bent and his hands clasped loosely around his knee. His long black coat was draped over the back of the rock like a slick of tar. His clothes were covered with a patina of ash and dust; his black patent leather shoes were stained and scuffed and travel worn. He was facing toward the silent truck, but his head was tilted upward and he was watching Albert's approach. His eyes sparkled; the face was slim and handsome and wore an expression of amiably smiling blandness that was entirely unsuited to the place and circumstances. He might have been sitting at the café in the square at Warwick, sipping coffee, watching the slave girls working at the fountains.

Albert pattered slowly down the little rise. There was a buzzing in his head; it was hard to think. He kept his expression calm.

"Hello, Albert," the young man said.

"Hello."

"I've been looking for you for such a time."

"Really? I've only been up there fifteen minutes."

The young man grinned. He was perhaps a little less immaculate than the images from Scarlett's memory—too much of the real world clung about him and his clothes. But she had captured his face perfectly. His thoughts flickered like a mirage above his head. Albert, as he always did in times of danger, seeking any conceivable advantage, automatically looked at them.

It was a mistake.

It was an abyss. A bottomless hole. His mind reeled; he stumbled and almost fell.

When he could see again, the young man was smiling at him.

"Yes, it *is* a peculiar sensation," the operative said. "Trying to read the mind of someone who is *already* reading yours. It's like a pair of mirrors facing each other, with nothing in the room. All you see is what you're seeing, which is what you're seeing, which is what you're seeing . . . and so on, into infinity. I'm surprised you didn't black out." He moved slightly. "But then, I've heard about your talents. I'm glad to catch up with you both at last."

The dark blue eyes twinkled. The silence in the hollow was deafening. Shadows extended from the mouth of the open truck.

Scarlett . . .

The buzzing in Albert's head redoubled. He felt a tingling in his fingertips, fiery threads of distress running through his veins.

"If you're thinking about Miss McCain," the young man said, "she won't be joining us."

"Is she—"

"She's exhausted, poor thing. Dead tired."

Albert looked at him. The buzzing became a roaring. His face contorted; he lifted a hand—

"Naughty, naughty," the young man said.

Something dark rose at Albert's side, blocking out the setting sun. Turning, he saw a section of the slope peeling upward off the hill. It was beautiful to look at, an iridescent, curling scoop of earth that rose above him like a rearing snake. Horror and wonder filled him. He stood transfixed. His hand dropped; his energy petered away. The roaring in his head was stilled.

The coil of earth tipped over and enfolded him. Albert managed one last frantic gasp—then the rushing sand and pebbles filled his mouth, stifled his breath, and snuffed his awareness out.

IV

THE SUNLIT ROAD

The Tainted had destroyed the other homesteads in the valley. They'd been systematic about it: the Fletchers first, then the Lakhanis, the Masons, and finally the McCains. Any survivors were driven higher into the hills, out beyond the safe-lands, and hunted down at leisure.

With some difficulty the girl kept her brother and herself alive. She took them to the north side of the valley, where there were high bluffs and cliffs that made progress arduous. They clambered to a ledge where bushes protected them from view. Here they ate bilberries and drank water from a spring in the rock, listening to the screeches of the predators and watching fires burning among the trees. They remained there for three days. On the second afternoon the girl risked leaving the boy and ventured down to the ruins of the Masons' smallholding, in search of blankets and supplies. In a cellar she located beer, nuts, and tinned meat; also ropes and an old tarpaulin. On her way back she became aware from excited yowls and whistles that her scent had been located. She ran to the river and threw herself in, floating half a mile downstream before struggling out and looping back to the safety of the cliffs. Her brother was where she'd left him, huddled in the tangles of a yew bush and drawing pictures in the dust with a stick. That night a squall came on. Soon it was tumbling in sheets. She rigged the tarpaulin between the bush and the rocks and brought out the food. They pressed together against the bluff, silent as two stones, with water pouring down the overhang. After their meal they slept. They did not stir till morning.

On the third day mist and rain hung between the hills. The fires in the ruins had burned themselves out. Gray twists of smoke rose here and there, frail cords attaching the Earth to heaven. A deep silence lay on the valley. The girl watched and waited; toward evening she noted the gathering of birds above the ruins and signs of animals venturing abroad. The following morning she broke camp, folding the tarpaulin and strapping it to her back with the ropes. She packed the remains of her supplies in her satchel, and she and the little boy came down from the cliffs.

It took two further days to reach the town.

Word of the massacre in the valley had penetrated deep into the safe-lands, and the outer roads were deserted, the homesteads locked and barred. The girl picked apples in the orchards and mushrooms in the woods. Once, she took dried fish from a smokehouse and left a note of apology on a scrap of paper wedged into the door. She didn't like the idea of stealing. She carried her brother on her shoulders for long distances and at other times let him walk alongside. The little boy was quiet, a part of him lost and left behind, still waiting for his mother in the valley. The girl was silent too, grim-faced, straight-backed. She did not try to hurry. There was no need. Nothing that had happened could be undone.

The town sat near the confluence of two rivers. In times past it had known flooding, and the base of its stockade was thickly sloped with protective rocks and stones, held in place by strips of wire mesh. Above this defense a wall of stakes rose high, punctuated by wooden watchtowers, from which yellow flags flapped merrily. A moat circled the site. It was a logging town, not large, connected with the world beyond the hill country by a single decent road. For the last half mile of the approach to the gates, the road ran between the river and the woodyards. There was activity here; the girl and her brother saw smoke rising from the sawmills, heard the rhythmic rasping of the blades. Sweetness laced the air: sap from the mills, clean water from the millstreams. Men and women in overalls cycled among the pines.

The girl had visited the town when she was very small, pressing close to her mother's skirts as she sold yams from the little horse-drawn cart. This had happened only rarely; mostly Florence and the lad Peter, being employed for such work, had gone instead. What memories she retained told of an enormous and noble conurbation, impossibly noisy, colorful, and complex. She was surprised by the dowdiness of the gate arch, the moss spotting the stockade.

It was a hot day; the girl and her brother halted for water in the shade of a pine tree beside the moat, fifty yards along from the gate. The boy drank with single-minded purpose, rivulets of water running down his chin. His red hair was stuck straight upright, smeared with chalk dust from the road. He lowered the bottle and let his sister take it. While she took a sip, he stared blank-faced toward the town.

"I don't like this place."

"We will get help here. There is a thing called a Faith House. They have a charity box for people such as us. They will tell us what to do."

"I don't like it."

"Be quiet, Thomas." She tried to imagine what her mother would have done. It was hard: already her mind had erected a stockade around her memories that was higher than the walls of the town. Her past life was inside it. If she wished to survive, she knew she must not look in. "We should clean ourselves up a little first," she said.

She kneeled on the bank and splashed her brother's face and hands before cupping water for herself. The moat was deep and clear, green with weeds. Fish moved in it, splinters of shadow flexing in the depths. They rose, held each other's hands, and went on.

Human voices murmured beyond the open gates, and sunlight warmed the backs of their necks as they crossed the drawbridge and entered the town. No one stopped them. They passed rusted bicycle racks, a postbox, a noticeboard in a bed of pretty flowers—and walked out into an open space. It was a broad concrete yard, set with trees at random intervals. The surrounding buildings were of timber and painted plaster, the colors faded, the surfaces cracked. The girl saw several shop fronts—a clothier's, a baker's—and a straggling cluster of market stalls. Townsfolk moved about singly and in little knots; dogs nosed through garbage or lay in the shadows of the trees. In one corner of the yard a metal cage, presumably a place of correction, sat atop four great tree-trunk legs, reached by a metal ladder.

Again the girl experienced the vaguest sense of disappointment at a childhood memory that had been found wanting. But there were people here—many people, with walls around them—and the prospect of safety for a time.

Without being noticed, they drifted to the center of the yard, where an immense trough sat beside a pump. The girl took off her satchel and the tarpaulin and set them against the trough. The tarpaulin was so heavy. It was hurting her back.

Her brother watched her. "I'm hungry, Carly. I want food."

The girl did too: there was the faintest smell of bread and biscuits in the yard. She looked about her, pushed her hair back. "All right," she said. "Come on."

They went across to the market stalls. Ten or twelve people were there. The girl hadn't seen so many adults in a long time. She held her brother's hand tightly, cleared her throat.

"Excuse me. Please could you help us? We come from up-valley, a few miles away. Our house has been burned. Our family is . . ." She cleared her throat again. "Our family is gone. We need a place of shelter, and—and food, please. Thomas is little, but I can work for it. I can work in the fields or in the mills. I'm good with my hands," the girl said, "and I'm strong." She hoped she was wearing her "open" face, the one her mother liked—smooth and clear, without the lines on the forehead. She hoped her anxiety wasn't showing through.

She could see sympathy in some of the faces as they listened, but also wariness, even fear, as if her words might carry some kind of contagion. Pairs of eyes glanced sideways at one another; gazes crossed and recrossed, weaving a net of unspoken meaning above her head.

"The Mentor . . . ," someone said.

The girl nodded eagerly. "Yes, I see. Should I talk to someone at the Faith House, then?"

"We could give them bread." This was a woman with kind eyes. "Bread or cake . . ."

"The new Mentor wouldn't like it. Best they just go."

A man nodded. "Go to Chard."

"Yeovil."

"Taunton. They'll let anyone in, there."

The girl blinked back and forth in bewilderment. "Well, where *are* those places?" she asked. "How do we get there? I don't have any money. Thomas, stay close to me."

"You can't stay here."

"But—"

"Best you just go."

"What is this? Who are these children?"

At first the voice seemed disembodied, as if it came from the air, from all around them. It was a plangent, rather nasal voice. The girl became aware of a slow turbulence among the adults, the mass of people parting slowly, like porridge stirred by a spoon. She looked up. A person in a long, black, collarless jacket, white shirt, and blue jeans was coming across the yard. He was a youngish man, well fed, with very bright blue eyes. A wave of sandy hair curved up over one eyebrow. He had pale pink skin, tight as uncooked sausage, with a bluish tint on the jaw. The shirt was collarless and buttoned tight beneath the throat. Like the white circle badge on his lapel, the thin white rim of the neckline suggested the neutral totality of the Faith House, the way it encompassed all things, all possible religions. He was not *of* the little market town—his clothes, his hair, his manner all screamed difference—but he walked through it with proprietorial confidence, unfurling like a flower wherever he turned his gaze.

He drew up in front of the girl and her brother. He stood slightly too close to them. Having regarded them both briefly, he studiedly looked away. "Where are they from?"

"From upvalley," the girl said. "Are you the Mentor? I'm pleased to see you. My name is Scarlett McCain." She cleared her throat once more and repeated her little speech.

She finished. The man had not looked at her while she was speaking, only squinted up toward the olive-colored foliage of a tree near the center of the yard. He had a pensive, frowning expression, as if seeking enlightenment from the fragments of sunshine that worked their way through the dark leaves.

The girl waited. The townsfolk waited.

Pink eyelids blinked, pale lashes fluttered. "And how was the house burned?" the man asked. "How was your family lost? I'm not quite clear."

The girl swallowed; her voice, when it came, was small. "The Tainted," she said.

A murmur of disquiet ran through the crowd; according

to their preferences, people muttered holy words and made a variety of sacred signs. The Mentor drew a circular path in the air with a finger, encapsulating the protective force of all approved religions.

"It is a just wrath," he said.

The girl stared at him. "What? I'm sorry. I don't understand. What does that mean?"

The Mentor did not answer her. His smile was regretful; he looked around the crowd. "As I told you in my address yesterday, friends," he said, "it is probable that this scourge has fallen upon us because of our immorality. There have long been deviant births in this district, and the ruling families have not implemented their responsibilities fully. Our society has grown corrupt and weakened. The gods are displeased. They send punishment. Yes, it is a just wrath. . . ." He gave a heartfelt sigh. "You know that, with my new Mentorship, we are taking pains to reverse this situation, but it will not be easy." He gestured at the girl and her brother but still did not look at them. "It means we have some hard decisions."

The girl did not understand the words, but she sussed the body language easily enough. She could read the adjustments of the crowd. The faces were smoothed out, the expressions blank and masked. All at once the bodies of the adults stood around her and her brother like a wall.

"We are citizens of your safe-lands," she persisted. "We have long traded here."

"It would be retrogressive to allow them shelter," the Mentor said. "If they come, others will follow."

"We're not asking to stay. Just some charity is all."

"You see the red hair, of course?" the Mentor went on. "The strange eyes? These are deviants, through and through. The younger child, in particular, is a little odd. Look at the listless way he stands. . . ."

"He's listless," the girl said, "because he's damn hungry. *I'm* hungry. Doesn't that mean anything to you?"

"He may well have other hidden blemishes, if we looked more closely. Birthmarks, defects . . . It wouldn't surprise me."

He reached out thoughtfully for the little boy. The girl slapped his hand away.

"Don't do that," she said. "Don't go near my brother."

There was a moment's horrified pause, then sharp intakes of breath.

"You *dare* touch me?" The Mentor pulled himself back, face contorted with anger and disgust. "Throw them out!"

His indignation was a signal; the crowd had been waiting for something, anything, to give clarity to the moral conundrum they faced. Perhaps the issue had been more delicately poised than the Mentor allowed. No longer. A woman beside him snatched at the girl's arm, yanked it sharply backward. The girl almost fell, colliding with other members of the crowd. All at once she could not see her brother. She heard a squeak. In a swell of panic, she fought herself upright, but other hands, stimulated by the bodily contact, excited by it, were reaching out for her.

"Thomas—!"

Hands seized her wrists, her arms, her thighs and calves.

She was dragged off her feet, hoisted aloft. The enthusiasm of the crowd fed off itself. There was laughter and hallooing. She was twirled along, flat on her back, helpless, staring at the sky. Across the yard they went. The moment lasted seconds and forever. She saw the arch of the stockade pass above her; with a raucous cheer, the crowd flung the girl free, limbs flailing, out into the sunshine, hard onto the wooden drawbridge.

An instant later, and the little boy was tumbling alongside her.

The people of the town spent a few more seconds indulging in their merriment before sauntering back inside—but the girl heard nothing of it, just the blood pounding in her ears. She got slowly to her feet, reaching out for her brother, who was standing beside her. She shared his smallness and his silence and his bafflement. She had cried out with the impact, but that was the only sound she'd made. She was too shocked even to swear.

They walked over the drawbridge and away along the curve of the road. A few men from the sawmills went past on bicycles, returning to the town. The hard sunlight beat at their faces. They neared the pine tree and the moat.

The girl stopped dead.

"Oh, gods, Thomas. We forgot the bag."

He looked at her.

"The satchel. We left it by the pump. We forgot the bag."

"You mustn't go back in there," he said.

"We've got to. It's got the fish and the apples, and some mushrooms. And the tarpaulin's with it too. We need that for tonight. If we can flag down a bus, we could go someplace else, maybe. One of the other towns. . . . We could barter a ride. And we need to eat. . . ."

Her thoughts were broken and confused. She couldn't think straight. She felt she was still being carried through the air.

"We've got to," she said again.

"No, Carly," her brother said. "Don't go back."

She smiled at him, smoothed down his hair. The only good thing about the whole mess was that they hadn't hurt him. He was as round-cheeked as ever. Perfect, not a bruise on him.

"I've got to, darling. I'll only be a minute."

His soft hand pushed its way into hers. "I'll come too, then."

"I don't want *you* going back inside, Thomas. They're not nice people." She squeezed his fingers. "They're idiots. I don't know what's wrong with them. It's just a little way past the gate. You remember the place, don't you? The pump. I'll be in and out in a moment. You know how fast I am. Quick and fierce as a wolf. Sit here in the shade, and you'll see."

But he wouldn't sit. He pulled himself away from her, scowling, his body rigid. Stamping his foot in the white dust of the road, he faced her down.

"I don't want this," he said. "Don't go back, Scarlett."

Anger surged inside her. This was the last thing she needed, him going all stubborn. He was so small and stupid and helpless and didn't know a thing. She wanted to beat her head against the tree and cry. "All right," she said. "Then *don't* sit down. You just stand right there. You're perfectly safe. Just stay on the side of the road. There are people going in and out all the time. Keep out of the way of the bicycles." She stared at him, all hot and harassed and fighting the despair. Staring at him but not seeing. Afterward, she could never quite remember the expression on his face.

"Wait here, Thomas," she said. "Wait here. I won't be long."

She turned and stumped heavily and quickly back toward the drawbridge. The Mentor had gone. The crowd had dispersed and was nowhere to be seen. Just pooling sunlight. A minute in, a minute out. That's all it would take. Might be better to walk, so as not to attract attention. Or just run in and get it over with. Either way, it would be easy. There was no one in sight. They'd gone back to their homes for tea and cakes or something. There was the open yard, the postbox, the market stalls, the cage.

And the pump in the center of the yard. She could practically see the bag from here.

The girl walked swiftly across the bridge. Before slipping through the arch, she looked back a final time.

Shielding her eyes, she saw her little brother waiting for her on the sunlit road.

16

She'd been dreaming again. As ever, the moment fled from her, the glow receded, leaving her alone among the shadows. She could never quite recall the details of what she'd seen.

Lying there, summoning (as every morning) the necessary strength to wake into her life, she felt the mark of the dream still wet upon her cheeks. But she was Scarlett McCain: she refused to open her eyes to *that*. She raised her hand to wipe her face—and discovered she could not do so. Bonds bit her wrists. Chains jangled. Her arms were painfully constrained.

Clearly another great day was about to begin.

Forcing herself awake, she found that she was slumped on a concrete floor. At her back was a metal pole, running floor to ceiling in the corner of a bare, gray room. Her hands were behind her, handcuffed on the other side of the pole. Around her was a mess of chains. Scarlett struggled into a more upright position and made a second unwelcome discovery. The chains began at the pole and ended at shackles on both her ankles. She was barefoot and bareheaded; her hat and boots and coat and any conceivable weapon were gone.

The cell was small, rectangular, and desolate, as cells in Scarlett's experience most often were. Another couple of poles along the same wall were unoccupied. There was a wooden door; a stool, presumably for the comfort of a guard or interrogator; and a window with iron bars. Through this, Scarlett could see a fragment of sky and the tip of a golden tower.

Not far from the stool was a pail of water, with a ladle resting in it. Scarlett, conscious suddenly of a pounding thirst and headache, did her best to ignore it. It was well out of reach. Even if it hadn't been, her hands were chained.

She made a series of awkward, chain-rattling adjustments and established that, given a little effort, it was possible for her to stand, squat, or sit. Anything more advanced than this was out. From a standing position she had a better view out of the window. The tower was revealed to be a Faith House minaret; beyond it, stretching to the horizon, were the red-roofed houses, spires, and crenellated water tanks of a great and prosperous town.

Scarlett stared at the shimmering vista glumly. "Gods above us," she said. "Milton Keynes."

A rattling made her turn. There was a watch slit in the cell door; evidently her awakening had been observed. The door opened, and a burly warder in a tweed jacket and bright red bowler hat came in. He had the usual attributes of a guard, namely a belt jingling with cuffs and truncheons, a face like a disappointed log, and a gaze of mute hostility. Scarlett instantly ruled out bribery, befriending, sweet-talking, or appealing to a nonexistent better nature.

"May I have some water, please?" she asked.

The man said nothing. In a leisurely fashion, he looked her up and down.

"Do you know what day it is? Do you know what has happened to my friend?"

The guard wiped his nose with a finger, completed his inspection, and went out. Scarlett heard the door being locked again. She swore briefly in its general direction and, with little else to do, turned her attention to her bonds. She tried various maneuvers, tugging and testing the pole and chains, but could find no weakness in them. At last, to save her strength, she sat down and composed herself, waiting for something to happen.

For the next two hours, little did. Scarlett had a single visitor: a cadaverous gentleman in a gray suit and bowler, carrying a measuring tape. He made swift assessments of her height, weight, and diameter of neck before tipping his hat and bustling off. Scarlett couldn't help feeling this was a trifle ominous. She closed her eyes and tried to meditate, but gave up almost at once. It had been while meditating in the truck that she had been surprised and struck down. She recalled little of it: footsteps outside . . . a silhouette at the door . . . Scarlett had assumed it was Albert come to apologize—until the world collapsed in on her. Meditation hadn't helped her then, and she wasn't in the mood for it now.

The cell door opened again. In came the slouching guard, followed by another person. Scarlett glanced up—then she raised her head at speed.

It was the Faith House operative.

He looked exactly as he had in Huntingdon: a lean youth in a long black coat that was a little too big for him. His fingers peeped from the ends of his sleeves; his belt was drawn to its innermost notch. His hair shone with oil. He was clean-cut, blue-eyed—and extremely young. Back in the motor-town saloon, he had seemed gauche and incongruous. Here, in the shadow of the brutish warder, he seemed incongruous still. He crossed directly to Scarlett, the first of her visitors to do so. Behind his back the guard looked on with scarcely repressed loathing.

"And there she is," the operative said. "My barroom friend."

Scarlett blew hair out of her face. "That's me," she croaked. "Going to buy me another drink?"

The youth looked over her with his calm, unhurried gaze. Her hat was gone; she imagined him exploring her thoughts at will and shuddered. He smiled at her. "Are you thirsty?"

"Parched. There's water in that bucket. My keeper there wouldn't give me any."

The young man glanced round at the warder, whose sullen expression curdled into fear. The warder reached for the pail. "I'm sorry, Mr. Mallory—"

"Don't touch it." The operative raised a hand; the warder flinched away. Crouching, picking up the metal ladle, the young man filled it from the bucket and brought it close to Scarlett's mouth. She drank greedily, water trickling down her chin. When she'd finished one ladleful, she drank another.

"Easily remedied," the young man said. "A little more?"

"No."

He stood, stepped back, set the ladle down. "Was that so difficult, Perkins?"

"No, Mr. Mallory."

"I'm sorry about him, Miss McCain. There are tusked badgers ferreting in the woods for dung that have better social skills than Perkins. And I'm sorry for your discomfort generally—and for nobbling you in the truck. It's just, well . . ." He grinned at her. "After Huntingdon, I'm not underestimating you again."

"Nor I you," Scarlett said. "How long have I been here?"

"I drove you down last night. Parked the truck right here at the Faith House. Brought them two fine fugitives and a heap of precious artifacts. I think I did quite well."

"And Albert? What have you done with him?"

"Ah. Albert . . ." The youth sighed; he clapped his hands. "Look, why don't we continue this conversation while we walk? Keys, Perkins, if you please. . . ."

The warder approached. Scarlett's legs were freed, her hands loosed from the pole. She got stiffly to her feet, ignoring the operative's proffered hand. "You're letting me go?"

He had a pleasant laugh. "Lovely. No, actually I'm taking you to trial. Well, I *say* 'trial.' Depends how you define these things. Hands again, please, Perkins. I can take it from here."

Scarlett's hands were recuffed at her back. On bare and bloodied feet, in ragged jeans and jersey, she limped after the operative and out the door. The guard remained behind.

The operative's coat swished gently as he led her down a

concrete passage. Scarlett went slowly, pondering the possibilities. Even with your hands tied, there were ways of killing a man, provided you had something stable to jump on and managed to get a leg hooked around his neck. Certainly not easy. Still, if she could get her bearings . . .

"I shouldn't bother with anything like that," the operative said over his shoulder. "You'll only do your back in. And breaking a man's neck with your thighs isn't exactly *classy*. Come beside me, so we can talk. Perkins wouldn't approve, but who cares? It's not too far to go."

Scarlett fell in alongside. He smelled of soap and solitude. "And Albert?" she prompted.

"Oh, you'll see him now. It's a joint trial. It's being held upstairs in one of the auditoria, which is a mark of the interest shown in you. Nice up there. Better than this dungeon."

"Where exactly *are* we?"

"Milton Keynes. The citadel of the High Council, in the center of the Sacred Compound." He chuckled. "You should take that as an honor . . . of a kind."

At the end of the passage was an imposing iron gate, emblazoned with the Faith House circle. Here, two armed men sat at tables, engaged in piles of paperwork. At the operative's approach, they rose and saluted. The gate was opened; Mallory and Scarlett went through.

"You seem surprisingly important," Scarlett said.

"Yes." Mallory smiled at her. "Of course, they hate me for it. They all of them hate me. They think I'm different— which I *am*. Think I read their minds—which I *do*. Think

I'd kill them and their loved ones in a heartbeat—which I bloody well *would* if they obstructed my sacred purpose. . . . And now we go up here."

The passage beyond the door was paved with terra-cotta tiles. Immediately opposite was a sunlit staircase, with arched openings overlooking the town. They were already high, and going higher. They began to climb. Below were spires and onion domes, and a colonnaded plaza shimmering in sunlight, dotted with flocks of drifting birds.

"Good view," Scarlett said.

"It is. They're building your gallows down there."

Scarlett hadn't expected anything less; still, as a conversation stopper it took some beating. They went on for a little way in silence. As they did so, Scarlett's thoughts flitted across various topics. She imagined shoving the operative out of one of the windows. She imagined bounding down the stairs, finding a roof to slide on, making a daring escape across the town. She thought of Albert again, and of Joe and Ettie, far away in Stow. . . . Another day lost! Only two to go! She thought of the alarm clock on Soames's desk, ticking down the hours. . . .

The operative walked beside her, smiling. It occurred to Scarlett that it might be better to talk to him and find out stuff herself, rather than simply let the bastard read her mind.

They arrived at the top floor of the building, turning into a terra-cotta corridor hung with tapestries and set about with glass cases, in which were objects not unlike the items dug up from the Buried City. Functionaries in white robes passed on unknowable errands, and gray-hatted guards stood at intervals along the walls. There was a scent of incense and wine.

"They live well, the High Council," Scarlett said.

"They do."

"Is this where you live too?"

"Not I. I travel the Seven Kingdoms, roaming the deserts, back alleys, and wastelands by the Council's sufferance and command."

"Doesn't sound *quite* so comfy."

"No. Still, I am content. It's more than I deserve."

Scarlett glanced aside at the thin, pale face. She remembered Albert's haunted expression at their first meeting, when she met him in the bus. "How did you find us?" she asked.

"By using my initiative!" Mallory turned sharply right across the corridor and through a gold-leafed arch, giving a casual salute to the sentry standing there. "Not long ago, a day or two after we met in Huntingdon, I bumped into a diminutive merchant-trader named Sal Qin. She was traveling alone—rather despondently, I thought, and with a furtive air. We got talking. I sieved her mind and discovered she had approached you both about a robbery in the north. Qin thought you had ignored the job, but I was less certain. I sent word by pigeon to contacts in Ashtown, who confirmed that a 'Mr. and Mrs. Johnson' had taken up residence in a local hotel. I had previously noticed," Mallory added, "that in towns you two had gone on to rob, the local inns often played host to a 'Mr. Johnson,' a wide-eyed simpleton who answered to Albert Browne's description. That told me all I needed to know."

Scarlett groaned aloud. "The idiot! I *told* him not to keep using that name!"

"And you were right," Mallory said warmly. "Well done. But he did, and so I headed north in haste, little expecting you would have already carried out the wicked crime. Your speed almost saved you. Luckily, I was alerted by a petrol seller at the Newark crossroads that a mine truck with two unusual drivers had recently taken the western road, and I was able to follow, discover your tracks, and take you into custody." He made a modest, urbane gesture. "And so 'The Ballad of Scarlett and Browne' comes to its inevitable end."

"I've never been keen on ballads myself," Scarlett said. "I don't like stories."

Mallory laughed again; there was warmth and sympathy in the sound. "You don't like your story, maybe! I understand that—I've also had to come to terms with the darkness in myself, with the horrible thing I am. By my labors I seek to cleanse myself. I fight forever against the shame inside me. . . ." He touched her sleeve. "And I think you know something about that feeling, too—*don't* you, Scarlett McCain?"

Scarlett said nothing. She looked at his fingers on her arm.

They had come to a set of enormous double doors of red-gold mahogany, inlaid with bands of bronze leaf. Two guards with gold bowler hats stood there at attention.

"The holy auditorium awaits!" Mallory said. "There will be at least one Council member, there will be dignitaries. . . . We must both be on our best behavior. Play your part well!"

Synchronized movements from the guards: the doors swung open. Scarlett was bathed in a flood of golden light.

It was an immense squared chamber, with a far wall of glass and a balcony beyond, overlooking the rooftops of the town. The glass doors were open; warm air drifted in, carrying with it the noise of bells and holy chimes from the Faith House complex below. Afternoon sunlight filled the chamber like honey in a bowl. The walls were lined with shelves of books in red and russet bindings. Scarlett and the operative walked toward the glass wall, between rows of tables at which sat men and women—black-suited Mentors and scribes with pens and paper files, some scribbling, most watching her impassively. Guards with pistols stood at side doors, through which Scarlett could see more shelves and ranks of cabinets. On a dais in front of the glass wall were seven empty chairs; before this, in the center of a clear area of floor, was a lower platform, and here was Albert, sitting on a stool.

He was small, hunched, and somehow misshapen, his proportions subtly deformed. What had they *done* to him? Hastening closer, Scarlett realized the effect was caused by what he wore on his head—an iron skullcap, bullet gray, with wires fixing it beneath his chin. The cap was massive: it made him seem frailer, younger than his years.

There was another stool alongside; Scarlett joined him on

the platform. The operative walked on, greatcoat swishing, and went to stand out on the balcony, alone.

"Hey," Albert said. Like Scarlett's, his hands were handcuffed behind him. His expression was faraway.

"Hey." She smiled at him. "You're looking good. Your bruises are symmetrical, at any rate. Are you all right, Albert? That hat—"

"Is just a bit heavy. It's there to . . ." He didn't bother finishing. "*You* know what it's for."

Scarlett suppressed a spasm of rage. On the balcony the operative was leaning on a balustrade, hands casually clasped, looking out over the town. "Did he hurt you?" she asked.

"Well, he buried me under half a hillside," Albert said, "so it *could* have been better. But I'm alive, so I mustn't grumble. Did he do anything bad to you?"

"Apart from knock me senseless, clap me in chains, and bring me to Milton Keynes? No."

"Good. Look, Scarlett . . . I'm sorry about earlier. In the truck."

"Forget it."

"If I hadn't got you mad . . . If we hadn't stopped . . ."

"He would have caught us anyway."

Albert shook his head. "No, but you were right in everything you said. I was stupid and pigheaded, and I hope you forgive me. I was worrying about Joe and Ettie."

"Yeah," Scarlett said. "Me too. Forget about yesterday. It's not a problem."

He brightened. "Thank you. I can't tell you how much that was weighing on me. I feel better now." He sat a little straighter, pushed his puny shoulders back. "Well," he said, "these are admittedly difficult circumstances, but we shan't lose heart! Always look on the bright side—isn't that what you say?"

Scarlett gazed at him. "It's me. Scarlett. I've never said anything so wet in my entire life."

"No? Maybe it was someone else. But look where we are!" Albert said. "*The headquarters of the High Council!* Aren't we lucky to get a glimpse of *this?*" With some effort, owing to his metal headgear, he indicated one of the open doorways on the far side of the dais. "Have you ever *seen* so many books and cabinets of treasures?"

Scarlett had already scanned the side rooms while looking for possible avenues of escape. Frankly, she was more interested in the sentries stationed at every door than in the endless bookshelves or the cases filled with artifacts. She could see tables too, on which were fragments of old texts held between sheets of plastic. Women with magnifying glasses were studying them, noting the details down.

"They're copying them," Albert said. "Hunting for lost knowledge." He leaned in close, spoke in a confidential whisper. "It's like with those ancient weapons we saw. *I think they're trying to uncover dark secrets of the past.*"

Scarlett nodded. Her chains rattled as she, too, bent in close. "Yes. It certainly looks that way. Quick question, though,

Albert—do you think that's *really* the most important thing for us to be focusing on right now?"

"Ah!" Albert drew himself up. "Of course. We *do* have other priorities. And I have good news on this front too: the operative's brought our truck here. We need to find it and drive it down to Stow. We've got almost two days left to save Joe and Ettie—there's still time!"

Scarlett regarded him. The thing was, he actually believed it. Believed it was possible. Believed it as they sat there, bound and helpless in the sunshine, with thirty guards around them, in the city of their enemies and with a bespoke scaffold being speedily erected for them in the square. There was something rather beautiful about that.

She gave him a bleak smile. "That's right," she said. "There's time."

A flurry among the functionaries beside the archive doors. Scribes rose, guards stiffened. A small, wide man in a jet-black suit was approaching between the copyists' tables and bookshelves. He bustled into the auditorium and made for the dais. His movements were brisk, his little legs covered ground at speed. He carried a wodge of papers under one arm.

A tall, lugubrious-looking Mentor stood. "High Councillor Bevan presiding!"

"Yes, yes, thank you. You may be seated." The councillor sprang onto the dais and flung himself into the centermost chair. He was an ageless round-faced man in small gold-rimmed spectacles. His skin was dark, his hair cut short on the back and sides; what few strands remained were ruthlessly combed across the top. He nestled his papers on his lap and peered myopically around the auditorium. "The purpose of the court today is?"

"The trial of the outlaws Scarlett McCain and Albert Browne!" the tall Mentor cried. "Also to discuss details of the execution ceremony and the accompanying celebrations."

"And these are the two offenders?"

"Yes, sir. Guilty of a dozen crimes of the very blackest stamp. Their latest are the Warwick theft I told you about and the assault on the northern mines."

The man gazed at Scarlett and Albert without expression. In other circumstances, namely at a distance and from behind the sights of a good rifle, Scarlett would have been happy to see a member of the High Council, who controlled the Faith Houses across the kingdoms. In this case she was determined to show no interest whatsoever. She slumped on her stool, looking bored.

"I see." Councillor Bevan nodded slowly. "It was Mallory who brought them in?"

"Yes, sir."

"The boy is the deviant, of course?"

"That's right, sir. Powerful. He's the one who caused the trouble in Stonemoor last year. Dr. Calloway was lost trying to bring him home."

"I remember. She went missing in the wastes. A sad outcome for us all. And the girl is evidently his enabler, who keeps him functioning. . . ." The man did not even look at Scarlett, but he kept his eyes on Albert for a time. He shook his head, adjusted his papers. "It's all so sordid. Such a shame. Very well. Now, in the course of their brief career I believe they have awoken a certain public interest, is that right?"

"They have a modest celebrity, sir. There's been a ballad."

Bevan made a face of mild distaste. "We've clearly apprehended them at just the right moment, Stevens. The public will be expecting a spectacular end, and we can give them one. Let's make a festival night of it. . . ." He trailed off, frowning; Albert was jiggling in his seat. "What's the matter with the lad? Has he been caught short or something?"

"I think he wishes to speak, sir," the tall Mentor said. "I'll have him restrained."

"No need. We're almost done. I assume we're hanging them?"

"I thought that was best, sir. Unless you want to break them on the wheel."

"Hanging's cheaper. And more classic, somehow. Tomorrow night?"

"Very much the intention, sir. They're building the stages now."

"Excellent. Nice bit of work for the carpenters."

"Yes, sir. I think we should make a fine show of it, if you and the other Council members are agreeable. We have three captive Tainted too, taken on a punitive expedition in the Oxford Sours. They are probably from the very group that ravaged Chipping Campden. They have been hobbled and subdued, but they are still alive and will rouse the audience to a frenzy."

Councillor Bevan nodded complacently. "Excellent. There are food shortages in the suburbs, and we had riots last night, out by the southern ruins, so this will be a distraction for the people. I may stop by to observe the show myself. Well, I think we're finished. Give the requisite permissions to all the local businesses. The slavers will want to run their usual stalls. . . ." He paused in the act of rising from his chair. "Yes, what *is* it, lad?"

Knowing that no possible human good could ever come from allowing Albert to make any kind of public utterance, Scarlett had been attempting to restrain him with a subtle series of kicks, curses, and elbow jabs. To no avail. He struggled to his feet, his head swaying awkwardly in his iron cap.

"Thank you, sir," Albert said. "I wished to make a personal plea to you. Not for ourselves but for two blameless friends, who have fallen into the cruel power of the Brothers of the Hand. Unless we return to save them, they will be devoured by owls. Can you find it in your heart to spare us for their sake, or at least send someone else to free them?"

He looked around. The sea of assembled faces was blank— apart from Scarlett's, which was busily groaning and rolling its eyes. Several guards advanced grimly in their direction.

The tall Mentor had also stepped forward. "I'm sorry, sir. I'll have him whipped."

"No, no. It's all right." Councillor Bevan looked at Albert. "My boy, this is a question of justice. Simply put, justice and order are what keeps our society together. Ranged against us are two types of evil. There is the evil that lurks outside our gates, and there is the evil in the hearts of unclean persons such as you. Your friends may indeed be blameless. *You* are most certainly not. I know of the Brothers of the Hand. They are a ragtag band of robbers who flourish wherever the hold of the Faith Houses is weak. Be assured we *will* destroy them in due time. For the moment, however, we begin with you."

He turned to leave. Albert gave a hoot of indignation; he stamped his foot upon the platform. "I refute that description!" he cried. "I am *not* evil! I may be an outlaw, but I was driven to this way of life by *your* persecution!"

"Albert—" Scarlett sprang to her feet. She could see the guards closing in, batons at the ready. "Now would be a *very* good time to master the art of shutting up."

"No!" Albert wriggled away from her. "I protest at the hypocrisy! If I am a deviant, as the councillor claims, so too is his servant in the stupid coat out there on the balcony! He has powers like me! Where is the 'justice' in this distinction?"

"A valid point," Scarlett hissed, "and one they will gladly discuss with you after they've cut out your tongue. Be *silent*!"

Albert made a complicated, indignant noise, then subsided. Councillor Bevan took off his spectacles; his voice was bored. "I appreciate your effort, girl. Wickedness stems in part from defects of birth, but also from moral ignorance, as your friend is proving now. Yes, certainly it is *possible* for deviants to be brought into the fold. Mallory provides evidence of that! He is a most useful and trusted instrument now, but

275

only because of his years of treatment at Stonemoor. Albert Browne rejected that opportunity, so he remains a threat that must be destroyed. Such is the brutal message of history."

He gestured toward the windows. Frowning, Scarlett followed his gaze. "History?" she said.

"Look out there, girl. What do you see?"

"The town."

"And beyond it?"

As at Warwick, so at Milton Keynes: Scarlett saw that the modern buildings were peppered with enormous ruins—twisted shards of metal, spires of concrete, half arches soaring into nothingness . . .

"Ruins," she said. "Products of the Cataclysm."

The councillor chuckled. "Hardly! *This* destruction was *much* more recent. It wasn't wrought by the Cataclysm but by deviants. People like the boy and Mallory. People with so-called talents." He smiled down at Scarlett briefly. "Is it any wonder we would prefer that not happen again?"

He clicked his fingers; at once, the room erupted into noise. The Mentor shouted orders, the guards congregated at the platform. Scarlett tried to speak to Albert, who had gone all stiff and still. Before she could do so, she was pulled apart from him and beaten to the ground. With blows and buffets, the outlaws Scarlett and Browne were dragged away down the central aisle and off to their separate cells. Peace was restored. The clerks and copyists of the Faith House archives returned to their paperwork. Out on the balcony, the operative gazed imperturbably into the sunlit void.

17

Curiosity. That was Albert's chief reaction. If it had been the councillor's intention to crush him with the horror of what he hinted at, or to overpower him with a sense of guilt, self-loathing, or shame, that intention failed. More than failed—it had precisely the opposite effect. Faced with the insinuation that his powers were linked to untold disasters of the past, Albert experienced a very simple response. He wanted to know more about it.

Day turned to evening, evening turned to night, night turned to morning. Light and shadow chased each other across the walls of the cell. Albert sat alone, in chains, his head resting against the punishment pole to alleviate the burden of the iron hat. His body ached, his heart was raw; he feared for the well-being of his friends. Yet in other ways he was at peace, even strangely free. It was a freedom that came from the knowledge—or partial knowledge—that he was not alone.

Over long years in the prison of Stonemoor, under the harsh control of Dr. Calloway, Albert had been taught to fear and despise the powers inside him. An essential component of this process—more effective even than the relentless program of tests and tortures that helped him associate his gifts with pain—was isolation. Albert was told that he was sick, that his illness barred him from participation in the world. Eruptions of the Fear tended to confirm this diagnosis. He and the other young guests of the facility were kept drugged and distracted, and thus isolated from one another too.

Albert had felt enough defiance to break out of Stonemoor, but—even now, living a life of liberation with Scarlett at his side—he still labored, deep down, under a feeling of his unique and solitary *wrongness*. Yet seemingly this was incorrect. He was *not* unique. Not at all. The words of the member of the High Council rang in his ears. "People like him" had caused destruction on an untold scale.

People like him. That was the part Albert focused on. Intended as a savage indictment, it felt to him almost like an offer of community. It felt like a validation.

Of course, if he wanted to find out anything more about it, he would have to keep himself alive, and that meant escape. Which was easier said than done. Rousing the Fear was one possibility—but the iron cap was clipped tightly to his skull and, try as he might, he could not shake it. The rest of his chains were firm too. Perhaps Scarlett might have invented a clever plan to strangle the guards and steal the keys. But strangling wasn't Albert's métier. So he sat and thought, and dozed and thought, until the new day dawned and he had perhaps thirty hours before Ettie's clock began its fatal chiming, far away in Stow.

Albert waited patiently. He felt his chance would come.

*   *   *

Sometime toward noon, two of the guards who had beaten Albert the day before reappeared in his cell, placed black sacking over his head, and removed him. He was led along unknown ways for an unknown distance. At last he heard the creaking of a door, a guttural command. The sacking was removed; brightness flooded his eyes. Somebody shoved him forward. Albert stood straight, blinking tentatively around him.

The cell was smaller than his previous one, and cleaner too. There were no punishment posts. Strong sunlight entered from the single window, and in this pool of light was a round café table. On the table, somewhat to Albert's surprise, was a bowl of fruit set on a white embroidered cloth, with a jug of water and two plastic cups alongside. There were two chairs pulled up to the table. In one of them sat Mallory, the Faith House operative, looking gaunt and pale and chilly. He had his coat on, the collar turned up around his ears.

"Albert! Welcome!" The operative sprang to his feet, ushered the guards out, and shut the door behind them. He indicated the room. "What do you think?"

"I like the doily," Albert said. "It really distracts from the shackles on my hands and feet, my metal skullcap, the bars on the windows, these iron chains."

The young man smiled. "Yes, it's the little things that make a difference." He waved a hand. "Shuffle over. Sit down with me. Take an apple. A celestine grape. Whatever you like."

"Thanks, but I'm worried about Scarlett. She's on her own somewhere, and I haven't seen her since yesterday. I think these guards are cruel."

Mallory shrugged. "They're just dull, unimaginative men doing their jobs as best they can. But don't worry—they won't do anything drastic to her. We need Miss McCain to look her best on the scaffold. Come on, sit down. I'm hoping to have a chat with you."

"Can't I see her?"

"Maybe after this. To be honest," Mallory added, as Albert sat diffidently in a chair with much clattering of chains, "I wouldn't want us to have this conversation in front of Scarlett. Frankly, her scowls alone would put me off." He grinned at Albert, selected a grape from a bunch in the center of the bowl. "It's much better to do this quietly. Just you and me, alone."

"We could have chatted quietly the other day," Albert said, "only you decided to bury me alive." He took a grape, bit into it. He was very hungry. The sweetness stung his eyes.

The young man grinned. "Yes. What did you think of the trick? Sudden lack of oxygen, bodily constriction . . . I find it good for awkward customers like you."

"Dr. Calloway would have been most impressed," Albert said. "I remember her praising me for just moving a flower petal a few feet across a room."

"Ah, did *you* do that exercise as well?" Mallory sat forward, smiling broadly. "So few ever managed it, even in Stonemoor! Practical, mind-controlled kinesis—Calloway's area of expertise. No wonder she liked you so much. Dear Calloway! She made me understand what I was capable of. She saved me, Albert, from the corruption of my nature." The smile faded. "Like she *wanted* to save you, too."

"I don't remember you at Stonemoor," Albert said.

Mallory nodded. "I was there. I came as a young boy, rejected by my family, ignorant in my wickedness. I left four years ago, chastened and enlightened. Calloway sent me off to a Faith House seminary, for further tuition with a man called Monk."

"I knew Monk too. . . ." Albert's eyes had darkened; looking at the window, he saw echoes of other windows, other bars, other barren rooms. He did not recall his own beginnings. Stonemoor was all he had ever known.

"We certainly overlapped, in any case," Mallory said. "Which room were you in?"

"Room 13B. It was the one next to the latrine."

"Not a cell I'm familiar with, sadly. I generally kept to myself in Stonemoor."

"Yes," Albert said. "Me too. It was best that way."

They sat there, gazing at each other. Both reached for the grapes at the same time.

"Of course," the operative said, "we no longer inhabit the same space. I have suppressed my inner evil, while you have luxuriated in it. I have remained true to Dr. Calloway's teaching, following the way of enlightenment and justice. You have become a rogue, thief, and mountebank, consorting with red-haired murderers and other felons."

Albert swallowed his grape and selected an apple. "When you put it like that, I suppose our paths have diverged a tad."

Mallory nodded. "'Diverged' is putting it mildly. And you have inadvertently brought a great grief upon me. After you fled from Stonemoor, Dr. Calloway went after you. She considered you too important to lose. Somehow, somewhere, she and her team perished in the wildernesses around the Thames. Her exact fate is unknown." He sighed, ran his fingers through his flop of oiled hair. "I remember the last time I saw her, here at the citadel. The sun was shining on her pale skin and black shoes, on her velvet headband, on the votive statues of the gardens. . . . She smiled and pressed my hand and walked away, and was lost among the totems." His eyes glistened. "She was like a mother to me, Albert Browne. Be relieved I don't hold *you* fully responsible."

Albert said nothing. He remembered the last time *he'd* seen Dr. Calloway, i.e., clonking her on the head with an iron bar on the edge of a cliff and watching her body drop like a broken puppet into the sea. He thought perhaps now wasn't the time to mention it.

Mallory drew himself back into the present with difficulty. "Well," he said, "I should probably get to the point. I know the festival organizers want to get you ready for tonight. But here's the thing, Albert." He smiled suavely, flicked back his coat, and leaned forward in a nonchalant pose upon the table. "You don't *have* to die."

Albert was biting into his apple. "I know. You can just let us both go."

The young man winced. "Well, *that's* clearly not going to happen. Scarlett stays here. She's an incorrigible villain. Everyone knows it. You know it yourself. But you—it's not so clear-cut. You're different, Mr. Browne."

"So I keep being told."

Mallory laughed. "Naturally. I only have to look at you to see it."

Albert looked down at himself and back at the apple. "I don't see anything."

"Precisely. You've had any number of appalling traumas the last two days. Explosions, crashes, close encounters with the Tainted . . . Then there was me, squashing you with a cliff. . . . Yet you're in almost perfect nick. All you've got's a couple of bruises."

"Actually, I've got lots," Albert said. "There are some real whoppers down below. I could show you if you like."

"Please don't, I beg you. All the same, you'll agree you got off lightly, given the carnage following you at every step. Poor Scarlett, in contrast, is *very* bashed about. . . . Now," Mallory went on, "this wouldn't be the *first* time you've survived disaster unscathed, would it?"

Albert thought of various similar incidents of his past. "I'm generally quite lucky."

"It's not luck, you fool! It's a talent! We've each got it, you and me both—it takes a lot to do us in. Then there's your *other* talents, too." He nodded at Albert's helmet. "The ones we're taking steps against right now. Dr. Calloway had a high opinion of you, and I respect that. Personally, though . . . I just don't see it. You were rubbish back there by the truck. Tried to read my mind, almost fell over. . . . Other than that, nothing. Zip. That girlfriend of yours did me more damage with a quick shove in a saloon."

Albert blanched; he looked uneasily behind him. "*Girlfriend?* I wouldn't let Scarlett hear you say that. It wouldn't go well for either of us."

"I don't believe you were *ever* that good," Mallory went on, ignoring him. "If you've got talent, it's totally chaotic. You certainly haven't the willpower to be at peace with what you are. But that's by the by. We were talking about tonight. . . ." He leaned forward again. "These are difficult times—the Tainted are spreading and the idiots in the Towns are squabbling. The Faith Houses need all the help they can get to impose proper order. And that means taking advantage of the Stonemoor project at last. It means using deviants like you and me." He smiled thinly. "Not everyone on the Council likes the idea, of course—some of them would be happy to kill us both. Stonemoor never sat easy with them, considering what went before."

A thrill of interest ran through Albert. "Yes," he said, "but what *did* happen before? What did the councillor *mean* yesterday, when he talked about the ruins out there? He said people like *us* had done it! What people? When? Come on, Mallory! You must know about this! Spill the beans."

The operative paused; he smiled quizzically. "Honestly, your life hangs by a hair, and *this* is what gets you excited?

What an odd little fellow you are. Well, you'd have got the answer if you'd stayed at Stonemoor. But you chose to walk out on your education."

"I walked out on torture," Albert said.

"Oh, man up!" Mallory made an impatient gesture. "Sure, there was tough treatment, but the truth is that creatures like us *can't* be treated with kid gloves. Would you mollycoddle a Tainted? No! So stop your gabbling and listen. I'm here to make you an offer. I'm authorized to say that your crimes are forgiven. You'll no longer be an outlaw. You can become a higher operative, like me. Obviously there'll be a period of adjustment, further training. . . . You'll need to go back to Stonemoor for a while. But *that's* no big deal, surely! Maybe you'll even learn the secrets you desire. . . ." He waited. "Just say the word, Albert! Gentlemen's agreement. Don't have to sign in blood or anything. Say yes, the chains come off, we stroll out of here together. You understand me?" He snapped his fingers. "Off and out."

"I can go?"

"Just like that."

"What happens to Scarlett?"

"Oh, she dies. But look, don't get distracted. Focus on what *counts*. And what counts is *you*."

Albert smiled. "Can I have an orange?"

"While you consider your answer."

"I'll eat it fast. You don't need me to tell you what I'm going to say."

Mallory gave a theatrical groan. "Come on! Scarlett McCain? She's really that important to you? You'd happily die for her?"

"I wouldn't care to live without her . . . ," Albert said. "That's not *quite* the same thing." He set down the empty orange peel. "Why not let her go, Mallory? Do that and we might have a deal. I'll come with you, do what you say. How's that for a plan? Only, you let Scarlett go."

The operative folded his arms, pulling his coat in tightly as if he felt the cold. He heaved the sigh of someone summoning immense fortitude. "Try to see it from our point of view," he said. "We've got a top-notch gallows built for you, and there's a sizeable crowd going to be there tonight. The pamphleteers will be out in force, the market traders, the sausage-and-pickled-cabbage men . . . We've got a whole vibrant business community who are depending on a proper show. They've put money into it! We can't just cancel! The people will get restless. Sure, there's a few Tainted getting torched, but that's just icing, and we need a cake. They've got to have someone center stage, and Scarlett will do very well."

"Get someone else."

"To replace Scarlett and Browne? What are we going to choose, a shoplifter?"

"Spin them a line. Tell them Scarlett's tipping you off about her accomplices—that there's a big conspiracy and we're just the start of it. Tell them you're having to torture her to get information, and you can't kill her yet. Put on a different show—jugglers or something."

"You don't know much about public entertainment," the operative said. "Jugglers? Then we really *would* have riots. . . . No, I'm sorry. Scarlett's fate is sealed."

"In that case," Albert said, "thanks for the fruit. I'd like to be taken to Scarlett now."

The operative regarded him, tapping the creases of his coat sleeves with his pale, thin fingers. "You know," he said, "this is all a lot of fuss about someone so . . . damaged. She makes us both look like paragons of contentment, and *we've* been experimented on like monkeys all our lives. What do you see in her? I mean, really?"

Albert went very still and quiet. A realization struck him. "Damaged?" he said.

"Well, obviously. I mean, clearly you know about her past." Mallory took an apple from the bowl, rotated it in his hand, looking for the reddest point. "You've slept at her side and ridden with her across the Seven Kingdoms. Clearly you'll have sieved her a hundred times."

Albert looked at him.

"You don't know?" Mallory frowned. His eyes widened. "You're not telling me—?"

"I didn't," Albert said quietly.

"I don't believe it. Oh, surely not. Come on. . . ."

"I never sieved her."

"Huh." Mallory made a sound of soft astonishment. His white teeth flashed; he bit into the apple. "I did."

Albert sat there, watching him chew, hearing the wet, complacent crunching. He sat there feeling the fury rise inside him. All the talk of executions, all the talk of gallows, none of it had roused in him quite the rage and distress he experienced now, to know that Scarlett's mind had been harvested by this cool, indifferent youth in his overlarge coat. The buzzing in his head was back; he felt shooting pains along his temples. He knew that if he wasn't careful, the Fear would come and, being bottled up by the iron hat, rebound upon him. He needed to exorcise it another way.

Mallory's eyes were on him. "I do believe you're upset. Extraordinary! There's even less substance to you than I imagined."

"Dr. Calloway didn't think so," Albert said. "She was still trying to persuade me to join her the moment that she died."

Mallory took another bite; he paused. "What?" He removed the apple and wiped his chin.

"She was still trying to talk me into coming back with her. She didn't perish in the wilderness, you see. She caught up with us. I'm afraid she died."

"What?"

"Just that."

"You're making it up."

"Take this iron hat off. Read my mind."

He sat, smiling at the operative from across the bowl of fruit. Birds sang on trees outside the cell. Mallory stared at him. Albert saw the edges of the doily lift and ripple in currents of unseen force.

"I do believe you're upset," Albert said.

The apple fell to the floor.

Albert's chair flipped backward; a tremendous force caught him, rushed him straight back across the room, slamming his body into the wall. Air was driven from his lungs. He was halfway up, his trainers three feet above the floor. The pressure redoubled. His world went dark; sheets of silver black flexed before his eyes. They cleared away. Mallory was crossing the room, coat swirling. He was almost upon him. His mouth was tight and twisted; there were tears in his eyes.

"Say that again," Mallory said. "Say what you did."

"Killed her," Albert whispered. It was hard to speak. "Bashed her head in and lobbed her into the sea. One of her little black shoes came off her as she fell. I saw it spinning away into the froth and cloud. Ooh, does it bother you?" he said. "Does it make you sad?"

Mallory made a noise between his teeth. The unseen force grasped Albert. For a moment he was crushed back against the wall, so that he thought his bones would break. Then he was lifted away. Air closed in upon his head, which was slammed repeatedly into the stones. The iron hat offered limited protection. He felt the back of the helmet grinding against his skull. Something snapped; Albert wondered if it was his neck.

The pressure subsided. Albert hung limp and bloodied against the wall.

The operative wiped his mouth with his hand. His breathing was steadying; he had control over himself once more.

"I suppose I should thank you," he said. "I'd been feeling

a little conflicted about leaving you here to die. Now . . . not so much. I'd do the job myself, but it'll be better completed on a public stage. It's all about the optics, after all." He turned. The force on Albert abated; he fell sprawling to the floor. "The guards will be along to take you to your precious Scarlett," Mallory said as he walked away. "I'll see you in the square this evening."

"Looking forward to it. . . ." Albert scarcely got the words out. By the time he did so, the door had already closed.

With difficulty, he pushed himself upright. Everything ached, his ears rang, he was seeing double. It was hard to move; still, he managed enough to know that nothing was broken. Nothing except the back of the iron helmet, perhaps, which rattled whenever he turned his head.

18

"My advice is to drop the scowls, darlings. Try to look innocent and noble. That way you'll maintain your popularity right to the end." The festival's stage manager stepped back from Albert and Scarlett and looked at them critically. He was a middle-aged man, doughy-faced and gray beneath the eyes. He carried about him an air of mildly harassed exhaustion, which Albert felt was forgivable: the fellow must have been very busy for the past day or so. He wore a black T-shirt and dark green jeans; his fingers were flecked with the white face paint he had been daubing on Albert's and Scarlett's cheeks to make them stand out on the scaffold. A boy in an enormous checked cap was helping him, carrying a tray of paints and powders, rouges, brushes, and scraps of rag. Albert and Scarlett lay in a corner of the condemned cell, chained to punishment posts, side by side.

"I'm not sure we *can* drop the scowls," Albert said. "Scowls are part of our look. They'll expect it of us. Or at least of Scarlett. I can try the noble innocence thing, if you like."

"Sort it between yourselves." The festival manager threw his white rag into the tray. "Well, that's all I can do. I can't work miracles. We'll fix the rest with lighting."

"Going to be a real show, boss," the boy in the cap said smartly. He was a chipper lad.

"I hope so, Ernest, I hope so. Okay, do you two rogues have any questions before I go?"

Albert felt the man would be disappointed to get no questions; it would wound his professional pride. He looked to Scarlett, who sat with folded arms staring out into space. Her coat, boots, hat, and gun belt (without its gun) had been returned to her. Her face had been painted a livid, deathly white that contrasted shockingly with the strands of her deep red hair. Albert had arrived in her cell to find the man and boy already working to make her presentable. She had been silent for the most part during the operation, and she said nothing now. Clearly it was up to him.

"How long do we have?" he asked. "What's the procedure? I want to do this right."

"No worries on that score," the festival manager said. "It's easy as falling off a log. At nine tonight, you'll be led up to the platform, where you can glower appropriately at the crowd. There'll be objects thrown—beets, onions, rocks maybe—but the scaffold's high, and usually they'll miss you. After a few safety announcements, the Tainted will be brought in and ogled by the crowd, and then comes your big moment. More things happen *after* the hangings, of course, but there's no point you worrying about that. What time's it now, Ernest?"

"Six-thirty-four, sir."

"Smart as paint, Ernest is. No flies on Ernest. I expect the party's getting started already."

"There's a crowd gathering out there," Ernest agreed. "Got hot-dog stalls and skull-toss booths in full swing."

Scarlett stirred for the first time. "Yeah? I'm glad *someone's* doing well out of it."

"Also, the ballad pamphleteers are at it again," the festival manager said. "Don't miss a trick, they don't—do they, Ernest? They've rushed off a new printing."

"Yep. 'The Life and Death of the Notorious Scarlett and Browne.'" The boy pulled a crumpled pamphlet from his back pocket. "I've got it here. Look, there's a lovely woodcut of your double hanging on the front."

Albert blinked. "Wait. How can they have done a woodcut of *that*? We haven't even been killed yet!"

"It's a souvenir," the boy said. "An execution special. *Got* to be done in advance. They'll update it for future editions, but the main points will be accurate enough. Crowd, gallows, you two twitching in the spotlight . . . I mean, there's not a lot anyone can get wrong."

"You think? There might be all kinds of interesting details they'll miss out."

"Oh, they've got plenty of details already." The lad adjusted his cap. "Check out this official 'Eyewitness Ballad' on the back. It gives the account of Miss McCain's repentance and conversion, just before the trapdoor opens. It's very moving stuff. Listen:

"She begged forgiveness of the crowd,
She wept and wailed and prayed out loud.
They put the noose about her neck,
At which she blushed and shouted, 'Heck!
I've done you wrong! I admit it so!
My time is up. I have to go.'
And then she—"

"That's *definitely* nonsense," Albert interrupted. "Scarlett wouldn't beg forgiveness of anyone. Or blush. And she's never shouted 'Heck!' in her life. She shouts lots of other things, some of which would be much easier to rhyme. No, it's inaccurate twaddle. I hope the people realize it. They shouldn't waste their money."

"Well, this is only a sample of what they're selling out there," the festival manager said. "There's painted mugs, too, and commemorative plates, and little dolls on the ends of ropes for the kids to hang beside their beds. At the very least you've got to admire the merchants' initiative. Now, you'd better both rest up. You've got a busy evening."

He rapped on the door to summon the guards. The boy tipped his cap. They departed with the makeup trays. The door thunked shut behind them.

Albert and Scarlett sat in silence in the cell. Darkness was growing in the room, the light shrinking along with their allotted time. Scarlett's hat cast a shadow across her face.

"Good to be alone," Albert said finally.

"Yes."

"Bit of peace and quiet."

"Yep."

He rested his head back against the post. "They've done your face up nice, I must say."

She snorted. "As pathetic attempts to find a silver lining go, Albert," she growled, "that's pushing it, even for you. If my face is anything like yours, I look like a funfair skeleton, like I'm already laid out in the morgue." She stretched her legs as far as her shackles permitted and gave an extended sigh. "You know what upsets me most about all this?" she asked.

"The merchandising? The cheap figurines?"

She gazed at him. He caught the glinting of her eye.

"I do know, of course," Albert said. "Joe and Ettie."

"That's right." There was a pause. They sat there. "Obviously, us being brutally killed in front of a massive baying mob doesn't thrill me either," Scarlett said.

Albert nodded. "Yes. Maybe the two things stack up about the same. But don't worry. We've still got time."

"Time?"

"To get to Stow before noon tomorrow. That's still our deadline."

Scarlett said nothing, but the way she blew her cheeks out told him she was skeptical.

Albert sat quietly, looking at the single barred window in the opposite wall. The light was a rich, deep blue. It had been a beautiful afternoon. All day there'd not been a cloud in the sky. He thought of the fens around the Wolf's Head, the furred reed heads rippling there.

"Albert," Scarlett said.

"Yes?"

"It may not work out quite the way we want tonight. You do understand that, don't you?"

He looked at her.

"I know," he said.

"Good."

There was a gentle breeze outside, flowing across the Faith House complex. Every now and then it broke in through the window, carrying to Albert the whistles of the men finishing the gallows, the hubbub of the distant crowds, snatches of music, sweet fragrances of food and wine . . .

"I can smell hot dogs," he said.

"Yes." Scarlett's tone had changed. "Albert—"

"I could just do with a hot dog. Lots of onions on it. Maybe a bit of pickled cabbage. Not mustard, though. Wessex mustard makes me burp something rotten. . . . Sorry, did you say something?"

Scarlett wasn't looking at him—her head was tipped downward so he saw only the crown of her hat—but he was belatedly conscious of the weight in her voice, the sound of it lingering in space.

"Yes, I did say something. I said: 'Albert.' "

"Did you? Yes?"

"I want to tell you something."

"About hot dogs?"

"Shiva, *not* about hot dogs. Or mustard. Or pickled cabbage. No. Something else."

She was very still. Albert, looking at her, found that her

stillness had communicated itself without him being aware of it. He was conscious as never before of his own body, of the position in which he sat. His breathing had all at once become quite shallow. He didn't move.

"Okay," he said.

"Though you bloody well know most of it already," Scarlett said.

He said nothing. The wind through the window dropped. It was silent in the cell.

"Scarlett—" he began.

"I know you're desperate for me to tell you," she said. "Well, if I'm ever going to, now's probably the time. So let's do it. If you shut up and listen, I'll tell you about Thomas. I'll tell you what you want to know."

Outside the window, the blue of the sky deepened into dark. Shade filled the room. Albert listened. He didn't move.

He'd been wrong, incidentally. That was the first thing to say. All those months Albert had thought it would be easier hearing it in her own words. He'd held back from sieving her— even before she'd worn the band, even when she took off the hat—partly because he'd feared the distress he'd feel. Mainly out of respect for her privacy, too, of course, but also because he didn't want to be exposed to the memories directly. He'd thought that hearing it from her own lips would somehow make it more bearable than stealing it fully formed out of her mind.

It didn't work out like that. He'd been wrong. The funny thing about it was that it wasn't the memory itself that was so painful, it was the struggle she had to process it, to give it voice. She was a broken jug, pouring out the story. Not just broken. Jagged, with sharp edges. She cut herself in the pouring, and she cut him, too.

"I left him in the road," Scarlett said. "I left him in the road in the sunshine and went back in through the town gates to get my bag. And they caught me. They caught me, beat me, put me in the cage. They left me there all night. I told them about Thomas. It would have been okay if we'd been together. I asked them to bring him to me. But they didn't. They put me in the cage and left me. I stood there, calling for him. All that night I was calling, thinking he might hear. Toward dawn my voice gave out. I just sat quiet in the cage. A little later, a militiaman came with a tray of food. He told me what had happened. A group of citizens had taken the law into their own hands the night before. They'd taken Thomas away to the iron posts beyond the crop fields, chained him up, and left him."

"Why?" Albert scarcely recognized his own voice. "Why do that to a child?"

"His hair color? His eyes? Something he said? Because he was small and irritating and in the way? I don't know, Albert. I just don't know." She was almost entirely shadowed now, except for where a pale glow from the window cut a crescent slice across her face. "Anyway, the militiaman opened the door to give me the food. That was a mistake on his part.

I knocked him down, took his gun and knife, ran away over the yard. It was early yet. The town gates were still closed. A man tried to grab me. I shot him with the gun. I climbed over the wall. I ran across the fields, straight through the ripened wheat. A farmer tried to stop me. I don't know who he was. He maybe had nothing to do with Thomas, nothing to do with any of it. I shot him, too. I got to the posts. The posts at the end of the fields. The people of that town, they had three posts there, two big ones, with the chains high up, you know, and a smaller one, with the chains low down. And the manacles on that smaller one . . ."

He waited.

"He wasn't there," Scarlett said. "Thomas wasn't there. The manacles were empty. While they'd kept me in that cage, something had come out of the forest and taken him away." She cleared her throat. "That's it," she said. "That's all there is."

No movement. He owed her his stillness, his numbness; it was all he had.

A peal of laughter came from far off through the window. Someone was beating a drum to welcome the coming night.

"You never know," he said at last. "I suppose there's a possibility that . . ." His voice trailed off.

"No." The hat moved. She was looking at him from the darkness. "Don't say it. Don't you dare say it. There's no way, and he isn't."

"No."

"The manacles hadn't been unlocked. They were still

closed. A beast came. That's it." She blew strands of hair away from her face. "After that," she said, "I don't know what happened. I think I wandered in the woods for a while, looking for my brother. A madness had come over me. I was like a beast myself. I threw myself down holes, dived through thornbushes, waded in streams, crawled over jagged rocks. . . . I found nothing. I lost my boots, my clothes were torn, I was a thing of blood and mud and rags. I went from village to village, town to town, fighting, stealing. I remember little of it. In the end, I came to Stow, and there the Brothers of the Hand found me. They took me in and saved my life, Albert. Say what you like about Soames and Teach, they saved my life back then. They gave me strength and purpose. It carried me onward for a time." She shrugged; her chains clinked in the dark. "And now I'm here."

"I wish that I'd been there for you," Albert said.

"What *I* wish," Scarlett said, "is that I'd got a rifle and gone back to that town and killed them all. The cowards who took my little brother."

They sat there.

"Thank you for telling me," Albert said.

"Sure."

"I appreciate it."

"Yeah. As I say, you knew most of it already. About me losing Thomas. You knew."

Albert sighed. He craned his head to look at her. How small she looked, crumpled in the corner of the room. How little there was of her. Without the grin, the gun, the swagger . . .

without that great spreading wilderness all around her to stride through and expand into, how small she was, in the end. He adjusted his position under the chains.

"No," he said softly. "I didn't know. Not really. You have to believe me. The things I picked up . . . it was just . . . random images, scraps of emotion . . . like photographs floating in the dark. I never sieved you for them, I promise. I just picked them up as they drifted by. It's nothing *like* the same as hearing it from you. This was real. This was me hearing it for the first time."

He waited. "Well," she said, at last. "Whatever."

"Scarlett."

"What?"

"You *will* find a way to get us out of here. You know that, don't you? When you put your mind to it, you always do."

"Yeah. Sure."

Albert's head hurt. It felt like his skin was pulsing against the inside of the hateful iron helmet. He could feel the anger building in him, anger for the girl Scarlett had once been, anger for the woman she was now. Speaking was something to distract himself, to break the momentum of his rage. "Another thing," he said. "It's not your fault. The guilt falls squarely on that Mentor of the town, the people who locked you up, the ones who . . . who took your brother from you."

The laugh she gave was not pleasant. "Oh, the guilt falls everywhere, like the burning rain. It falls on everyone. It sure as hell falls on me."

"You were a child, like Thomas," Albert said.

"That's no excuse."

"They stopped you from going back."

"Because I'd left him."

"They had to lock you up to stop you, and even *that* didn't work. You broke out! You fought them off! You went back—"

"I left him," she said. "I *left* him on the roadside, and I went around the corner and I never saw him again."

"You cannot blame yourself."

Chains rattled furiously. It was like she fought herself, alone in the darkness. "Albert, that's all that's left for me *to* do."

19

Even deep inside the building, you could hear the roaring of the crowd. It penetrated the layers of brick and stone, reaching the underground corridors by which they approached the square. It was a constant hum, deceptively soft and almost swallowed by the clatter of the guards who marched them to execution. But Scarlett knew that when they came into the open air at last—when they stepped out beneath the scaffold—the noise would hit them like a truck. It would be such a sound as to make the head spin and the ears bleed. It would not be easy to think or remain calm.

Two guards ahead, two behind, two on either side: the men seemed to have been chosen for their size, stockiness, and general ability to block out light. They kept so near to her that Scarlett could not move an inch independently in any direction, but only shuffle forward directly behind Albert. She looked at her partner's stiffly bobbing skullcap, his defiantly upright posture as he walked toward his fate. Poor Albert! If the Fear came now, his powers would be bottled by the iron hat and only give him extra pain.

No one spoke. The guards were coolly focused; the ritual

had begun to which there was only one conclusion. They proceeded in silence till they came to a flight of stone steps leading up into the dark. Here the phalanx halted. All at once the noise of the crowd swelled above them; a reddish glow spilled down the steps and bathed them all like blood.

"This is exciting," Albert said.

A door closed; the light cut off. The festival stage manager pattered fussily down to meet them, a clipboard in his hand.

"What time do you call this?" he said. "It's a poor show being late for your own hanging."

Scarlett glowered at him from behind the guards. "We'll try to do better next time."

"They're just starting the dancing now. But the crowd is growing boisterous. I need to get you out there before they rush the stage." He took an enormous watch from the pocket of his jeans. "*Where* is the other? I hope there has been no hitch! I'd better go and see. . . ."

He bustled away along a passage. The guards remained in position around Scarlett but perhaps relaxed a little, giving her more space. Albert turned to look at her.

"What 'other'?" he said. "Who's he talking about?"

"No idea. I thought it was just us." She eyed him. "You okay, Albert?"

"Couldn't be better, considering the circumstances." He seemed calm enough. "You?"

"Peachy."

"I saw you were doing a bit of meditating, back there in the cell."

"Yeah. It helped. Though it would have been better with the prayer mat."

"I've always wondered about your meditating. It seems a curious art to have learned from Soames and Teach. I can well believe they taught you about robbing banks, cutting throats, shooting innocent bystanders. . . . But *meditating?*" He shrugged. "I guess it's a rounded skill set, if nothing else."

Scarlett snorted. "Soames and Teach didn't give me the mat. Someone else did."

"Someone else! Who? A burglar? A swindler? A passing hoodlum? I'm all ears."

"Not *all* my previous acquaintances happen to be criminals," Scarlett said. "I'll tell you some other time, maybe when we're *not* standing in the shadow of the scaffold."

"You're right. Perhaps it's not the moment." Albert moved nearer. "Listen, before things get crazy: keep an eye out for the mine truck when we're aboveground. I was just about conscious when Mallory parked us the other day. He's left it somewhere outside this building. There's a thin minaret close by."

"A minaret . . . ," Scarlett said slowly. "Sure."

"We'll need the truck to get to Stow, of course—and it'll help us save Joe and Ettie. Soames won't bring them out unless he thinks we've got the goods. It *has* to be part of our plan."

Scarlett gazed at him. "Yeah. The truck . . . I'll keep watch for it. No problem."

Well, it was better like this, of course. The sheer force of his daft and mindless optimism was keeping Albert safe, insulated from what was about to happen. Scarlett was glad of that; she hoped it would carry him through, right to the end. And as for her . . . strange to say it, but she *also* felt okay. A weight had been removed from her when she'd told him about Thomas. It felt good to have shared the knowledge of her little brother. It made his memory stronger. For so long she had been the one person in the world who remembered his existence. Now, just for a short while, there would be two.

A flurry in the corridor. The guards swung aside as if on hinges, revealing the festival manager returning. Trotting ahead of him was a tiny person with cropped gray hair, a coat of black leather, and boots inlaid with silver filigree. Scarlett blinked in surprise. Beside the hulking militiamen the merchant-trader Sal Qin seemed even smaller than when they'd seen her at the Wolf's Head Inn. Events had diminished her. The gleam in her eyes had dulled; her wrinkled face was etched with care. Her tiny hands were tied. She was roughly shoved alongside Scarlett and Albert, and the guards closed up around them.

"Sal!" Albert cried. "What are *you* doing here?"

The lines around the merchant's mouth flexed sourly. "Well, they're not putting me in the balcony seats, if that's what you mean. They're hanging me, too."

Scarlett frowned. "What for? Not our Ashtown theft?"

"The very same. That horrible youth with the oversize coat arrested me, and here I am."

Albert's eyes had widened. "I'm so sorry! It doesn't seem quite fair."

"Tell me about it," Sal Qin said. "All I did was make an

innocent suggestion in a pub. As far as I was concerned, you two bozos didn't even agree to do the job!"

"Things got complicated," Scarlett said. "If it's any consolation, we *did* end up stealing a truckload of good stuff, which shows your original idea was sound."

Sal Qin scowled. "Yes, what comfort that gives me. It makes my suffering worthwhile. Now I'm having my neck stretched for my trouble, and the worst of it is that no one's even going to care. That flouncing manager assures me I'm bottom of the bill. While I'm out there taking my last breath, everyone else will be watching you."

"Don't worry, Sal." Albert leaned in; he spoke in a conspiratorial whisper. "All is not lost. Why? Because you are in the company of the legendary Scarlett McCain! She is a master of strategy and guile! Even now, she is doubtless putting the finishing touches to a clever escape plan. Look at her face behind the greasepaint—see the raw cunning in her eyes!"

The merchant-trader looked at Scarlett skeptically. Scarlett knew full well that her face displayed nothing but hopeless fury, but she was saved from interrogation by a whistle from above. The festival manager beckoned; the guards began to move. Scarlett, Albert, and Sal Qin were bundled up the stairs. For a few seconds they stumbled on in darkness, with the noise of the crowd reverberating like the growling of a beast. Ahead of them, red cracks marked the outline of a door. It swung open. There was a swirl of smoke, the touch of chilly air. A gale of sound buffeted Scarlett's ears. She saw Albert and Sal Qin stagger back as if on the deck of a listing ship. She steadied her own legs, clenched her jaw—no, she would *not* be daunted. A moment later the stairs disgorged them. They were vomited out upon a stage.

Scarlett had once spent time in Milton Keynes, assessing the chances of doing a robbery there. In the end, she had decided against it: the place was too well defended, with sharp-eyed militiamen and Faith House operatives loitering on every corner. But she had taken the opportunity to visit the shrines and precincts of the Sacred Compound, marveling (despite herself) at their size and wealth and splendor. Perhaps she had walked through this very plaza, boots tapping across its concrete emptiness. . . . If so, it was difficult to link the memory with what confronted her now. A violently congested mass of color, noise, and movement spread out before her like an inland sea. Faith House buildings rose like illuminated cliff faces on every side. Strings of colored lights looped between the columns of the porticos and zigzagged twinkling over pediments. The sky was flat and black, but the ground flickered as if with starlight, the dazzle cast by lanterns hanging on innumerable poles. All across the plaza, open-sided tents glowed like fireflies, housing entertainments and distractions of every variety—merchandise stalls and cafés, inns and pop-up slave-booths, eating joints and sweetmeat bars. And in between them all, darkly teeming, surged the crowds of the Faith House capital, enjoying the pleasures of execution day.

The platform on which Scarlett stood was at the edge of the square, behind one of the alehouse tents, in an unglamorous area of beer kegs and rubbish bags. But a raised gantry ran away from it toward a three-part stage, set front and center of the main Faith House wall. Here was the focus of the festival: a slim white gallows of extravagant height, soaring higher than the portico of the building behind. Scarlett had to admit that the carpenters had done a decent job. The great squared post rose from the middle of the platform. From its top jutted an enormous cantilevered beam, ending in a T-shaped bar. Over this looped two strong white ropes, terminating in spotlit nooses. Right now the nooses were low, at a convenient neck height, but the far ends of the ropes were anchored to iron hoops on the platform floor. Battalions of sturdy men stood ready to hoist them high, so Scarlett's and Albert's final moments would be visible across the square.

And this was only the centerpiece. There was a smaller scaffold to the left of the main stage with a trapdoor beneath the noose, presumably for Sal Qin. On the right, an immense pyre of brushwood burned in a circular metal pit, casting a baleful glow over proceedings. High above it, projecting springboards showed where the captive Tainted would be propelled out into the flames. Farther off was a stage with a company of dancers undulating under spotlights. Scarlett tugged reflexively at the bonds around her wrists. She noticed Albert looking at her, all staring eyes and stark white face paint. She smiled grimly. "The kid in the cap was right," she said. "This *is* a real show."

Their arrival had been spotted. Nearby sections of the audience gave a frenzied cheer and raised their drinks in ironic salute. The movement rippled away into the dark. In a cordoned area beside the stage, seminaked men with drums began to pound out a dramatic beat. The dancers set to with renewed vigor. Flames rose from the firepit; far off across the square, an open-backed lorry bearing something beneath an enormous tarpaulin began to inch its way toward the stages. The crowd parted, screaming, cheering. The platform shook.

"All this effort is for us?" Albert shook his head in wonder. "They really shouldn't have."

Sal Qin glanced at Scarlett. "How's your clever escape plan coming along?"

"Working on it."

"Working on it fairly urgently, I hope."

In fact, Scarlett could see only one possible line of attack. Her wrists were bound in front of her, but her fingers were free. There were a dozen men, armed with revolvers and truncheons, waiting to escort her along the gantry. . . . If she was fast, she might kick one or two off, might wrest a gun from another. Then things would get interesting, if only briefly. They would still be surrounded by a thousand enemies, still be in the center of the square . . .

It was pathetic and suicidal, but it was the bare bones of a plan. And it was all she had.

A swift, lithe shape pattered up the steps onto the platform, his long coat trailing behind him. Mallory, the operative, had joined them: dark and handsome, smiling. He shook hands with the festival manager, spoke a few words to him. Then he looked at Scarlett, who desperately tried to think of something, anything, unrelated to what was actually on her mind.

Mallory grinned. "Good job I took that nasty iron band out of your hat," he said. He nodded at the captain of the guards. "Keep the girl ahead of you during your walk across to the scaffold. Have a gun pointed directly at her back. Don't let her get *anywhere* near your men. You understand me?"

"Yes, sir. The boy too?"

The operative patted Albert's iron cap fondly. "No. She's the dangerous one." His eyes widened as he met Scarlett's gaze again. "Well, *that's* not a very nice thought, Miss McCain. It's not hygienic, and it's a waste of a good truncheon. Plus, would I *really* bend that way?"

"I think you might," Scarlett said. "One day I intend to find out."

The operative chuckled. "Looking forward to it. All right, Sergeant, we'll move across as soon as the Tainted are in position. Any problems, I'll be there too."

The drums beat on. The lorry had reached the far platform, beside the firepit. Mentors climbed aboard and, in a flurry of practiced movements, pulled the tarpaulin aside. Three wheeled cages were revealed: in each a thin white form was crouching. The trilling of the crowd reached a new pitch of hatred and revulsion.

The festival manager clicked his fingers. The guards moved. Scarlett felt a gun jabbed against her kidneys. They set off along the gantry toward the scaffold. They went in semidarkness; spotlights from the Faith House roofs were trained elsewhere.

"I must say," Albert said, "this is all very nicely choreographed. Everyone's busy looking at those dancers now. What's going on there?"

On the separate platform beyond the Tainted's cages, a score of performers in implausibly colorful costumes were cavorting against a backdrop of badly painted cardboard buildings.

Scarlett groaned. "As if the evening wasn't bad enough. It's a Faith House Mystery Play."

"Ooh, that sounds interesting."

"Well, it bloody isn't. It tells the story of how the Mentors saved the Surviving Towns. You watch—there'll be a naff Cataclysm any second."

Right on cue, fireworks went off at the back of the far stage. The crowd crowed in delight. The cardboard buildings toppled. Papier-mâché rocks came hurtling from the wings. The performers cowered and shrank in cartoonish terror. Yeah, it would be the usual—a stylized rendition of the Cataclysm, followed by the chaos of the Great Dying and the Frontier Wars, with dancers starving, fighting, and perishing theatrically in all directions. Soon, no doubt, men in overtight white leotards would lope onstage to depict the emergence of the Tainted in the Wastes, followed by the first Faith House missionaries, bringing mustachioed justice to the fractured Towns. Scarlett looked away. She'd seen Mystery

Plays performed a dozen times, and they didn't appeal to her even when she *wasn't* walking to the gallows.

She turned inward on herself, breathed slowly, just as if she was on the mat again. She did her best to shut off the noise and chaos, focusing instead on the essential things, the threads by which their lives hung suspended. Separating them, arranging them. Looking for a way out, for a final opportunity . . .

But she could see nothing that could help her. Just the scaffold, with its death-white double branch, framed against the black of the sky. Just her bound hands. Just the armed guards; the operative; the vast buildings blocking any hope of escape . . . And all around, far as the eye could see, the thrumming malevolence of the crowd.

She could not run. If she tried to jump off the stage, the mob would tear her to pieces or knock her down and drag her to the gallows. A scissor kick to the stomach of the nearest guard would end with the same result.

Was there a way?

She couldn't think of one.

They passed the smaller gallows, where Sal Qin was ushered to the side. A gaunt-faced gentleman in a gray suit stepped forward. It was the man who had taken Scarlett's measurements in her cell. With a series of polite and attentive gestures, he arranged Sal Qin upon the trapdoor, then hurried across to ready Albert and Scarlett too.

"There and there, if you will. . . ." He pointed to two enormous blue crosses taped to the floor. "Stand with the ropes in front of you. . . . That's right. I'll have to take your hat off in a moment, miss. I'll be sure to do that at the last minute. Sir, your iron cap remains on throughout, of course. You'll see I have made allowances for that in the diameter of noose. . . ."

He chattered on. The festival manager was fussing around as well. The operative had wandered past to the edge of the platform, where he waited in an attitude of polite interest. Scarlett stood as directed, looking through the oval of dull white rope. She looked aside at Albert. Something of the magnitude of the moment had at last penetrated his defenses. He was gazing all around him. His shoulders had dropped; his face was sad.

"Hey, Scarlett," he said.

"Hey."

"I never thought I would see something like this."

"Try not to worry. It'll be quick—that's all that can be said for it."

"Look at poor Sal! Look at us! Look at those three Tainted, too. . . . See how they shrink from the flames, how they crouch at bay in their cages. They surely have enough intelligence to understand their coming fate! I am sorry even for them."

Scarlett sighed. "Well, that's maybe going a *bit* far. But I'm glad you're still *you*, Albert. Stupid, softheaded, kind . . ."

"But I'm not, Scarlett. I'm not. I'm *none* of those things. I'm angry right now. Really angry. I don't think I've ever *been* so mad."

"I'm sorry to hear it."

"I'm shaking with it. The pain in my head . . . the Fear . . . I'm finding it hard to breathe."

She looked at the iron hat that trapped his powers in. It was a pity he couldn't have harnessed that anger long ago. . . . "Try to ignore it," she said. "It'll all be over soon."

Albert said something else, but his words were lost to her: at that moment, the Mystery Play on the far stage came to its conclusion. The old-time Mentors onstage ended their triumphant dance, cutout towns sprang up from the floor, the drums built to a thrashing frenzy. The lights went out. The drums stopped. The square floated darkly on a wave of ex-pectant crowd noise, lit by the flames of the firepit and the starlight of the dotted lanterns.

Then brightness. Spotlights strafed the platform, illu-minated the outlaws Scarlett and Browne standing at their nooses. A tsunami of sound rose and struck them. Scarlett looked below at the baying faces of the mob. She breathed in the screams, the shouts, the blood lust and expectation. Objects were thrown onto the stage. Something hit the side of her face.

"Did you hear that, Albert?" she called. "I swear there were a few cheers. One or two of them must like us!"

He did not answer. He was stiff and still, his head down, all fight gone out of him. As she watched, he started to shake his head mindlessly from side to side. It was a sorry thing to see, especially with the horrible iron hat. She looked away. The men on the drums had begun the final beat—slow, rhythmic, quiet at first, but gradually escalating. The noise of the crowd subsided. This was it, the best bit: the climax of the night.

The polite executioner shimmied forward. He approached Sal Qin, standing like a child in her leather coat and silvered boots. How small she was. How immense the rope looked as it was placed around her neck.

Now to Scarlett. Gently, almost apologetically, he removed her hat. The noose was put round her neck, to a roar of approval from the crowd.

The man flitted away; from the corner of her eye, Scarlett could see him attending to Albert too. Poor Albert, still shaking his head furiously, shaking like a dog. People in the crowd were laughing at him. Things were thrown. She saw Albert stagger; he did not look up.

Scarlett gritted her teeth, looked out into the dark, away from the executioner at his podium, away from the man at Sal Qin's trapdoor lever; away from the three strong men beside both her and Albert, their hands tightening on the ropes. Yes, they were readying themselves now. She felt the noose take the strain.

She let the whole thing fade out—the noose, Albert, Qin, the animalistic crowd. She took a deep breath. It was fine. It was good. She'd always lived with the knowledge that one day her single great mistake would be unlived, that she would loop back round and out of the town gates and back across the drawbridge with their flecks of silent fish, back to the tall, dark pine tree and the sunlit road, with her brother waiting for her there. It was good. It was going to happen now. It was the way it had to be. Already she could see the sunshine on the stones and grass, the heat haze on the path. And on the path . . .

She smiled out into the light.

A thump. Something rolled onto the platform and struck against her feet.

The road was empty; the sun went out. Scarlett looked down at her boots.

An iron hat lay spinning there.

She turned. Time stopped. Albert was standing at his noose, his head bowed. He had finished his shaking. He was very still, taut as a drum. His hair, freed from the hat, spiked outward like a jet-black star.

There was an expression on his face she had never seen before.

He lifted his head. The cords tying his hands burst open.

He raised his arms.

20

lbert let it come. There was no holding back this time. *Scarlett, her brother, Sal Qin, even the poor trapped Tainted:* he held their suffering in his mind and let it fuel his rage.

There was no thought for himself, no thought for the consequences. Why bother? They were all going to die anyway. That was the beauty of it. Everything was simple when you stood at a rope's end. And the iron hat was there to help him. It kept the pressure bottled up till the very last moment, when he finally shook it loose, maximizing the buildup of the Fear.

It happened so fast that he scarcely knew what he was doing. But he didn't care. He let the power burst out in all directions, sweeping away everything in its path.

The cords on his hands broke first; then the bodies of those nearest to him. The gentleman in the gray suit was blown away, his bent finger still discreetly raised to give the signal for the hanging. The festival manager was blasted out across the crowd, still holding his precious clipboard. The guards who had held his rope were gone like leaves in a storm. Even the operative, Mallory, standing louchely at the corner of the stage, barely had time to raise a hand before the force hit him, carried him off with his coat draped over his head. He passed through the flames of the firepit and struck the side of the lorry beyond, leaving a scorched indentation. Burning, he spun away across the square.

Albert didn't notice any of this. He stood with his arms out, fists clenched, letting his fury free.

It smashed against the mighty gallows post at his back, cracking it at the base.

It bent the fire in the pit, arching the flames out and over the screaming crowd.

It broke upon the cages of the Tainted, sending them skidding across the platform.

Albert stood there, sightless, uncaring, the power flooding out of him.

The cages toppled over the edge of the platform, plunged down, and smashed against the concrete of the square. The bars split open: thin white shapes sprang forth. Howling, they leaped over the heads of the nearest onlookers and vaulted far into the crowd. And now the crowd surged outward. Some people were on fire; others simply fled—the terror of the Tainted was on them. The frenzied tide overran the nearest stalls, smashing them down, sending stoves and firepits tumbling. Lanterns struck canvas. Fires licked up. The tents themselves were aflame.

The platform cracked beneath Albert's feet. Behind him,

the scaffold post broke like a rotten twig. It toppled backward, crashing against the concrete pediment of the Faith House building and wedging at an angle there. A rope from the cross-beams whipped up and out, flexing like a cow tail. Its noose caught the side of Albert's face, stinging him into sudden consciousness. He flinched at the pain, swaying where he stood. The flow of power was tripped. The force inside him died.

Lights revolved before his eyes. He was empty, spent. . . . All at once, he realized that he was kneeling on the ground, and that someone was swearing loudly and colorfully, close by.

With an effort of will, he forced himself to concentrate. The platform was torn in two. The main gallows post hung tilted behind him, stretching up into the dark. The other, lesser scaffold was gone. Below the stage was an expanding ring of emptiness—laced with burning stalls and bodies—and beyond it, still retreating, the panicked, shrieking crowd.

The swearing intensified; a person clambered up over the shattered edge of the platform.

"Scarlett?"

A small body levered herself into view. Gray hair, silvered boots. It was Sal Qin.

"Now I *know* why I tried to hire you," she said. "I've got to admit that was spectacular, though you nearly broke my neck more quickly than the noose would have done. Luckily, all my ropes snapped when you shot me halfway across the square."

Albert tried to focus on her. "Where's Scarlett?"

"Anglia? Wessex? The Burning Lands? You blew us all to hell."

Sharp anxiety washed across his confusion. "That's not good. . . . We need to find her."

"What we *need* is to get out of here." Sal Qin darted across the platform, where random items—shoes, knives, truncheons, guns, bowler hats—marked where the guards had once been standing. She picked up several weapons, offered one to Albert. "Pistol?"

"Not for me, thanks."

"No, I don't suppose you've much call for one."

A faint voice issued from above. "When you've finished yapping, could someone possibly get me down from here . . . ?"

Albert looked up; he followed the line of the toppled gallows. Scarlett was hanging by her legs and fingernails halfway along, twenty feet above the plaza floor. Her hands were tied; she could not grapple the post to get safe purchase. The gallows rope dangled in loops beneath her streaming hair—and the noose was still round her neck.

Albert gave a mew of alarm. He tried to stand, but his body felt unresponsive, as if it belonged to another. "I'm coming!" he called. "Just give me a minute! I'm a little woozy."

"I don't *have* a minute. I'm slipping."

"Hang on!" He forced himself upright, began a valiant hobble toward the post.

"I'll go," Sal Qin said.

Albert hesitated. "Are you sure?"

"Of course."

"That's very kind."

Scarlett slipped slightly. Her neck and voice were now

noticeably constricted. "Either of you," she croaked. "Any order. In your own time."

"Allow me." Sal Qin put a knife between her teeth. She ran to the tilted post; with unexpected dexterity, she scampered up. Reaching Scarlett, she sliced first through the rope that bound her neck, then the cords that tied her wrists. She retreated. Scarlett grappled at the post, dangled securely by her hands and ankles; in moments she had skittered to a safer level and dropped back to the platform.

"Thanks, Sal." Scarlett took possession of two pistols and a knife and tucked them into her belt. "You too, Albert." She pushed a strand of hair out of her face, smudging her white face paint, and looked out into the fire and the dark. "Right. What are our options?"

Sal Qin was checking the cartridges in her gun. "A heroic last stand."

"Stuff that. We can do better. Albert—how are you feeling?"

Albert had been surveying the square. Waves of humanity sloshed against the buildings at its perimeter, seeking exit through the gates. He saw white shapes racing through the shadows, jumping at people, bringing them down. Desperate shots were fired. The Tainted dodged and leaped and sprang. There was evidence of militia activity coming in their direction too—ranks of bowler-hatted figures stealing toward them between the burning tents and tilted lanterns. One group had come up the underground steps from the Faith House and was assembling at the end of the gantry.

"I'm getting stronger with every moment," he said. "But we're trapped."

"No, we aren't. Not yet." Scarlett raised a gun and shot a militiawoman who had ventured out onto the stage; the woman spun on her heels and dropped away from view. "We need to move," she added. "It's not just the militia we've got to worry about now."

Albert followed her gaze. He knew what he would see. Yes: far out beyond the roaring firepit and the tents, a thin youth in a burning coat was limping toward them.

"He mustn't get near us," Albert said.

Sal Qin grimaced. "I know. But I don't see a route out."

"You've already shown us the way," Scarlett said. She pointed at the toppled gallows. "We go up there and onto the roofs. Sal—you first. I'll help Albert. He's weak, not to mention naturally cack-footed. When you get to the top, give us covering fire."

Exactly what Sal Qin's past consisted of Albert had no idea—but it was clear she was no stranger to tight situations. She didn't discuss, she didn't argue. She simply acted; with a skip and a bound she was away and running up the post. Now it was Albert's turn. He wasn't about to discuss or argue either—but that was about as far as his enthusiasm went. He sighed, stepped onto the post, held out his arms, looked somewhere vaguely in front of him, and began walking.

"Well done, Albert." Scarlett's voice came from close behind him. "I'm right here. Just relax now. Ignore the shooting."

Which was pretty much Albert's motto at the best of times. Perhaps it benefited him that his outburst of the Fear had left him almost comatose, since his terror was dulled almost to nothing. Yes, the militiamen on the ground were already firing. Yes, the post was steep, slippery, and not nearly as wide as he would have liked. Yes, the drop below would have broken all his bones. . . . Somehow, he kept it all at one remove. He kept on climbing.

Ahead of him, Sal Qin had reached the roof of the portico; she hopped up onto the triangular stone pediment and disappeared from view. Instants later, her gun appeared at a cornice and began firing down. Bullets from the militia passed in front of Albert's nose and thumped into the wood of the post. From the sounds at his ear, he could tell Scarlett was shooting back; wild vibrations told him she was probably doing little jumps on the beam, adjusting position as she coolly picked off their enemies, one by one.

He paid no attention, placed one foot after another, trudged onward. . . . Surprisingly quickly, he found himself at the place where the gallows crossbeam wedged against the side of the pediment, and he was able to scramble over the concrete and fall onto the small tiled roof of the portico. He righted himself quickly, peered back the way he had come.

Here came Scarlett, walking backward, shooting with both hands. She was farther down than he'd thought, a black silhouette framed against the flames of the firepit. Sparks of gunfire perforated the night. The militiamen were advancing across the square. He glimpsed bodies lying on the platforms, wounded men crawling for shelter . . .

And a slim young man in a smoldering coat, almost directly below.

There was a wrenching, grinding squeal. The gallows post began to shift along the pediment. Something was driving sharply against it—a vast force shoving it aside.

Albert reached out and over the cornice. "Scarlett! Quickly!"

She'd felt the movement, she knew the danger. She spun on the post, sprang upward with two mighty leaps. . . . The post sheered sideways, out from under her boots. She gave a final flailing jump, jacket flapping, hand outstretched—

Albert grabbed hold of her wrist. With a tremendous effort, he took the strain, hauled her up and over the concrete sill. The post tore free of the pediment. It crashed away. Scarlett landed awkwardly on top of him. She was heavier than expected. Her hair fell soft against his face.

In an instant she was up again and dragging him to his feet. "You all right, Albert?"

"Yes. Well, I may have grazed my knee. . . ."

"We can amputate it later. We can't stay here—Mallory might pull this whole portico down. Sal, we need to get up onto the main roof. Come on, Albert—it's only a tiny climb."

For once she wasn't fibbing. The base of the main Faith House roof was not much higher than the ledge on which they stood. There were joints between the blocks, a drain-pipe, and windowsills to aid them. They were beyond shooting distance from below. With such factors in his favor, Albert managed the ascent quite easily, only treading on Sal Qin's fingers once, only kicking Scarlett in the eye twice; in short order he reached the tiles.

As he did so, he chanced to look away, along the line of the building. They weren't the only ones seeking to escape the square. On the next wing along, a thin white figure was also climbing, teeth bared, nails stabbing at the stones. Its hair whipped white against the moon. It glanced across: for a moment Albert felt the weird brush of its gaze upon him. Then it vaulted over the roof crest and disappeared. Now Albert felt something else—Scarlett prodding his backside from below. He levered himself up and onto the roof and left the chaos of the square behind.

The Faith House was vast and its roof system intricate, a fact that helped their chances of evading detection. It also complicated their chances of locating the mine truck. For many minutes they negotiated a shadowed landscape of tilted planes, hunting for a thin minaret similar to the one Albert remembered seeing on his arrival. They scrabbled up and down steep tiled surfaces, shuffled along narrow crests, bypassed ranks of chimneys, belvederes, and towers. They crossed covered walkways, looked down into silent streets, cul-de-sacs, and lanes. They heard whistles, howls, and gunshots too, but the noises seemed increasingly remote. Steadily, the noise of bedlam waned. Only once was there an alarm. Sal Qin startled a flock of roosting birds, which rose from the roof as if the tiles themselves had taken wing. Scarlett immediately led them in a different direction.

"Got to be careful," she said. "Mallory will be watching out for signs. He'll see."

They came at last to an area of flat roof in a remote portion of the complex. A single minaret sprouted darkly above them. There was a yard below it, surrounded by tall buildings, black windows, and silence. A humpbacked shape sat along one side of the yard, wreathed in shadow, its gun turret pointing out at nothing.

Albert nudged Scarlett. "See that? The truck!"

"I see it."

"It looks quiet."

"Yeah. Very tempting." She tapped her fingers on the tiles. "Too tempting?"

"No."

"Okay. We'll rest a moment, then try to climb down."

They crouched between the chimneys. Albert sat with his back against the brickwork. The Fear had left him feeling faint and nauseous, but his strength was returning. Columns of white smoke rose behind them; they could just hear distant shots and screams.

"Sounds like the Tainted are still on the rampage," Sal Qin said. "Should keep the Mentors busy for a while." She skittered up the nearest roof slope and peered over the top.

"For an honest merchant-trader, Sal seems very good at this sort of stuff," Albert said.

Scarlett was checking one of her pistols. Her face was an inhuman mix of smeared white face paint, gunpowder, and blood. Albert supposed his own was much the same.

"Sal's done well," she said. "But you did great. Shaking off the iron hat, I mean. Bit last-minute, arguably, but still . . ."

He nodded. "I had to wait until I was really upset."

"Did you? Truly?" She shrugged. "I think you do yourself an injustice. I think it's there for you whenever you want, whenever you need it." She put the gun away, pulled out the other. "But we won't argue. How did you know that you could get the hat off, though? You just discover it was loose?"

"No, it'd been broken for a while. It was our friend the operative, actually. Earlier today. When I had an interview with him."

That made her pause. "What?" she said. "*Mallory* did it? Deliberately?"

"No. I'm afraid I goaded him into it. I was rude, unfeeling, and brutally confrontational. Basically, I just imagined I was you. And it had the right result. He got very cross and gave me what I believe is termed a thorough roughhousing." Albert indulged in a small, cracked chuckle. "And the back of the hat split when he drove my head repeatedly against the wall. I knew then I could probably get it free."

He watched as Scarlett assimilated this; he waited for her congratulations.

"Hold on," she said. "Let me get this straight. So you knew

you could take the hat off all this while . . . you *knew* we could escape . . . and you didn't bother to tell me?"

He grinned affirmingly at her. "Yes. And a good thing, too. I managed to keep things believable."

"Believable? You little bore-worm! I thought we were going to die, right up to when the rope tightened round my neck!"

"I had to," Albert said. "Don't you see? Mallory would have read your mind. If you'd known about the hat at any stage over the past three hours, he'd have known about it too! Then he'd have had it mended, we'd all have been hanged, and you'd have been left feeling so *awful* about yourself." He paused. "Though not necessarily in that order."

"Funnily enough, I've actually been feeling pretty awful *anyway*," Scarlett growled, "thinking this was going to be the end. I was so sure of it that I—" Her face dropped in sudden realization. "I told you about Thomas and everything."

There was a silence. "Please, Scarlett, don't regret that," Albert said. "Don't regret that, whatever else you feel."

She shook her head, said nothing.

"Scarlett . . . ?" He reached out, touched her hand.

Scarlett's eyes narrowed, her face hardened. She raised her gun, pointed it in his direction, and without words pulled the trigger. The noise of the shot was deafening; Albert staggered back in shock, flailing his arms, clawing at his chest.

"Scarlett—! *Why . . . ?*"

"Oh, for Shiva's sake. You're not hurt." She rolled her eyes and pointed past him. "*That's* why."

Albert turned and looked. Where the Tainted had come

from he couldn't say. He had heard nothing. Perhaps it had stolen up from the wall below. Now it stood crouching on the edge of the roof, a few feet behind him. Moonlight shimmered on its bone-white skin, on its yellow teeth, on the blood flowering around the bullet hole just below its shoulder. It scrabbled at its wound, took a step back, lost its footing, and fell away. Albert heard it crash against something, a rattle of tiles as it slid down a lower roof—finally a distant impact as it hit the yard below.

Albert swallowed; he peered down, glimpsed the body lying there. "Think it's dead?"

Scarlett's eyes were steely. "I don't know. Takes a lot to kill them."

Sal Qin came tumbling, sliding down to join them. "What the hell was that?"

"I'll tell you what it was." Scarlett shoved the gun back into her belt; she pushed her hair out of her eyes and stood up tall. She glared round at Albert and Sal Qin. "That was the last bloody thing that's getting in my way tonight. Albert, get up. Sal, get ready to do some final climbing. We're going to shin down there, take that truck, and make a midnight drive to Stow. And no one—not the militia, not the Tainted, not the Mentors, not that bloody operative—is going to stop us. And when we get to Stow, we're going to find Joe and Ettie and we're going to rescue them from Soames and Teach and their sodding band of Brothers before the alarm clock rings at noon. Then we're going to go somewhere nobody can find us, and

I'm going to have a bath, eat a meal, and sleep for at least a week. *That's* what the hell that was. Are there any questions?"

There was a resounding pause.

"Nope," Albert said.

Sal Qin scratched her chin. "Well, it would mean slightly more to me if I knew who any of those people were."

V

HIGH NOON

For her afternoon's vigil, the old woman had chosen a dry patch of sidewalk where the high street did its dog-leg turn between the laundry house and the bike racks. The laundry was closed after lunch on a Tuesday, and foot traffic was low, so she would not be directly under people's boots. She was opposite the Goat pub too, so she got the double bonus of good roasting smells drifting from its gardens and coins tossed by its customers as they headed in and out. Best of all, the spot was a sun-trap. Between three and six, light pooled against the wall behind and warmed the prayer mat nicely. In the general way, the old woman was prepared to forgo food, alcohol, finery, and other pleasures of the flesh. Sunshine was one luxury she *would* take.

She had settled herself cross-legged, with her cloak wrapped round her to keep off any chill. Her hood was back, and her long white hair and brown sun-creased face were bent forward, welcoming the light. Right now, in mid spring-time, it was warm enough to do without her extra blanket, and she was comfy. The first hour of meditating went well. Her mind roamed far afield, away from the town and off across the Wilds as far as the Iron Mounds and the Rubble Sea. She ran with the wolves of the forests and flew with the crows above the crags. And when a cloud bank passed over and the chill to her hands interrupted the vision at last, she found four coins in her saucer that had not been there before.

She was watching the clouds passing overhead, turning the rooftops from yellow to gray to blue, and so to yellow again, when an odd kerfuffle along the high street caught her ear. She thought it came from the jewelry quarter. A breaking of glass, a shouting, the frenzied ringing of a handbell . . . She paid it little attention. It was perhaps another stupid Faith Day ceremony. She'd long lost track of them.

Presently the disturbance moved off in the direction of the Marsh Gate. The old woman was pleased about this. At six, the bells would ring out in the Faith House, summoning worshippers to their observances. It would get busy *then*, sure enough, with stolid, respectable folk parading in their evening best—the men in their suits and polished shoes, the ladies with their powdered brows and gems of dark obsidian. All eager to see and to be seen.

Right now, thankfully, it was quiet. The old woman continued her meditations.

Her mind was just ascending to a higher plane of enlightenment when something heavy dropped onto the mat beside her. There was a flurry of movement and a volley of muttered swearwords. Before the old woman could react, she was shoved unceremoniously to one side. With a squeak, she toppled sideways onto an elbow, legs still crossed, bottom tilted high above the mat. From this unexpected vantage point, she opened her eyes and squinted across at her new companion.

A thin redheaded girl was settling herself beside her, half on, half off the prayer mat. She was all legs, arms, scowl, and sharp angles. A knee hit the saucer, spilling its coins. The old woman's spare blanket was kicked away by a wriggling boot. The girl wore dark clothes and had a cylindrical leather box hung about her neck. She also had a small leather bag; she dropped this, chinking, between the folds of her legs, which she was in the process of crossing. The old woman caught sight of a belt with knives, odd tools, a gleaming pistol . . .

The glimpse was gone; the girl had snatched up the blanket and was draping it over herself, shrouding her head in an impromptu cowl.

Seconds later the old woman heard a thrum of hobnailed boots upon the road. She glanced away along the high street. Men with bowler hats were approaching, silhouetted against the sun.

"Say nothing!" The hiss came from beneath the blanket. "Say nothing, or I'll shoot you. I have a gun pointed at you this moment under the cloak."

The old woman made no audible response but pushed herself back into a sitting position. Beside her, the girl was finishing arranging herself, swearing softly all the while. The head beneath the cowl was lowered in an attitude of deep contemplation. As the old woman watched, however, a pale-skinned hand emerged from the blanket, holding a coin. This was inserted into the box around her neck. The hand retreated. All was still.

The noise of feet came closer. Three militiamen, bowlers

far back on their scalps, guns in hand. They moved at something between a jog and a run. They did not break stride as they passed the mat but rounded the corner and were gone.

The old woman scratched at her eyebrow. "They'll be back," she said.

The girl beside her remained quite still, but her voice drifted from beneath the hood. "Not a word. My pistol hasn't gone anywhere."

"Did you kill someone?"

"No."

"A robbery, then."

For an instant the small, fierce face was visible, pale as a ghost-badger in the shadows of the blanket. Green eyes burned at her. A short way up the street, the footsteps of the men had paused. They were engaged in an agitated conversation.

"You should rest your hands in your lap, like this," the old woman said. "Palms up, so the evil in you can drift away. In your case, that might take some time."

A scowl beneath the blanket. "I don't need your sodding advice."

"It's freely given, unlike most things in this world. Take it or reject it as you choose."

"I will."

"Fine." The old woman stretched her arms out like a rackety seabird on a guano-caked ledge. "Now shift your bony backside up. You're hogging the sunlight. Or, pistol or no pistol, I'll let out a caterwauling that'll loosen the wax in your ears and bring the militia scampering on the double."

There was a short hesitation. All at once, the girl shuffled up a little. The pursuit was returning along the road.

When they finally drew level, the men were red-faced and out of countenance. They were accosting bystanders, knocking on doors, making strident inquiries of the landlord at the Goat. The girl kept her face lowered, flicking furtive eyes at the old woman to check out the way she sat. She had folded her hands together the precise same way the old woman did.

A militiaman approached the mat. "Madam, we seek a fugitive."

With a heavy sigh, as if drawing her consciousness back from far regions of the Earth, the old woman raised her head. "A fugitive? What man do you chase?"

"No man! A girl, allegedly, though from the description you'd think it was a beast from the black marshes. A wild-eyed harpy, all hair, teeth, wickedness, and spite, who's just nicked six black tektite earrings from Bob Barnett's jewelry store. She escaped over the rooftops, then dropped to earth again, like horse dung spattering in the street. Have you seen her passing?"

"My spirit has been elsewhere. I think I heard swift boots running toward the park."

"We've been that way. Didn't your companion see anything?"

"I doubt it."

"Can I ask her?"

"She is deep in meditation. Also it wouldn't do much good. She's deaf and dumb."

"Not massively helpful, then. . . ." There was a hint of reproach in the militiaman's voice. "I respect the sanctity of your mat, but she had better hope the Mentors don't hear of her infirmities. . . ." After a pause, he raised his bowler and hurried off to join his fellows, who were proceeding with their inquiries down the street.

The two hooded figures remained quiet for a time.

After a while, a voice came from beneath the blanket. "Why didn't they accost us?"

"Because they know something *you* don't know. This mat is holy ground."

The girl made a derisive noise at the back of her throat. "Hardly. I am looking at its threads close up. I see dirt, crushed cake and biscuit crumbs, and things that I hope and pray are raisins."

"You see all and know nothing. At the very least, those men have standards. Of courtesy, for example. Dignity, courtesy, and respect for others and their property."

The noise was repeated at greater volume. "More fool them! I *have* no standards. I believe in nothing!"

"The box round your neck says differently," the old woman said. "What's it for?"

"Cussing."

"Not robbery or violence? Not roughly manhandling a devout mystic during her holy devotions?"

"Cussing."

"Mm." The old woman stirred. "Well, you'd better put another coin in the box, hadn't you?"

"Yes."

"For that 'sodding' back there."

"Yes! I know! *Shiva!*"

"Ha! Make it two coins."

"Dammit, how about we make it three?" The girl did so, with quick and practiced fingers. She was peering from under the blanket now, looking up and down the street. "In any case, the fools are gone, and so shall I be shortly. I won't have to put up with your wittering any longer."

The old woman made no further comment. She breathed deeply. Her small hands were wrinkled, the color of stewed tea. They lay palm up on her lap. The tattered folds of her cloak spread around them like the petals of a discarded flower. A large black fly landed on a bony protrusion, possibly a knee, and worked its way along. It hopped onto a finger and sat there, cleaning its front legs. The old woman didn't stir.

"I see you are one of those fools who respect all life," the girl said after a while. "No matter how foul or depraved."

"This fly?" The old woman sighed. "No, I'd gladly squash the little bastard, but that would entail moving, which would disturb my deliberations. I'd even be tempted to eat it—I haven't had any food for two days—only I know what it's been sitting on, farther down the gutter, not far from where you are. I therefore tolerate it as a temporary pest and irritant. Much as I do with you."

The girl snorted again. They were silent then, the two women and the fly. Presently the fly departed. The girl made vague signs of doing likewise; her movements, however, were slow and indecisive. It was warm in the sunshine, and the ragged cloth was surprisingly comfortable. It felt good not to be running for a time.

"How's it working out for you?" the old woman asked. "Being a common thief?"

"It's all right."

"Bit stressful, I should imagine."

"It's better than what came before."

"Black gems from the tektite fields—stardust from the Cataclysm. What will you do with the jewels? Wear them?"

"Hardly! I give them to my bosses. I get well paid for— Gods! What was *that* noise?"

The old woman chuckled. "I can snort just as well as you. Louder and longer, if I hear something that amuses me. So you're the sap who risks the gallows, while cruel men take the profit? Nice."

"I have gainful employment, at least," the girl said after a pause. "I make my way in the world. I do not starve or eat flies."

"Oh, don't kid yourself. You eat flies."

There was no reply. They sat on the prayer mat, side by side. Traffic on the street was increasing, as workshops closed their doors and people came in from the fields. A coin was thrown spinning into the saucer.

The old woman detected a compression in her companion's silence, a buildup of indignation or tension. Sure enough, when the girl finally spoke, her voice was harsh and swift, like a dagger pressed to the throat. "Don't lecture me, you old hypocrite. That stuff about flies! I may be on a leash, but you—you're a puppet of the Faith Houses! I ought to shoot you right here and have done."

The old woman shrugged, looked left and right. "What have *I* to do with the Faith Houses? Do you see the Mentors squatting with me in the gutter?"

"That means nothing! You live in the town, which they control. If they didn't approve of you, you would be dragged off to the Felon Fields for the wolves to take!"

Now it was the old woman's turn to hesitate. "You're right in part," she said at last. "They tolerate my methods, though they dislike them. Meditation is taught in the Faith House itself—meditation and humility before a shiny portfolio of gods. They cannot very well object to me practicing it. Still, they would prefer I do it in the gardens of the House, not here. I am less tidy than they would like. . . ." She gave a grateful flourish of one hand as a passing child threw a penny at the saucer. "Bless you, my dear! Bless you! . . . In fact," she went on softly, "I am entirely free of them. Do you want to know what the secret to this freedom is?"

The girl shrugged beneath the blanket. "Tell me."

"This mat. The Mentors' influence ends at its fringes. While I am on it, I am elsewhere. My mind takes off. It ranges far and wide, across the Seven Kingdoms, beyond the Burning Regions and the sea. . . ." She smiled, her teeth neat and pearly white. "I escape the Mentors. I escape my fellow townsfolk, too—the prying cruelty of the women, the beery bravado of the men. I escape the limitations of this stupid old body of mine. I also escape my imperfections, of which, believe it or not, there are several. There are no constraints when I am on this mat. Right now, you are no longer in the town. Don't you feel it?"

"No."

"Close your eyes again."

The old woman could not see the girl's face beneath the cowl, but there was a quality to her stillness that suggested she might have followed the advice. It lasted approximately five seconds.

An explosion of annoyance. "Ah! This is stupid! I have no interest in any of it!"

"Then why are you still sitting here?"

"Well . . . it's busy on the street. It'll be easier to slip away soon."

"As to that, in a few minutes the six-o'clock rush begins. Better go now, if that is what you desire. Or stay with me awhile longer. There are techniques I can teach you if you choose. Paths that lead to enlightenment and freedom."

The girl snorted. "You'll want something in return, no doubt. Payment and such."

"No payment," the old woman said. "Your company is enough."

"Huh. Now I *know* you're lying." She was hunting about for scraps of cynicism to feed on. Even so, she didn't go. "You say you can escape anything on the mat?" she asked.

"Anything."

An extended silence followed. Patience being one of the techniques in which the old woman was proficient, she only smiled and closed her eyes. She let the sunlight begin its work of healing on the wounded girl. She didn't need to see under the cloak to know there was a hole right through her. Big enough to fit a fist in, or a heart. The sun and the mat and all the skills of meditation would never fill that hole, but they could cover it over, maybe, given time.

The old woman was almost asleep when she heard her companion get to her feet at last. She didn't open her eyes. "Well?"

"I've got to see some men about some jewels. But if what you say is true . . ."

"Come back whenever you're ready. I'll be here."

21

From a distance of several miles, Albert could see the hill town of Stow rising white and red above its safe-lands, the sunlight glinting on the terra-cotta roofs. Beyond, the forested ridges of the Wessex Wilds straddled the horizon, but the safe-lands were a sea of harvest fields. Men and women worked among the burnished rows of wheat, heads bowed, scythes flashing. Few glanced up as the armored truck sped down the center of the straight white road. It did not slow. It had been going most of the night and all of the morning. They were nearly there.

Using binoculars he had discovered in a rear compartment, Albert studied the details of the town. He saw the road rising to the broken gate; he saw the ancient defensive walls—rings upon rings of toppled stone—spilling down the slopes to merge with thickets of buckthorn. He noted the dovecotes and pigeon lofts, the sharp rooftops, the cypress trees that fringed the hillside. To the south was a jumbled slurry of favelas. On the northern ridge the disorder of the warehouse district rose to a low summit, where a squat black dome protruded. Albert focused the glasses on it, imagining the giant owls within.

"There's the bell tower," he said.

"What's the time?" Scarlett was driving. She did not take her eyes from the road.

"Just gone eleven. Got less than an hour."

"Fine. Should take us twenty minutes from here." She spoke over her shoulder. "How are you getting on, Sal? Albert—go see if she's done."

Albert ducked through the driver's hatch into the rattling shade of the cargo hold. Sal Qin was kneeling at the far end of the mesh cages beside a stack of wooden boxes. She was just heaping a final load of earth and pebbles into the topmost crate. As he approached, she patted it down and fixed on the lid, then got up with an air of satisfaction.

"That's the best I can do," she said. "Think it'll fool them?"

Albert considered the boxes. They certainly *looked* the part. They were genuine crates from the Ashtown mines, each one stamped with the Faith House circle. They were nicely heavy now too. It was just a shame they didn't have any artifacts in them. When they had located the truck in Milton Keynes the night before, they had found it (predictably) empty, apart from seven unused crates that the Mentors had ignored. These were now full, thanks to the pile of stones and dirt they'd collected by the road at dawn. Seven plausible-looking crates . . . not a huge number, not by any means a proper lorry load, but surely enough to gain admittance. Enough to get Soames and Teach excited. Enough to get them in.

Providing no one actually looked inside. . . .

"It's all about convincing the Brothers at the door," he said. "This should be enough for that."

Sal Qin wiped her hands doubtfully on a rag. "Seems a risky plan to me. Far too many variables. Too many things to go wrong."

"Scarlett says it'll be okay."

"Mm. I've only met Scarlett twice, and she's already nearly got me executed. Forgive me if I don't dance a hornpipe of triumph quite yet. And when the crates *are* finally opened?"

Albert looked across at the biggest crate of all. It was long and sturdy, and safely padlocked, and kept apart from the stack of smaller ones. "None of it will matter then."

They clambered back into the driver's cab. Scarlett hadn't moved. She had her hair tied out of her face with a piece of thin cord. The sunshine was unsparing: it showed her bruises and torn clothes, even the weal on her neck where the noose had tightened. It also showed the cool, determined light glittering greenly in her eyes.

"All set, then, Sal?" she said. "Happy with what we're doing?"

The little merchant-trader perched on the passenger seat. She took up a leather bag beside her and readied it in her lap. "'Happy' is putting it a trifle strongly. I think the scheme is mud-rat crazy, and I'm sure I'll never see either of you again."

Scarlett grinned. "That's the kind of endorsement we like."

"Don't forget I've met this Mr. Teach of yours," Sal Qin said. "He was a man who smelled of violence."

"I've never beaten him in a swordfight yet," Scarlett admitted. "And he's *almost* as good as I am with a gun. But

348

that's beside the point, because we're going inside their base unarmed. . . . Got our bag of weapons?"

"I've got it."

"Good. Thanks, Sal. Assuming we avoid unpleasant death, we'll rendezvous with you later, in the cemetery outside the city walls."

"Yes, yes, I know. In the cemetery, under the shadow of the cypresses, among the haunted tombs . . ." Sal Qin sighed and shook her head. "Why you couldn't have picked a simple coffeehouse to meet in I'll never know."

"Coffeehouses are busy. It's nice and quiet among the graves," Albert said.

"As I'm sure you'll find out, one way or another." Sal looked at her watch. "All right. I'll bring the things you re-quested for the journey—*if* I can get them at the market. I'll be at the cemetery at one o'clock, and will wait as long as I can. You'd better let me out here."

The road was rising out of the plains, past twists of rusted machinery and scattered heaps of mottled stone. Stow's gates hung open above them. Albert could see washing fluttering between the houses. An iron weathercock turned lazily on the top of the Brothers' tower.

Scarlett applied a boot to the brakes; the truck swung to a standstill at the verge. Sal Qin got out, carrying the bag of weapons, and gave them a brief ironic salute. The truck revved away, following the curve of the hill. Albert looked in the side mirror: Sal was a tiny figure walking after them up the road.

The gates of Stow were skewed and open, stained black

349

by ancient fire. If Albert had been susceptible to eerie fancies, it might have given him the impression of a demonic mouth, hanging horribly, welcomingly, agape. Fortunately, he wasn't.

There were guard huts beside the road, where unshaven sentries sheltered from the heat of the sun. They saw the Faith House symbols on the truck and waved them past. The truck reached the crown of the hill. At the final turn Albert glanced back over the flatlands they had crossed, at the ribbon of road stretching away into the haze.

He could see nothing on it. Nobody was near.

"You do know he'll be coming, Scarlett," he said.

She slowed the truck. Grubby-faced children with baskets of fruit were walking up to the gates from the fields. She let them pass, the engine idling. "He's got to get Milton Keynes under control first," she said. "It was chaos last night. The riots are probably still going on."

"No. He won't delay. He read your mind often enough to know about Joe and Ettie. He knows we'll be making our way to Stow. He'll be coming after us, right now."

Scarlett looked at her watch, honked the truck's horn. The last of the children gave little jumps of fright and skittered out of the road. "Better get the job done quickly, then," she said.

"The thing is, Scarlett . . . after what happened in the square, I'm tired. If he shows up—"

She stretched out and patted his arm. "You did the job once already. I wouldn't ask you to do it again. Don't worry— we'll rescue Joe and Ettie and vamoose. *Before* he comes."

They rolled under the fractured arch and into the town.

A cobbled road led on toward a busy marketplace, but Scarlett turned right, along a narrow street. Residential houses were left behind. Albert saw warehouses and workshops, a brewery set back behind high walls. He had a sudden memory of the prison walls that had surrounded the gardens at Stonemoor, sealing his childhood in.

"You were correct about Mallory," he said softly. "He's from Stonemoor too."

Scarlett nodded. She had that little half smile at the corner of her mouth. "Makes sense. You and him. There are similarities, and I don't just mean his power."

Albert frowned slightly. "I don't know what you mean. He's nothing like me."

"You don't think so?"

"Of course not! That swanky suit. That stupid coat. That ridiculous oily flop of hair."

"I'm not talking about his *looks*, Albert. It's his personality, what's inside."

"I swear he wears some horrid perfume too, which— *What?* How can you say that? He's vicious, and cold, and murderous, and wholly unscrupulous, and—"

"I know. But under all that swagger and smarm, he's got the same . . . unworldliness as you." Scarlett paused. "Well, not *exactly* the same. When I found you on the bus, I thought you were ill. Like there was a fever burning inside you. Mallory's got it too, and I don't think it ever leaves him."

Albert pondered this in silence. "You took my fever away," he said.

"Well, you got me out of a hangman's noose, so I'd say we're about even. What's the time?"

"Eleven-twenty-six. It's maybe getting a *little* bit tight."

"Then," Scarlett McCain said, "it's a good job that we're here."

The road rounded a corner, still ascending the side of the hill. Now, having reached the top, it ran straight and level between ranks of warehouse fronts toward an abrupt dead end. An immense wall of brick and plaster rose up from the dirt. It had a single squared opening, big enough for a bus to pass through, sealed with a metal door. Scarlett drove the truck steadily down the road toward it. Squinting up, Albert could see the stained black dome of the owls' bell tower showing beyond the wall. A few minutes less than a week ago, he had left this place to begin the journey north to Ashtown. They were back at the headquarters of the Brothers of the Hand. Somewhere inside, Ettie's alarm clock had almost run down.

The truck came to a halt before the great square door. Scarlett turned off the engine. Dust settled. On a wooden walkway raised above the road, a man sat in a rocking chair, reading a newssheet. He was a doughy, rather shapeless individual, with a face like an undistinguished potato. He wore a white shirt and gray jeans, and his tweed jacket hung over the arm of the gently rocking chair. The smallest finger of the hand that held his newssheet was cut off at the base. On the wall at his elbow, a black horn mouthpiece hung by a communication grille. There was a thermos flask and an empty bowl on the stoop beside him.

The man glanced up at the truck incuriously and returned to his paper.

"Here's the watchman." Scarlett took a piece of gum from her pocket, unwrapped it, and put it into her mouth. "Just got to get past him."

Albert regarded the man. "Doesn't look too hard."

As he spoke, the watchman leaned toward the ivory mouthpiece and spoke into it briefly. At once, a door in the wall opened and six enormous men filed out. Each sported a black slouch hat, an unshaven chin, a white shirt of eye-popping tightness seemingly painted onto his muscular torso, a gun belt dripping with weapons of every size and description, and a pair of steel-capped boots. The tallest had to fold in half to get out of the door. The shortest could have fitted Albert snugly under the crook of his armpit and would probably have enjoyed it. Their eyes were chips of ice, their horny hands hung bent and ready by their guns. They lined up on the walkway, facing the truck. The watchman sat back in his chair.

Albert swallowed. "It could be hard*ish*, I suppose."

"Yeah. That's our welcoming committee," Scarlett said. "Well, let's get it done."

They got down from the cab. The sun was high. The edges of the warehouse roofs were scalloped by pools of shade. Flocks of black birds hunkered on the gutters; otherwise, there was no sign of life in that long, deserted street. Albert closed the cab door. He looked back down the road. They were near Stow's highest point, and he could see for miles above the chimneys, out beyond the town. A wind was blowing from the east, running in silver waves through the crop fields. The route by which they had come was a white thread fading into blank blue distance. . . .

There was a soft ache in his head that hadn't been there before.

He stared out at the distant road.

"Albert," Scarlett said.

The watchman was waiting, rocking gently in his chair, his silent gunmen standing alongside. He was pretending to read his newssheet. He waited for Scarlett's shadow to fall over him and only then condescended to look at her.

"All right there, Walt." Scarlett nodded at the watchman, then at the other Brothers. "Boys."

The watchman's scalp and chin were covered with whitish stubble. Albert felt you could have lopped off his head, turned it upside down, and stuck it back on without much altering matters. He regarded Scarlett with his dark little eyes. "You're cutting it fine, girl," he said.

Scarlett chewed her gum steadily. "We're here, aren't we? We've got the stuff they want. We just need to go in to show them." She stood casual and calm in the dust of the road.

"I bet you do." The man took a watch on a chain from a pocket in his shirt and inspected it in an offhand manner. "Dear me, you're almost out of time."

"Just have to let us in," Scarlett said. "We've done the job that was asked of us, and now we're back before the deadline. It's easy."

"Doesn't *look* like it was particularly easy for you," the watchman said. He ran his gaze over Scarlett's and Albert's bloodied faces, their ragged clothes.

"Well, not as easy as it would be to punch your nose backward," Scarlett said. "That much is true."

The man's eyes became flinty; the rocking of his chair slowed. "You didn't ought to talk to me like that, McCain. Not in your position. I watched you all those years when you were Soames's little favorite, and you never once gave me the time of day. All hoity-toity you were, and look at you now. Groveling to get in. I've a mind to let the clock run down."

"You do that, Walt," Scarlett said. "If my friends die, the first thing that happens is—I drive away and take these treasures from the ancient past with me. Soames and Teach won't have them. What do you think they'll do to you?"

The watchman scowled. "We could just shoot you here. That would be simplest."

"Go ahead. If that's what the boss has ordered."

There was a silence, broken only by the squeaking of the watchman's chair. Albert felt fairly sure the men *would* let them in. If they'd wanted them dead, it would have happened already. But it was almost noon. He thought of Joe and Ettie being led into the great domed chamber. He thought of the chains rising up into the dark. He imagined the eager fluttering of the owls. . . . Whether or not owing to the tension of the moment, the pain in his skull was increasing. There was a throbbing pulse behind one eye. Probably it was just the aftereffects of the Fear, but—

His head jerked up.

For an instant, he'd had the sensation of something subtle probing at his mind.

Up on the stoop, the chair stopped rocking. The watchman shrugged, as if disclaiming responsibility for the perversity of the world. "All right, McCain. They're waiting for you inside. But we ain't letting you in without due process, that's for sure. No guns, no knives, no nasty surprises allowed, as I'm sure you understand. We're going to check you and the truck." He clicked his fingers; two of his men stepped forward. "Raise your arms."

Albert stood still and silent as he and Scarlett were frisked for weapons. He kept his face as impassive as he could, but his heart was thumping in his chest. A great agitation was upon him. He wanted to move, to run—to rescue Ettie, yes, but then keep fleeing, away, away from the youth who followed him. How weary he was! How weak! He could not face him. He *couldn't*. He just didn't have the strength.

He looked across at Scarlett. She was the picture of indifference, chewing her gum, staring out at nothing while one of the giant Brothers patted her down like an attentive bear. How weary she was, too; how bruised and battered by events! Albert knew the toll that the last few days had taken on her. Yet, as so often, she projected nothing but defiance. In the gleam of her eye, in the movement of her jaw, in the insolent calm of her posture, she refused to acknowledge any weakness whatsoever. Simply in the way she stood, she defied the world and its horrors—and Albert, watching her, felt his own pulse slow, his sinews stiffen. His jaw set hard. He looked away along the road.

Finding no weapons on their persons, the Brothers had entered the truck. The rounds of ammunition in the machine-gun turret were located and removed, the cupboards and compartments searched. Only the crates were left. The men stood back. Walt the watchman levered himself from his chair; with Albert and Scarlett following, he went to the rear doors to inspect the consignment for himself.

"This all?" he said. "Not many boxes."

Scarlett chuckled. "No, but their contents are precious indeed. Ancient, cursed artifacts from the Buried City, constructed by doomed generations of the past."

The watchman rubbed the bristles of his chin. "Says you. I should open them up and see."

"By all means. Choose any you like."

"This big one with the lock."

"Of course. I have the key. But be aware that as well as being cursed, they're also fragile, and might turn to dust if the full light of the sun shines on them. We've already destroyed several priceless items that way. Still, I'm sure Mr. Soames will forgive you if you bugger up another on his doorstep. Better safe than sorry, after all."

The man frowned. He blinked at the boxes in indecision.

"Go on. Take a peek," Scarlett prompted. "Part of the mechanism will probably disintegrate in the noon light, but hey, go for your life. Soames and Teach won't mind."

357

A range of emotions played over the watchman's face—curiosity, cupidity, caution, fear. His hand hovered over the padlocked crate. Albert waited. Ettie's clock ticked down.

"All right," the watchman said. "You can drive in. You'd better hope you impress the bosses with this little lot. I'm not impressed. Looks like a load of tat to me."

"Cheers, Walt. Spoken with your customary generosity and grace." Scarlett gave him a beaming smile as he stalked away. She shut the rear doors firmly and set off for the cab.

Albert did not follow her. He had a feeling of chill unease, as if a finger of cloud had passed over the sun. What was it? That odd ache in his head, that same invasive prickling . . .

The watchman had returned to his chair. He motioned to his men. One spoke into the black horn mouthpiece, gave an order. There was a clanging. The metal barrier in the great brick wall began to rise.

Scarlett was at the cab door. "Come on, Albert. Let's go."

"Coming." He started forward—and all at once cried out. Pain flared inside his head—a sudden sharp, thin probing. He felt a presence that was not his own. He pushed his fingers hard against his forehead, writhing with the motion.

The sensation died. Albert breathed out, hid his face behind his hands.

"Albert?" Scarlett was at his side.

The barrier rose. The watchman had settled himself back in his chair. "Better get on with it," he called. "Mr. Soames is waiting."

Albert raised his head slowly, turned to look toward the

east. Out in the sunlit fields, beyond the walls of Stow, a small white dust cloud was whirling along the road.

Scarlett saw it too. "Is it—?"

"Yes," he said. "It's him."

"Soames is waiting," the watchman said again.

Albert delayed no longer. The decision was simple enough; he had already made up his mind. In ten minutes, the cloud of dust would get to Stow. That didn't leave time to do what had to be done inside. There were no alternatives that he could see. He swept his hair out of his face, as if brushing his exhaustion away. "You take the truck in, Scarlett," he said. "I'll be along in a minute. I've got something to attend to first." He addressed the watchman: "She'll go in alone, Walt. Not me. I'm staying here."

"Hold on, hold on. . . ." Scarlett raised her hand at the watchman, at the guards standing impassive by the door. "Just hold on a second," she said. "No, Albert. No. There is absolutely no way—"

"It's very simple," he said. "You go in and get Joe and Ettie. Follow the plan. Give Soames what he's asked for. I'll delay our friend out here, then catch up with you."

She looked at him, then out at the little cloud of dust that came like an arrow across the fields. A muscle moved in her cheek. Her lips were white and thin.

He smiled at her. "I've got to, Scarlett. It's the only way."

"You'll catch up with me?"

"Yes."

"Well, how's that going to pan out?"

"It'll pan out really well. It'll be fine."

"No," Scarlett said. "It really won't. I'll stay with you. You can't face him on your own."

He caught hold of her hand. "The clocks are almost run down. You said so yourself. What have we got, ten minutes? Come on, you *know* you've got to go in. For Joe and Ettie. It's easy."

"Easy like your mission was easy?" the watchman called. "Gate's open."

"Albert—"

"You've *got* to go in."

They looked at each other.

"You going to kiss each other goodbye?" the watchman said. "Don't let me stop you. It's a free country." He sat back, grinning, in his chair.

Scarlett pulled her hand away. "Well, I think it's a stupid plan," she said. "I'm just putting that out there." She scowled across at the watchman, climbed back into the cab, and slammed the door. "All right—show's over, Walt. Just me. I'm driving in."

"You're to drive straight through the warehouse to the room of clocks. They're waiting for you there. You know where to go."

"Give Ettie a hug from me," Albert said.

She frowned at him, her hair disordered, her face pale. "I don't need to. You can hug her yourself in a bit."

But he was already looking away from her down the road.

22

There was one brief instant, as Scarlett was in the act of driving through the gate, when the emotional pulls before and behind her reached equilibrium. At that moment, with the truck half in darkness and half in sunshine, with Joe and Ettie up ahead and Albert at her back, the twin tugs to her heart were in perfect, awful balance. She felt suspended as if on a taut string, as if a length of wire cut through her. The pain it brought was keen.

But also fleeting. The cargo lorry drove on, into the shadows of the warehouse. Albert receded behind. A grim-faced Brother pressed a switch on the wall, and the metal barrier began to rattle down, closing off the street. With that, the string was cut. Scarlett could no longer go back, and the pressure inside her eased a little. The choice had been made. Her route ahead was clear. She took her boot off the accelerator, let the truck idle forward through an empty, dusky space. Men gestured for her to go on. She drove under cones of electric light down a long, bare hall.

It was a way that was familiar to her, though she had never driven it before. The maze of ancient factories and storerooms was the home and headquarters of the Brothers of the Hand, a miniature cosmos of illegality, where the rules of Soames and Teach held sway. As she went, she saw all the old chambers, each steeped in its particular significance. There, to the right—the whitewashed training rooms, where men boxed and wrestled and learned the arts of sword, garrote, and knife. There, to the left—the passage that led to the concrete gun range, where Scarlett had sought to shoot her past away. Next, the lorry turned at right angles toward the central hall, rolling through the ruined quarters, with their littering of broken walls and half-demolished rooms, their piles of practice safes and padlocked doors— a place where any conceivable heist could be planned and trained for. Now came the dormitories (and, somewhere, the little room where she had slept those first horrific days, screaming out her fury and her guilt), then the dining hall and map room. Finally, the corridor that led to Soames's offices, where they'd interviewed her, accepted her, welcomed her. . . .

Memories hovered wraithlike at the windows. Scarlett ignored them, kept her gaze fixed forward. Far ahead, grainy in the shafts of sunlight wafting down from distant windows, she saw the double doors to the room of clocks. The doors were open. Scarlett checked her watch. Five minutes to twelve. Almost noon. She felt a bead of sweat build at the side of her forehead, run quickly down her cheekbone to her jaw. Irritably, she wiped it off. She had no use for *that*. It was time for the final interview. It was all about the performance now.

And she had to do it on her own.

Without Albert, she felt oddly naked and incomplete, almost as she had on her first arrival here so many years before. Albert . . . She thought about him behind her, waiting in the road. How weary he was, how spent. He was even more defenseless than her. But he too had made his choice. She thought of the one who was coming—of Mallory's competence, his ruthless exertions in service of the Faith Houses, his unbridled power . . . And Albert had to face him without her at his side.

So many partings.

Anger at what she was being forced to do flooded through Scarlett. She gritted her teeth, pressed her foot on the gas, and accelerated through the open doors into the room of clocks.

It was as the watchman said. They were waiting for her there.

A little group was assembled at the far end of the hall, under the glow of the arc lights, in front of the desk and the wall of clocks. It was like they'd been carefully posed—probably *had* been, knowing Soames. For once, he himself was not behind the desk; his wheeled leather chair had been parked nearer to the strings of chains and ropes that rose like the stems of obscene plants through the dark center of the hall. Close beside him were Joe and Ettie, and beside *them*—intimately, threateningly close—stood the lithe figure of Teach in his patchwork coat, his sword held loosely in his hand.

She drove the lorry at speed across the hall, swung aside at the last moment, reversed it toward the four figures so the rear doors were facing them. She switched off the ignition. In the sudden wave of silence, she spat out her wad of gum, took the last piece from her pocket, and folded it into her mouth. Then she got out of the cab.

She'd parked it well. The group was ranged in a semi-circle round the doors like a little expectant audience. Scarlett strolled toward them down the side of the truck. As she did so, she took in the essentials—the things that might help keep her alive.

There were four other Brothers she hadn't previously clocked, standing back in the shadows of the wall. Teach's bodyguards, their faces hidden beneath broad, flat caps. Scarlett didn't need to frisk them to know they'd have the full complement of weapons strapped to various extremities. If fighting started, they would expertly weigh in.

The spotlight glittered off Teach's skull, off Soames's massive shoulders. Teach was balefully relaxed. Aside from his sword—which was in any case more than enough—he had his gun ready at his belt. Soames had no obvious weapon or defense in view. Today he wore a deep brown suit with mustard pinstripes. A yellow handkerchief jutted from his pocket. His hands rested on the swollen marrows of his thighs. On one ample knee sat a tiny alarm clock, decorated with white and yellow flowers.

The hands were almost at the twelve.

"Mr. Soames, Mr. Teach." Scarlett stepped with a swagger into the amphitheater of light. She grinned round at them all.

"You always did know how to make an entrance, my dear," Mr. Soames said.

"True." Scarlett turned away from him. "Hello, Ettie," she said. "You okay?"

The little girl gave her a smile of welcome. There was no surprise there, no fear or agitation, just simple pleasure at Scarlett's arrival. She seemed the same as in the parlor of the Wolf's Head Inn. Perhaps her hair was extra tousled, her dress more scuffed and torn. She was sitting on the floor next to a mess of paper and a tub of crayons. She was busy drawing.

Unlike his granddaughter, something of the privations that Joe had suffered during the week had left their mark on him. Was he perhaps more stooped? Were the lines on his face more deeply etched? But his gnarled hands were clenched close to his sides. His bony chin was up, his eyes flashing defiance at the wicked men around him. It made Scarlett's heart full to see his calm composure, his quiet dignity.

"Hey, Joe," she said. "I got here."

The old man inclined his head gravely. "I never doubted it."

She smiled at him.

"Though I also predicted you'd cut it bloody fine."

Scarlett cleared her throat. "Yeah, well. We had a few holdups along the way."

"Holdups?" The old man's nostrils flared, his eyebrows bristled. "I'll say you did! Look at that clock! It's two minutes to twelve! They don't *do* units of time much smaller than that!"

"Yes. All right. I did my best."

"Well, it wasn't really good enough, was it? These bandits have been readying me for the owls! All morning they've been at it. They've weighed me, they've doused my shirt in meat oil, they've even picked me out my own personal chain!"

"I'm sorry to hear that, Joe," Scarlett said. "Don't fret. I've come to set you free."

"Good. Because it's *your* fault in the first place that we're here."

Scarlett's grin faltered. "Now look here, you old buzzard—"

From his seat, Soames gave a deep and reverberating chuckle. His mop of gold curls bounced with pleasure. "Ah, families, families! Surely they are sent to try us! I am only glad, my dear Scarlett, that you have found another to replace the one you lost. Perhaps this horrid old man is something of an acquired taste, but his sweet child is another matter." Folds of skin swelled against his shirt collar; the great pink head bent in Ettie's direction. "We've had some lovely conversations, she and I. Not conversations of a conventional sort, naturally. She is more interesting than that. She communicates with the sweep of a pen, the blot of a color, the curve and intensity of a line! But no doubt you know all this already." Behind the golden spectacles, Soames's tiny eyes gleamed brightly in their pouches of flesh. "In short, it will be hard to say goodbye to little Ettie. But say goodbye we must. All that remains is to decide the manner of our parting. Which brings us, Scarlett dear, to *you*."

It was just the kind of florid welcome Scarlett had been expecting. She used the moment to gauge the relative positions of her enemies. Soames and Teach in the inner ring, four others farther out. The owls above. The chain hoists close by. And behind her: the truck doors. Aside from the bodyguards, everything was within a few feet. It was pretty much as good as could be expected. Which wasn't to say it *was* good, but nor was it entirely bad.

"Yeah," she said. "But before we start, Mr. Soames, why don't you turn that clock off? As you can see, I'm here."

Mr. Soames smiled vaguely. He said nothing but only looked toward the little alarm clock on his knee. All at once, as if triggered by his gaze, it sprang to life. It bounced and quivered and jittered along the surface of his leg, emitting tinny, piercing rings. It was a strangely unpleasant sound, and there was something vile about the clock's mad gyrations. Scarlett, Joe, Ettie—even Mr. Teach—watched in fascination. It was like seeing some small, insane creature in its death throes. You had the urge to put it out of its misery, to find a hammer, a mallet—anything that might silence it with a blow.

Mr. Soames extended a great, pink, meaty finger and gently moved a lever to halt the thrashing bells. The sound ended.

He smiled round at them. "Noon," he said.

There was an intense rustling high above, a fervent and frenzied hooting.

"The owls know it," Mr. Teach said. It was the first time he had spoken. His bald pate shone white like a death's-head under the arc lights. He glanced up into the shadows of the bell tower. "They know what an alarm clock's ringing means. They know what happens after that. It always triggers their blood lust. Sometimes they start taking pieces out of each other."

Scarlett stepped forward. "Good, because that's all those feathered gits will be having for lunch today. When the clock struck, I was already here."

"True!" Joe cried. "I can vouch for that." He clapped his hands together briskly. "Well, clearly it's time for Ettie and me to go. We'll leave you to discuss the rest of it. Don't bother getting up, Soames. We can find our own way out."

He made as if to step away; at once, Teach's sword swung up to meet his throat. In the great wheeled chair, Soames's hulking shape leaned forward, bringing with it a curve of shadow. "You *were* here, dear Scarlett! But what do you have with you? *That* remains to be determined. Certainly you have not yet transferred artifacts from the Buried City into our hands, as per the agreement made a week ago. And noon has sadly passed." His mouth pursed wryly. "So you see, the outcome is already ambiguous, my dear."

Scarlett smiled. "And here I was thinking you'd play fair."

"As to *that*, it all depends on what you've brought us." Soames made an expansive gesture. "Perhaps we'll forgive your betrayals in a flash. Perhaps you'll all be able to stroll merrily on your way, peppered with Mr. Teach's kisses and congratulations."

"I could happily skip that last bit," Joe said.

"Or *perhaps* it will work out otherwise," Soames went on. "Who can tell? You have something to add, Teach?"

"I do." One of Mr. Teach's little quirks was that whenever his sword was naked in his hand, he could never quite keep it still. Its razored tip kept making little jerks and jolts—small, practiced cuts and incisions, as if it was rehearsing cutting through a heart or neck. It twitched now, but the rest of him was still as stone. "I have a question," he said. "Where is the boy?" His eyes were fixed on Scarlett. "Where is Albert Browne?"

Scarlett gave a noncommittal wave of the hand. "Albert? He's waiting outside."

"Why?"

"It's a gesture of good faith. You know he has certain . . . abilities. I would not want you to distrust us in any way—particularly in this sensitive moment. Thus Albert remains outside, and I come in unarmed."

"I don't believe you," Teach said.

"Ask Walt. Albert's out there now."

Soames's bulk shifted with sudden impatience; he glared over his glasses at Scarlett. "If you mean Walt the watchman, we're certainly *not* going to ask him anything. In any case, the boy's whereabouts are of considerably less interest than the contents of that truck. You went to Ashtown?"

"As you see."

"You robbed the mines?"

"We robbed them. We took the very best artifacts we could find."

"Excellent!" Soames clicked his tongue with satisfaction. He settled himself back in the chair. "I've got to confess, I'm excited. This is suspense, isn't it, Joe? This is theater. Put out the bunting, Mr. Teach, get the drum rolls started. Scarlett, my dear, it's over to you."

In recent years, Scarlett had amassed considerable experience selling dud religious artifacts to the credulous and hard-of-thinking in towns across the kingdoms. To do this, she had learned the art of the poker face, of maintaining a blithe self-confidence in the teeth of all the evidence. Circumstances were slightly different here—the stakes were somewhat higher—but in essence they were the same. So, moving back toward the truck, she didn't let herself dwell on the brute reality, which was that none of her crates contained anything remotely valuable. Soil, stones, and roadside chippings were all they had—all of them, bar one.

She felt the intensity of Joe's gaze on the back of her neck. She felt Teach's hard scrutiny, the soft brush of Soames's little eyes.

It was all about the performance. Scarlett gave a sweep

of the arm, unclipped the rear doors, threw them open, and stepped dramatically aside.

There was a silence. Mr. Teach made a long hissing noise between his teeth. Mr. Soames was a solid mountain in his chair.

"Oh, crap," Joe said.

Scarlett looked in. It had to be said that the seven boxes didn't look quite as impressive as she'd hoped, having been thrown about a fair bit during her nifty swiveling maneuvers in the hall. Aside from the one big, heavy crate, still firmly in position by the door, they were scattered rather messily around the inside of the mesh cage. But at least none of them had burst open. That was something.

"Well now," Soames said. "Either my glasses have misted up with sheer sweaty anticipation or that truck looks half empty. What do you say, Teach?"

"Less than half full, Soames. Not even a third."

"What was the agreement?"

"A cargo lorry full of the choicest treasures the Buried City could provide."

"Precisely." Soames's head glowed with pink asperity. He took his handkerchief from his pocket and dabbed various planes and portions of his face. "Scarlett Josephine McCain," he said, "you came here to us many years ago in dire need. Let's make no bones about it, you were a dead girl walking. Another week, another *day*, and you'd have died bubbling in a ditch or been strung up in the market. We took you in, do you recall? We fixed your body. We fixed your mind. We gave you the skills that even now sustain you. Can you look me in the eye and truly say that this meager pile of battered boxes justifies such investment?"

To be honest, Scarlett couldn't. With an effort, she maintained her languid smile. "Ah, but the number of boxes isn't everything," she said. "It's what's *inside* that counts. And these are the richest pickings of the Ashtown mines! Eerie mechanisms of ancient days, rust free and miraculously preserved! You will marvel at their quality and shiver at the strange knowledge they must contain!" She waved her hand at the largest crate, her head tilted to one side.

Soames flinched. "Don't flutter your eyelashes at me, young madam! I feel quite ill."

"Agreed," Teach said. "It's like a wolf flirting. And you can stop your huckster spiel as well. We're not fools queuing outside a Faith House, who'll be gulled by fancy words."

"Seeing's believing," Scarlett said. "Let me show you."

As she spoke, there was a distant noise of uncertain nature. The floor of the great chamber shook. Flakes of black dust dropped like snow from the dome of the bell tower.

Soames and Teach glanced at each other. "Something going on outside," Teach said.

"I don't know *what* that is," Scarlett said. Her stomach corkscrewed. *Albert* . . . She ran her tongue over dry lips.

Teach's eyes narrowed; he pressed his sword point against the ground and leaned casually upon the hilt. "Not having us on, are you, girl?"

"Would I do that?"

"I think you're capable of anything. That boy of yours. Out there. Up to no good."

"It's nothing to do with me."

"I hope not," Soames said. All semblance of humor had dropped from him as surely and silently as the flakes of dust falling round them. "Well, the men will go and see. . . . But *we* have talked enough. Mr. Teach, stand beside Joe and Ettie. If, when Scarlett opens the first box, we are not satisfied by what it contains, be so good as to kill the old man. If, when she opens the second, the same pertains—you may kill the little girl. We will give their bodies to the owls, and Scarlett will ride with them to the tower. Scarlett—please proceed."

"Sure." Scarlett kept her eyes studiously away from Ettie. There was perhaps the slightest moment when her gaze touched Joe's and she caught the desperation there. She turned to the truck, made as if to reach for the biggest crate, and moved her hand away.

Teach had seen her pause. "Why not that big one?"

"That is the finest artifact. The rarest and most valuable. I thought I'd work up to it."

"No. Start with that."

With just the barest suggestion of reluctance, Scarlett pulled the largest crate toward her, and over the edge of the truck, so that it began to tip. It was very heavy. She eased it downward, let it sit there, propped between truck and floor, facing out toward the desk.

Hard to be sure, but she thought she could hear a

scraping sound, a distinct vibration from within the crate. What with the ticking of the clocks on the wall and the background humming of the lights, it didn't carry to Soames or Teach or anyone else.

Soames tapped his fingers on his knee. "Well? Let's see it."

"I don't believe there's anything in there at all," Teach said.

"Oh, there's something," Scarlett said. "Trust me."

There was a handle on the top of the long, thin crate, to help swing the lid clear. A padlock secured it. She took a key from her pocket, unlocked the padlock, flipped it open, tossed the lock away.

She took hold of the handle and looked round at her friends and mortal enemies alike:

Soames leaning forward, mouth open in expectation.

Teach readying the sword behind Joe's neck.

Joe standing gaunt and still.

And Ettie. Ettie smiling up at Scarlett, crayon paused in her little pink fist.

Scarlett grinned at her and winked.

Then she opened the crate.

23

Staying put. Just staying put while she went in. It was one of the hardest things Albert had ever had to do. After that, the waiting-for-his-death-to-come-to-him bit was easy.

He stood at the end of the street, in the shadow of the wall, listening to the metal barrier rattling down behind him. It slammed with harsh finality, cutting him off from Scarlett and his friends. Which was precisely what Albert wanted: it made things simple for him.

He looked at the silent warehouse buildings on either side of the road. They weren't derelict, or even run-down, but they were sick—the windows dirty, the colors faded. There was a tightness, a tiredness about the town of Stow that reminded him of the faces in the sanatorium rooms at Stonemoor. No one was about. The six gunmen had gone back inside the building, and the only person visible was the watchman in his chair. At least *he* seemed happy. He had picked up the thermos flask beside him and was pouring a yellowish soup into his bowl.

Albert adjusted his gaze beyond the rooftops. Away in

the fields, the cloud of dust had become a black car racing toward the hill. It passed out of sight toward the gates. In five minutes it would arrive.

He spoke slowly to the watchman. "These old workshops, Walt. Whose are they?"

The man had taken a spoon from his pocket and was prodding at the contents of his bowl, as if mildly surprised by what he found there. "They belong to us," he said. "To the Brothers. Storage and such."

"Anyone there now?"

"Not at this hour. Dawn's the witching hour for our boys. They run home to bed."

Albert nodded slowly. "That's good. I shall be meeting with someone in a minute," he said. "Here in the road. You might want to go inside. Or somewhere very far away."

"Private conversation, I take it?" The watchman took a mouthful of soup.

"Something like that."

The man nodded, gave him a rough salute with his spoon. "Oh, well, in that case naturally I'll just desert my post and nip inside for a bit, leaving Mr. Soames's gate untenanted while you have your little chin-wag. Nothing easier. Delighted to do it for you, unknown youth. You just take your time."

Albert looked at him. "Really?"

"Shiva's sister! Of course not! What's wrong with you? Don't you understand sarcasm?"

"Not entirely." Albert smiled faintly. "I never quite got my head around that."

He stepped off the sidewalk and out into the full glare of the sun, moving a few yards away from the entrance to the warehouse. As he did so, he felt an invasive presence in his mind again. It moved slowly, rootling amid his thoughts, like a starved dog nosing in some bins. It was growing in strength. Albert did not try to expel the presence: he knew what it was doing. Fixing his location, checking his motivations. Good. He wanted to be found.

Behind him, the watchman's attention had been recaptured by the soup. Albert could hear the rasp of the spoon, the rhythmic squeaks as the rocking chair started up again. He stood with his trainers in the dust and his arms hanging loosely by his sides.

Shadows clustered like spectators in the doorways of the buildings. The flocks of birds had gone from the roofs. The road was deserted. Small curls of dust danced in the sunshine, as if unseen children were running across the street.

The probing in his mind abruptly stopped. Having satisfied itself he was going nowhere, the presence drew back. Albert was alone again. He thought about Scarlett. He thought of her in the house of her enemies, entering the hall of clocks. Again he felt the compulsion to go after her, to be at her side like a companion should.

But he couldn't do that now. It was too late.

The long black car swung round the corner at the far end of the road, coming from the direction of the town gates. It morphed and melted in the heat haze, as if reluctant to fix on any consistent form. Heat deadened the sound of the engine.

Coming fast, it slowed abruptly, pivoting in the road when still two buildings distant. It came to a slanting halt, stood silent, black, and glittering, dust rising from the wheels.

Albert waited. Behind him, he heard the creaking of the watchman's rocking chair.

The operative, Mallory, got out of the car. What with the haze, his form snapped and flickered, now in two pieces, now three, now one. He hadn't been driving; he was too important for that. He shut the rear door, walked a few paces out into the road. Something occurred to him. He stopped, went back, spoke in at the driver's window. At once the engine started; the vehicle reversed, turned sharply, drove back the way it had come.

The young man was alone in the middle of the road.

Albert and Mallory faced each other down the long strip of Tarmac. The operative seemed physically unaffected by events of the night before, but his coat was charred at the edges and peppered with burns. A corner of it flapped in the breeze. His hair flicked across his forehead.

Albert adjusted his jumper, pulled his trousers up a little. One day he was going to have to get a better belt. He flexed his fingers, gave a soft, wry smile.

"So here we are," he said.

Mallory squinted, held his hand to his ear, said something Albert couldn't catch.

"What?" Albert called. "Didn't get that."

"I didn't hear what you said."

"Oh."

The watchman looked up from his soup. "You could try getting a bit nearer," he said.

Albert squared his shoulders, moved slowly up the road. The operative had come to the same conclusion, independent of outside advice. He too was walking nearer through the dust.

They stopped again. Now they were ten yards apart.

"This is better," Mallory said.

It was the first time Albert had got a good look at him since their conversation in the cell. And he had to admit it— Scarlett was right. It was like standing in front of a cracked mirror. There was something in Mallory he recognized, even as it made him recoil. Not in the overlarge coat or oiled hair, not in the bland smirk that consistently played around his face. It was in the eyes. There was a fire burning there that Albert knew well. He knew it, because it burned inside him too.

The years at Stonemoor had created that fire—the experiments, the punishments, the rote-learned guilt and shame. Those things were gone, but the fire remained, for it needed no external fuel. It subsisted on itself, on its interior pain and rage. Albert had continually tried to smother the flames in himself, only to find them bursting out uncontrollably as the Fear. By contrast, Mallory's fire *was* controlled: he tended it constantly, stoking it, enjoying its heat. His outward self was cool and icy, but within the prison of his self-control was a furnace that had spread to occupy every inch of his being. There was no softness there, no ease, no generosity remaining. It had all been burned away.

Albert felt great pity for him.

"Sorry about your coat," he said. "I see it's got a bit charred."

"It was my best one, too," Mallory said, grinning. "But I'll live. I must say, I was surprised by what you managed last night. It was a pretty trick with the iron cap. I wasn't ready for it at all. And after that—well, I didn't think you had it in you."

Albert nodded. "I regret the destruction I caused. I hope it's over now."

"Over?" Mallory's smile grew quizzical. "Hardly! We've quelled the initial panic, the fires are out, and two of the Tainted lie dead in the square. We haven't found the other yet—but we will. Frankly, though, the whole situation is a dog's breakfast. The problem is, Albert, people are fundamentally stupid. Perhaps you've noticed that? If the crowd hadn't lost their head and charged about like brainless sheep, there'd have been very little damage—and I'd have got to you before you legged it over the roofs. And now there's a lot of anger among the citizens—directed as much against the High Council as against you. They blame *us* for the debacle." He shook his head. "It's amazing how much trouble two selfish little outlaws can cause."

"Well, you should have left us alone," Albert said.

"Oh, you're *much* too annoying for that." The young man adjusted his cuffs with his cold white hands. "Look, we both know where this is leading, but before you start wailing and pleading, I've got to be honest with you. I can't let you off this time."

Albert looked at him. "Before I start *what?*"

"Wailing and pleading. Begging for your life. You had your chance in the cell at Milton Keynes. That was then, this is now. After the mess you made back in the square last night, any idea of a truce with the Council has gone out the window. You can get on your knees if you want and bawl to the fourteen heavens, but it won't make a fig of difference. Sorry."

"I don't actually *want* to beg for mercy," Albert said.

"No?" Mallory gestured mildly at their surroundings. "It's just you're not running away with your skirts over your head, like usual, so I naturally assumed . . ."

Albert held up a hand. "I've waited for you on purpose. I'm here to make you an offer."

There was a moment's pause. Then Mallory laughed. His eyes crinkled in appreciation. "I see what you did there," he said. "Nice. Pity we don't have a bowl of fruit to share this time. Well, go on, then. I've got ten minutes before the car comes back. What *are* you offering me, Albert Browne?"

"It's simple. I think you should join forces with us."

"You mean with you and Scarlett?" The grin broadened. "I'm honored, but . . . are you sure she'll be around? I sensed your anxiety earlier when she left you. How do you think she's getting on in there?"

Albert was wondering this too. The massive silence of the building was cold against his back. Scarlett would be in with Joe and Ettie now, opening the lorry, bringing out the crates. . . . "She'll be doing fine," he said. "She'll be out in a few minutes, I'm sure."

The burned coat flexed. Mallory put his hands into his pockets. He made a little rocking motion, sunlight gleaming off his shiny shoes. "I like your positivity," he said. "Me, I think she's already dead. But let's talk about your offer. You want me to become a bandit too?"

"It's nothing to do with being an outlaw. I want you to be free. Free of the Faith Houses, free of the Towns."

The young man nodded slowly. "I think I know the kind of freedom you mean. Drinking rainwater out of puddles. Eating roast mud-rat with your fellow outcasts under the stars. A carefree life of deprivation and squalor, far from civilization . . . Nope, it doesn't appeal too much, I'm afraid."

"Mud-rat's actually quite tasty," Albert said, "if you skin and soak it right. But you're missing the point, Mallory. You need to think about who you're working for. You were up in that Council chamber with us, back in Milton Keynes. You heard what that man from the High Council said. He called us *both* deviants. How does that make you feel?"

The youth shrugged his narrow shoulders. "It makes me proud. Proud because I *am* a deviant—a deviant who has successfully controlled his darker impulses. I was monstrous when I came to Stonemoor. I have been molded, reshaped, renewed. The wicked child has become a better man. . . . But we've already talked about this, and you, my friend, have lost the chance of joining me. However, I'm pleased to say there's another promising crop coming through at Stonemoor, so I won't be alone much longer."

Albert's skin went cold. "More children like us?"

"Not like *you*, I hope! With luck they'll join me soon as valued members of society. Then we can get on with fixing all the problems that beset our towns. The Tainted, the dissenters . . . and the criminals like that dozy Brother over there."

He pointed beyond Albert to the rocking chair a little way back along the street. The watchman had finished his soup. His head was back, his hands clasped over his belly. He was enjoying the noonday brightness. The chair moved slowly. His eyes had closed.

"*He's* not the problem," Albert said. "You are. And you're fooling yourself, because you'll *never* be valued by society. Don't you see? That's the issue. The Mentors loathe and fear you."

"Yes, they do. They do. And rightly. I loathe and fear myself."

"Well, that's hardly healthy, is it? Meanwhile you carry out all the most horrible jobs for them, jobs they're too weak to do themselves, and they tolerate you because of it! But as soon as you stop being useful, that tolerance will end. Then you'll be on the scaffold too, like me."

The edges of the operative's coat fluttered. Air shifted round him. His face showed anger for the first time.

"You know it's true," Albert said.

"Baloney." Mallory spoke with sudden crispness. "*You* went to the scaffold, Albert, because of your life of crime. *That's* the truth you can't bring yourself to acknowledge. Our kingdoms are split and broken, and the powers in them have the right to impose order and civility. If not—what happens? Thieves will flourish, the Towns will fight each other, the Tainted will overrun it all. People like you and me have caused great mischief in the past. It's the role of the Faith Houses to ensure that doesn't happen again. I have shouldered that responsibility alongside them. You haven't. That's why we're here."

Albert felt a force brush against him; not powerfully yet, but enough to make him take a step back. He took a deep breath, stood upright, pushing the force away in turn. "And what about your *other* responsibility?" he said. "Your responsibility to others like you, to the weak and helpless, to the infirm children, to the people cast out by the Towns?"

Mallory made a dismissive sound. "We have no responsibility for *them*! Our societies must be *strong*—that's the only way we can survive. Defectives and deviants are not part of society and must consequently be rejected and cast out. That's why we have the cages, the posts out in the fields. It's a time-honored tradition that helps to ensure— What's this? You're not *crying*?" He broke off, frowning. "I do believe you *are*."

It was true that Albert's eyes had misted over a little. For a moment he was elsewhere. He was back with Scarlett in the cell, listening to her story. . . . He stood with her in sunshine, looking at the empty iron posts. . . . All at once he felt an overwhelming sadness—not only for Scarlett and her brother, but for himself and Mallory too. They were all lost children. He took a deep breath and wiped his sleeve across his face. "I've got a prediction," he said huskily. "They'll come for you, one day. As soon as they have no use for you, they'll come. At night, unexpectedly, and in numbers. You're an enemy in their house. Your powers won't save you in the end."

They gazed at each other. Over on the stoop, Walt the watchman's rocking chair had stilled. He was emitting little snores.

"Well," Mallory said, "it's been nice. But there's not much more to say, is there?"

He lifted a finger. A yellow stone rose from the dirt of the road, darted sideways like a hummingbird, and struck Albert on the side of his head.

Albert gasped and almost fell. He put his hand to his temple, felt the blood running down.

"Please," he said. "We don't have to do this, Mallory."

The operative didn't answer. He glanced across the road. A spar of wood, propped against the wall of a warehouse, came to life with malign intent. It launched itself forward, spinning brightly through the sunlit air. Albert flung himself to all fours; the spar whizzed over his head and away, skidding to a standstill in the earth.

"We don't have to do it." Albert's jumper was halfway up his back. He got shakily to his feet, spat dust from his mouth. "You and I are no different! You're hurting yourself, too."

"You do talk nonsense," Mallory said. "Besides, what's all this 'we'? You aren't going to do anything! You let all your power out last night, up there on the scaffold. It was only the purest chance you didn't kill your friends. And now it's gone and there's nothing left for you to fight with. You should have learned to be precise—like me."

Five more stones rose from the curbside. They hovered ten feet up, trembling with force. Albert looked at them. *He* could make stones move with his mind too. He thought of sitting above the mine shaft at Ashtown, in the peace of evening, just a few short days before. But it had been quiet then, and he had been calm. There was no way he—

"*This* is better than lifting flower petals," Mallory said. "Let's see, which shall we choose to brain you? Eeny, meeny . . ."

Albert's teeth clenched. He pushed his bloodied fringe out of his face. A surge of anger passed through him, manifesting outward as a gust of air—

—which made the operative's hair flutter gently and his coattails waft. Mallory didn't so much as sway where he stood. He looked down, watching waves of dust break into nothingness against his shoes. "Was that delicate breeze something to do with you?"

"Might have been."

"Honestly! Where's the energy? Where's the panache? If you'd learned self-control, you wouldn't be so weak! You'd be able to do something like this."

The stones dropped diagonally, raining down on Albert. He dodged one, but the rest connected, making him cry out in pain. He raised an instinctive hand. A strong counterblast of air cracked against the operative's chin, knocking his head back.

"*Stop* this," Albert said.

Mallory stepped away, rubbing at his neck. "Ow," he said. "Well, I suppose that's a *little* better. Still feels kind of apologetic, though. Come on, man, put some welly into it."

He looked across at a workshop frontage, pointed his hand toward its door.

Desperation swelled in Albert. There was no time to think. "Stop, Mallory! We're the same, you and I!"

"Prove it, then." Without effort, Mallory pulled the door clear of its hinges, sent it slicing horizontally out across the street. Albert made a frantic gesture; the iron door went spinning past him, carved straight through the brick wall on the opposite side. The wall collapsed; parts of the roof above slid sideways. Tiles and beams spilled down into the road.

Over on the stoop, the watchman woke with a yell. He sat up in the rocking chair, staring all around him. Albert was doing some staring too, looking at his hand.

"Well, now we're getting somewhere!" Mallory cried. "*That* was a nice deflection! Where'd it come from?"

"I honestly don't know."

"And that's your problem, right there. You don't like to look at what you are. You've shut yourself off from it. Got to relax and embrace the darkness—like I do."

He clicked his fingers. A beam came dragging out of the

debris and flipped across at Albert, who with a jerk of his arm sent it at ninety degrees up the road toward the operative. Mallory swayed aside; the beam whirled past and plowed into the Tarmac, sticking up from the surface like a javelin.

Mallory's face shone, his eyes gleamed bright. "Better and better! When you don't stop to worry about it, you *can* do the basics, after all! But this is kid stuff. What about something that requires a bit of *real* finesse?"

His gaze flicked past Albert. He looked through the clouds of swirling dust to where the watchman was tiptoeing quietly away.

"No!" Albert said. "Please don't . . ."

Wood scraped along wood. The rocking chair shot forward along the wooden platform. It scooped up the watchman, who let out a squawk of pain and fright, bounced a few feet farther—then rose with him into the air.

"Please, Mallory—put him down!"

"You're going to have to show *real* control here," Mallory said. The chair swerved sickeningly close to the metal door and swung back along the street. "Come on. Can you intercept him? Can you halt him? Can you bring him safely back to earth . . . ?"

The chair whizzed past close to Albert's head. He had a brief vision of the man's slack face, his hands gripping the chair arms. Mallory snapped his fingers. The chair rocketed up and over the nearest warehouse roof and in silence fell away. There was a distant crash.

"Nope," Mallory said, smiling. "Guess not."

Albert stood dead still. He felt a cold, white rage rise through him, up through his limbs, through the marrow of his bones. It was not the Fear but an icy detachment born of moral revulsion. It was new to him. The anger was there, but he felt quite calm. "You killed that man," he said.

"Well, yes. Unless he got caught on a washing line. Landed in somebody's big pants."

"You murdered him. . . ."

. "Oh, come on. Murdered? He was a Brother! A thief! And a killer himself, in fact. Hadn't you bothered sieving him?"

"No." Albert could hardly speak. "The only thing I knew was his name."

He turned his head. There was a pile of tiles from the broken roof lying on the ground. Albert looked at them. He moved his eyes. The tiles rose up and shot like bullets at the operative. Mallory flinched back as the tiles were pulverized on the invisible barrier that surrounded him. For a moment he was lost in a reddish cloud of clay dust. The cloud settled. The operative stood straight again. He brushed the dust from his shoulders. There was blood at the top of his forehead, where a fragment of tile had got through.

He put his hand to it, regarded his fingertips briefly.

"Well," he said.

Albert was already looking down at the road. He did so with cold dispassion, willing it to move. The surface broke open, split apart like the top of a freshly baked cake. The crack ran out along the center of the road, the Tarmac ripping, lifting up, heading straight toward Mallory. The operative jumped to avoid being carried upward, stumbled back, and fell. Albert walked in his direction, peeling the Tarmac like the rind of an orange. It curled over the operative like a gray dead wave.

Mallory sat up, sent a concussive force along the center of the road, shattering the Tarmac into fragments, striking Albert headlong. Albert had erected a protective field of air about him; even so, he was hurled twenty feet back along the road against the front of the Brothers' building. He smashed against the brick and plaster, embedding himself deep in the wall.

His eyes had difficulty focusing. He looked along the ruined road, saw two operatives tilted at odd angles, struggling slowly to their feet. Their faces were pale and newly serious. Their hair hung ragged. They made adjustments to their dirtied sleeves.

Albert shook his head to clear his vision. He prized himself out of the plaster, dropped lightly to the ground.

"I want to thank you, Mallory," he said. "You've shown me a very good way to focus. I think I can see it now. I'm more relaxed. I feel at peace with what I am. But you made a mistake, too." He raised a hand. The wall began to bulge behind him. "I wasn't reluctant to fight you because I'm *weak*. It's the reverse. I've too *much* power, and you've just let it loose. So, now . . . tell me what you're going to do."

He snapped his fingers. Metal squealed, stone tore. Pulling the front of the building with him, Albert started forward through the smoke and rubble.

24

Even at the moment the Tainted was released from the crate, Scarlett had no clue what she was about to do. There were too many variables, beginning with the creature itself. Which way would it spring? Would it even spring at all? The restorative powers of the beasts were legendary, but this one had already been shot, fallen from a high rooftop, and been squashed in a not-especially-large box for twelve hours. That combo might surely quell its insane ferocity. If it hesitated, stumbled, or just lay prone and disoriented, as it had when she and Albert had hastily imprisoned it the night before, there were plenty of persons in the hall capable of finishing it off—and Joe, Ettie, and Scarlett with it.

She needn't have worried. It was almost like she'd coached the thing. The moment the lid was flung aside, there was an explosion of savage movement. With a screech of hatred, the white-limbed form uncoiled from its prison. It leaped straight out of the tilted crate, saw Mr. Soames's chair directly ahead. Teeth bared, fingernails clawing, it made a single bound—and launched itself at Soames's face. The energy of the impact was such that the wheeled chair shot backward, struck the front of the desk, and toppled over. For a brief second a pair of conical pinstriped legs could be seen flailing beside the Tainted's swiping arms. Soames didn't have time to make a sound.

Scarlett was already moving too—almost as fast as the Tainted, away from the truck in a different direction. Where it leaped high, she hugged close to the ground, riding the fleeting instants during which everyone else remained motionless in shock. She went for Mr. Teach. Before he could react, before he could choose between killing Joe, saving Soames, or warding off Scarlett's hurtling attack, she had bowled into him, striking the pit of his stomach with the crown of her head. His sword went flying. He collapsed, gurgling, beneath her; as he did so, she plucked the gun from his belt and, in the same movement, rolled over him and away. Her left hand caught up the sword. Now she had two weapons. She was on her feet again, turning to Joe.

Give him his due, the old man hadn't been sluggish either. He was scooping Ettie up, grappling her under his arm. He looked at Scarlett. "To the truck?"

"You got it." Scarlett broke off to shoot one of the four Brothers, who was raising a gun at her from the edge of the hall. Teach was still spluttering at her feet. She lowered the pistol to kill him too—and at that moment the whole hall shook with two immense impacts from outside. The floor seemed to tip, the very hill it stood on shuddered. Scarlett was thrown to her knees. Clocks dropped from the shelves. The four arc lights above Soames's desk went crashing down—three shattered and went out; the last remained on, buttering its radiance hot and thin across the floor. The darkness beyond was all the darker. Scarlett could hear cries of panic from the men, the trilling of smashed clocks, the snapping of the Tainted's teeth.

She clambered to her feet, swung the gun around. Too late—Teach had gone. Joe was stumbling with Ettie toward the truck. She ran to join them. Lesser reverberations shook the building. High above, a split had opened in the side of the bell tower. A thin shaft of daylight speared downward from the rim of the dome, cut through swirls of grainy darkness, and lost itself halfway up the wall. The interior of the dome showed faintly now. She glimpsed the tops of the chains, shimmering dully—and also a grid of intersecting rafters, on which immense pale forms flapped in consternation, seeking to draw back from the light.

Joe loped down the side of the truck; Scarlett kept pace with him, sword out, pistol raised.

From across the hall came sounds of running feet. Over by the toppled arc light a bent, white shape scurried nimbly out of sight. Someone screamed.

Teach's voice called at a distance: "Seal the doors! Lock them! Seal it in!"

"You've got to drive, Joe." Scarlett wrenched open the door of the cab. "I'll cover us from the back. Make for the doors at the far end—see where that glow is? Bust them down if they're shut."

Joe had his arms round Ettie. He was cradling her head with his hand. He paused and looked at Scarlett. "That earthquake—"

"Albert, I think."

"But what—?"

"Gods know. Just drive for the exit—*if* it's still there."

Joe nodded, dropped Ettie inside. He scrambled after her, sat blinking at the controls. Scarlett turned, ran toward the rear of the truck. As she rounded the doors, she almost collided with one of the Brothers; he had a sword stick in his hand. He swung it at Scarlett, who ducked—the blade embedded itself deep in the side of the door. She jabbed at his leg with her own sword; he fell back from her, howling.

Scarlett kicked the Tainted's crate away, hopped up onto the back of the truck. She called over her shoulder. "Joe! Drive!"

"I've barely figured out how this thing works—"

"Drive!"

The engine puttered gently into life. Away in the dimness of the hall, a frenzied volley of shots rang out—someone shooting in sheer terror. A man ran from left to right and was gone again. She heard the Tainted's cry. Scarlett slammed one of the rear doors shut, crouched at the other, gun at the ready.

She could hear the engine idling.

"What are you *doing*, Joe?" she shouted. "Are you trying to find the turn signals or something? Just get us *out* of here!"

The engine roared, the truck started forward. Scarlett steadied herself in the doorway.

"Good! Go!"

Joe put his foot down; they veered erratically away across the hall. A slight, bald figure stepped out of the dark, coat flapping like torn shadows. He had a gun in his hand. He fired six times; bullets sparked and rang off the door by Scarlett's head, leaving an even line. Scarlett fired back, a single shot. Teach's leg gave way; he tumbled back head over heels. Scarlett grinned thinly, made to close the rear doors. As she did so, the truck struck something on the ground and jolted up onto its left-hand wheels, gears grinding, engine roaring. Scarlett lost her balance, fell backward through the doors— and out of the truck itself.

She landed hard on concrete, rolled briefly, came to rest facedown.

She raised her head, blowing hair out of her eyes. Joe had accelerated again. Good—he was doing well, he was giving himself a chance. They had only just started closing the hall doors when the truck reached them: it swerved, knocked against one, scraped along the other—and a moment later was somehow through. Frightened men pushed; the doors slammed closed behind it. She heard bolts being driven home.

Scarlett got slowly to her feet. There was blood on her face. Her shoulder throbbed, her ears rang. She had lost the sword, but the gun was still in her hand.

Fine. Now it was only her.

All the doors to the hall were shut. It was very dark in the room of clocks. The sliver of light from the broken dome did not reach the depths where she was. That one fallen arc light was still there, a good way off, fluttering feebly, spilling its dying light across the floor. You could see a mess of wires close by it; also the edge of Soames's chair, one of his shoes, a red-black stain spreading out across the concrete. . . . Nothing else.

Scarlett stood quiet, listening. It was warm in the blackness. She heard a few last clocks ticking on the wall. She heard groans, sighs, and scuffles in the dark . . . noises of growling and chewing, the sobs and coughs of dying men. It was like standing in the stomach of a beast.

Still, whatever was going on outside didn't seem *much* better. Great thrums and crashes sounded, reverberating against the dome. It might have been the Cataclysm come again.

She grimaced. At least it seemed Albert was giving a good account of himself.

Now all she had to do was find a way out.

Scarlett pushed her hair back and swore silently under her breath, a process that generally helped her think. It worked again. She remembered the door to Soames's personal chambers, set in the wall beyond the desk. Perhaps they had forgotten to lock that.

She started off, moving soundlessly through the dimness. The first thing she found was not the door. It was Mr. Teach. He was lying sprawled on his back, not far from where she'd shot him. Close by was a pile of bricks and mortar that had presumably fallen from the dome. His head was propped against the debris. The bullet wound in his thigh was bleeding profusely, making the patches of his long coat gleam. His black eyes glinted in the dark, watching as she drew near.

Scarlett squatted close beside him, but not *too* close. She had her gun held ready.

"Well," she said.

"Well." Like Scarlett, Teach spoke in a hoarse whisper; he did not want to attract attention. He raised his head, looked stiffly around. "It's eating my colleagues, I think, so we're good for a moment or two. Where's my sword?"

"Lost it."

"What? You only had it two minutes. Give me my gun."

"Why would I do that?"

"I'll need it to shoot myself when your pet comes near."

"Nope, sorry. What's the best way out of this dump?"

Teach gave a mirthless grin, which pulled the skin of his face drum-tight. "There isn't one. All the doors will be bolted. You're trapped in here."

"Come off it. You and Soames must've had a backup option for an attack like this."

"To be honest, we never predicted *this* particular eventuality. A living Tainted brought to us in a box? Someone dismantling our base from outside? You've got to admit, it's unusual." Teach coughed; the cough became a sigh. "Ah, Scarlett, I knew you were good when Carswell brought you in all those years ago. Just a ragged, bloodstained scrap, but so much fire in you. So much inventiveness. With this you've exceeded my expectations."

The floor shook; dust fell from the ceiling. There was another distant crashing, less dreadful than the ones that had gone before. Whatever was happening outside, it was coming to an end.

"What *is* that boy of yours doing out there?" Teach asked. He made an effort to rise, then fell back again. "Poor Soames. He never guessed what either of you were capable of. I told him. I warned him. I should have killed you both at the Wolf's Head crossroads."

"Yeah. You really should have." Scarlett got to her feet. "Well, see you around."

The black gaze dropped from her face to the gun in her hand. "Aren't you going to kill me? Don't make my mistake. Now's *your* chance to finish things."

Scarlett looked out into the dark, where something monstrous moved among dead men. "I think I've finished things pretty conclusively. Anyway, I'm not like you. The answer's no."

The man chuckled. "So—the final ruthlessness is still lacking! That always *was* your weakness, girl. You had that softness in you from the start—since the tragedy that brought you here."

Scarlett looked in the direction of the flickering light. The door was somewhere beyond. Locked or not, she had to try. But she did not know where the Tainted was. ... . "You and Soames looked after me—in your own fashion," she said. "So I'll spare your life now. That's my parting gift to you."

"Some gift," Teach said, "to mortally wound me, then leave

me helpless to be eaten by that thing. . . . But I'll accept it in the spirit with which it is meant. And so, before you go, I will give *you* a gift too."

"Not necessary at all. Goodbye."

"Oh, but it's a gift of hope. . . . It concerns your brother."

Scarlett had already begun moving off. Now she froze. "What?"

"Thomas. Wasn't that the name? Tethered to a post and eaten, when his sister was away."

"You'd better be careful," Scarlett said. The gun was heavy in her hand. She did not look back at him.

Teach's voice was failing. "Don't be cross! I have nothing but sympathy. . . . I know how terrible guilt can be! Yours was halfway to killing you when Carswell made his intervention. Even now it eats away at you, close beneath the surface. . . . But I have good news for you. I don't believe the child *was* taken by beasts."

All expression left Scarlett's face. Like ink on wet paper, it ran down the slopes of her cheeks and dropped away. "You're lying," she said. She opened her mouth again, but the curse she wanted would not come.

"Leave me, then."

She lifted the gun, turned round. "No. Speak. You've got five seconds."

"Ah, so you decide to be ruthless *now*? Good! I'm glad to see it." Teach smiled painfully. "You know, I think you've grown complacent in your misery, Scarlett McCain. It's become almost comfortable for you, the knowledge of his death. But I can take that comfort away, so you never sleep easily again."

"Two seconds."

"I merely speculate. On the borders of Wessex where you lost your brother, slavers go in search of children. They raid Cornwall; they slip across the straits to Wales and bring them back in little boats. But these are dangerous expeditions. They are lazy men. They look for alternative sources of livestock for their fairs. What is easier than stealing children from the punishment posts? Slipping along, untying them, placing them in cages, riding away? Who is to know or care? The *Towns* do not want them! The Towns want them dead! They can be taken far away and sold to people who do not care about their defects or their crimes. If a child is young and well, if it has some unusual quality—bright red hair, for instance—so much the better. Off they trot to be a slave in some godforsaken border town."

Scarlett's gun was motionless. "I don't believe you. You're making it up."

"I have dealt with such slavers many times."

"But Thomas . . . You don't know this."

"Speculation, as I say."

"It was animals," she said faintly. "Animals . . ."

"Maybe. But maybe, if you'd traveled at once to the nearest slavers' fair, you might have found him waiting for you. Instead of which, you began drinking and fighting your way across Wessex." The bald head drooped into shadow as Teach

400

gave himself over to a spasm of quiet coughing. "It's not your fault, naturally," he said. "No one told you."

"You could have told me," Scarlett said. "If any of this hogwash is true, which I doubt."

"Why would I tell you? You were useful to us. We valued your anger, your talent, your reservoir of pain." Teach chuckled; he raised a hand and wiped a bubble of blood from his mouth. "There was a void inside you. No hope, no doubt. Nothing but certainty and guilt. See how strong it's made you, Scarlett! You should be grateful to me." He gave a faint sigh. "But *this* is your gratitude—you destroy my life and livelihood and grind me into the earth."

Scarlett stood above him. "You truly knew this? All along?"

"I *don't* know it, not for certain. It's a possibility."

"You *guessed* this . . . and you never told me?"

"I'm telling you now. So, you see, perhaps you might have found him, if you'd searched and persevered. Instead, you gave yourself up to despair and darkness, and he is gone." There was a silence. "And that is my gift," Teach said, "and my revenge upon you. There is nothing more to say."

Scarlett looked at him. She raised her hand, pushed the hair out of her face. As she made the movement, Teach tensed. Perhaps he expected her to fire the gun or strike a fatal blow. When she did not do so, he made a soft, sad, almost disappointed sound. Wincing with pain, he raised himself up onto his arms. Then he crawled away from her, out of the light and into the darkness of the hall. One moment he was there. The next no trace of him remained.

Scarlett scarcely noticed him going. She stayed where she was, staring out at nothing.

Perhaps you might have found him, if you'd searched and persevered.

Scarlett did not move.

Somewhere in the dark there was a sudden rushing, followed by a gasp and a protracted rattling cry. Then silence. Then a scraping, bumping sound, which started near and receded with inhuman speed—something heavy being dragged away across the radius of the hall.

Scarlett did not react. She stood quietly in darkness, letting the chill of Teach's words percolate between her bones and sinews, around the trembling surfaces of her lungs, and across the contours of her pulsing heart. It dripped down into the fibers of her being, reaching her remotest parts, freezing them, cracking them with their touch. The cold penetrated to every recess. Her mind slowed; her blood grew thick, her heartbeats soft and torpid. Her eyes shut. Her limbs, her fingers, all the extremities of her body twitched, as if they were closing down.

In that moment she came very near to dying—quietly, alone, and in the dark. She did not need the Tainted, though if the thing had fallen on her she would have done nothing—indeed, she would scarcely have noticed it. She was almost nothing herself now, a shadow among shadows. All the fight, the pain, the crystal certainties of the rage and guilt that had sustained her down the years were gone. Even that had been stripped away.

If you'd persevered . . .

From far off came a metallic crash. It sounded as vast as a roof collapsing, and also sharp and intimate, like the ringing of a bell. Scarlett opened her eyes. With that noise, the threads that still attached her to the world twitched her back to life. She thought of Albert, Joe, and Ettie—all in mortal peril.

She took a slow, shuddering breath, as if she were getting up from the prayer mat or waking from deep sleep. She stood straight-backed and upright, her hands loosely at her sides. She was Scarlett McCain again, alone and in the dark. She listened, breathed, began to think. . . .

Then she began to move.

With a few more steps she had rounded Soames's desk. The floor was a graveyard of smashed clocks. Feeling her way among them, she made it to the door.

With infinite caution, she tried the handle. . . .

No. No luck. The door was closed and bolted. There was no escape that way.

From somewhere out in the hall behind her came a soft and furtive noise. Resisting the desire to freeze, Scarlett forced herself to rotate, forced herself to move back into the room in the direction of the sound. On stiff legs she walked to the shelter of the desk. Without any swift movements, she eased herself behind it and crouched there, waiting.

She had Teach's gun but no firm idea of how many bullets were in it. And she could not risk opening it to check. The noise had stopped. She pressed her head against the wood, counted to three—and peered round the side of the desk.

She saw the ragged oval of light spilling out around the toppled arc lamp. Around it only darkness. But there, at the very fringe of the light, something with long hair was crouching.

She heard a snuffling and a restless clicking of teeth.

Scarlett stopped breathing. Cold sweat beaded the back of her neck.

If she stayed still, perhaps it would move away. It could not smell her, surely—not at this distance, not with all that blood smeared around its mouth. . . .

The thing's shape shifted; it was bending forward with its thin arms splayed out at the sides like a reptile or a spider, lowering its nose close to the floor. It was searching out her scent. Scarlett knew that as surely as if it had told her. She pressed herself tight against the corner of the desk. The thing stopped moving. Scarlett was motionless too.

Teeth clicked twice. Silence . . .

Then the shape rushed toward the desk.

Scarlett sprang to her feet and launched herself over the top of the desk. As she landed, something collided against its side. She scrambled onward in blackness, making for the center of the hall. As she went, her hand tightened on the gun—Teach's gun, with its unknown number of bullets.

She heard the rapid movements of the thing behind: the slap of feet, the scratch of nails. Now was the time to shoot—but it was almost impossible to bring herself to stop. . . . The frantic piston work of her thigh almost jolted the weapon out of her grasp. Scarlett's jaw clenched. *Damn it—stop running!*

She swiveled, dropped to one knee, sighted blindly behind her into the dark, and pulled the trigger. In the flash from the muzzle, she caught an instant's glimpse of a white face, a blur of gray-white hair, an oncoming open mouth of dripping teeth. Then darkness again.

She fired twice more. Each time, the face was nearer. Each time, it occupied a different spot as the thing veered side to side. With the third bullet, the sound of running feet collapsed into incoherent thumping and thrashing. The creature howled; something scraped against the toe of her boot. She pulled the trigger again—but the gun was empty. She tossed it away, jumped back, and collided with a dangling mass of cold, hard fronds. For an instant Scarlett thought she was trapped by something immense, tentacled, and alive. She opened her mouth to scream—then realized what it was.

The owl chains.

Noises close by. Scarlett grasped at a single chain. She hoisted herself up, hand over hand. She went feverishly fast, imagining the bloodied face lunging at her from the darkness. Up, up, up . . . After a few moments she stopped, hung there in darkness, listening to the clinks of the gently swinging chain.

Nothing.

Maybe she'd killed it with the shot.

Maybe it was dead or dying. . . .

From directly below she heard a gentle scraping, as the thing dragged itself along the floor. It reached the base of the chains. She imagined it looking up toward her.

The chain twitched as unseen hands took hold. It shuddered as unseen hands began to climb.

Scarlett swore feelingly into the cavernous dead space. Pressing her boots tight against the chain, she went on scrambling upward through the void.

The air grew warmer as she went. It carried a thin and acrid scent—the smell of must and feathers, of blood and old dry bones. The only light was the distant arc lamp, a pulsing heartbeat in the cavity far below. Scarlett's arms ached; her skin was cold and hot; sweat dripped into her eyes so that she could scarcely see. From time to time she glanced back down and saw the eyes of the thing that followed staring up at her along the twist of chain. Above her was the mass of the great black pulley wheel that worked the chains, with the grid of owl beams faintly silhouetted beyond. Right now the beams seemed still and silent. Scarlett wasn't deceived. It was a silence of anticipation.

Death above and death beneath, and blackness all around.

She passed through the grainy spear of light slicing down from the hole in the dome. Scarlett scarcely had the strength to climb now, but the oscillations of the chain were growing stronger, the movements below faster and more urgent. She made a final effort—and all at once found herself drawing close to the first of the beams.

It was not very far away; if she reached out, she could pull herself on. She hesitated. The sour smell was very strong. She heard the faintest clinking in the dark.

Claws snatched at her boot sole. Scarlett kicked herself free, hurled herself out across the space, landed on her stomach across the beam. It was a foot wide, thickly caked in soft white droppings. Her legs dangled below. Scrabbling desperately, she swung herself round, so that she lay straddling the beam. The chain beside her was swinging violently. There were vibrations on the beam, too, as something large came hopping and fluttering along it. Scarlett pushed herself up, got shakily to her feet. She was facing the crack in the dome; she began to shuffle toward the splinter of light.

The chain clattered: a shape leaped from it, landed in a crouch on the beam behind. It stood with awful fluid ease, limped forward. A white arm extended—hairless, black-veined, with broken nails upon the hands—and reached for Scarlett's neck.

Something bigger, whiter, faster hopped along the beam behind the Tainted, snatched down, and caught it by the head. The Tainted was plucked up and off the beam. The owl hopped back: and now, all around Scarlett, the silence was pierced by hoots and screams, the darkness exploding into a frenzy of wheeling gray fragments. Scarlett did not watch or linger. She stumbled toward the brightness up ahead.

At the end of the beam, the skin of the dome had ruptured in a hemorrhage of broken wood and blackened tiles. With the last of her strength she threw herself against the hole. Splinters bit into her hands, spurs caught at her clothes.

Warmth bathed her, sunshine blinded her. Scarlett scratched and tugged and wriggled, gave a final desperate push. . . . At last, almost insensible, she clambered up through darkness and fell outward into light.

It was a world of dust and silence. The roof of the dome was a black curve, the prow of a ship surrounded by white cloud. A thick, soft layer of dust hung swirling in the air, weakening the sun, reducing it to a pale, brown, vinegary disc directly overhead. Scarlett rolled away from the hole and flopped back against the blackened lead, feeling its pitted dryness, shielding her eyes with her arm. Visibility was not good: the chimneys and rooftops of the town protruded like sea rocks through the mist, and the fields beyond were smears of yellow-blue.

Scarlett lay motionless against the dome. Presently the sun began to burn through the dust. It warmed the lead and bathed her skin. She raised herself and sat at the highest point of Stow, looking down upon a scene of ruin.

The landscape of the town had changed.

Many of the old factory buildings that comprised the headquarters of the Brothers of the Hand had partially collapsed. One area near the entrance had been entirely ripped away. The remaining portions of roof had sagged as if their beams had melted in the noonday heat. Other metal beams jutted blackly; standing portions of brick walls stabbed like knives into the swirling dust. Several neighboring warehouses had been demolished too: great piles of rubble sloughed like mudslides into the road outside the Brothers' door.

It was very quiet. The smoke cast a suppressing pall over the town. But there *was* movement and there *was* life: just a little of it. Away in the center of the road, the cargo truck from the Buried City lay on its side, surrounded by strewn bricks and other debris. And standing beside it . . .

Standing beside it, on a clear patch of ground, were a child and a man. They were upright, unsupported. They seemed okay; they seemed uninjured. They were holding hands.

Walking toward them down the remains of the street was someone else.

The slim, slight figure of a youth.

It went slowly, limping a little, away from the broken warehouse. Scarlett leaned forward. At first glance she could not quite tell. Her eyes were too bleary, and it was too far away for her to properly make out the shock of black hair, the saggy jumper, the silly white trainers that seemed too big for him. But she *thought* she knew.

Then the child lifted its arms and ran to him, and she *was* sure.

"You did it, Albert," Scarlett said. "Bloody hell."

With that, she lay back against the roof. It was all the swearing she had strength for. The rest could wait until she'd figured out how to get down.

25

They were frying goose eggs in the kitchens of the Wolf's Head Inn that morning, and breakfast was being served. The taproom was filled with the scents of bacon, porridge, and fresh wild honey. Behind the bar, Gail Belcher performed prodigious feats of coffee pouring while her barmaids flitted among the booths with racks of toasted sourbread and pots of bilberry jam. Albert watched them from his bench beside the window. It was his favorite time of day.

He had no strong opinion on the nature of the afterlife; still, if he'd had to take a punt, he would have hoped for something similar to this. At that early hour, the inn's guests were clean, sober, and convivial. Nobody was fighting. Traders sat with cultists, cultists sat with furriers, furriers sat with frog hunters and Anglian oystermen. Sunlight spilled through the mullioned windows, and the low black beams rang with quietly animated chatter, with the clink of cutlery, and with occasional outbreaks of flatulence from the oystermen. Such fragile communality, Albert felt, was something to be cherished. He had toast and honey at his elbow and a pile of purple cushions at his back. He had slept well in a feather bed. No one was presently trying to kill him. He could have done without the oystermen, who were in the next booth along, but otherwise he felt content.

Best of all, his friends were there.

At a nearby table, Joe and Sal Qin were playing a post-breakfast round of cards. It was a vigorous, even unsubtle, game, which seemed to involve both players stealing cards from their opponents' piles and snatching them back with obscure words of challenge or rebuff. Both were cheating with equal bravado. He spotted Sal plucking two cards from her jacket sleeve, while Joe had at least three stuffed down the back of his trousers. Albert was pleased to see it. The journey to the Wolf had been arduous, and it had taken several days for everyone to recover. Joe and Sal, at least, seemed back on form. And as for Ettie—

Almost as if she'd heard her name, a diminutive blond shape materialized on the seat beside him. She had three colored pencils in her mouth and a sheet of paper in her pudgy paw. Hand and paper were abruptly thrust under Albert's nose.

"Is this for me? Thanks! It's lovely."

The scribbled coils of interconnecting lines seemed particularly cheerful today, the colors as complex and vibrant as the atmosphere of the room. Albert propped the picture against the coffee jug and patted the child's head. He had observed Ettie closely since her rescue, anxious that there might be repercussions from her ordeal. But her talent for being blithely unaffected by events remained intact. She was a happy soul. Everyone at the Wolf's Head liked her; the furriers gave her twists of otter pelt, the oystermen gave her colored shells, even Old Mags Belcher fed her sweetmeats from her rocking chair by the fire. Albert found her increasingly fascinating too. In her small and silent way, there was much to be learned from Ettie.

"Can we tempt you to a game, Albert?" Joe had swiveled on his chair. For an elderly man who'd been recently kidnapped, menaced, and threatened by owls, who'd driven a lorry through a collapsing building, crashed it, and pulled his granddaughter from the wreckage, he seemed in decent fettle. "I suggest rattlesnake or sabers. Sal's lousy at both of them."

Sal Qin was stuffing a pipe with heather tobacco. She snorted rudely. "Hah! Says Joe."

Albert smiled. "Not for me, thanks. I'm waiting for Scarlett."

"Sure she's not already here?" Joe squinted at the nearby booths. "She's got so many bruises, she blends in with the cushions."

"She'll be up in her room," Albert said. "Sleeping or meditating, I expect."

The old man grunted. "She hardly ever gets off that mat these days. We barely see her."

"Is it any wonder?" Sal Qin struck a match against the side of her boot and lit her pipe. "The poor girl's been through a lot. She faced off singlehandedly against a Tainted, a posse of man-eating owls, *and* a bunch of gangsters! Plus, a friend of hers blew up half a town! It's not surprising she's got plenty on her mind."

Albert drew himself up. "Actually, Sal, it was only a couple of warehouses I destroyed—*not* half a town."

"Ooh, yes, that makes *all* the difference. Pardon me for exaggerating."

"Well," Joe said, "knowing Scarlett, she'll soon be out and about again, kicking assorted arses up and down the kingdoms. This latest ordeal will no doubt join all the other hidden traumas that make her the sweet-natured pacifist we love so well." He shuffled the pack of cards. "Now, to more important things: Rattlesnake it is, then, Sal?"

The little merchant-trader nodded. "All right, but I'll whip you at it as I did before." She blew out a circle of aromatic smoke. "When Scarlett *does* show, Albert," she added, "you might want to tell her I'd like to chat about your future plans. It's been almost a week, and you both seem fine now. Not to put any pressure on you, but I reckon you outlaws might still owe me a job. . . ." She winked at him and turned her attention to the game.

Albert sat back beside Ettie in his booth and took a thoughtful bite of toast. He had to admit it—they probably *did* owe Sal twice over. First, it was *their* actions that had helped make her a condemned fugitive, wanted across the southern kingdoms. Second, it was only thanks to her that they'd got back to the Wolf's Head at all. Neither he nor Scarlett had been in any state to arrange their escape from

Stow. It was Sal who had met them in the cemetery and spirited them away from the smoldering town. It was Sal who had sold Scarlett's bag of weapons to raise cash for the buses. It was Sal who negotiated the borders and led them all on the final grueling march across the fens. . . .

You both seem fine now. . . . Well, they were certainly better than when they'd reached the inn. Albert had been in a state of complete exhaustion, and Scarlett was stumbling and silent. But the Wolf's Head had quickly worked its magic. It had done them good to hear Gail Belcher's hearty welcome and to find their possessions laid out in plain, comfy rooms, as if they had never left. Even so, they'd mostly slept the first few days.

So how *was* he doing, one week on? Physically he was well. Inwardly it was hard to say. His fight with Mallory remained with him—it was almost as if he were still there.

Shutting his eyes, he could still see the buildings toppling around him, the ground being torn and twisted, bricks swirling in the sky like flocks of evening birds. . . . He could still see the rooftops being dragged from their moorings, the walls upended, the endless storm of strike and counterstrike as he and his enemy circled each other in the center of the road. . . . Sometimes they'd been invisible to each other, swathed in plumes of smoke and cloud; next, they'd drawn so close they might have clasped each other's hands. It was a ceaseless dance, a game of advances and retreats, of impulse and sleights of thought, where solid things were hurled and smashed and gathered up and thrown again. A game where the world could be reshaped like putty, where Albert's only constant was his dark reflection, his shadow, the figure in the tattered coat—a creature of increasing desperation . . .

And then, quite suddenly, he'd been alone, with only a mountain of shattered debris marking the place where Mallory had been standing. Slabs of steaming concrete, blocks of fallen masonry . . . A few small fragments rolling down the giant cairn. He'd watched them till they stopped and then kept watching, the silence thudding in his ears. . . .

"Drifting off again?" a voice asked.

Albert opened his eyes. Scarlett was standing above him, a tray of breakfast in her hand. Her bruises were fading, her cuts healing well. After Stow, she'd seemed gray and distracted, like she'd lost something there. She was still pale and rather thin, but her face was clear and she was grinning. There was the old green sparkle in her gaze.

"We're not robbing a Faith House right now," he said. "So I'm allowed to lose focus as much as I like. Yes, I was drifting. Care to join me?"

"Don't mind if I do. Hey, Ettie. Nice drawings."

Scarlett sat, somewhat carefully and stiffly, opposite the little girl. Her hair was damp and hung loose around her shoulders. She took a spoonful of porridge. Albert poured out coffee.

"You all right?" he asked.

"Never better. Albert, what the hell is Sal Qin doing over there with Joe?"

"Playing rattlesnake. It's quite a lively game."

"I'll say it is. She's just pulled a card out of his trousers. They're at it early, too."

"I'm not sure they ever went to bed."

Scarlett raised an eyebrow. "They get on surprisingly well for two old codgers. Think that's why Sal is hanging around? Think it's Joe?" She bent in close. "You ought to sieve their deepest desires and find out."

"I wouldn't dare. It would put me off my breakfast. Actually, Sal *says* she's waiting for us. Says we owe her a job."

"Well, she can wait a while longer for that. No more piddly heists for us, Albert! We've just destroyed the Brothers! We broke out of Milton Keynes! We raided the Buried City, trashed Warwick, and tore up half the kingdoms! The pamphleteers can stick *that* up their execution specials." Scarlett waved a porridgy spoon at him. "Besides, right now we're not doing anything for anyone. The notorious Scarlett and Browne are having a bloody good rest."

"You seem in a perky mood," Albert observed.

"I am. Food, kip. Bodily healing. See that hairy fensman at the bar? I beat him at an arm wrestle the other day."

"That's good. I played dominoes with Ettie yesterday and lost."

She grinned at him. "Sounds like we're both back to normal. I must admit, you're doing better than I thought after your run-in with Mallory. No bits dropping off, no limbs gone. I'd have expected at least a missing toe."

He looked down at his bruised hands, his torn jumper, his ragged trouser legs. His trainers too had seen better days.

"Under all of this," he said, "I'm fine. Which is mostly thanks to *you*, Scarlett. All those times you told me just to let my powers free—you were quite right. I didn't fight it, back there in Stow. I didn't fight myself any longer. That helped me out a lot."

"Glad to hear it." As usual, she wasn't interested in dwelling on things that were gone. She finished up her porridge and pulled a plate of eggs across. Albert took a sip of coffee.

"It's a shame about Mallory," he said. "He'd suffered a lot in Stonemoor. I tried to reason with him, but things got slightly out of hand."

"Slightly."

"Yes."

"Do you think he's dead?"

Albert frowned. "I don't honestly know. There were rather too many buildings dropped on him for me to see. If he isn't, they're going to need a pretty big spade to dig him out." He shrugged. "But he hasn't turned up here yet, so . . ."

"That's good enough for me." Scarlett was busy forking up her egg. Albert looked at her. He wondered if it was a sensible time to tell her what he'd decided on. She was in a decent mood, which meant he was less likely to be punched, or throttled, or poked in the nose with an eggy fork. But the chances still weren't zero. And, hairy fensmen aside, he didn't believe she was *quite* as robust as she claimed. There were gray rings round her eyes, and still that air of slight distraction that she'd had ever since she'd climbed down from the Brothers' tower. But if not now, when? He had Ettie

417

beside him, and her patterns were blue and green and somehow calming: they gave him the confidence to try.

"Speaking of Mallory," he said, "there's one thing I've been meaning to talk to you about, Scarlett. Even if *he's* gone, this isn't going to end. He told me there are other children out in Stonemoor, with talents just as strong as mine. The Faith Houses are still experimenting on them, twisting them, indoctrinating them. . . . It won't be long before they let them loose into the world." He looked out of the window, took a deep breath. "And it makes me realize, too," he went on, "that I've been trying to ignore my own past all this time. I mean Stonemoor, of course, and also where I came from, and what I actually *am*. . . . And, and I can't go on neglecting it any longer. I need to find out more. So what *that* means is I've come to a difficult decision, which—" He flinched back as Scarlett stretched a sudden hand across the table. "Are you reaching for that spoon?"

"I was reaching for the salt."

"Oh, fine. It's just I know what you can do with spoons." He cleared his throat. "Where was I? I've kind of lost my thread."

"I don't know. I wasn't really listening. I've got an idea," Scarlett said. "Let me just finish this; then why don't we go outside a moment?" She glanced round at the busy taproom, at Joe and Sal Qin at their game, at Ettie's silent industry. "I've got something to tell you too, and I'd rather do it there."

* * *

Outside the Wolf's Head, it was a golden morning. The sun hung low; the fens were a burnished sheet of flame. Two of Gail's daughters were cleaning the guests' bicycles in front of the sheds. Their voices sounded coarse and happy on the fresh, warm air.

Albert and Scarlett found a small veranda below the cobbled yard, with a bench that overlooked the sunken pasture. Hens and geese were wandering peaceably on the grass. Scarlett sat in a pool of sunlight; she pulled her knees up beneath her chin and folded her arms across them, gazing out across the marshes. Her hair shone with a deep red glow. It dropped in curls around her face. It seemed to Albert, sitting there beside her, as if she'd almost been made new again. All the rips and tatters on her clothes were rendered invisible in the brightness. Her weariness, her bruises—all the evidence of ill usage—were temporarily smoothed away.

"What is it?" he said.

"It's about Thomas." She didn't wait for him to react but plowed on almost in a flurry. "Right at the end," she said, "back there in Stow, Teach told me something about my brother. I don't know if I believe it, or what it means, but . . ." She looked at him. "But I want your opinion, Albert. I want you to hear it too."

He sat quiet while she told him, hunched forward a little, staring at her face. It was different from the other time. When she'd spoken of Thomas back in the Faith House cell, he had been motionless in horror; here it was a different kind of concentration. Scarlett's voice was calm and considered, and *he* felt calm too. The peace of the Wolf's Head was on Albert, the peace of sunlight and the morning. He had a peculiar feeling in his stomach. He could feel a small grin stealing over his face. He didn't want to acknowledge it because he didn't yet know what Scarlett was feeling. He sat there on the bench and said nothing once she'd finished. He could hear faint yells from Joe and Sal's card game drifting through the taproom window. Out on the fens, a heron broke clear of the reeds and flapped awkwardly into the sky.

"Obviously, in some ways, things are no different," Scarlett said. "Taken by slavers? It was a long time ago. Anything might have happened since. And Teach might be wrong, of course, or lying."

He nodded. "That's very true."

"All the same," she went on, "don't you think . . . doesn't it suggest that there's just the smallest speck of a possibility that—" She stopped. She caught his eyes.

It was no good; he couldn't be the one to say it. He looked back at her and waited.

Scarlett just gazed at him.

"Well, what do *you* think?" he said.

She gave a great sigh. "I think he may be. But if he is, it's somewhere far away."

And all at once, a great burst of happiness rose up in Albert, rose unstoppably the way the Fear used to, starting in his belly and spearing up and outward through his chest, to the tips of his arms and fingers, to his face, his eyes, his smile. He launched himself sideways on the bench like an ungainly tiger and grappled Scarlett close, wrapping her round, squeezing her tightly to him. She was so surprised, it took her several seconds to fight her way free.

"Ow!" she growled. "Get off! For Shiva's sake! I *was* lots of little bruises, and now I'm one big fat one! What was *that* for?"

"For what you just said." He grinned at her. " '*He may be.*' For those three words. That's all."

Something in her face had lifted. "I mean, it's not much," she said.

"It's not quite nothing, either."

"No," Scarlett McCain said. "It isn't."

They sat on the bench in companionable silence. Slowly, laboriously, the sun was breaking clear of the fens. The world was bright and flat and steadily expanding around them. It was why Albert always liked mornings; they were alive with possibility.

"You know what *I* reckon we should do next," Scarlett said, after a time, "is mosey southwest for a change. The Faith Houses will be searching for us, so we'll stay one step ahead if we go somewhere new. Also, Gail tells me there are some sizeable slave markets in those parts. We could pay a little visit to them. Who knows—maybe there'll be some men there who might remember transactions from long ago—or be *persuaded* to remember them." She smiled at him, showing her teeth.

Albert nodded slowly. He still had tingles of excitement in his fingers. "Good idea. I'm sure there are *lots* of ways of jogging a slaver's memory. We can throw in a couple of bank jobs, too," he went on. "Just to keep our hand in. It would stop us from going stale. And there'll be plenty of Faith Houses to rob—and maybe some *other* notable locations to track down. . . . The southwest's a very interesting region."

"Isn't Stonemoor that way too?" Scarlett asked.

"I think it might be."

"Excellent. We can call in there as well." She prodded his shoulder. "Because don't imagine you're wandering off on your own, Albert Browne. All that waffle about your past and discovering who you are. . . . If you tried doing that solo, you'll fall down a hole within seconds, or get lost or something equally useless. If that's what you need to do, I'll help you. We're a team, and we do everything together—slavers, Stonemoor, *and* a second breakfast."

"You can't *still* be hungry," he said.

She sprang up from the bench. "I'm half starved," she said. "And so are you. Come on."

They walked together back toward the Wolf's Head. It occurred to Albert as they went that Scarlett knew his mind just as well as he knew hers. It wasn't a bad feeling. Outside the sheds, their bicycles were glinting in the sunshine. Ettie was sitting on the inn steps, drawing. Soon enough they were spotted; then came the squeal of welcome and the little girl running toward them over the yard.